ONLIEST

ONLIEST

J. DANIEL BATT

to Aisleyn—
in a world of echoes, you are my true story

to Mae and Alires—
you brought me closer to the stars
than I could've hoped

"All things are drawn toward what is like them, if such a thing exists.
All earthly things feel the earth's tug...
And things that share an intelligent nature are just as prone to seek
out what is like them."
—Marcus Aurelius

PROLOGUE

THE MEMORIES OF THE BARLGHAREL

Composed 2970

Between the stars, there are no seasons. Shadows of dead worlds drift in the void, but there is no laughter. Perhaps small nebulae, lit with their own faint fires, float without aim, but there are no voices. In the vast gulf—a gap far larger than the human mind can comprehend—perhaps wonders wait to be discovered. But not life.

Life does not spread through the cosmic distances. It roots itself on the microscopic worlds that hug the warm stars.

Life is a coward. It never ventures far from the blanket of the solar winds, and the dusting of magnetism that sparks the skies above its head.

Between the stars, there is only loneliness. And in time, madness.

This is a fact as constant as the tick of hydrogen spinning in its singular electron shell. Unalterable. Between the stars is death, and only fools aim to cross it.

The great starship Olorun launched, with its own teeming masses, toward another sun. Between the stars, beyond that border, loneliness gripped it. And then madness.

Its builders had conquered the interstellar challenges: food, energy, propulsion, habitat, radiation, laundry, medicine, and more. They were ignorant of life's desperate pull back inward, back to the star that birthed it. Remember, life is a coward.

Olorun launched as the pinnacle of human achievement. The builders utilized every known advancement in the construction of the behemoth starship. It roared out of the Sol system like a dragon in rage.

Kapteyn's Star lay ahead as its target. The red dwarf hung nearly thirteen light years from Sol. It was bright enough to be viewed by children looking through telescopes, yet the star itself was a visitor to our galaxy. Torn from the Omega Centauri cluster millennia ago, it was a much cooler star than Sol, burning nearly 3500 kelvin less.

Rolling in orbit around Kapteyn's Star were two super-Earths: Kapteyn-b and Kapteyn-c, named Àpáàdì and Òkè respectively. Àpáàdì was five times the size of Earth, and it orbited Kapteyn's Star every forty-eight days. Òkè was seven times the size of Earth. The system was ancient, possibly over eleven billion years old. They are worlds twice the age of Sol itself. In millennia past, the just-waking beasts upon their surfaces could look up at night and see Sol wink into existence, forming from the clouds of stellar matter.

Òkè was cold. Dead as the grave. A world that wished to sleep away the eons before it. It stayed silent, and its ghost would not even venture forth to haunt.

Quite different from Òkè, the closer brother, Àpáàdì, was a gray marble with blue veins of running water coursing across its shattered surface. There are oceans of water, but they are coursing under forested surfaces. The word "temperate" crept into scientific reviews of the globe. Tempered. A calming, beckoning world.

Why go to such a different place? It circled in the habitable zone—a range of space around each star where the requirements for life are apt to flourish—and was the closest star to Earth with such a find. Odd, alien, and enchanting.

Àpáàdì called to the new life around Earth. "Come to me, you young ones. Beings such as you once stepped from my oceans. They have long since left, but I am still here, waiting. My forests wait for your children to run barefoot through them. My clouds wait for your eyes to marvel at them. Swim in my seas. Bring life to my ancient shell. Come."

And life called to life. Deep called to deep.

Truly deep inside the human heart, that call echoed. Humanity heard it. A magnetic pull twisted their heads to that part of the sky, and the builders gazed across the gulf.

The twinkling of stars was a cruel joke. They appeared close enough to pluck from the sky. The phantasmic darkness between Earth and distant suns was vanquished. All to make us leap across the gap.

When we recognize the danger, it's often far too late. We were out from the shore, unable to swim back. The dark fathoms circle. There was no foundation. Nothing below. Nothing above. Alone. Alone. Alone.

These were the thoughts that haunted the crew of Olorun as it breached the interstellar medium. Who heard them first amongst the thousands in that metal hull? The Captain? Or a young child? A worker deep in the lower levels, close to the hull, close to the thin barrier between life and death, his hand pressed against the metal, feeling the pulse of the void? When did the maddening reminders encroach? Perhaps someone foolishly reading Lovecraft late at night? Who first opened the doors to the madness of truth?

It did not matter. The uncontainable fact of the void would've encroached upon them somehow.

Don't make the mistake of comparing the space between stars to the simple exercise of circling the globe or navigating to the Moon or Mars. On the red soil, on the peak of Olympus Mons, the warmth of Sol can still be felt on your skin. The tug of gravity is still there, although, in such a minuscule degree it goes unnoticed. The dunes of Mars gaze upon the oceans of Earth. It is a risky trip but still within the neighborhood. Help is just a call away.

Out here, where Sol and Kapteyn's Star are just dots in the peripheral, loneliness was real for the first time.

A thousand Earths—a million Earths—could careen through this frozen vacuum without touching. In a gulf so immense, madness was nature.

Olorun blazed into the gulf and tore into the insanity between the stars.

1

THE TIGER, THE GIRL, AND THE STARSHIP

"I only wonder there were not comets and earthquakes on the night
you appeared in this garden."
—G. K. Chesterton, *The Man Who Was Thursday: A Nightmare*

Across the roiling space between stars, the generation starship Olorun lumbered, and deep in its spinning, cavernous hull, a girl lazed.

Under the light of a false sun, against the gentle current of the great river Lokun, a tiger named Eku swam like a god and, stretched out on the great cat's back, her limbs dipping below the water, lay Syn, the young queen of the abandoned starship. Her clothes, forgotten fabrics gathered from empty homes, rested strewn on the bank. Her skin, already dark as the tiger's own stripes, soaked up the faux sunlight.

Above them both, watching them laze in the warm afternoon, floated a white porcelain, oblong-shaped bot named Blip.

"There're demons below the mirror," Syn whispered, her eyes shut and her feet bobbing across the waves as Eku paddled from side to side. Each word was hung onto as if wanting to be a song.

"Stop it," Blip spoke in his nasal tone. His white shell displayed a blue pixelated face. A series of blue lights arranged in two circles provided him eyes, a thin line for a mouth, and, when needed to emote, a pair of eyebrows. Right now, his mouth turned down in a visible frown, and he rolled his eyes.

"Maybe the river has no bottom. Maybe there's a kingdom below. Maybe they're just waiting for us to sleep, and they'll swim up to steal us away." She opened one eye—just a sliver—to glimpse Blip's reaction.

"Please," he muttered, turning away from her.

Syn lifted herself off the tiger and leaned over to stare at her reflection in the water. "I see one now." She held a finger above the mirrored face. "Look at those evil eyes and that wicked grin just waiting to launch out from the other side and gobble you up."

He dropped to just an inch above the water in a smooth motion that was at once free fall and then instantly a solid stop, floating motionless in the air. The water below him rippled and her reflection distorted and disappeared. He gave an audible sigh—a simulation of the reaction since he had no lungs.

"Ahh, Blip. Don't do that," Syn whispered, "No reason to get bitter."

"I'm not—"

"Besides, you're starting to irritate Eku." She reached a hand above her head and stroked the tiger's neck, curling her fingers below its ears. The tiger purred—a rumble that shook her entire body. "See? Don't upset the kitty."

"I don't see a kitty," Blip spun around. "I see a predator."

Syn rose up off of the tiger's back, "She's a softy." Her fingers kneaded into the great cat's fur. "She's as programmed as you. You know she can't hurt me."

"It is impossible to completely program a tiger. With the right circumstances and provocation, her untamed instincts will take over, and you'll see how dangerous she truly is. If you survive."

"Hasn't happened yet."

Blip stared at the tiger. "You keep her happy."

Syn leaned in and whispered to Blip, "Maybe I'm the dangerous one." She stretched out her own fingers with their long nails, each painted in a bright cacophony of colors—orange, red, silver, and pink. "See. I have claws too."

"You are not," Blip huffed. "You do not."

Syn slipped off the tiger's back, landing with a plop in the water. She held a finger to her lips. "Shhh. Someone might hear."

"There's no one else to hear."

"Oh yes there are. There are thousands aboard," She cupped a hand to her ear. "They're just dead." She leaned in close. "Shhh. Do you hear that?"

"What?" Blip asked, rolling his eyes.

"Nothing. I hear nothing at all," She stretched out her arms and spun, "Everyone else is gone. I'm all that's left. In this big 'ol ship!"

"That's not your fault," Blip said.

"Oh, I don't know that," she smiled at him then shut her eyes and dove under. She swam through the clear water toward one of the waterfalls. It thundered in a constant downpour against the false rocks. Syn came up, her head under the stream—a dark shadow veiled by the mist.

Eku paddled to the shore and plodded out of the water. She shook, and the fountain of water sprayed for meters. Blip had been watching Syn as she swam and had been ignoring the tiger. The spray of water showered the bot's shell, blurring his blue-hued face.

He flew away and yelled, "Stupid thing! Watch it."

Syn stuck her head out of the falls. She couldn't hear the interaction, but she had seen enough of it to understand the situation. "Play nice," she scolded, "Or..."

Her words dropped off, and she shot a look skyward.

Blip saw her gaze and turned to see what had captured her attention.

Far above, beyond the thin wisps of clouds, a bright light shone, streaking toward the ground.

Syn swam out from the falls, covering the distance between her and Blip quite fast. "A shooting star?" she asked as she watched the falling light and its long streak of a tail.

"Inside Olorun?" Blip asked, his voice edged with sarcasm.

"What is it?" Syn said.

Within seconds, the descending streak slammed into the ground several kilometers away—far enough that the curvature of the Disc allowed them to see the impact point and the plume of smoke and dirt that had just been sent up. The horizon swept up and away as the landscape followed the inside edge of the spinning habitat ring. Whatever the streaking light was, it had landed in the jungle but nearer the edge, near the settlements—the first level of houses that formed the wall of the Disc.

Syn ran her fingers through her dark hair. Like the tiger, she shook her head to shed the water. Her cloud of hair became a halo around her dark face. "Let's go," Syn said.

"I'll go," Blip countered, already moving in that direction. He picked up speed on his way over the water.

"No!" Syn shouted, stamping her foot on the ground.

Blip halted and turned around. He cocked an eyebrow up.

"You're not leaving me behind again," Syn jabbed a finger at him. "Wait."

She strode further out of the water and picked her clothes up from the bank. She dressed quickly, throwing the tattered garments over each other in a mismatched array.

Blip hovered, eyeing the crash point, ignoring Syn, his constant wobble betraying his eagerness to investigate.

From a nearby branch, she lifted up her collection of chains and necklaces and put them around her neck. From the ground, she picked up her spear—a long carbon-fiber piece she had made herself. Mirroring herself, the spear was ordained with bright silks and threads at one end and smears of paint along the shaft. She stepped up to Eku and ran her fingers through the large cat's fur. "Now we can go."

The three moved ahead at a brisk pace before Syn decided to launch into a full run. She was lithe—thin, tall, and graceful. She knew this world, knew these trees and these paths. She flowed naturally through them and began to pick up speed as she let her body fall into the run.

Beside her, Eku paced, her orange and black pattern strobing through the shadows of the overhead trees. They crossed from underbrush over crafted sidewalks that were now decaying through lack of use. The grass overgrew edges of many walkways.

She turned onto a path, knowing it led out in a straight line toward the section they were aiming for. Once Syn's feet hit the walkway, running lights along the edge of the path sparked to life, glowing a pure cyan. Each step was bathed in crystal blue illumination. The ship awoke for Syn—perhaps it was designed for human interaction, and since she was all that remained, the ship awoke only for her.

The pathways, like much of the ship, served double duty. The sun above was fake—the column around which the Disc rotated was lined with sunstrips that glowed and produced the natural lighting that covered the Disc. But it was still light energy, and the ship was designed to conserve as much as possible—the pathways, the roads, the tops of buildings, all of these intended by the builders to collect the light and convert it back into energy for the ship. If light fell on plants, they would use it. If light fell on manufactured surfaces, it would also be used. A conservational loop perfectly tuned.

And now, something had entered that pristine world.

Syn darted ahead—now only a half kilometer away from the crash. The lights glowed against her skin, and she looked like an angel flying through the forest

A simple cleaning bot blocked her path. The puck-shaped unit scrubbed away at the debris, picking up stray branches. The bot, like all of its kind, performed its job well. It could respond and talk back. But that was all programmed—the only smart bot inside Olorun was Blip. Blip stood apart from all of the thousands of other bots that managed the world of the Disc.

Syn leaped over the cleaning bot in a single vault and didn't miss a pace. Ahead, the thin column of smoke rose.

"Can't see it. Can't be big," Syn said. The impact loomed ahead, smaller than she had expected.

"Slow," Blip said.

"Anything?" Syn responded. Blip's sensors often detected things invisible and overlooked by her.

Next to her, Eku gave a slight growl.

Syn eyed the tiger and added, "Either of you?"

Both the bot and Eku slowed and took their next advances with care, each cautious for their own reasons.

Syn brought her spear up.

"What is it?"

"I don't know. It's new. I'm getting a strange pingback."

"A bot?" Syn asked. They were inches away.

Blip's shell shifted to green, and he began to probe the surroundings at a more precise level.

The trees opened up—the impact had been in a small park area, behind some grassy knolls. The light was scattered by the overhung boughs and deep foliage. The column of smoke rose up, stabbing the sky. Already a dozen different response bots were moving in. Each were thick cubic units with treaded tires and various attachments to deal with the different crises that might arise. Several were spraying down a bit of fire that had caught a few trees nearby—a white foam billowing around the flames. In the midst of those, a few of the square medic bots swarmed. Even though Syn was all that was left, they mobilized in response to any disaster, assuming assistance for the now-absent humans.

The center of the impact, surrounded by other bots, was a small crater, a mound of dirt blown up around it.

"Perhaps a piece of the sunstrips fell off?"

Blip gave a nod. "Maybe."

He moved in closer and sounded a slight, high note. The other bots froze at his command. In a moment, they each backed up, clearing the space around the impact.

Syn peered over the edge, waving the thin smoke away. She

gasped. Inside the crater, blackened and dented, laying in a mound of dirt, was Blip.

But Blip was next to her. She moved her eyes between the Blip bot in the crater and the Blip floating next to her. There had only been one Blip. Since the beginning and for always. There was only one Blip because there was only one Syn. He was her assigned companion. They had woken up in the crèche together and had been together since. His white face was the first thing she had seen and her first word was, "Hello."

"Blip?" was all she could let out. Her eyes were wide, and her mouth hung open. Something clattered on the ground next to her, and she realized she had relaxed her grip on her spear. Her hand splayed open. Again, she mumbled, "Blip?"

Blip flew in to hover above the burned replica. His shell glowed green—an unnatural bright beacon against the dark verdant surroundings.

"What is going on?" Syn insisted.

"I don't…" Blip started.

"It's you," Syn said, pointing at the copy of Blip in the smoldering hole.

"No, it isn't."

"What is it?"

"I don't…"

"Don't say you don't know. There's only one of you." She glanced at a random disc-shaped cleaning bot. "There's hundreds of cleaning bots." Near her, recording and documenting the incident, was a small spherical eye-bot, its red case bright against the green foliage. "There's tons of these." She turned back to Blip, "But there's only one of you!"

"I know," Blip said as his surface turned back to white. He flew back to her, looking eye to eye, "It's a companion bot."

"A companion for who?"

"I don't…"

"Don't say that!" she cut him off.

"But I don't!" he shouted back.

Syn knelt and reached out a hand, edging close to touch the copy in the hole. Eku growled in warning. She glanced up at Blip.

He nodded. "Try it. It won't respond to me. You sometimes have better luck than I do."

She held her hand above it, sensing for heat. It had come down like a star, blazing through the sky, lighting the nearby trees on fire and blasted a hole in the ground several feet deep. It was charred and smashed. But it didn't radiate any heat. She placed her fingers on it—cool to the touch. She shook her head.

Syn was convinced it was a companion bot now. Anything else would be blazing hot—nearly on fire—but not a bot like Blip. Not a companion bot. Blip was quite unlike any other bot she had ever known. He wasn't affected by temperature like others. He was never cold, never hot. He was the best, fastest, most intelligent bot she had known. And bots were all she knew.

It didn't respond. She wrapped her hands around it and lifted. Like Blip, it was incredibly heavy. This one felt even heavier. She struggled to lift it from the ground. "Need some help," she grunted.

Blip made no reply.

She twisted and waddled with the extra weight in her arms.

"Blip?" she asked, turning and placing the bot on the sidewalk, "Who is this?" And then, knowing that the only companion bot on the ship was the one assigned to her, Syn whispered, "Whose companion is this?"

Inside, a thin line of hope flared. *Could there be someone else on the ship? Someone who needed a companion?* Syn looked around. Was that person watching them even then? Was it someone else who believed they were alone? Syn glanced at Blip and another thought rose, a thought she never guessed she'd have. *Blip knows everything. Did he know about this companion? Did he know about the other person? Was he lying?*

Blip caught Syn's gaze and looked up above them to the shining sunstrips, unaware of the far-off storm forming in her thoughts. He blinked at the sunlight piercing the treetops. There, in the center of Olorun, was the axis around which everything rotated. They called it the needle. Fastened to it were the sunstrips—bright panels creating the illusion of sunlight in this artificial world. "I...I've never met this bot." He was going to say the he didn't know, but he knew what response that would bring.

From behind her, a small chirp went up. Syn turned and peered back in the crater as she brushed the soot from Blip's twin off her hands.

At the bottom of the hole, buried in the dirt, a small piece of red metal wriggled.

Syn bent down and reached into clear the dirt away. "An eye-bot," she said. It had been under the bot when it hit, smashed into the earth. Syn scooped out dirt on its edges and then plucked the vibrating bot out of the soil. She brushed off its crimson surface and held it up. It opened its iris and eyed around. Without a thank you, it attempted to lift off and fly high up overhead. It managed a few inches from her palm and then dropped suddenly back down. It blinked and shuddered, attempting to rise up again. It knew one thing—fly and record, and now it couldn't do one of those things.

Syn patted its head. "Okay, you're a bit hurt. Calm down, and I'll take care of you." She sat the bot gently on the ground. "Wait there." Syn stared at it and then back at the companion bot. "So what now?"

Blip nodded, "I'll check records. I'll do some digging. There has to be something to tell where he...it came from."

Syn narrowed her eyes, "That's all?"

Something brushed her side. She glanced down to see the red eye-bot nuzzling against her. Saying thank you. She patted it. They weren't as smart as Blip, but they were on the level of a pet—a dog or a cat. If you show a little attention, they were pretty loyal. She had never been able to get them to do tricks, though. "Give me second, and I'll get you fixed up."

Blip scooted back, "What do you want me to do?"

"Are we alone?"

Blip just stared, unanswering, as if she had asked the dumbest question at the moment.

While there were still areas to comb through, in years, they hadn't heard or seen anyone else. She knew they were alone. She was alone—the only human for light-years.

Her gaze darted downwards. She muttered, "Can we at least investigate?"

"Where?"

"The needle?" Syn stared up.

"You were there yesterday. You floated around in the zero-g for hours. Did you see a companion bot yesterday?" Gravity was normal at the base, but high up, in the center at the needle, there was no gravity.

Syn shook her head and jabbed a finger toward the unmoving bot next to her. "But then where did it come from?" She had wanted to say, *and why have you been lying to me?* But she wasn't certain, and the possibility of driving Blip away frightened her. That had always been a real fear. The only other living thing. The only other thing on the ship with a voice. He wasn't human, but he talked. He was her friend. And she was always scared of losing him. If he was gone, then she'd be alone.

"I don't know. Maybe there's a storage bay in one of the towers. I'll start looking. I'll tell you if I find anything."

"Please..." she started.

He sighed—a sound she hated.

Syn paused before she retorted. *Perhaps he was telling the truth.* She so wanted him to be telling the truth. And if so, this had to be affecting him as well. She couldn't imagine what it would be like to discover an exact copy of yourself after thinking you were the only one. She patted Blip's shell, "That's fine. Take your time."

He would get to the bottom of it, she knew that. He was the fastest thing in the ship. He could solve anything—access anything. If there was a secret on the ship, he'd figure it out. Syn nodded, sighed in relief, and then rubbed Eku behind her ears, running her fingers through the cat's thick fur.

She tapped its shell. Another living voice like Blip. Another friend. Syn allowed a small smile at the hope. "Can we fix him?" Syn asked.

"Get a mover bot. Take it somewhere I can analyze it."

Syn nodded. "The garage?" The garage was her own personal workshop. There she could do some of her own analysis.

"Fine," Blip said.

Give him time, she thought. *Trust him.* And at the same time, far back in her mind, *why are you trying so hard to convince yourself?*

She held up her hand with the resting red eye-bot. "Okay, little one. Let's get you fixed up." With an eye on Blip's fallen twin, she thought, *and let's figure you out.*

2

THE WORKBENCH

"Once you grow past Mommy and Daddy coming running when you're hurt, you're really on your own. You're alone, and there's no one to help you."
—Octavia Butler

The large garage door slid back into the ceiling, and the lights in the workshop flickered on to reveal a large metallic room with benches all around. Broken bots, components, and wires cluttered every space. In the center of the workroom, a large canvas lay draped over a vehicle, hiding it from view and elements.

Syn sauntered in, kicking at piles in her way until she reached the back counter and plunked the red eye-bot down. "Give me a second."

Behind her, Blip motioned at the various worker bots following him, and the silver spheres lifted the quiet shell of the fallen companion bot onto one of the wider workbenches near the entrance.

Syn gripped the screwdriver closest to her and hissed through tight teeth, "My ship. My Olorun." Her own words startled her—had she spoken aloud? She checked herself—Blip's hearing was powerful.

She tapped the screwdriver against the tabletop. *How could there be another companion bot anywhere on this ship? Especially from the needle?*

She had played up there over and over and over! They had explored every nook possible. If it was her world, it was coming unraveled, and she was scared as to what might fall loose from the seams.

The other bots assisting settled the white shell of Blip's twin on the metal workbench as Syn nodded and whispered, "Thanks."

Blip dared, still confused, "I don't think he'll work again."

Again, she insisted, "I want answers." She dusted the bot's surface. A chunk of grime resisted, and she leaned in, scrubbing at the spot with a dirty towel. A pang of empathy tugged at her. *How must Blip be feeling? How bizarre this must be for him? To encounter his twin?* Syn wondered how she would react if she woke up to discover an exact duplicate of herself. She shivered at the thought and pushed it from her mind.

"I'm trying to find them," he muttered. "I'm resilient, but I don't think I could survive a deadfall drop like what he experienced. He's not damaged on the outside, much, but if we can break open his shell, I suspect he'll be scrambled."

"Why do you assume it's a 'he?'" Syn narrowed her eyes and looked sideways at him.

He seemed oblivious to her questions and continued, "I'm surprised he wasn't flattened."

"You're a horrible detective," Syn said. There was the tone of teasing—her mock insults were part of their usual banter—but this time, she meant it.

"Syn," Blip said, pulling back toward the entrance of the garage. He raised his eyebrows, feigning shock.

Syn smiled. "You're not Sherlock Holmes."

"But you could be Watson."

She snagged a wrench from the table and chucked it at him, but he deftly dodged it.

Syn turned back and ran a finger along the white companion bot. The shell was dented in several places. A large, oblong indentation ran up its spine. A star field of smaller dents, many of them pea-sized, littered the rest of the casing. Syn held the flat edge screwdriver above the plate and began to pry against the loose panel. Blip shirked back—

a slight movement but still obvious. *Did Blip feel pain? Could this new one feel pain?* The bot on the table didn't stir, so she pushed further.

Thin smears of dirt covered the inert shell. Dingy and drab stains occluded any hint of its former pristine nature. Syn glanced over to Blip. Blip stood in contrast: gleaming white, shining to a perfect polish.

Syn whispered to the broken bot on the workbench, "Wake up." She ran a line across the dents, hoping for a seam, a hint of a crack that she could wedge the screwdriver into so she could work on the bot's brain. All other bots were easily disassembled, reassembled, and repaired. Not this one. And thus, not Blip.

"Can you help?"

"It's clean."

Syn waved a hand over the carcass. "Clean?" Anything but.

"Clean. The brain is empty."

"You know that? It talked to you?"

"No. It didn't talk. That's the point. I can't find anything. I keep scanning its neural-net, and there's not a single response. The core is clean."

"Then can we at least open it up. Maybe the memory core is intact."

Blip made no move.

Syn raised an eyebrow. "You guys have a memory core, right? Like the others?"

"You guys?" Blip coughed.

"You and your twin here." She tapped the shell with her screwdriver.

Blip continued to circle around him, scanning. "I don't know if he's anything like me."

"You've been scanning him for a bit now—you and I both know he's nearly identical."

Blip narrowed his eyes but said nothing.

Syn stepped back and leaned against the workbench, taking the chaos of the garage in. Years before, she and Blip had made their way through the homes and the garages on the third and fourth tiers just south of the jungle. The man who lived in this one had been named Alileen. And he'd loved to make things. His house was filled with different tools and half-finished projects. Countertops were littered with opened bots, their guts spread open to be resembled. On first glance, they can look like an odd array of noodles and plastic pieces. Wires peppered the tables and discarded plastic bits had been smashed into the floor from constant trodding. If it could be opened up, he had done so and then left it laying around. Appliances, bots, anything that he could tinker with was there. Syn had felt a quiet bond with the man whose space was a memorial to curiosity and ingenuity. *Crack things open. Find out how they work. Get them back going again.*

Together, Syn and Blip had repaired most every type of bot in the Disc: a mass of wires and electronics, translucent bundles of thread wrapped in tight configurations around anti-grav motors, primitive CPUs, and TyTech strips. She had learned each bot's makeup and constantly tweaked them—often improving them. The hovering eye-bots now flew faster than ever before thanks to her alterations.

Behind her, something clinked. She turned and saw the red eye-bot wriggling on the bench. "Oh! Sorry. Forgot about you for a second." She leaned in. "So, what's wrong?"

The eye-bot stared up at her, unblinking. "Well, that's odd—usually your iris is constantly in motion. Is that the problem? Did the crash jam your iris?" She ran a finger across the lens and saw the circular iris start to shutter and stall. Over and over. "That's it. Okay. I think I can fix it. Must just be jammed a bit hard. I think I have a replacement one."

She sat the red eye-bot down and looked through the scrap parts scattered across the bench. There were no deactivated, whole robots. If she could get it moving again, she would. She hated the idea of a bot just stuck on her bench because she couldn't fix it.

She rifled through a few drawers and piles while Blip floated around nudging and prodding the companion bot electronically. Syn stole a glance but not much had changed—he just rotated clockwise around the bot as if he was stuck in orbit—the gravitational pull of the other so strong, he'd be stuck like that forever.

"Found it!" She held up a duplicate iris, a silver circle of layered pieces inside a solid set of rings and motors. "Just need to open you up and we'll pop this in, and you'll be back to normal."

Syn patted the bot. "This might feel weird. Just trust me. I won't hurt you."

She picked up a small black metal tool and ran it across the seam along the bot's circumference. Its case hissed and popped, and she pulled off the top part of its shell, the one housing the clear lens that made up its eye. Its internal systems were all revealed: a tightly packed collection of chips, gyroscopes, wires, and a small strip of organic tissue. The secret to all of the bots, Syn had discovered, was some portion of lab-grown brain tissue that kicked up the level of processing. Blip had said it was the only way the builders could get true AI to work—the human brain, he had said, was quantum in nature, and no machine was able to get there without some tissue assistance. Blip had called it TyTech. It always weirded Syn out a bit when she had to prod around inside the bots while fixing them.

The old iris unit popped off despite the bot's wriggling under her fingers. *Was it anxious? Did robots get nervous?* She knew it was not in pain, but it did jostle more once the lens and iris were gone—discomfort probably from its primary sensor being dulled. *Everything must be blurry,* she thought. The new piece slid in easily.

"Calm down," she hushed, then held a bit tight as she grabbed the top part of its shell and popped it back into place. Once she felt the give and heard the expected click of the magnetic clips joining, she relaxed her hold, patted its head and said, "There you go."

With a nearly inaudible whirr, the eye-bot focused with the new iris. It closed and opened a few times. Then the eye-bot popped straight up off the workbench, whistled once, and then flew out of the garage door into the open air of the Disc.

Blip sighed, "Wish my counterpart were that easy."

Syn allowed herself to relax and slid down to the ground, plopping her legs straight out. Fixing things had always calmed her. The anger and anxiety had melted away. The delicate work required so much focus—the random butterfly of thoughts just faded. "Sorry Blip. This must be frustrating you as much as it is me."

"I'm not frustrated. I'm confused. I just don't understand how..." he clipped his sentence short and then after a pause said, "I don't understand how it came to be. Where it came from."

Syn narrowed her eyes. *That's not what he was going to say.*

The minutes passed by in silence. The minutes built into an hour. Over and over, Blip floated in a slow arc around the other companion, scanning and rescanning, his casing glowing green as his various sensors did their job.

Syn sat on the ground, feeling the exhaustion of the day. She yawned, surprising herself. "Oh, that's not good." She stood up and grabbed a scanstick from the table—an all-purpose scanner tool for bots that detected levels of various electrical activity inside, the status of their anti-grav generators, and other critical information. She walked over and began to move the stick across the bot with careful precision.

"I think I've searched for most everything that thing will tell you," Blip said.

Syn smiled. "Ya, but at least it'll talk to me. You've been doing your thing for a while now and haven't told me a thing."

Blip paused and looked at her. "What's the stick saying? Have you picked up a reading on its primary systems?"

She glanced at the tool and was surprised to see no reading whatsoever. She thwacked it against the palm of her hand hoping to jostle it to life and then ran it back over the white surface. Grimacing, she said, "Nothing. I'm getting nothing."

"Ya. That's why I haven't given you any of my readings. I haven't any. Nothing. Not a single thing. Even for the inert systems—the default ones—there should be a basic reading even if this thing was off. Antigrav generators never cycle entirely down. But nothing is registering. Either this thing has a casing that prevents any reading, or it has never been turned on before."

Syn ran the scanstick over it again. "That's impossible." She slapped it on the table once and glanced at its small screen. Nothing. She smacked it against her palm. "Oh, come on. That's not possible."

Irritated, she hit the stick against the bot on the table, "Come on, you stup—"

The companion bot's case flashed red, casting a crimson glow on every surface of the garage.

Both Syn and Blip leapt back. Blip's own white case reflected the red, causing him to look as if he had been drenched in blood. The light flashed again, and then in a grating, alarmed tone, the companion bot bleeted out "J. One. Three. Zero. Two. Room ninety-nine. She's in J1302-99. J1302.99."

Just as quickly as it had sparked to life, the red light dimmed, and the room was only illuminated by the sparse blue lights lining the edges.

"What was that?" Syn shouted at Blip, her back against the work-bench. She had snagged a wrench and was holding it with white knuckles in case the thing attacked.

Blip was frozen, staring at the inert bot. He stammered, "I...I don't..."

This time, the wrench Syn threw hit him with a sharp clang, and he jostled back to focus.

Syn pointed a finger at him, "Don't say that. I'm sick of hearing you say that you don't know. That's garbage, and you know it." She jabbed the finger at the lifeless bot, "That thing just rattled off some address. To a room. And said someone was there. Blip, is there someone else on this ship? Who was he talking about?"

"I..." Blip started but paused as Syn wrapped her hand around another silver-colored wrench on the table next to her. Blip paused. "We'll find out."

Through clenched teeth, Syn growled, "You're absolutely right we will."

Blip turned and looked out at the darkening Disc. "It's too late now. We'll go in the morning. It's too far away, and it'll take a long time."

She searched her memory. *J. What lift was Settlement J closest to?* He was right. Her mind was tired. She couldn't place the settlement. Couldn't think of how to get there. It wasn't close, she knew that. "Ugh," she said, "You're right." She dropped the wrench, and the clang filled the garage. "First thing tomorrow."

She walked out into the night through the open garage door, nearly tripping over Eku, who had fallen asleep on the path out front. She dug her fingers into the cat's fur and said, "Let's go Eku. Bedtime."

The cat yawned then stood, and the two walked to her tree, fading into the darkness, leaving Blip alone with his mirror image lifeless on the table before him.

3

JOURNAL ENTRY: FIRST MEMORIES

The Unauthorized Journal of Syn
Section 7
Composed 2759

My first memories were of the white porcelain room that I later discovered was called Integration Bay One. It was also called my crèche. Integration. I was the one being integrated. Blip and I have celebrated that day as my birthday. I'm sure that I technically had a birthday, but from what I can discover, the transition from fetus to child didn't include a mother. Or a father. Just a Blip.

That's right. I was born in a machine, and I stayed in that machine for several years. The pod tinkered with me while I hibernated. I do remember dreaming, odd shapes, things with frightening eyes, and then words and smells and colors, all jumbled together. My brain was soaking up the constant feed of information that they sent me.

And the definition of "they" isn't easy to answer. While the former inhabitants of the ship, the ones whose bodies are now glistening in the moist dirt of the body farms, were intelligent, they weren't the ones that created me. I thought, at first, they might have been. Perhaps those first few weeks, maybe months, of searching through the Disc was a search for my creators. Maybe I'd run across one of them that would see me and exclaim, "Syn! You've woken up! You've found us!" That was my hope. With each new house we entered, I replayed that scenario until it faded away.

Blip helped me dig up the records. I was planned long before the ship was launched. I was the Eve—an engineered human that was just a bit stronger, smarter, and faster, and I was designed to be the first on Àpáàdì, the Earth-like planet formerly known as Kapteyn-b. I was supposed to be woken up, though, right before we made planetfall, not decades before. My designers were on Earth. I suspect I had a real mother, or at least, an egg-donor. But that egg and me were nothing alike. The videos explained how they went through each line of DNA and custom-tooled me. Entire sections of the nice TGAC code were pulled out and reinserted with others. Maybe some animal. Maybe something unseen before. I know I can see as well in the darkness as the big cats that now prowl. I know that I can hunt better than most anything I've encountered out there. I'm fast. I can do a kilometer in two minutes.

For all that comprehensive planning before the ship left Earth, the morons on the ship screwed it up. The entire mission went to the sewers, and someone woke me up way too early. I'll be an old woman when we hit Àpáàdì. If the idiots had at least left me alone, the ship would've woken me up right as I entered the elliptical plane of Kapteyn's Star. If that had happened, all of the ship's mission and plans would've worked out. No, there wouldn't have been any of the actual ship inhabitants to make it, but at least one human would've stepped foot on the second Earth. Humanity would've made their home on two different planets. Not now. Idiots.

A blinding light hung in the center of the integration room and it hurt to look at. My eyes hurt. My ears hurt. I woke up, slamming my head against the slowly opening glass. The shock caused me to puke. Yes, the miracle of birth—my first few moments—was me hurling the vilest green crap from my weak stomach onto the glass in front of me. I stumbled out into the ship, my first few steps, covered in my own green vomit, rubbing at my eyes and screaming because they burned. Every sound was horrible. My ears were working for the first time, and I just wanted to drown myself. I didn't know that's what I wanted. I just knew I wanted to plunge into something that would block out all of the sound, all of the madness, all of the absolutely insane sensations.

Being born is tough. Don't call someone a "baby" as an insult. Babies are tough as nails. Babies come out and manage to make the whole bloody, nasty affair look cute and adorable. They cry a little but then in moments are cooing against their moms. I didn't get that luxury. There was no mom to grab me and hold me tight and say, *I love you. It's okay. Shhh. There. There.*

No, instead, I got the taste of my own puke and Captain Pote's deep voice exclaiming, "Welcome to a new world. You are the hope of our entire endeavor. We are all anxious to meet you. We can't wait to find out who you are. We've planned for you for decades, but you are unknown to us. Don't lose heart just yet, little one, you carry the greatest responsibility on your shoulders ever given to a human. You will be the first of humanity to settle a new Earth. You will be the first one to descend to our future home and ensure its safety and survivability for us. You are both forerunner and, in a way, our guardian angel. You will protect us on that planet from forces we have yet to understand. So, prepare yourself. Use these next few weeks to make yourself ready, and I look forward to having you sit and join my daughters and me for dinner. Happy Awakening Day, little Eve!"

The video shut off and there I stood, a naked little six-year-old, just told that I would be the savior of this people. My feet stuck to the floor because of my own puke. I left a green set of footprints from my birthing capsule to the couch. I found a blanket, and I curled myself up in it, blocking out the light, blocking out the sound, blocking out the torture of this new world.

Since this is confession time, and I'm honest with you, you should know I pissed the bed a lot back then. Okay, I didn't even know what a bathroom was until day two. Imagine that, of all the instruction videos they could have thrown at me, the location and proper use of the bathroom, was one scheduled for day two. The second day—day two! Can you believe it? Seriously, they were morons. When you're born, the one thing you want is silence and food and then a place to relieve yourself. Babies get diapers. Not me. I got a great big bed to turn into my own personal litter box.

The first video, after Captain Pote's wonderfully inspiring message, was on the education plan they had set up for me. I'm pretty sure that first video used the word "pedagogy." Why did they think I would care about that? These geniuses had launched an interstellar craft with a mini-world, a small self-sustained version of Earth in a great rotating Disc, and they still didn't understand children. They didn't understand humans.

Maybe that's why the whole thing went to the sewers. They knew engines. They figured out laundry, and they figured out life support. The food was solved. General biology and the entire balance of private geo-system was planned out meticulously. But they still couldn't prepare for the uncontrollable insanity of humans.

It's been years since they all died, and the ship's systems are working correctly. The ship is still flying at top speed toward Àpáàdì. The Disc still spins. Gravity still works. The food producers in the lower level farms are still growing food at a break-neck pace. There's more food than I can keep up with. The air is pure and clean. I'm healthy. The water in the great river Lokun still flows.

But the humans are all dead. Each and every one of them except me. Captain Pote killed seven himself in those last days. He had piled the bodies up in his office when I found him. He had ended up stabbing himself straight in the head. Ugh. I think the blood is still on his desk.

They all went mad. Anger and greed and fear.

And someone had also managed to wipe the system's memory of the records of those last few months. I don't know what sent them all into a raging mania. I don't know what started the "Madness." There's no exact moment recorded for when it happened. No luck finding that precise info. But I know they're all dead, and they're dead because they killed each other. With knives and sticks and bricks and anything that they could bash into another person's skull.

Humans.

To Hell with them.

4

———————

J1302-9_

"The life of the dead is set in the memory of the living."
—Marcus Tullius Cicero, *Philippics*

The world hung frozen and silent around her. She yawned, and the soft noise of her breath filled the quiet of her world. The treehouse was draped in the sapphire of nighttime from the false moonlight from above. Across the room, with a deep, rumbling, stuttering snore, Eku slept, curled up and looking more like a housecat than ever before. A few other housecats slept around it, one tabby nuzzled into Eku's thick coat for warmth.

All were sleeping. All were still. But there was no Blip.

He was never there in the middle of the night. He didn't sleep. He didn't power down. He'd come and rest beside her as she dozed off every evening, but she knew that once she fell asleep, he was up and about, onto the tasks at hand. Reviewing repairs, analyzing the environment, checking on plants.

Or that was what he told her he was doing.

Syn narrowed her eyes and stood up. In that quiet hour, her own body felt loud. Perhaps he was somewhere else entirely. Olorun was huge, and she was quite small.

As she stepped out of the main room and descended the stairs, a thought bloomed. Blip had nearly eight to ten hours a day away from her. He could live an entire other life in that time. And she would never know it. *What was he doing right now?* Perhaps late at night, he would meet up with not just another companion bot, but with many of them. Perhaps there were secret meetings every single evening without her. Perhaps tonight they were holding a funeral for their fallen comrade. Was Blip secretly mourning the loss of a hidden friend?

Syn shook her head as she stepped through the wet, cold grass in her bare feet. The chill bite sent shivers up her spine.

Syn stepped out of the trees, into a small clearing, and the thought echoed again. She muttered, "Who can I trust?"

Did she hear a response in the wind? Did the leaves rustle and say, *you're alone?* And again, the tree creaked: *all alone, little girl.*

She closed her eyes and took a deep breath. The air wafting over the river filled her senses. A smell mixed of the spreading moss from the far banks, the racing fish, and the moist spray from the rapids created a sharp tonic. If she had been groggy from sleep, she was now fully awake. Far, far away, behind the rush of the river, she heard the slight buzzes of bots floating across the Disc. Above her, clearing the air, were the jellyfish: massive bots unburdened by gravity floating across the sky, pushing the clouds around. Beyond that, she heard the crunch, crunch lumbering steps of the treemovers—the spider-like giant bots that served as the caretakers of the forest. The entire artificial ecology—an ecology of bots—never stopped their toil. She wondered, *did they have some hidden world they built, behind the walls of the Disc, that they escaped to when I'm not looking?*

So not everything was asleep. *Was Blip with them?*

The wind moved down the Disc and whipped the loose fabric of her pants around her. She only wore a thin blanket across her shoulders, and the breeze yanked at it, threatening to rip it from her. The world was painted in blue and black. A bruised world. Perhaps this was the true sight of the world. Perhaps daylight was a mirage, she thought. Perhaps it was only at night that the truth was revealed.

Again, that dark, bruised voice in her skull whispered: *all alone.*

And a single tear ran down her cheek.

She stared up at the curving Disc towering far away and reaching up above them, its end veiled in the shadow. Blip was somewhere out there, but she did not know where.

She shivered again, but the wind was not blowing.

What else is out there?

The single set of doors were shut tight, and the string of lights parallel to the center slit were black. A fan behind Syn, far behind, whirred up slowly, juttering a few times as it did, cycling air through the vents above, a hollow sound through the empty corridor.

Syn slid an orange paint-covered finger across the wall as the running lights at her feet lit up. She smeared the orange paint in a half-meter long line. "There."

"Room J1302-97," Blip said as he floated up to the large doors.

"We're looking for J1302-99."

Their hunt had led them to one of the settlements on the side opposite of her tree—this was the side that she had explored only recently in detail. They were near the thirteenth level of the settlements. The entrance path around this level opened up on one side to look out at the Disc and the sweeping jungle that moved off in both directions. The jungle twisted up and disappeared into the clouds above their heads. There were still several corridors, like this, that she had not touched. They spent most of their time in the jungle or by the water or, more and more often, floating through the zero gravity of the needle. Yet, the settlements had to be accounted for. It was still amazing to her that after several years of being awake on Olorun, there were still a few places they hadn't ventured. The settlements had begun to bore her—they all seemed the same. House after house after shop after office after store. It was an endless repetition of a boring life.

The settlements were a collection of houses stacked several high along the outside edge of the Disc, providing a wall and a border for the world of Olorun. The dense, hill-laden jungle named Aja (Syn's home) thrived in the center of the ring.

Blip twisted up in the air, peering down the metal corridor lined with doors. "I know. But that's what's weird. The rooms stop at 97. There is no 99. This is the last room on the thirteenth level here."

Syn looked back from where they had walked and counted off the doors, reading the numbers above the access panels. "91. 92. 93. 94. 95. 96." She pointed at the one ahead of them. "97. Okay. Did we hear him wrong?"

"You could've. I didn't. He said J1302-99."

"Maybe it's not a room."

"What else works according to that numbering?"

"It's not 99. 97 is the only room here. It's the last one. And we've never explored here."

"Let's open it up."

From down the hall, Eku walked—a large shape emerging from the darkened corridor into the blue light of the floorstrips activated by Syns presence.

"Eku!" Syn shouted, running to wrap her arms around the tiger's neck. She pulled back and looked at her hand and then at the cat's neck. "Oops! I got some orange paint on you."

"She's an orange cat. Won't make a difference," Blip said.

Syn dabbed another finger into the small pot of orange paint in her hand and tapped her finger across her forehead leaving nine dots above her eyebrow from left to the right. "There. We both have paint." She smiled and held up her finger to the tiger. "Look we found somewhere new." She leaned over and in a hushed, dramatic tone, she breathed out, "And a mystery."

Syn stood up and walked to room 97. "It always surprises me when we come to a place that's new." She nodded at the orange mark. "These are everywhere." Their first explorations throughout the ship were panic-infused creeps fearful of what might jump out at them. When it became clear that they would be crawling over the ship for years, Syn had found some paint to mark their progress.

Those little dabs of paint now felt pervasive. Few doors remained unmarked.

"We've almost explored the entire Disc. We would've gotten to this spot sooner or later, whether that bot had said it or not."

"Doesn't it worry you?"

Blip looked sideways as the access panel slid open and revealed a digital interface array. "Step closer. It's out of power."

Syn took a couple of steps, glancing between her fingertips and then out across the railing to the sweep of the Disc. As she stepped within a meter of the access panel, it lit up with its common green interface.

"Thanks." Blip sent over a quick command line, requesting the door to open. "And what do you mean?"

Syn stepped back from the access panel, and it went dark, eliciting a muffled grunt of irritation from Blip. "What will happen when we run out of places to explore? What happens when every wall has an orange mark?" She looked around, gripping the edge of the rail and staring out at the Disc.

"None of this will be new ever again. We'll be locked in without any place to explore. Maybe we should just let this door stay shut. Maybe we should plan to leave one mystery and always keep it a mystery. At least then we'll always know that there's something we don't know, something that we haven't explored." She spun on Blip. "I'm scared of the same old thing day after day after day. What happens then?"

Blip sighed. "Breathe."

Syn took a deep breath and snarled, "That's good. It doesn't change the fact that your twin is the only thing new we've really encountered. I know what's going to happen when we open that door."

"He's not my twin, and *I* don't. That's why I was trying to open it."

"We're going to discover the same boring room with the same white and grey acoustic panels on the wall with the leftover clothes and half-eaten meals, and maybe, somewhere, a screen will be left on to some children's show, and Barney the purple dinosaur will be singing as we enter. That's it! How do I know that? Because that's the same thing we've encountered everywhere else. If it isn't Barney, it's some band or TV commentary or documentary about Earth. Oh, and don't forget the dead bodies. They'll be sprawled out somewhere in the most uncomfortable positions. But that's it! Nothing new! Nothing amazing! TV, food, death, and gray walls. Olorun's great legacy." Her voice had reached a level of pitch he hadn't heard for a while, and the last few words clipped out in a panicked state.

"You're having an anxiety attack. It's going to be okay." He floated close, moving within an inch of her. Not close enough to touch but close enough to be able to if she wanted it.

"Blip? Don't you get it? It's over! That bot was the last great mystery, and once we solve that, it's over! We will live the same day over and over and over. Like that movie...*Ground...Grounder Day!*"

"*Groundhog Day?*"

"Yes! Except we're not trying to get anything right! We can do the day perfect, but we're stuck."

"It's going to be fine."

"How do you know that? How can you say that?"

Blip sighed and started, "I—"

"Don't sigh. I'm not your problem." She spun around and began to walk the other way.

"This was your idea! I said I could do this without you! Are you okay with me checking this out on my own? I can ask Olorun to open the door!" Blip shouted after her.

"Of course you can. You always can." Syn turned on her heels and pointed. "But that's not what's going to happen. You don't get to talk to the ship when you're not happy with me."

Blip floated back, "Not happy with you? What are you talking about?"

"I'm not freaking out. I just can't get why you're not!"

"Wait— did you hear yourself? I didn't say..." Blip moved in close and began to count, his voice deep. "Twenty. Nineteen." With each number, his voice hushed a bit more.

"You know what I mean. I'm not getting the words right," she said, seemingly oblivious to what he was doing.

"Sixteen. Fifteen."

Syn took a deep breath.

"Ten. Nine. Eight."

"I'll open your door. But some point is coming…" She nudged past him and walked to the door, the floor light sparking up as she passed and the access panel now glowing orange. "Some point is coming when we won't get to open a door and experience anything new."

"Four. Three. Two."

She tapped her fingers on the panel, throwing in the same code Blip had started. She looked back over her shoulder, "And doesn't that scare you? Like you're some fish stuck in some can, and you're never going to get out."

In a whisper, he said, "One." Blip gave a sound like a sigh himself after a pause. "Please stand here so I can open it?"

Syn sighed, shaking the brief panic free, and pulled the makeshift spear closer. "I've been waiting for you." Syn nudged the floating robot, "Besides, I thought you could do anything."

Blip's eyes went narrow, "I have great big memory banks, but I can't keep it all up inside me. There are a few things that I get on info drip from Olorun. She's the one that has all the info." Blip faked a cough.

She hated when he talked about the ship as if it were alive. It creeped her out. He didn't do it often, but occasionally, he would throw out a line like that and make her anxious—to think they were crawling around inside a living thing. Maybe it was even the thought that if Olorun was alive, then what did she know of Syn? *Had she been watching everything? Is she watching now?*

She stepped forward. The panel lit up. "I'm here. Shut up and open the door."

The lights on the door flashed green.

Syn smiled, "Nice."

Blip made a metallic sound like a grunt.

Syn rolled her eyes, "Fine. You can say it."

In a deep voice, Blip declared, "Open sesame!"

Syn sneered, "Welcome to Olorun. Now let's see the last great mystery."

The inner gears of the door ground to life, clunking over and over. The split in the door widened, and Syn bent back into a defensive stance, her arms pulled tight, gripping the makeshift spear tighter. Only darkness lay ahead. And then, a smell familiar and stomach-churning rolled out—undisturbed, unfiltered, stale air. Syn coughed and pulled out a stain-spotted yellow cloth, wrapping it around her mouth.

Eku crouched and growled—a deep, rumbling sound.

She coughed again, forcing herself not to gag, swallowing the bile back down. After a moment, Syn whispered, as if facing a tomb, "Light please."

This room had apparently not been opened since the Madness had swept through the ship and everyone died. In the center of the room lay a body, face down, clothed in the deep purple wear of the science crew. A few thin strands of blonde hair lay against the skull. Something, perhaps a rodent, had torn away at what was left, leaving only the brilliant white of skull. Most of what was left was hardened flesh and bone. All muscle and meat had been ripped off and digested by something small enough to get into these nearly impenetrable suites.

"Her name was Agan'ja. She was thirty-five and worked as a botanist in the soil farms," Blip said, cross-referencing some database from Olorun with what he picked up about the room.

The room felt frozen. The newly-entered light illuminated the thick particles of dust kicked up by Syn's steps. No sound. Nothing. Now she did wish for the childish songs of Barney. Anything to break the sense of entombment.

"Remember that old movie *The Mummy?*" Syn asked.

"Which one? Fraser, Karloff, Cruise, or Wolfhard?" Blip had moved into the kitchen, but she could still his green glow through the slit in the doorway.

Eku walked through the living room sniffing at every chair, corner, and wall—undisturbed by the corpse in the entranceway.

Syn paused and thought through the options. "All of them. This is

the disturbing of the crypt. The thing you're not to do. And then..."
She smacked her spearpoint hard against the door to the kitchen and shouted, "And then the Mummy gets you!"

Blip spun in the air, his body shifting from green to red in alarm. In a moment, his shell drained of color back to porcelain white. "Not funny."

"Pretty funny."

"There's nothing here."

Eku seemed to growl in assent.

Syn walked through the hallway into the back bedroom. Everything in the suite was undisturbed. Books on shelves. No food out. Compared to most places they had searched, this one seemed oddly prepared to be left alone for all time—everything perfectly cleaned and arranged. "Maybe."

The bed was made with a green and yellow striped comforter. A normal decor choice on this side of the Disc. Syn had identified different groupings of style and taste of those that were here before —some were gaudy in their color choices, some were muted, some relished old cultural patterns. Some had clung to more recent, subtler choices. But the styles never varied much from their neighbor.

Syn walked into the bathroom and gasped. She was presented with an elaborate series of mirrors. Before her stood a large, full-bodied mirror with angled panes on all sides. She could see herself from nearly every angle. "Lights," she whispered, and the bulbous glamour lights around the edges lit up.

"Ouch," she grunted, closing her eyes as they adjusted to the brightness. When she opened them, the effect was dizzying. More than just five Syns surrounded her. A hundred copies of her receded back through the corridors of the mirrors—a hundred Syns all standing at attention. The orange dots across her forehead reflected back and seemed to float before her. She moved her hand in the air and watched the copies all echo the movement in perfect synchronicity. *Yet, was there a delay? Would she have known if one had refused? Perhaps, twenty copies back, that one didn't respond as fast,* she wondered.

A Syn that was not completely Syn. Just a bit out of step. Out of rhythm.

Or maybe instead, she imagined, she was peering into the past and was seeing all the Syns that she had been before. Young Syn, stepping out of the crèche and exploring Olorun the first time. Curious Syn next—always looking in every door and every room without much thought. But that extinguished fast. Curious Syn was the first to die. Oh, she kept a token of curiosity to remember her, but the Curious Syn would never survive the wilds of Olorun. After that had come Sad Syn, then Angry Syn, and then Hopeless Syn and then one after another—none of them capable of doing the job that needed to be done. Survival required that those parts of her, those echoes of who she was now, be cut off and thrown away with no precision. She was standing because none of those others could. She was the survivor that had been birthed in their passing.

Beside her, Eku stood and growled, snapping her attention back to the now.

"Ya, girl. Just me. Nothing to worry about." She tapped the mirror with the point of her spear before turning away. "They're just me. They're not real. They can't hurt you."

Before exiting the bathroom, she examined the counter and opened up a wooden jewelry box. Inside were a variety of beaded necklaces. She picked one up that was carved from wood and decorated in a variety of blue designs. She slipped it over her neck to join the others. She searched through the box and found a small orange tiger carved from some soft stone. "Look Eku, it's you." Syn clipped the pendant to the end of the most recent necklace to join her collection. "There, that way you're always with me even when you're not."

She turned back to the living room, and Eku padded after. "Nothing here. This wasn't where the other bot meant."

As she came around the couch, her foot snagged, and she stumbled, catching her balance after a couple steps before falling to the ground. "What the?" Behind her, half under the couch, was the shattered shell of a vacuum bot.

Blip floated in. "Are you okay?"

She pulled the bot out and picked it up. "I have discovered a remarkable thing." She held up the vacuum bot. "A broken bot." She held her arms out straight and let the heavy construction drop to the group with a loud clang as its plastic pieces shattered, spraying across the room. "Just like every other bot on this ship."

She walked over to Blip and leaned in, pressing her nose against his white surface. "Know what?"

Blip floated without response or expression. With as mechanical a response as he could muster, he replied, "What?"

"Just like you will one day." She stepped back and pushed him away. "And you're going to leave me all alone."

She walked back to the entrance and kicked the corpse's skull, detaching it from its spine. It rolled across the floor before stopping against a table leg. "This was stupid. A waste of time. We should be opening that bot up. Or going back to the needle or something."

"I'm sorry," Blip said.

Syn stared at him. *An unusual response for him.* "What for?"

"I'm sorry we didn't find anything new."

She glanced down at the necklace and fingered the orange tiger pendant. "Oh, but we did. See?"

"That's very pretty," Blip said.

Syn grinned, "See. I knew you liked tigers."

"That's not what I—" Blip started, floating after her.

Syn stepped to the door as it slid open and interrupted him, "We've got a long ride back home. Theater's on the way, and I want to watch a movie. You can choose. Come spend time with me or go talk to your girlfriend Olorun."

With that, she stepped outside and breathed, "Lights off," dropping the apartment into pitch blackness, leaving Blip floating alone. The door behind her to the outside shut with a strained hiss, cutting off the sound of her receding footsteps.

5

───────

THROUGH THE FOREST

"Think, now, if the accomplished whole be Heaven,
How wonderful the anxious years of slow
And hazardous achievement—a destiny for Gods."
—Yorùbá Creation Myth

Syn had fallen asleep during the last minutes of the film and woke when Blip nudged her.

They moved in quiet from the Theater to her tree. She wanted to talk with Blip, quiz him more on the recent strange events, but instead she just squeaked out, "Stay with me until I fall asleep. I don't want to be alone."

Blip gave a single nod of agreement but chose to not respond.

From the darkness of the forest, from the false night created by the dimming of the sunstrips, walked a dark shadow. Syn froze. As it approached, she relaxed. Eku. The tiger. Her tiger.

She wrapped her arms around its neck and buried her face in its fur. Eku's flesh was warm, its body rose and fell with its steady breathing, and deep inside, like from a hidden furnace, the slight start of the rumbling that would be a purr began.

So, with Eku by her side, she chose to walk. She wanted to step

40

through the jungle with the power of Eku beside her. She wanted to be in her tree. Yet, she also just wanted to take her time. She craved shelter and sleep and the lull of a long walk.

It was only a few kilometers. Syn could see her tree peaking up over the other trees. It was enormous and seemed to stretch forever. It was the one sight that was visible wherever they stood on the Disc. From the other side of the Disc, looking up, she could see the small green dot that was the tree's top, and it was still visible against the mass of the rest of Aja. There was so much green in the jungle preserve, but her tree was somehow greener. It was darker, and it called to her. She felt like she should've named it Lighthouse. She could see it from great distances and was pulled to it over and over.

The first time Syn had seen it, the call deep inside her was there. But she was also scared. It was larger than anything except the Towers and the Disc itself. From kilometers away, it felt enormous. It was easily twice the height of the other trees. Its branches were visible, darting above and through the treetops. It somehow overshadowed and unified the trees. Those twisting branches seemed like the arms of some mother trying to bring her children together. Syn had seen movies of mother birds and their outstretched wings cradling their chicks along. The tree's branches always felt like that protective, leading nudge of a mother. It directed, it protected. She knew it was all in her head. It was just a tree. A giant tree perhaps, but she knew that it didn't have any special magical properties. There was no magic beyond what she could carve and program together from other parts. There wasn't some great god-planted tree in the middle of the garden that she was pulled to. It was just a tree, and no gods had raised it up.

Looking up at the tree for the first time, there was a part of her that seemed to pause at the enormity of it. It was the tree of all trees, and it was beyond imagination. She couldn't believe that the builders who had designed this ship had thought far ahead enough to consider a tree. No, this tree was simply tall because it was the cage-fight winner in evolution's tournament battles. The other trees hadn't won the genetic monopoly. Just this tree. And as it grew, it overshadowed others. She had called it the Queen of Trees. A Red Queen sitting on her throne.

Syn moved from tree to tree and stepped through the underbrush. The forest was meant to be managed and taken care of. In her exploration of the Aja jungle, Syn had taken note of at least nine different type of forest worker bots whose entire job was keeping it cleared and managed. There were tree trimmers, refuse cleaners (small spidery type bots that crawled through the underbrush), tree doctors (these were drilling into the trees, analyzing samples, and injecting various chemicals to help the trees continue to live)—just a sample of the bots in the forest. But several years without humanity and the floor of the forest was a mess. It delayed her travel and that delay just shouted at her: the tree is special. She didn't know why, just that it was.

It was quiet tonight, and the sunstrips above were powering down. The forest at twilight was just perfect. The animals were just beginning to wake up or go to sleep. The forest crackled as insects took flight. Leaves rustled as things moved from their burrows and stiff breaths issued from underneath the green packed into every corner. Small creatures taking their first few breaths of the evening, determining the changes of the day and hoping for prey, or to avoid being prey.

Syn still kept her spear close by. The animals that were about, like Eku, were all programmed to avoid humans. They preyed upon each other, but Syn knew she was safe. Still—she knew there were still places unexplored, so she kept her spear nearby. There could be monsters in the dark surrounding her, but she was confident in her ability to protect herself. Yet, she was glad Blip was here. No matter how confident she felt, he always emboldened her.

She pushed through foliage and dense brush before she reached the trunk of the tree. She felt incredibly, wildly, unbelievably small. Like she was an ant staring at an oak tree.

Syn stood there at its base and just stared. She breathed deeper. A few minutes of reflecting, of standing, and she could've sworn the tree was breathing in sync with her. She would exhale, and it would inhale.

She would inhale as it exhaled—carbon dioxide to oxygen to carbon dioxide. Over and over.

She walked with quiet steps, her bare feet padding along the wooden steps, and moved around the trunk, her hand tracing along the rough bark. The bark changed every time. It had grown underneath her fingertips. A crack would be smaller from one day to the next, or larger. She could never predict the changes the tree would make to itself.

She always wondered how her living amongst its branches had changed its future. Looking up, she thought its outer branches were arcing up more, cradling the treehouse, and thus, her. *Was it protecting her? Did it know who it was?* She wondered, *When I sat at its peak, did it feel as satisfied as I did that first time? Had it been waiting for me? Had it been growing slowly in anticipation for me living there?* She hoped it had. Every night, for just a few seconds before darkness took her, she imagined she could hear its wooden heart beating deep inside its ringed depths. Ka-thud. Ka-thud. Slow. Slower than the spin of the Disc itself. Ka-thud.

Tonight she walked into her main room and fell onto cushions, into the mass of stuffed animals—piles upon piles of them that she had scavenged from across the ship. Blip floated by the door, and Eku crawled up next to her. Syn's eyes shut, craving that steady beating heart. Ka-thud. Ka-thud. Each slam of that imagined heart pulled her deeper into sleep, below the waves. Ka-thud. And she slept.

6

———————

THE TEA PARTY

"Before us is the dream of a million souls. A new Eden lies ahead. We are the stewards of the hopes of all that came before and the gratitude of all that will come after."
—Captain Pote

"A very merry unbirthday to me!" Syn sang out, her arms raised above her head, tea splashing all over Captain Pote's table. Her mouth was wide open, and she bellowed out the notes. "And a very merry unbirthday to you!"

Next to her, in the odd array of light from various fixtures, was Blip. He bobbed, floating a few feet off the ground. He chirped in his nasal voice, "I have work to do. Please, let me go."

Syn fell back into the padded chair with a thump, crossed her arms, and glared, "You promised you'd do this scene. And you'd do it right here." She wanted to add, *I thought you were doing work these last few nights. Where were you?*

Blip spun away so Syn couldn't see his eyes. "I did not."

"Liar." She pitched her white cup against the ground, and it shattered. Her voice was full of false anger, and she wore a grin. With a

44

laugh, she continued singing, "Twinkle, twinkle, little bat, how I wonder what you're at!"

At the sound, Eku gave a grunt from the far corner of the room where she slept. She lifted her head, looked around, and then went back to sleep, snoring softly.

Bits of porcelain rattled across the light wood floor. It didn't add anything to the mess of the room. The entire house was in complete disarray. Syn had raided this house over and over for keepsakes she could take back to the great tree, back to her home. She often came back to stage her various productions. It wasn't a theater, but it was the biggest house along the south edge of the Disc, and it felt the closest to family. It had been Captain Pote's face, with his daughters in the background, that she had first seen when she had woken up in the white room. His large jowls and smiling face had been a calming influence in those first confusing moments. She had always felt drawn to him and his family. When she discovered that the video message played when she first woke had been a recording made years before and that Captain Pote and his family had been dead for decades, she had cried for a long time. She had wanted to run away the night she had found the Pote house and walked in on the Captain's daughters, who were now just withered corpses. Instead, she sat down at the dinner table, the same table she was hosting her tea party at now, and she wept. She had fallen asleep with her head on the table, and when she had woken hours later, she cried again. She would never know the family that she had hoped for. Those first several months in her crèche—an isolation and integration room where she was brought up to speed on the Starship Olorun, was dotted with several pre-recorded messages from Captain Pote and even his daughters. His oldest daughter, Stace, had been the one that recorded the most and to whom Syn had felt the deepest connection. She had imagined staying up late talking to this bright-eyed girl. She had wanted to ask her so many questions that the videos and instruction tutorials never answered. But Stace's body was blackened with decay, and her blue-knit flex suit hung loosely on her splayed-out corpse.

Syn would play those videos, reciting the lines. In isolation, she memorized each response from others when conversations happened.

Her favorite was a video greeting that Pote and his daughters had recorded in the evening. The setting was the very room she was in now. Pote would enter, the camera behind him, and announce, "I'm home!"

The girls would run out and yell, "Daddy." Syn would mouth those words in unison as they shouted it.

"So what did you do today?" he would add.

Syn would mute the girls and fill in her own details, "Blip and I played, and then we watched videos about big buildings on Earth. He made me eat some nasty green things called asparagus. But I tricked him and spit it out when he wasn't looking."

That video was played over and over, even after she left the white room, and she would fill that space with details of her own day.

"The ship's greatest advancement, our most powerful technology, is the people in the ship." Pote, started each of his monthly "State-of-the-Ship" addresses with those words.

Yet, in that house, now empty and absent, Syn couldn't escape the fact that Pote and his daughters rested in a dirt field two levels down below the base, amongst a field of the dead, dissolving in the body farms. After much digging, Syn had discovered a final, horrifying video of Pote's last days, defending his family from the marauding passengers. Pote had killed seven himself before someone slammed a pipe wrench over his head and shattered his skull.

Blip flew around the table in a fast arc to float above the chair holding the stuffed bear that served as the Mad Hatter. In a wild, lilting voice, Blip shouted, "Move down!" Then he whipped over to the next chair, the chair that Syn was sitting in, and bumped her hard.

She teetered and then fell with a crash into the stuffed bunny serving as the March Hare. She cackled with laughter as she lost her balance, landing hard on the ground and giving a triumphant "Whoop!" She picked up a fallen tea cup, a tiny white piece with pink trim, and flung it high in the air. "That's it, Blip!"

Blip rocked and smiled. "More tea, Hare!"

The March Hare was in no position to provide more tea. When it landed on the hard ground, it sent up a puff of dust before settling.

"March Hare, get back into character," Blip said, narrowing his eyes.

Syn leaned over and picked up the stuffed rabbit up and waved him in the air, moving his arm as if he was responding to Blip. "Excuse me, sir," she said, in a gruff voice meant to serve as the March Hare, "I have decided I have had quite enough tea for today and instead am going to watch the clouds float by. Come join us, our fine friend. Tell me what shapes you see as they float above." Syn flopped him back to the ground and fell back staring up at the dark ceiling that was covered in cobwebs and numerous stains.

Syn spread out her hands and closed her eyes. "That one looks like a shark." There were clouds in the Disc, but they were sparse and thin —the airflow was so limited that the clouds didn't have much space to build up in. She had never seen cumulus clouds in real life. The large fluffy ones. She had also never seen a shark in real life. Both were as fanciful to her as the Earth from which the Olorun had departed. Images in videos replayed hundreds of times, but nothing tangible. They were not things she had sensed on her own. Only her imagination held them. Eyes shut hard, she said, "And that one looks like a farm tractor." She had seen a farm tractor. There was one parked not too far from the tree. She had never been able to make it work, but that was not for a lack of trying.

Blip floated down to rest beside her. His eyes narrowed. "Perhaps I see a caterpillar. A great big worm moving through the sky."

Her smile grew twice as large as she leaned into him and whispered, "I love you."

Blip shifted his voice lower and replied with, "I know."

Syn's smile grew even bigger, and she giggled in delight. "I'd like some music."

The robot gave an audible sigh, and a moment later a thin tune, its notes light and slow, filled the room. Despite the domestic surroundings, they were still on a ship hurtling through space—a ship integrated with countless processors and interfaces, all of which Blip could access at any moment.

Syn muttered as she turned the edges of her mouth into a small grin. "No. Not that. You can't reply with 'I know' and then not play John Williams. Please get it right."

Blip sighed. "Are we done with the tea party?" As he spoke, the music shifted into a familiar rising anthem.

"The tea party has evolved, dear Blip."

Blip sighed again. "Devolved."

"Watch the clouds. After all, we must be in Cloud City."

"You truly belong here with us among the clouds, princess."

It was Syn's turn to sigh. "I'll be Leia tomorrow. I'm Alice today." She held Sir Hops-A-Lot up in front of Blip and said, "Can I put bunny ears on you?"

"You were Sleeping Beauty three days ago. Baba Yaga the day before that. And Luke Skywalker the day before that," Blip whirled in the air and floated down next to her, positioning his eyes to the ceiling. "It gets a bit tough to keep it straight."

"You're a computer. Put it in a database. Timestamp it. Retrieve when necessary." *This feels so much better*, she thought. Her suspicions had grown like a weed, thin and invasive at first, and soon consuming everything good around it

Another tease, *use that big brain*, was on her lips when the entire room shook. She let out a cry and flattened both hands to the ground to steady herself as the place rocked. Teacups slid from the shaking table and shattered on the floor. The entire room vibrated, and a bookshelf in the corner tottered then tipped over with a large crash.

Then an enormous, deafening boom sounded, and Syn brought her hands to her ears.

Syn shouted, "What's happening?"

Eku came to her haunches, growling.

Blip didn't respond. He turned smoothly in the air and darted straight to the front door and out. The shaking of the room and the entire house seemed to have no effect on him.

The sound ebbed away, but furniture was still crashing to the floor. Several books from a high shelf landed with thuds. The window in a far room, perhaps the kitchen, exploded and was followed by the tinkling sound as shattered glass fell to the floor like rain.

As the shaking lessened, Syn jumped to her feet and chased after Blip, Eku quick on her heels. "Where are you going? What's happening?" The room was still rocking back and forth, and she was far less steady than she had anticipated. She gripped the wall to keep herself from falling and moved toward the open front door with one hand braced against the wall. Paintings that were hung by small screws and nails vibrated off of their hooks and crashed to the ground.

The light from the bright outdoors, light that streamed through the jungle known as Aja, poured through the narrow passageway and lit the front room.

The whole jungle swayed as the vibrations rippled through it. From here, looking out on the edges of the Disc arcing up on either side of her, she could see the quake like a wave, moving through the treetops. As the wave moved, birds, thousands of birds, flew up from the green tops. They squawked and hooted and screeched as they fled their branches. Eku hunched low to the ground and growled with every vibration.

In front of her, moving his gaze across the open air of the Disc, floated Blip. His eyes were gone. His facial features were gone. He was simply a white porcelain ball hanging in space, thrumming with a thin blue light that strobed in and out.

"Blip?" Syn said as she walked up to him. Her knees were wobbly, and she could feel the ground move below her. Whatever it was, it had lessened, but the after-effect was still reverberating beneath their feet.

Blip didn't respond. His blue light shifted to orange. The strobing ceased. He was just an orange glowing orb before her.

"Blip?" she asked again.

Nothing but a hum. She shook her head. Blip's humming sounded more like the fans that broke down from time to time along the towers that served as radials from the Disc back to the needle. When those were on their last legs, the engines would start to hum just as

Blip was now. A wash of worry hit her. *Was Blip broken?* Had the quake affected him far more than she had thought?

She reached a hand out above him, her palm flat. Her skin was illuminated by the orange light, changing her pigment to resemble a pumpkin. Her voice sounded weak as she tried again to speak, "Blip. Please?" She was scared now. When she woke up every day, he was there. Usually chiding her for sleeping late. And when she went to bed, he was still there. He would sing to her before she slept most evenings. His voice was horrible, she had finally concluded after her binge study of music, but it was still familiar, able to lull her into a deep sleep and reminded her that all was right with the world. What if she never heard that off-key voice again? What if he never sang to her as the light from the sunstrips faded into the late evening? What if she never heard those sour notes again? What would she do?

"Blip? Please!"

Once more, with insistence, she yelled, "Blip!"

The orange light flicked off as if someone had flipped a switch. Only the white sheen of his thick plastic hide lay underneath her outstretched palm. She rested her hand on him.

Blip's blue face returned in an instant. He shouted, "There's been an explosion!"

7

INVESTIGATING

"How is it, ye ravens—whence are ye come now with beaks all gory, at break of morning? Carrion-reek ye carry, and your claws are bloody. Were ye near, at night-time, where ye knew of corpses?"
—*Hrafnsmál*

"An explosion? Where?" The words seemed to be from a fantasy, much like the Tea Party they had pulled from *Alice in Wonderland*. There had been moments of concern in the past, but the ship was remarkable in its ability to self-repair. If something went wrong, there would be a small army of robotic responders to manage the issue. There had never been an explosion before. The closest was the impact of the companion bot a few days past. And the scurrying robots put out that fire.

For every other incident, she cried out in alarm, and Blip had turned to help her, and then the other robots, most smaller than Blip, were there to manage the problem. There had been the broken water line. Syn's fault. They had been racing, and she had tripped on a waterhead by a path. It hadn't been a big emergency, but the water, under pressure, streamed up into the air several meters. Syn had given a sharp laugh, and before she'd stopped, the repair bots were there.

They had pushed her away and then went to work. All told, the incident had taken less than a minute.

There had been other problems. Wildlife. Plant disease. But nothing that would alarm Blip like what she was witnessing on his face.

Blip stuttered, "Behind...Behind..."

"Where? What exploded? Is the ship in danger?" It was impossible to grasp anything large enough happening that the entire world could be damaged. But she had watched enough science fiction that she knew that might be a possibility. They were on a ship moving through the stars. Moving from one star to another. An interstellar journey. Perhaps this would be the day the journey came to an end.

The fallen companion bot had invaded her world just days before, and now this explosion was shaking the very walls. Her large world seemed tiny suddenly.

Blip whispered two soft words, "The gate."

Syn put a hand to her mouth. The gate was in the needle. The gate was the one part of the ship she'd never managed to get past. Blip could open up anything but the gate. Every access panel, every gateway, every room. Blip was the master skeleton key, and the obstacles never daunted him. Oh, he was reluctant, more often than not. The more Syn wanted to explore, the more Blip rejected her decisions. Every door presented a possible threat to him. In the end, he'd open them up, and they'd continue their exploration and scavenging. But then none of them were The gate. She felt like every time she uttered it, it should come out in all capital letters. THE GATE. It was a massive hundred-meter edifice and completely impenetrable. There was a part of her world that she had never seen before. They didn't know what lay on the other side.

"On this side?"

"Behind the gate. That's all I can figure out."

"I thought you couldn't tell what was happening behind the gate."

"I can't." Blip was already moving up the Disc toward the nearest tower to ascend to the needle around which the Disc revolved. "I simply measured the waves in the Disc and across the rest of the ship.

I calculated back the origin of the tremors. Whatever caused that, it's behind the gate."

"Wow." That was the only word that came to her.

"Let's go," Blip said.

Syn shook her head, attempting to shake loose her confusion. She stepped after him.

"If it's the gate, it's going to take a bit to get there."

Blip nodded and turned toward her bike. "Twenty-two minutes. At top speed. Probably longer."

Syn smiled. Even in the face of danger, Blip was still joking.

She had the ship down to pure memory. She knew the closest path from one place to another. Yes, the gate was a bit away from here. They'd have to make it to a tower, and then, if the elevator was working, ascend the massive five-kilometer-high strut that followed the outside of the Disc, alongside the tiered housing units, until it intersected with the needle. Then, they'd have to go up two or three levels in zero gravity and maneuver a few more kilometers. Even with all of that, the trip couldn't take more than fifteen minutes. He was challenging her. He was hoping that she'd feel the challenge and dart ahead without becoming distracted, which was her usual M.O. His hopes were well-rewarded.

Syn sped toward her bike.

Close behind her, Eku sniffed, and Syn looked back. Syn shook her head. "You can't keep up. We have to go fast."

Eku didn't move. Syn took a few steps and rubbed the cat's neck. "It's fine," she said, "It's okay. You play. Go have fun."

Eku stayed put though, unwilling to leave without her.

Syn smiled, scratched the tiger again and straddled the bike—a quick version known as the Ogun model. Syn loved this hover bike— its blue finish, the way it sloped forward like a tiger, ready to pounce. It was sleek and beautiful, and she felt like she was hugging an arrow shot through the air.

The Ogun hovered above the grass. Like Blip, it used magnetic induction to hover above the metal surface that lay just below the jungle soil.

As she touched it, it sprang to life. Like most everything else, it responded to her touch. She was all it needed to come alive. She was the code that unlocked it. There had been keys on doors and different vehicles when she had first ventured out into the Disc, but they were of no concern to her. The ship was hers alone.

8

OGUN

"And he dreamed, and behold, there was a ladder set up on the earth,
and the top of it reached to heaven. And behold, the angels of God
were ascending and descending on it!"
—Genesis 28:12, ESV

Like a rabbit hopping up out of the weeds, Blip jaunted ahead and pointed far down the Disc. "Go to 17. Hopefully, the Jacob there is still working after that."

"16 is closer," Syn said.

Blip nodded as she pointed the Ogun out from the house. "Yes, but closer to the blast. I'm hoping that 17 wasn't damaged at the top," he said.

Syn paused, took her hands off of the bars, and looked at him. "You think the Jacob lifts are damaged? Near the needle?"

"Maybe. I don't know. Olorun is struggling to deploy scanners and assess the damage."

"How's that possible?" Syn couldn't understand that. The Olorun was the ship and the ship responded as fast as Blip, as fast as thought.

"I think the whole system had to reboot. I'm not getting my feed."

"Blast," Syn said. She understood the feed between Blip and the ship. He interfaced with the system and had access to everything through his connection. Always on. Always present. This was the first he had ever said there was a delay with it. He mentioned it so casually that Syn wondered if he had encountered this before. He wasn't freaking out. He wasn't frightened. For him, losing his connection with the ship was something that just happened. That frightened Syn, sending a cold sensation washing across her. It was proof he wasn't telling her everything.

Syn steered the Ogun toward 17. With a single tug, the hover shot off. Even at this speed, it would take a minute or two to get to the bottom of Tower 17, and then they would have to get in the Jacob lift.

The air whistled alongside them as they sped forward. There was music to the sounds: the hum of the engine, the slight off-key whine as they careened across the surface, the metal frame straining in the tight corners, the rush of the wind as they roared past the blurring scenery. It was a soothing echo of what Syn imagined flying would be like.

They moved through the various buildings and structures. The Disc's rises resembled a stacked city, designed in organic shapes to lessen the artificialness of it all. At the base, the structures were spread out. No congested alleys or streets. Yet, no single path was a straight route. The designers of the Olorun loved curvy roads. Since the ship had been manufactured, since it was all artificial in nature, the goal was to make every bit of the design feel natural. Sidewalks and roads all curved through foliage. Sightlines were broken up.

Ladder 17 was nearly one hundred meters in diameter at its base. It curved up, following the outward bulge of the Disc and the tiered houses and green spaces of the rise. The houses and buildings followed the curve and ascended past the clouds. The upper residences had housed the older members of the crew. As the levels went up, the gravity lessened. This was an attractive option for the elderly, for those of the crew that were past 100. With less gravity, they had more mobility, less fear of falling, far more strength in managing everyday items. So it went—the younger at the base, the older far up the rise. It was an unintended physical hierarchy of age. Syn had discovered this fact in her scavenging and exploration of the residences. The decor of the houses changed the farther up the rise she went. A scattering of toys at the bases. The residences became odd geological strata of the lifespans of its crew.

Syn slowed and drifted next to the tower's base. The Jacob lift opened up in the center of the strut. As they approached, the lift doors slid open.

Blip gave an acknowledging beep. "Grab your spear."

Syn narrowed my eyes. "Up there? No lions, or tigers, or bears up there, my brave little toaster."

Blip just stared back. "I'm concerned."

Syn narrowed her eyes but went back to pull her spear free from the makeshift sheath she had crafted on the side of the Ogun. The spear was nearly five feet in length, and Syn had crafted it from several carbon-fiber pipes (it was as light as a feather) and managed to cold-weld a carbon-fiber knife she had shaped to the tip. Syn could hit nearly anything from at least forty to fifty feet away. She had taken down a lion that had escaped the zoo in their second year. She hated to do it, but he had been chewing up the cats and dogs in the Anatolia neighborhood, and he had to die—the closest the Disc had to a serial killer. The animals had been docile, programmed deep in their DNA toward a tameness. But that change in nature was only a guarantee with humans. She was safe, but the lion still possessed its primal urges to hunt and feed. And now, it seemed, to hunt alone for the sport of it.

Reflecting on the moment, she had been frozen in fear, her stomach rolling in anticipation. It wouldn't kill her—couldn't kill her. But if she walked away, its spree would continue and other animals would die. Or perhaps, this would be the one animal that fought its programming. Maybe it would break free of its reins, charge her, and she would die. Then, Olorun would tumble through space, empty of all intelligent life except a single robot named Blip. She shook her head. Imagination run amok. Very little could hurt her here.

A strange thought formed far back in her mind. If she had conceived of her own death, Blip had as well. *Would Blip knowingly choose to live his existence alone?* Perhaps he kept the other bot secret so that he had someone else in case Syn died.

And she would die. At some time. Clearing through the dead bodies in the Disc had convinced her of that. Everyone died. Perhaps, her death was years from now, but she would die. She knew it. And so did Blip. *So why had they never talked about it?*

Syn stared up the length of the Jacob lift. The tower stretched to the sunstrips, and its end was obscured in the clouds. Far above them, attached to the Jacob lift, an Orisha mask stared down, seemingly oblivious to the commotion. The masks had been created by the Builders and each was different. The one above her was a rectangular construction with a long, long chin, slits for eyes, and a thin mouth below an angular nose. The masks were hundreds of feet tall and could still be viewed down here. They were mounted on each lift and created a somber feel when viewed; each of them were silent like sentries, looking over life on the Disc.

"Express ride to the top?" she asked.

"No stops," Blip said, as much to her as the Jacob. The inner doors of the lift shut, and the outer doors to the chute closed. The elevator lifted up—it was a gentle motion.

Syn put a hand on the wall. Smooth and clean. They cruised upwards at an incredible speed, but they did not feel it. Without the open window to the world below them, they would not have even noticed.

They broke the fourteenth level, and the canopy of the Aja jungle fell below them. The dense green foliage blocked out the individual paths that snaked around the outside. They soared higher, and the world of the Disc opened up below them. Syn sighed and thought, *Mine.*

Below her, splitting open the Aja jungle was the river. Her river. *And He separated the waters from the waters…* The various populations that inhabited the ship had each given it their own name. Some had called it the Euphrates. Others called it Shui. The few Russians that had assisted with the construction of Olorun called it the Volga. Syn had named it Lokun, in honor of the people that had ultimately launched the craft. She had forgotten most of her language course work from that first year, but she remembered that word. The Lokun was beautiful, stretching the entire distance around the base of the Disc. The ship's Disc—a large ring—rotated around the center needle of the ship's fuselage. The rotation produced gravity. It was nearly 32 kilometers in circumference and four kilometers wide. Almost 128 square kilometers of surface for Syn to play and live upon.

The Lokun zig-zagged from edge to edge, its course allowing it to form eddies and currents and pool in places and bottleneck in others. At three different intervals, from the rocks built into the walls of the Disc between the rising settlements, waterfalls pushed the river along.

The water came from the great bodies of water that surrounded the Disc. The biggest danger of space was the radiation. Earth had its atmosphere and magnetic system to divert and absorb the harmful radiation. The atmosphere of the Disc wasn't capable of that. It was not thick enough. Instead, in a secondary, insulating layer around the entire Disc, an ocean of water floated. It was impossible to get to and impossible to disturb. There was enough water in the shield to flood the Disc and more; easily a kilometer-thick extension on both sides of the Disc.

The river fed back into it. The water filtered to the settling ponds below before it moved back to the surrounding ocean shield. Then the water would pour back into the river, pushing it along. Compared to the water in the shield, the Lokun was a mere trickle. But laying upon it, floating with its current, it felt mighty.

Syn had once taken a boat out without any true intent and allowed herself to float along. For four days, she laid in that boat, circling the Disc. She felt like she was in orbit. Over and over, she saw the same sights move past. She laid there without sleep as the sunstrips along the needle faded into darkness, and the projected stars, a representation of the outside, were allowed to show their light. Her fingers hung in the water, and the small fish would come taste the salt from her fingertips. They nibbled at her skin and then darted off when she moved. She drifted between sleep and awake, allowing the lull of the world, the hum of the engines, and the thrum of the rotating Disc to hypnotize her.

She dreamt that she had stared into the deep of the Lokun, and there, below its mirror surface, was another world. In that other world, there was another Syn, another girl, looking up. Her hair, her eyes…her. But with a different voice and a different mind. Someone human to share this world with. Someone with flesh and blood and tears and anger and fear. Someone beyond Blip and Eku and the animals and the dumb bots. She loved Blip. He was her closest friend. But that night, she had felt very alone. She drifted through the waters and wondered what it would be like to hear another human's voice, not through some recording, but with her own ears. Would the voice be different if it had been formed with human vocal cords? Would it sound different to her tiny ears if the words had escaped warm lips, crafted with a thick tongue that was moist with spittle? Would the conversation be different if the other person had to pull their hair from their eyes like she often did? If they had to sometimes pause the conversation to run and use the bathroom?

Syn had hung from the bow of the boat and let both hands deep into the water. She saw herself there and saw that reflection mouth other words than the ones her own lips formed. The reflection was living. It was thinking. It was another, and she wanted to fall forward and embrace it, pull that other close to her own chest and feel the thump, thump, thump of its heart and the warmth of its breath against her neck. She wanted to feel the sweat of the other's skin and let her mutter, "It's okay. You're not alone. I'm here."

But that had been something near to a dream.

She pulled away from the glass, the view of the river Lokun, and thought, *I say blast it to the shadow girl, the girl below the waves. Olorun is my world, and the rule of it comes with the thorn of loneliness. Who cares? I'm a god in this little place and…*

"Why are you lying to me?" Syn said, her eyes surveying her world.

Blip turned away from the control pad and looked at her. "Excuse me?" he said, his voice low and careful with a hint of confusion.

The ignorant tone he replied with set her off. She wheeled and pointed. "Stop lying. Stop it now."

Blip moved back, appearing stunned by her words. "What are you…"

But he couldn't get the words out. Syn interrupted, "The other bot. The other one like you. You knew about it! I saw it in the way you approached it. You were surprised by its arrival but not by its existence. You were surprised that it had crashed. Where do you go at night? When has the feed broken down before? Who was that companion bot? What's the explosion about? You know all the answers, and you're not telling me a thing! I want answers." She was furious. With each sentence she stepped closer to him, her finger pointed at him and spit flying from her mouth. "Stop lying Blip!"

Deep inside though, a small voice spoke, *you're going to send him away.* For a moment, the voice caused her to stagger, and she only finished with a stunted, "Stop…"

Blip stuttered at her pauses, "What are you…" and then, "I'm not." Finally, after her final word, Blip replied, "I…" But he would never finish that sentence.

9

───────

THE JACOB

"Sometimes it is the people no one can imagine anything
of who do the things no one can imagine."
—Alan Turing

The Jacob came to a sudden stop, and they were thrown up, slamming hard into the ceiling. They were over halfway up the tower. The further up they went and the further from the base of the Disc they climbed, the lower the gravity was.

They drifted back down to the floor. Syn's blood floated around them in small droplets. Syn was bleeding—she put a hand on the back of her head and brought it back, wet and red. *Dammit!* she thought. The interruption in her confrontation had been so sudden that her anger was replaced by shock and without the fuel of anger, she was embarrassed that she had attacked Blip like that. *It had all just come bubbling out. It was all there under the surface.* She shouldn't have said it, she thought, and at the same time, she thought, *I meant every word. I want those answers.*

"Are you okay?" Blip asked, staring at Syn's hand just as she was.

Her cheeks reddened at his kindness. She didn't deserve it. "I think so." The injury stung, but not as bad as others she had. Syn fell often.

She had broken bones and the bots were great about stitching her up as fast as they did nearly anything else on the ship. Their repair work didn't stop the pain, though. Yet, she didn't feel she was as hurt now as she had been before. "I think I'm okay."

Blip floated around. "I think the Jacob is dead."

"Dead?" Syn pushed off and maneuvered to the window, trying to glance up at the needle. There was nothing that she could see wrong. "Everything looks okay."

Blip was talking to the controls and allowed a soft "Hush" to escape as he did so.

Syn thought, *stupid bot. Just do your job and don't boss me around.* He could pay attention to two things at once. He didn't need to concentrate. Syn concluded it was just an act. *He wants to be more human than I want him to be.*

The screen on the control panel beeped. Blip whirred and narrowed his eyes. The panel beeped back at him.

"Rude," Blip said, offended.

"What's…" Syn couldn't even get the words out before she received another "Hush" from the football-shaped robot.

Syn spun in the air and aimed toward the door. With a small push of her feet against the back wall, she propelled herself forward. It didn't take much effort to move in the near weightlessness this high up. Syn loved the sensation, though—fun, absolutely crazy fun. She would venture up to the needle just to enjoy the wildness of spinning and wheeling unencumbered through the air.

Syn put her arms out in front and braced herself as she moved toward the door. Her fingers gripped into the fine crack between the windowed Jacob doors.

Blip still argued with the control panel. She never could figure out exactly how he worked with the different interfaces and AIs on the ship. Sometimes they seemed stubborn and unbendable to Blip's desires. There were others that he could just connect with and rewrite their entire processes. Yet, she was amazed at how, given enough time, he could get them to do anything.

Syn pulled at the doors. They were over four kilometers high in the air. Syn had heard of a fear of heights in the films she watched. But on the Olorun, this seemed so odd. All someone had to do was to look up and see the ground above them. Wherever you were on the Disc, you were looking down at the ground (or up, depending on how you wanted to describe it). So, yes, they were high up, but this high up, they were also near weightless. If Syn stepped out, she would slowly start to drop down. Slowly.

There was a hatch up above, along the underside of the needle, and she could climb from here. *Stay close to the tower and push yourself up.*

The doors began to open. There was a tremendous amount of pressure on them, and they were difficult to budge.

Blip whirred and shouted, "Stop!"

Syn glared back at him. "I'm not one of your machines." He could try all he wanted to get the Jacob to turn on and take them the rest of the way, but her way seemed more fun. Syn continued to pry at the door.

Blip flew up, inserted himself between her and the door. He turned and bumped her arm away with the back of his head. Syn lost her grip, and the doors slid shut with a slam.

"Blip!" Syn said. She swatted at him, and he whirled out of the way. "Stop treating me like a baby. I know we're high up but I can float to the top. We'll just use the hatch."

Blip wobbled in the air, buffeted by the hard slap. He just narrowed his eyes and then zipped to look eye-to-eye with her. "It's not about that. There's almost no air out there."

Syn paused. No air? What did he mean? "Blip, what are you talking about?" Outside those doors was the Disc. She could look down, and though they were nearly minuscule dots, she could still see the trees and houses. There was the small rectangle that was the soccer field. A lake twinkled below them. The reflection of the sunstrip rolled across its surface.

Blip sighed.

Syn scowled. She hated when he did that—it was a sure sign to her that he thought she was being stupid. "I'm not dumb," she scolded back. She pushed away and crossed her arms. "We're taking too long. I just want to get up there."

"How high up are we?" His tone had changed. He had dropped the scolding, but he was now purposely talking in a lower tone, spacing out his words, making sure Syn clearly understood him.

Syn remained unmoved. Her arms were crossed, her chin down, and she stared at him through narrowed eyes. Around her, her dark hair floated in the gravity. She grunted, "Schoolmaster Blip."

"Fine. I don't have to explain it to you. Just do me a favor," Blip moved back to continue his argument with the elevator, "And stay away from the..."

"Oh, great Blip, please don't withhold your wisdom from my tiny little mind," she growled. Yet, inside, she did want to know what he was going to say. She wanted to know why she could not go up and float to the needle. And he knew she wanted to know, so instead of a lecture, Syn was on the edge of begging him to instruct her. Syn slapped her hand on the wall. She felt as if she could never outgrow him. He would always have something more that she needed from him. She would always be in chains to him that were forged from her continued and seemingly never-ending ignorance.

"Really?" Blip quirked up an eyebrow.

Syn scowled and thought *Stupid Blip*. Yet, she nodded. It was slight —maybe not even a nod, just a move of the head.

It was enough. Blip turned and raised himself up. Syn was floating several inches off the ground. Blip made sure to move, so he was looking down at her—not much, just so his eyes were an inch higher than hers. Perhaps it made him feel more like a teacher. Whatever the reason, Syn wanted to grab him and punt him down the Disc.

She spat out, "So, little football, are you going to tell me?"

Blip sighed again. "As I was saying, how high are we?"

Syn just stared.

Blip allowed a moment of tension, and then he continued, answering his own question. "We're 4.5 kilometers above the base of the Disc. How does the Disc have gravity since we're in weightless space?"

It was Syn's turn to sigh. "It spins."

Blip nodded. "Yes, it spins. And because it spins, the Disc has gravity. However, the closer we move to the axis point, the needle around which the Disc spins, the less gravity there is. All of the air in the Disc is also under the pressure of the gravity being created by that spin. Oh, there's air up here, but the air is far denser the further down the tower you go. When you're at the base of the Disc, the air is at its densest. It's designed that way. When you hop in the elevator, we pressurize the elevator so that the air pressure is the same as it is at Disc base level. The needle is pressurized too. We work hard so that you experience the same air pressure everywhere you go."

Syn frowned. She hated when he used the word "we." It creeped her out. She knew there were other AIs on Olorun—although they were all dumb bots. Blip was unique—a distinct, individual mind like hers. Yet, he still talked to the other machines with their varying degrees of technology. She knew he had assembled a team of bots that worked to make life easier for her. But the "we" was just weird. It made her feel that there was a whole world of conversations going on that she was not a part of. Her frown deepened, and she thought, *we? Why not "Us?"* but she didn't say anything. Again, her doubts surfaced. She wanted to shout again at him but no, not now. This wasn't the time.

Blip continued, ignoring her frustration. "But if you go out those doors, the air pressure is significantly less than when we are down at the base. So much so, that you'll suffocate."

Syn looked over her shoulder. *Okay, I hadn't thought about that.* She just thought she would slip out and float all the way up to the hatch and save the day. It had to be that easy. Except it wasn't, and she had nearly opened that door and killed herself.

She'd have been like all the other humans: dead on Olorun. Sometimes she felt like the ship was just waiting for her to die. She was the lone person on a ship that had housed thousands. Of all those people, she was the only one not dead. The only one living. As if she was the holdout. Perhaps the ship was readying to do something new but waited on her to die like some little gnat buzzing around.

Syn let her arms down. It wouldn't be her. She wasn't going to die. She'd listen to Blip and live, despite how much she hated to. She had no desire to be like the other fools on the ship—she didn't want to be one of the other dead bodies she had discovered. She grinned and thought, *sorry, Ship, I'm here to stay. You can try and get me to open up doors and kill myself, but handy Blip and I would always be there to thwart your plans. So keep on waiting. The rest of your plans can wait. I plan to live a long, old life.*

Yet, Syn wasn't sure how old she wanted to be. She was seventeen. Did she want to be alone for the next seventy to ninety years? When the ship had left Earth, the average person lived past 200. On the ship, the oldest person had been 120. There was something about space travel that limited the upper range. Would she want to live another 106 years all by her lonesome? She had Blip but…

The more she thought about it, the more tempting opening those doors and falling out into the airless space above the Disc became. She imagined it. She'd be the one survivor whose body they couldn't process. If the ship were ever found, there she'd be, floating above the forest, above the great tree, like some watchful angel. Maybe the children who would find this place on some distant world would call her that. The Floating Angel.

"Syn?" Blip said.

Syn shook her head.

"Were you daydreaming?"

"No," she lied.

Blip looked at her. Then he turned and went back to the control panel. "Besides, if you would give me just a few more minutes before you tried to kill yourself, you would have discovered—"

Suddenly, the elevator lurched forward. Syn floated back to the ground, and the sensation of gravity slowly increased. They were moving. Blip had done it. He had convinced the Jacob AI that they shouldn't be stuck in the lift four kilometers above the ground. She thought, *yay Blip!* Although there was no way she was going to let him know how happy that made her.

She floated around. There was the pull to the floor due to the movement up, but they were still in low gravity, and she bobbed around easily. "Thanks," was all she felt comfortable muttering.

"Want to know how I did it?" Blip said.

She glanced at him. She did. She was always fascinated how Blip worked with the other machines. But she didn't want him to know that his stories were interesting. So she just gave a hrmpph and said, "How?"

Blip smiled. "I threatened it."

She narrowed her eyes. "You did what?"

Blip's smile grew a bit more, "I threatened it!"

Syn smiled. *Oh, the tiny robot is happy with himself. Big tough Blip has gotten tough with the elevator.*

"How'd you threaten it?"

Blip chimed, "I told it that if it didn't respond, we'd let Bob use it exclusively." He winked at her, and she let loose a wild laugh.

"That's mean." Bob was one of the maintenance bots. A large puck-shaped thing, notorious for cleaning up messes and walking away dirtier than he had begun. He tended to drag the mess with him too. One of the other lions had killed an emu and dragged its corpse onto the south edge of the lake and then stalked off, obviously bored with its catch. Bob to the rescue. The mess was cleaned up, but Bob did not realize that part of the emu's leg, the part shredded by the lion, was stuck to its back clamp, and he was dragging it wherever he went. A trail of blood and feathers. That was not the first time, either. Bob made more messes than he fixed. And the two could never talk to him about it. He was very focused on his tasks.

INTO THE NEEDLE

Obi nkyere abofra onyame
"No one shows a child the sky."
—Ashanti Proverb

"We're here." Blip moved up and stood in front of the doors. When he spoke next, his voice had grown quiet. Concerned. "I'm going to black out the lights. I want you to be cautious. I'm going first."

"Blip, what are you scared about?" Syn asked but still picked up her spear and gripped it hard. She pushed toward him, now in full zero gravity.

Something had happened up here. Something big. *Maybe space pirates!* Syn thought. She knew there was no such thing and, if there were, Olorun was way too fast for anyone to intercept them. Besides, they were between the stars. A molecule in the sea—far away from anyone else. Nonetheless, something had happened. She risked Blip's ire. "Space pirates?"

He sighed a great Blip sigh. "No." Only one syllable this time. Definitely on edge.

"Fine," she said and moved behind him. He dropped the lights, and they were plunged into complete darkness except for the amber glow of the control panel. Blip chirped something in its direction and that too went completely dark. Syn shivered—Blip was genuinely concerned.

The door to the elevator opened soundlessly, and they met an equally dark scene ahead. A few warning lights shone in different, scattered locations across the expanse, but they were small and red and didn't provide any clarity of the actual scene.

"Blip?" she asked, her voice barely above a whisper. Without realizing it, and as much as it was possible in zero gravity, she had crouched into a fighting stance, ready to spring at whatever could be out there.

The lights were off, and they were entering a den where something perhaps waited. The entire ship had shaken in the wake of that explosion. The longer they stood there, the more she began to imagine that there was something dark and dangerous, with a predatory heart, on the other side of that blackness. Something waiting there for them. She couldn't hear its beating heart, but she was sure could feel it. Feel its dark anger. Feel its hunger. She was sure it wanted them. Wanted her. Wanted to devour her.

Blip gave a brief hum. It was almost unheard. A thin red light, thin as a wire, moved across his back. He was scanning the area.

"Nothing there," came his voice. Again, nearly a whisper.

Syn hated this—it was odd to feel frightened on the ship. The ship was hers.

The lion. The prowling pack of former house dogs. These were things they had expected or at least knew might be a problem. They had been given some warning.

"Can we turn on some lights?" Syn asked, keeping her voice as low as possible. She was avoiding another reprimand, and he wasn't in the mood to ignore her.

Instead of answering, Blip shone a read spot beam from the center of his head, lighting up the area a few feet in front of them. They were in one of the access tunnels that led to the central hold and beyond that, the gate. There were still 200 meters of tunnel between them and the main gate room where the tunnel spilled out, joining with the others from the various towers across the Disc and several more dropping from the engine bay, electronics, and central computing hubs.

The access door to the bridge was directly above the gate. But beyond the gate? Syn had no idea. Neither she nor Blip had managed to open it. All of the scans and ship schematics simply showed nothing more than the access controls for the Bussard ramjet at the front of the ship. After months of consideration, she had assumed that the gate was impregnable because of the ramjet. The ramjet magnetically scooped up hydrogen to be used to power the engines. The amount of radiation near the ramscoop had to be incredible. Syn had been afraid she would light up like a candle if she were able to get there. So, she gave up trying. The ramscoop worked. The engines worked.

The ramscoop was gigantic. It was not the size of the Disc, but it was at least a fifth the size of the Disc, and the Disc was enormous.

"Let's go," Blip said as he floated out of the Jacob and down the tunnel. Syn floated behind, giving a small kick against the back wall. She trailed her spear next to her and readied herself.

Syn paused and thought, *oh. Why hadn't I connected the dots earlier?* Space pirates might have been the preferable option. If the ramscoop was broken, this whole trip might come to a quick end. The scoop did more then pick up spare hydrogen—it also protected the ship from rocks and micro-meteorites. *Perhaps that's the source of the explosion.*

They moved into the darkness. The air was still. Syn gripped her spear so tightly she thought she might squeeze straight through it, that it would crumble under her grip. She cringed and thought. *Why? Why am I so scared?* This wasn't the first time she'd explored something unknown on Olorun.

This wasn't even the scariest place in the ship. The body farms had to be the scariest. The thousands of corpses slowly turning into soil, the white skulls popping up from the ground like strange mushrooms. The body farms were bathed only in blue light until the planting began. It was always silent there. Always still.

She had zipped through these tunnels hundreds of times before. They would race these when they were bored, moving from the engine hold to the gate as fast as they could. Blip would take one tube and Syn would take the other. There was nothing here. The animals didn't make their way up here and neither did the bots.

"What's that smell?" Something sharp and pungent hung in the air, like fire. "Blip, something's burning."

"Give me a moment. I wasn't focused on smells." He paused and a moment later said, "That's...That's...No." His speed increased, and he zipped through the tunnel. He could propel himself through the magnetic induction embedded in all of the ship's surfaces.

Not Syn. She had to swim like a frantic fish. Or get to where she could push off of something and use that to increase her speed. "Blip wait! What is it?"

Blip then said something that was unbelievable. "Gunpowder." Then he was out of the tunnel and into the main hold before the gate, a good fifty meters ahead of her.

Syn stood frozen. She knew what gunpowder was. In their constant visits to the theater, binging on film after film, they had gone through a western phase. She was particularly in love with the *True Grit* renditions. A lone young boy seeks to conquer the wild world around him. That theme resonated with Syn. In the third remake—the 2045 version with Caleel Wastonbi, there was a scene in which Wastonbi, reprising the classic role of Cogburn, decided that he wanted to send a message and loaded the mine under the hideout with gunpowder and set it afire. The land became a living hell. The final confrontation took place against that orange glow and the world itself had erupted. It was a twist that was not in the original two films, but it was beautiful. Syn knew the power of gunpowder. That was gunpowder: lighting the entire world on fire, turning the distraught wild west into an uncontrollable inferno. But gunpowder didn't belong on starships. Syn was sure he had to have said something else. She had to have misheard him. There was no way that she was smelling gunpowder. And yet, as she thought of it, there was a smell of sulfur and fire, sharp and pungent. A tang that stung the inside of her nostrils.

Gunpowder.

Syn maneuvered to the floor, aimed, and pushed herself as hard as she could after the white little bot.

THE GATE

"riverrun, past Eve and Adam's, from swerve of shore to bend of bay, brings us by a commodius vicus of recirculation back to Howth Castle and Environs."
—James Joyce, *Finnegans Wake*

The tunnel opened into a cavernous room. In the vast steel room, floating aimlessly, Syn felt smaller than an ant. Though the ship was an unfathomable distance from Earth, Olorun still had bugs. The ship had quite a large array of insects. She hated most of them. So many of them were nuisances, but it had been decided by the Builders and explained to her in one of the introductory videos that certain insects were important to "the balance of the macro eco-system." She was convinced the Builders were idiots.

The gate itself loomed before them. Not David and Goliath. This was David and Jupiter. The gate was over 100 meters high with a circumference of 314 meters. It was several meters thick and consisted of three different iris mechanisms—opening and closing upon the circular entry.

And something had dented it.

The gate's irising blades were bubbled in its center. Something significant from the other side had pushed the blades in this direction.

"Whoa," Syn said.

Blip wasn't looking at the gate at all. Instead, he was carefully moving in a circle, scanning the edges of the gate room.

Blip finished a 360 turn and swiveled to point upwards. He searched through the dark corners below and above them. Syn didn't need his sensors though. She could hear it. She could feel it. They were alone.

They were always alone.

"It's fine, Blip," Syn said as she pushed gently off of the metal floor and propelled herself up to the center of the gate.

"There's no one here." Blip circled one more time as if he needed to convince himself.

"Blip, who could be here?"

He didn't answer. Instead, as he swung around, he zipped up toward her and stopped hard in the air. Syn felt a tinge of jealousy. She couldn't do that maneuver. An object in motion tends to stay in motion. An object at rest tends to stay at rest. When Syn moved around in the zero gravity of the needle, she had grab something to slow her momentum. Not Blip. The little bot could stop hard. Syn shivered. It was creepy, as if the rules of physics didn't apply to him.

"What caused this?" Syn held her hand above the oversized bubble in the gate. The large blister itself was localized. The entire gate hadn't ballooned out. Just a small two or three-meter section in the center.

"An explosion."

Syn glared at him and smacked him with the edge of her spear. He wobbled, straightened and looked back at her. "What was that for?" he asked.

"Don't be sarcastic."

"An explosion caused this." He moved closer to the center of the Gate. In her mind, Syn imagined themselves as Jack standing before the door to the Giant's castle. So tiny as to almost be unseen. Yet, there they were. And judging by the dent, the giant on the other side was angry.

"You determined that before. I felt the explosion. What exploded? What went boom, Blip?"

"I don't know."

"Did a bot go boom? Did a bitty bot make a big boom?" Syn was having fun. It would annoy him. But he was the one with answers, and he wasn't giving her any. She hated the way he parsed out info as if Syn had just woken from her crèche.

"There is nothing on the other side of this."

"That can't be."

His voice firmed, and he repeated, "There's nothing on the other side of this."

Syn did the same. "There seems to be something on the other side. Big dent." She pointed as if he couldn't grasp what she was staring at. "Big dent. Big boom."

"Syn, you are an annoying pest. Listen to me. There is nothing on the other side of the door. Something had to hit from outside. Maybe a meteorite."

"Isn't the ship supposed to protect against those? The ramscoop?"

"Well, obviously it did not."

"Obviously what? You're sure it's a meteorite?" He was starting to make her angry.

"It had to be. What else could it be?" He spun and came to eye level with her. His words came out sharp and precise. "There. Is. Nothing. On. The. Other—"

He never finished the sentence. From the other side of the gate, a single tiny tap sounded. Just once. They both turned and looked. Then another tap came. Two taps. Spaced apart.

"Debris settling," Blip explained.

Syn started to believe him until two more taps came. A distinct rhythm. Tap. Tap. Fast, together. Then a pause, and another tap. Tap. Tap. Pause. Tap. Then again.

On instinct, Syn rapped against the metal with her knuckles. Tap. Tap. Tap.

The tapping stopped

Syn's eyes went wide, and she stared hard at Blip. He looked up at her and then went pure green, turning on every single sensor he could.

"Space pirates," Syn whispered.

His green glow pulsed over and over as Blip used every detection method possible. After a minute of the green glow and no tapping, Blip turned back to his normal white porcelain shell. "There is nothing there."

"Tap? Tap? Tap?" Syn said, rapping her own knuckles on his hard shell.

"There's nothing there!" he shouted back at her.

Syn pulled back. He had yelled at her. The two had fought before. They had disagreed. But he had never yelled back at her. In her mind, he was exactly what he was named: a companion bot. He was there to help her. To advise her. Deep inside, she had always assumed that meant that he was also there to ultimately obey her.

Syn stayed there, her mouth hung open. He hovered, glowering as well.

A voice, smaller than an insect's wing, whispered, "Help me." The words were thin, like ice. Nearly silent above the background hum of the gate room.

Two words.

THE VOICE

"Smoke and dust, the stuff of simple myth trying to be legend . . ."
—Marcus Aurelius

Syn kicked out and swam toward the gate. She slammed both hands against the metal, gripping into the thin edges of the massive iris blades. "What was that?" she shouted, but she didn't wait for an answer. She yelled again, "Hello? Who was that? Hello?" She shouted over and over and heard nothing.

Blip was speaking, but she was not listening.

Syn had heard someone. She had heard another voice. A human voice. She continued to shout, trying to get the voice to respond.

Blip yelled, interrupting her mania. "Stop! I can't hear!"

He was right. Syn was yelling so loud, they wouldn't be able to hear if the other person was responding.

Syn shut her mouth, but she could not stop her mind. So many possibilities raced through her head. It had sounded like a girl. Like she was hurt. But Syn couldn't be sure. Her mind ran. *How could there be someone else on board? Maybe a ship hit us? Another Earth ship? When Olorun launched, it was supposed to be the fastest ship ever. It's possible they made faster ships. But ships that could catch up to us?*

The thoughts stacked on themselves. *Perhaps it wasn't a human. Perhaps it was just a bot that had gone haywire or was injured and malfunctioned. But how had a bot gotten out there? Maybe it was one assigned to the ramjet, but we'd never heard of any bot being placed out there.* She and Blip made sure the bots were well taken care of. They were all checked up on regularly. She could tell you most of their names and what they were doing—she had named all of them herself. There weren't many that even came up to the needle, let alone managed to get through on the other side of the gate. But perhaps one of them had the access codes to open the gate. She and Blip never considered that one of the bots might be assigned duties on the other side.

"Are there any bots missing?" Syn said.

Blip looked at her, his expression empty. "What?"

"Are there any bots missing? Could that have been a bot?"

"On the other side of the gate? Seriously?"

"Stop disbelieving me. We're not getting anywhere with that. Just answer the question."

Blip sighed. He gave a slight nod of his head. He turned to analyze, but she caught him roll his eyes. A few seconds later he said, "No. They're all accounted for. 272 independent bots. Not counting any of the plant growers or field maintenance. Over 1089 deactivated without any change." After he had spouted off the facts that he was reading, he narrowed his eyes, "Just the same as always."

Syn whispered to him, her eyes still on the iris of the gate, her fingers lightly touching the metal, "Who said that?"

"Maybe it was a recording." Blip moved back and floated. "Maybe it was an announcement." He came up to Syn. "Maybe we didn't hear it. Maybe it was a mass hallucination."

"You're a robot. That's not possible. Besides, you know what we heard."

Blip waited and then gave a brief nod.

"So can we just wait and see if they talk again?"

Again, Blip gave a subtle nod. He understood that this was important to her. There might be someone else on board the behemoth known as Olorun.

So they waited. And listened. They floated inches away from the iris of the gate like tiny dots before some ancient edifice. Nothing broke the stillness of that empty cavern. Nothing moved, and no new lights shone. It was only the two of them in the quiet dark.

Minutes passed, and they still heard nothing. Syn was frozen in anticipation and fearful to break to moment—fearful that the instant she chose to leave, to call it quits, the voice would sound, and she would miss it. Minutes turned into hours, and they still didn't move. Nor did they hear anything. It was a tranquil quiet. Far away, the Jacobs' ratcheting whirrs could be heard as the lifts went up and down transporting an array of bots performing their business between the various levels of arch-wall structures. But nothing moved in the gate room. And nothing spoke.

Blip's voice broke the spell. "Syn, wake up."

Syn's mind drifted. *Wake up. Why would he say that? I am awake. My...*Her eyes were closed, and when she opened them she was drifting about the room, in a slow tumble away from the gate. She had fallen asleep. Syn shook her grogginess away although it didn't help much. Syn gently swam toward the gate, toward the bubble. "How long has it been?"

"That we've been waiting?" Blip asked, "A few hours. I don't think we're going to hear anything."

Syn ignored him and pressed her face close to the bubble and said aloud, "Are you there? I want to help."

As expected, they heard nothing. Syn put her hand on Blip's head. "Okay, let's go."

"Where?" Blip asked.

Syn paused as she aimed herself at one of the tunnels. She replied, "The bridge."

Blip nodded, and they darted up (or down depending on perspective) toward the hatch to the bridge along the wall of the gate room.

13
____

A BRIDGE OF LIARS

"How cheerfully he seems to grin, how neatly spreads his claws. And
welcomes little fishes in, with gently smiling jaws."
—The Caterpillar, "Alice in Wonderland"

Syn placed her hand on the hatch and stopped. No, she didn't
want to be up here anymore. At that moment, something stole
over her. It wasn't a chill, although she felt very cold inside.
She felt alone. And at the same time, she felt very not alone. Something had invaded her world, something she had not met. And she
knew nothing about it.

At that moment, Syn wanted to be back in her tree. She wanted to
be in her bed—to shut out the vastness of the gate room, of the Disc,
of Olorun. She wanted to make her world as small as possible, to go
behind the walls and lock the doors.

But that wouldn't solve anything. There was something on the
other side of the gate and she knew nothing of its nature. There was
an unknown on Olorun.

Syn started to punch in the commands on the control panel to
open the hatch. Then, she paused.

She did know something about it. It knew her language. She had

81

understood it. She thought to herself, *would a space pirate, some cosmic adventurer, know my language? Maybe there was some universal translator, but really, did they work that fast? No.* There had been urgency, inflection. The voice—the girl—knew Syn's language. It was Syn's language.

Was it Syn's voice? Quieter, yes. Strained, yes. Scared, yes. But Syn could hear herself saying those words. She mouthed the words as they descended: *Help me.* Then again, she breathed them out, nearly silent, inaudible except for her own ears. "Help me." Blip didn't stir. He didn't hear. Or perhaps he didn't care. But Syn could hear her words, and they sounded so much like the other voice. Maybe they had been Syn's words. Her voice on the other side of the steel.

Or perhaps Syn had imagined it. Floating before the hatch to the bridge, the fear of the gate ebbed away. She was less certain she had heard what she thought she heard. Perhaps it had been an echo. Maybe they were her own words. Maybe they were in her head. *But Blip had heard them.* Maybe the other words were clipped? Had she said something that would sound like "Help me?" Was there something she had done that made the cavern echo her own words back to me? Maybe.

The hatch to the bridge popped open with a quiet hiss. As the door slid sideways, the light from the dozens of screens shone through and lit Blip up in a soft blue hue.

"After you," he chimed.

"Gentleman," Syn said, spear tight in her fist.

The bridge was a series of arcs, descending as they spread from the main tube. The walls appeared as windows out to the stars. They were not windows. There was no glass there. They were computer displays—perfect resolution, clear as glass, and as precise as reality itself. It was like looking through actual glass onto the fields of the Disc. The screens showed the field of stars that surrounded the Olorun. Before them, in the direction the bridge faced, was the nose of the needle, and beyond that the Bussard ramscoop arrayed in a skeleton framework of arcs and a wired webbing laced between them. The ramscoop wasn't solid. It was a massive net. A web set out to catch the flies of stray hydrogen and other particles that the ship could convert into energy or other elements to replenish their always dwindling stocks.

Syn walked to the center of the bridge and turned around. Lights blinked, images flowed past, and the metrics of the ship were displayed in graphs, raw digits, and other scrolling information. It was all here at her fingertips—the entire run of Olorun. On one screen, the biological and mineral balance was accounted for: hydrogen, oxygen, nitrogen, potassium, iron, and much more. Each had a target value, and the ship readjusted systems to achieve them. Too much carbon dioxide in the air? The ship would begin the collection of the increasing molecule and divide it into carbon and oxygen. The oxygen could then be mixed with hydrogen and added to the water supply. The free carbon would be combined with free hydrogen to create methane—a fuel that was used in micro-heating throughout the starship. This was one method to keep things in balance. There were hundreds, and Olorun was always planning ahead, working to resolve potential problems before they arose.

On the other side, charts spread out describing the intricate underworld of the Disc where so many dumb bots worked: the body farm, the fields, the hive spaces, the under-solar generators, the filtering ponds. Syn was always astounded by how much else was happening below her feet when she walked the Disc. It was easy to forget that there were layers below layers between her feet and the emptiness of space.

It had been several years after first setting up home in the treehouse before she had ventured into the Underworld. Oh, there was a proper name for it: Strata Level One. Strata Level Two. But to her, it was always the Underworld. Standing in the Disc, the sky reached up and up so high, to the very ground on the other edge. Nothing was pressing down on you from above. In the Underworld, that wasn't true. The roofs were not low, but they were still there. Twelve feet high was the average height of the rooms. Some were taller. A few, the body farms, in particular, were much lower.

The settling ponds themselves were impossible to navigate—at best there was a foot above the water level in those spots where the water from the entire ship was filtered slowly through the depths of rock and then back to the ship. All of the moisture was moved through that very bottom level.

Along one screen, the engine performance of Olorun was analyzed and displayed. This one had schematics floating above themselves, projecting up off of the screen with a wave of her hand. The screens stayed flat until she chose to interact with them. But with a simple motion, they expanded and filled the space around her—a very real three-dimensional visualization of whatever they were projecting. For the engines, she was able to move and manipulate the different parts and examine the flow of fuel from the scoop back through filtration and processing to the engines themselves. The engines themselves were cold and quiet now. They were in a drift sequence. Floating ahead with inertial mass only.

"Oh," Blip said from her right.

Syn floated to him and hovered near the center bay of screens. The one in front of him had no diagrams. There were only numbers and an array of tiny dots blinking on and off in such a fast succession that they made no sense to Syn. Blip was gathering some data—he could read that, but she couldn't. "What is it?"

"Something is wrong." Blip's eyes went off and then so did his mouth. He became a white porcelain football floating above the green-lit screen. "A second," his voice chimed, far more robotic and manufactured than was normal. He was in deep calculation. This wasn't like being on the Jacob when he was trying to convince the elevator to ignore its programming. This time, he was downloading key information. "A minute more on calculations. I want to run this a couple times to make sure." His voice had a bit more color. Less monotone now. Maybe he was hopping through the information at a better pace.

So Syn sat and watched the various micro squares turn on and off. She became hypnotized by their flashing and almost fell asleep until she heard his voice, "Okay. I've got it."

"What do you have?"

"It's bad," he said.

"Don't try to soften it. Just tell me." Syn hated when he evaded answering. Nothing was ever positive when he did it that way. It always made the news feel a bit larger to her, but she usually listened more after he took that approach, just as she was then.

"Okay, so um…"

Computers that stuttered had to be the stupidest thing ever. "Get to it," she said.

"Something's wrong with the gravity," Blip said, and she saw him pull back a small distance. Not more than an inch, but he shifted when he broke the news. *Was he scared?*

"What's that mean? How much?"

Blip moved closer but still kept his space. "Not much now. But it will mean a lot soon. A whole lot."

"Isn't the gravity controlled by the spin of the Disc?" Syn asked, leaning closer to the screens.

Blip spoke aloud, although Syn knew it was only for her benefit, "Give me a visual of the Disc."

The computer spoke back, its voice deep and feminine, "The Disc is thirty…"

Syn cut it off, "I know."

Blip interjected, "Show me the spin of the Disc now compared to the spin of the Disc when Olorun launched."

The single image of the Olorun now inhabiting the air in front of them split into two identical sized copies. Olorun then and Olorun now. The colors had faded. All along the outside of the ship, black lines and small dent marks appeared. The skin of the ship itself was now bright white, bleached from the decades of constant radiation bombardment without any form of protection.

But the biggest difference was the spin. It wasn't much, but while watching, after the fourth or fifth spin, it was obvious the more recent version was slower. And if it was slower, "The gravity is less now than when we started," Blip said.

Syn shook her head. "Can we live with it?

"It isn't a great difference."

Syn's hand traced through the air. The Disc was spinning slower.

Gravity was less. But there was so much else happening there, she could not figure out why. The energy being pushed into the Disc to keep it spinning was the same. The weight of the Disc was nearly the same as it had been. Although that wasn't entirely true—there were a few tons' difference. In the scope of things though, that was nothing. She just couldn't figure out why it was moving slower. She walked through the sparks of light hanging around her, moving her hand to grip and rotate the image of the Olorun in the air. She spun it around to get a good profile look at the Disc spinning about the needle. Beautiful. Slow. Steady.

"I don't know. I can't explain it."

"You have all the information you need to make this analysis?" That had been a line of thinking that Blip had trained her in early on. She had to make sure that she knew all of the details before she hypothesized. It was the result of having an AI as a mentor. Data was king, or at least all of the data at her availability. Anything that was obscured could be a potential spot for answers. For Blip to have supposedly analyzed everything, a bit of a connection and explanation for the slowing Disc should appear. But nothing?

"Yes," Blip said.

Syn grabbed the edges of the Olorun hologram before her and pulled out. The ship's image expanded. She did it again and zoomed in on the part of the needle where the gate would be. With her thumb and index finger pressed together, she turned the various pieces of the needle around, looking for anything. "Is this now?"

"The image is accurate as to the last full ship analytical scan performed at 0200 hours, earlier this morning," the computer answered.

"You mean the explosion?" Syn asked.

The computer responded, "Yes."

Syn turned to him. "You've already done a scan? I hate when you read minds." Syn said, although she truly didn't. It was always something that made her want to hug him right after he did it. She smiled and thought, *it's freaky how well he knows me.*

"Ya, it was what I was wondering," Blip said.

Syn raised her eyebrows at this and stepped over to him. "You did? Did you ask the computer about it?

Blip hesitated.

"What is it?" she asked.

"Nothing," Blip said, "I'm just verifying that I understood everything the Olorun replied with. There's no connection. The explosion didn't seem to result in any decay of the rotation of the Disc. The decaying speed had been occurring for a lot longer before the explosion happened."

"Did the slowing cause the explosion?" Syn asked.

"I…Hmm…Maybe," Blip said and then spun around to interface with the computer again.

Syn smiled. She had stumped him. She muttered, "'Bout time."

"And that's a no," came Blip's fast response.

She grunted and crossed her arms. "Fine." She turned back to the design of the ship. Something about the image was bothering her. Something about the numbers. Syn wasn't a math genius, but she could hold her own. Everyone on the ship had to know complex algebra. She wasn't great at physics, but she understood the gist. This type of modeling was where she fell down. Nonetheless, something was annoying her about the images and figures floating around. Something that seemed off.

Propulsion. That was it.

"Blip, how much fuel is left?"

Blip coughed and narrowed his eyes at her. "Computer, can you give me a quick summary of the overall total engine expenditure since launch?"

The computer replied, "In fuel?"

Syn nodded. Blip said, "Yes."

"Thank you. Give me a brief moment to verify the data." The moment was brief. Maybe a second at most. Then, the screens around her pulled out the full bar graph showing monthly and yearly fuel use for overall propulsion.

"There," Blip said. He shone a light out to highlight in the air above some small number.

Syn just raised an eyebrow.

"The fuel being used, and the overall drag on the ship doesn't equal the current speed and projected mass. Based on fuel expenditure, we should be moving a lot faster than what we are now." Blip spun around and worked the calculations out on one of the screens near Syn. He mumbled to himself, "See. At this speed, the fuel should've been a lot less. At this fuel rate, we should be traveling much faster. There it is. If I...No, almost there." He gabbed to himself and ignored her. This calculation was critical. He went silent.

Syn stood in the middle of the quiet, blackened bridge, waiting for Blip to come back up for air. All but the screens were dark. There, around her, floated the blue diagrams of the ship, glowing in bright lines.

"No, this is far worse than what I had originally predicted. I knew it was bad, but not this bad..." Blip stopped mid-sentence, realizing he had uttered more than he intended. He turned to face Syn.

She glared. "Do you think these have..."

Blip just stared at her. Not at the figures. Not at the numbers. Not at the diagrams in the air around them.

"Blip?"

He just stared at her.

"Did you know this was happening?"

Blip didn't respond. Although she could've sworn she saw a momentary, half-second flicker of his eyes when she asked the question.

"Blip, are the explosion and the gravity and the fuel connected?"

"No," he finally spoke. "There is no way they are connected."

"Did you know about this before now?"

"I knew."

It was her turn to stop talking. She glared at him, eyes furrowed, jaw clenched. *Stupid Blip. He knows something that he isn't telling. What else is he hiding?*

He continued, "I knew that something was off, but I didn't think it would matter. I didn't think it would be this bad, this fast. We're still moving through space. We're still going to be on this ship for a few more decades."

She turned and placed her finger on the glowing number he had highlighted. "Not according to this."

He glanced at where she pointed. The numbers were a stream of information, but what they were spelling out was simple. They were burning too much fuel. They either didn't have enough to make it to Àpáàdì, or when they arrived, the ship wouldn't have enough to slow their speed.

"Blip," Syn said, "If I'm understanding you, and from what I can grasp, if these figures are right, we are burning through our fuel faster than we should be. Either we stop that, and this trip takes a lot longer, or we don't, and we burn up too much fuel, and we can't slow down when we get there? Is that what you're saying?"

"What's it matter?" Blip said.

Syn's jaw must've dropped down to her feet. "What's it matter?" Her voice was louder. She waved at the numbers scrolling around us in the dark room. She wanted to pluck them from the air and rub them in his face. How could he not grasp the problem? "Olorun won't reach its destination! We're stuck on this ship forever now! How can you say that?"

His voice lost all emotion. "The mission is dead, princess."

Syn didn't think. She didn't breathe. On the word princess, she slammed her fist into his white hide, and he went sprawling through the air. "I'm not a princess!" Syn shouted, her fists balled up, screaming at him. "I'm not a princess."

He turned and righted himself without effort and flew back at her. Syn jerked back in fear that he was going to charge her. Instead, he moved right up to her, nose-to-nose. "The. Mission. Is. Over." Each word was uttered sharp and distinct. "Over." He repeated the last word, drawing it out long and loud.

"No!" Syn shouted.

"Over. They're dead. All of them. Even if you land on the planet, even if you make it there. In a few decades, maybe a century, you're going to die. And then what? What's it matter? We have a good life here on this ship. Let Olorun do whatever Olorun wants to do."

Syn narrowed her eyes. Her head spun. *Why was he talking about the ship like that? As if it was autonomous?* It was automatic, but at best, the ship was still a dumb bot—a massive dumb bot, but a dumb bot still the same.

"What are you talking about?" She couldn't believe it. Blip had always been the one to tell her of the plan of the ship and the ship builders. He had gone through the great vision and the goal for the ship. He had described the exit from Earth and the need to move humanity elsewhere. He had been the one to go one for hours describing the great interstellar initiative of the years before that led to the building and launching of Olorun. Syn couldn't believe what she was now hearing. "It's your mission!"

"It's a dead mission. It was a dead mission from before you awoke. These numbers don't matter." With that, he signaled to the computer to shut the display off, and the blue floating images blinked out. They were left alone in the dark room, silhouetted against the star fields in the windows. "Let's go back to the Disc. To the treehouse." He turned and moved to the door.

"Blip," Syn said. Her eyes staring out at the starfield in front of them.

He stopped and turned around. "Yes?"

"Why can't I see the ramscoop?"

"Huh?"

Syn stepped closer to the primary display, the one that showed what was ahead. The star they were aimed at, Kapteyn's Star, was barely a pinpoint of light from this angle. There was nothing but empty black space there. "Where's the ramscoop?" Syn pointed ahead of them.

"This is an image of what's ahead of the ship," Blip said.

"I know that. Where are the cameras positioned?"

"I don't know."

Syn spoke into the air, "Olorun, where is this camera located?" She tapped the image ahead of her.

Before Olorun could respond, Syn caught the faintest wisp of blue light from Blip.

"Blip?"

"I want to go back down to the Disc," he replied. And with that he was back to the door.

It was all quite clear at that moment to her. She whispered a question she had asked several times before, but this time, she knew there was a different answer than before. "What's on the other side of the gate?" Her words were faint.

"I do not know." There was something in the way he said it— maybe the flatness of the words. Perhaps they came out just a fraction of a second faster than they should have. She was certain. Blip had just lied to her.

"You're scared of what's on the other side of the gate." Syn still looked out at the stars. "There's something on the other side, and you know what it is. No—I take that back. You know who it is. There's someone else on Olorun, and you know about it. And I think you've known about it for a long time."

Syn walked toward him and tapped the top of his head, "And you know how to open the gate." It was her turn to walk to the door. She pushed off and floated to the hatch before he could respond. Syn floated through the five-foot gap and then popped the hatch open below into the gate room.

There it was. The gate with its odd and conspicuous bubble. It looked like a zit and the more she stared, the more she was sure it was going to explode.

Blip's shadow entered the cavern, and he came to hover beside her.

He started, "Syn—"

"Open it," she said, not allowing him to get anything in. She didn't want the excuses. She didn't want the explanations.

"Syn—" he started again.

This time, louder, "Open it!"

"You don't know what's on the other side."

"But you do." She tapped her spear against his shell.

"Not exactly. I didn't know there were people alive over there."

"People? Alive? More than one?" Syn flung her arm out in gesture at the behemoth door before them. "There's living people over there?"

"There must be. But I don't know how."

"Stop it with the thousands of cryptic sentences! What are you talking about? What's on the other side? Where does that gate go to?"

He did not respond. Instead, they floated in the emptiness as the engines hummed behind them. There were no sounds beyond that.

Then he spoke three words which rattled her and took her breathe away. "There's another Disc," he said.

She shook her head. She rubbed at her temples. She staggered at the shock of his words. She struggled to catch her breath. She had heard him, but it was unbelievable. *Another world?* After several moments, she found the words and asked, "Another Disc?"

She wanted to be angry. He had just shared the most significant piece of information ever. She was furious. But she was also stunned, and her words coming out were nothing more than a single croak.

"When the Madness struck here, it struck there first. This was before you were even woken up."

Syn knew the Madness had started before she was awoken. She had been activated after everything on the Disc went to Hell. Blip had always called the plague of killing and insanity *The Madness.* It made sense. Finding corpses torn apart, entire families slaughtered, and a perfect world devoid of humans felt like madness.

Blip continued, "From what I can tell from the scant files, it was the same: disease and killing—it was the identical story as on this side. But they went a step further. They burned their Disc. Someone or several people set fire to the residences. The bots couldn't respond fast enough. Everything went up in flames."

"How do you know this?"

"It's what Olorun told me. But everything was destroyed. The food stocks. The farms. The bots themselves. Gone. I did not say anything because there was nothing over there. An empty shell."

"What about the knocking? The voice? You told me everyone on Olorun had died."

"That's the truth." His voice was indignant. He wanted her to believe him. Syn wanted to believe him. "That's what Olorun told me."

Then a thought crept in. She had never had reason to doubt anything until this moment. Finding out that Blip had hidden facts made her question everything. "How can you be sure Olorun isn't lying?"

Blip bobbed side-to-side as if shaking his head. "She is not like me…"

"Not a liar?"

"No! That is not what I meant. She is not a thinking machine—She is not independent. Just a dumb computer. One big giant dumb bot. That is all. Info in, info out. Tell it what to do, and it will do it. It cannot lie."

Syn raised an eyebrow, but it went unnoticed by Blip in the darkness of the gate room. "Obviously, it did. You did. Someone is alive over there."

"I know."

"Blip, you don't get it. There's someone else on this ship. There's someone else out here."

"I'm sorry."

"You know how lonely I've been. You know how much I wanted someone else."

"I'm…" He didn't finish the line, but there was sadness there.

Syn dared, "What? You don't know? What's at the end of that sentence?"

Blip stayed quiet.

Syn glared, "You're what?"

Blip's words were soft and quiet, "I'm here."

Syn hung her head. "Just open it."

"Olorun told me that all of the colonists died. If something is alive over there, it's not—"

"Open it."

Blip flew away from her, plunging downwards away from the bridge hatch—although in the gate room, there was no up or down. "Blip!" She kicked out and tried to follow him, but she was slow.

There was nothing to propel herself against. Syn was forced to swim in the air. She could gain speed, but it took a while. Then he was gone from her sight, having flown into one of the dark shadowed places in the corners of the room. "Blip!" she shouted.

"Over here," he said. She couldn't see him, though, and instead, followed the sound of his voice.

After a couple minutes of slow swimming, she made her way to him. He floated in the very bottom corner of the room, against the far edge, a place entirely draped in shadow, far away from any of the tube lights, the hatch indicators, or emergency lights.

"Blip, are you running away from me?"

"No."

"Why won't you open the gate?"

"If we're going to do this, can we be smart about it?"

"What do you mean?"

"I'm not opening the gate. It's too big. Too obvious. Remember what we heard from the other side."

Help me. Syn remembered the soft voice so clear. The first words from another human's throat to her ears.

"The Madness struck that side worse than here. It's not safe. If there is someone alive, if Olorun is wrong, then they're probably dangerous."

Blip nodded.

"You suspected this the entire time." Again, the urge to punt him across the room washed over her, and she did everything she could to push it back down. "So what's your plan, oh great wise liar?"

"Stop that." Blip paused a second before continuing, "There's an alternate access hatch here."

Syn stared ahead of her. It was solid metal. There was nothing distinct. Just the wall that surrounded the circular irised gate. "Where?"

Blip flashed something and a small, thin razor-line of white light appeared in a circle about two-feet wide. "It is only for bots. Only for companion bots. Only for us. There are fail-safes built into the entire ship—places only companion bots can access to keep those in our care safe."

Syn shook her head. "You knew there were other companion bots? You said you had never seen another one when that thing crashed."

He nodded but did not answer. Instead, he aimed himself at the wall. The white light dissolved to reveal a small opening just wide enough for her to crawl through. If Syn had been a boy, if she had been anything other than her petite form, she wouldn't have made it. It was designed for Blip-sized bots and thin girls. "I'll go first. Have your spear?"

Syn nodded. It was still clutched in her hand. She didn't want to talk. She seethed. *Lie after lie after lie.* She kicked at the wall and pushed ahead of him, darting for the opening. "Liar," she grunted.

Blip grunted. "Wait! Do you have everything? Your spear?"

She nodded again, feeling the reassuring weight in her hand, and motioned back to him, giving him the middle finger as she moved into the tube. For a moment, she reached to halt herself, thinking of Eku. *No, she'll be okay. Leave her in the happy place. She can be queen there in my absence.*

"Fine," he said and followed after.

14

JOURNAL ENTRY: THE ZOO

The Unauthorized Journal of Syn
Section 16
Composed 2757

I'm alone here on Olorun. That doesn't mean I haven't had to fight. I have often had to intercede for something smaller— animals attacking other animals. Most of the time, the bots assigned to feed them keep to their schedule, bringing up manufactured meat from the lower food levels. However, if the big predators don't get their food allotment, some of them have gone a bit haywire. And some of them, like the lion, found a new joy in the hunt.

But I've also discovered when not to kill. Along with the lion, a tiger had escaped from the zoo. These were the largest of creatures that were of any concern. There were zebras and giraffes and monkeys. Those I let out myself. They needed to be able to romp around free.

I know I'm safe. They can't hurt me. It's hardwired into their DNA. But they can still hunt the rest of the animals. Survival of the fittest and all.

My first steps into the Zoo told me something was wrong. It was quiet, and the Zoo was never quiet. Set near my tree, the Zoo was arrayed in five wings, spreading out from the center. I had always been a bit on edge when I went into the Zoo. Unlike the rest of Olorun, it was the one place that didn't light up when I entered. I suspect it's because random lights coming on and off would upset the animals, but for whatever reason, the Zoo didn't respond to my presence. Never had. And so, it was different than anywhere else we explored.

The animals in the cages knew me, as I was the only one visiting them, but they didn't trust me. At first, Blip and I had considered letting all the animals out. But then, we realized that it would cause more trouble than it would solve. Besides, the bots were fairly good about keeping up on the food and checking in on the animals. The Zoo ran itself.

All that changed the day the Zoo went quiet. And it went quiet because most of the animals had escaped. All of the gates had opened at once. One of the main locking switches at the front gate had faulted out and opened everything else. I had watched *Jurassic Park* and always thought that sort of thing couldn't happen…until it did. I have a theory it was one of the monkeys. Those things were crazy smart, and I'm sure one of them got loose and then tried to break its buddies out, accidentally opening up the gates for the others.

Blip and I ran down the list of the ones that had escaped after securing the ones that hung around. We had worked for several weeks to capture and bring several back. Some were just impossible to catch. The foxes in particular were quite challenging. We were getting to a bit of status quo as the predators started hunting the other escaped animals. I didn't like the thought of them dying, but it was the natural order. Just needed to work to keep it in balance.

Then the lion had started killing for fun. I hated to do it, but I had to take that one down. It was pretty lazy, and it didn't take much stalking to kill it. I hunted the beautiful beast, and when I found it, I stabbed it straight through with my spear. It was for that hunt I had made my spear originally. It did its job, and I never went out without it again. Designed to go first, to point the way, to keep me safe, and to draw blood. It did all four well.

Now there were wild things in Olorun, and so I had to keep myself safe. Blood spilled in Eden.

A few of the bots had tried to stop the lion. Lion vs. Bot—it was a great fight, but the bots didn't stand a chance. The protector bots had been designed for deterring humans. They tried to stun the lion. I think it gave the lion a bit of a tickle. Useless.

A small pack of hyenas had been let out. Three of them. We tracked them but decided to leave them alone. They were pursuing only rodents—we had enough of those that we could use the help—and stray birds. They were small enough that I was certain we could curb them before they caused any problems.

Then, there was the tiger. It had killed an emu on the bank, but unlike the lion, it didn't leave the carcass out. It had dragged it away.

I was fearful it had, like the lion, started killing for fun. It would be dangerous to the rest of us.

The tiger had left the lake and returned to where it slept each night. Neither Blip nor I could figure out where it was hiding. We had thought of different ways to canvas the area. We had tried my tree, and while it's incredibly tall, it still gets lost in the canopy, and the field of view is limited. We ended up make a sniper's nest from one of the Jacobs. It's how I knew I could force the doors open. Blip had convinced number six to only go up a few dozen feet, just high enough to get a good view of some of the beast's hunting grounds and low enough that we could get to it if we spotted it. We pushed the doors open and just hung out there. For days. We had stocked up on snacks, and Blip had flown out a few times to get me a few extra items from the tree or one of the reserves. Then one night after the sunstrips had faded and a subtle cerulean hue lit the entire Disc, we saw something move between the trees.

It was smart. It moved from bush to bush to high weed along the eastern end of the lake. We never did catch a look at the black and orange patterning, but we could see it clearly by how the foliage moved. We followed as the disruption in the leaves moved further toward the rise of living structures along the curve of the outer wall of the Disc.

It stopped from time to time, and we were sure we had lost it. The movement of the brush would stop and all would grow still. Far away we heard a small bird squawk but other than that, our world was silent and still.

Then it moved again. Finally, after minutes of watching this odd, random advance, the tiger broke from beyond the shrubbery and walked atop a stone bench and stood, staring behind it, daring someone—daring me. It knew I was following. It never looked at us, but there was a moment that I knew it was aware of our eyes on it. How? I don't know. But it knew I could see it. It knew that its secrets were about to be revealed. But as it could not see who it sensed, the tiger shivered and then leaped from the bench onto the tile floor and walked into one of the main houses, a green condominium along the first-floor level. It disappeared in the shadow of the open doorway. It was going to sleep, aware that morning was coming soon.

I wouldn't hunt it at night. It was too awake. Too alert. Too dangerous.

15

___

THROUGH THE MIRROR

"For now we see in a mirror, dimly, but then we will see face to face.
Now I know only in part; then I will know fully, even as I have been
fully known."
—Paul, *1 Corinthians 13:12, ESV*

The gate assembly was thicker than she had imagined. They floated through the quiet corridor until Blip flashed red and stopped. The light of the access tunnel went out.

"Blip?" Syn said, a flood of fear washing over her.

"It's fine," he stated in a whisper, "Just be quiet."

Always cautious Blip, Syn thought.

"Let me ahead. I'll try to open it up," he said.

She felt him push past her as she hugged the wall.

In front of them, an opening appeared. Only a faint glow of red lights was visible and that was broken up by harsh shadows. At best, the light was a glow cast from some far-off source. Syn couldn't see much but she could smell something. Acrid. The air was pungent and the stench of chemicals wafted through the corridor. She took a breath and felt her throat burn. Her nose felt like it was on fire, and she started to cough. She struggled to hold it back, but the impulse was too powerful. One hand clamped over mouth, she began to cough. The sound echoed through the access chute and out into the major room.

Blip whirled around. "Stop," he hushed.

It did no good. She continued to cough, her eyes watering with tears and her face turning red. She let loose her spear and brought both hands up to her face, trying to stifle the fit.

Blip glared and then flew out of the opening, into the room. For a brief moment, between coughs, between the haze of her watered eyes, she saw the red glow cast on Blip's shell, and he looked like some ghastly spirit risen to haunt her.

The fit continued, but after a minute, it lessened until she was only hacking with an irritated throat. The air was still noxious in her nostrils. The smell was worse than anything she'd smelled before, save the air hovering the body farms, but even that smelled organic. The body farm produced chemicals that spoke of life and death. The smell from the other side of the gate was something else. It was unnatural. Unreal. And Syn hated it.

She floated there, bumping against the edges of the tunnel, wiping the water from her eyes. *They've heard us. They've heard us*, she thought. She wasn't sure who "they" were. Blip seemed certain they were dangerous, and she'd accepted that fact on this side of the gate.

A moment passed and the fit subsided, she took shallow breaths, working to avoid more irritation. Again, it was only her and the hum of the engines. Where had Blip gone?

She started to speak when the red-hued orb of Blip flew back down to the front of the opening. "It's okay," he said. "The room on this side is empty. He glanced back behind him, "Well, not empty." He scanned around and motioned with a slight nod at the floating debris littered around them. "Not like our side. But there's no one over here. No one heard you." Then he floated close to her. "Are you okay?"

Syn shut her eyes. His lying had hurt her. This brief moment, as he demonstrated he was still concerned for her, worked to heal that, and she recognized it. It wouldn't resolve everything, not even the majority of it. But it helped a bit.

She nodded. "I'm fine." She pushed out toward him. "It smells horrible."

Blip turned on a few additional sensors. "Yes. There's been a fire here."

"The explosion?"

"Yes, that. And more." He moved ahead of her and went up past her view.

She followed after, pulling herself out of the access point. As she exited, she heard a small whoosh and looked back to see that way vanish. Just as on the other side, if there was a hatch there, she couldn't tell it. It was simply a wall. A huge iron wall. She followed the wall up and out. The room was bathed in red glow from several orbs floating in the center of the room. Large chunks of debris and machinery floated around. There was no clear path from one side to the other. Only crimson, mangled chunks of metal before them.

In the depths of the room, she lost the far chunks in a haze of smoke. Something had been burning on this side. The smoke still pumped from somewhere unseen. She could see the clouds of white smoke billowing up and out, continually filling the space.

"Stay close," Blip said.

She nodded. She didn't need the reminder. She hadn't expected this. Although she wasn't sure what she had expected.

Nostalgia caught her. Not for the location but for the experience. In the early years, after descending into the Disc, she'd explored day after day. Every morning brought a new site and unexpected danger. The trek they were making now was foreign.

"I missed this," she said to Blip as they pushed off from the edge toward the center of the room.

Blip didn't respond. Perhaps he didn't hear. She was glad that he hadn't acknowledged because she felt embarrassed as she uttered it. A bit immature.

They moved further into the room. They grappled and rolled around larger chunks of machinery. Each piece dented and smashed as if they had been mauled by some gigantic hand attempting to create a snowball. Yet, the pieces were twice her height. *How did they get them up in the room? Where had the machines come from?*

Amongst the debris, scorched bots floated. Several had been fused together in the heat of the explosion and formed a ball floating in the space before them. *Why were bots up here?*

On the other side, it was called the gate room. She did not want to call this the gate room. Those words were accompanied by a sense of awe. On the mirror side, this room brought only waves of revulsion. There was nothing reverent in the array of debris and the sickening smells and the wafting smoke.

On the mirror-side… She thought about that word. They had done just that—passed into a mirrored version of their world, as if passing through the glass itself.

If the other side was the gate room, then this was the mirror room. "The mirror room," she muttered aloud.

Blip paused, his pace already slowed by the growing amount of debris in their way. "Huh?"

"This side is a mirror image.

"Through a glass darkly..." Blip quoted.

"Paul," she said.

"You remember."

Syn pulled at a piece of debris. As it spun, a ghastly visage stared up at her. Syn gave a startled gasp.

Blip halted and spun toward her and then followed her stare.

The debris she had just moved around was not metal. It was a body. Burned and ravaged beyond recognizability.

Syn swam around it. The body was still. No breathing. It continued its rotation until it faced away from them, and Syn felt a wash of relief as the face disappeared from view.

Blip nudged it. "It's dead."

"Scanned it?"

"Very dead. But that's not all."

The body slowly rotated until it faced up again.

"Oh," said Syn as she caught a look at the blackened face. There was no surprise this time as she studied the corpse. She had seen her share of dead bodies. They were everywhere until Blip had programmed some dumb bots to haul them off to the body farms. Even years past their clearing of the Disc, they still found an occasional set of bones in the wild, its flesh torn from it by the animals roaming free.

"It's a child," Syn said.

Blip nodded. "Maybe. About your height. I think it's a girl. Caught in this fire."

"Was this the person we heard tapping?"

Blip wobbled his head in a gesture reminiscent of a shrug, even though he had no shoulders. "Maybe."

Syn's eyes went wide. "She was still alive then. You knew about the hatch. You could've rescued her. We could've rescued her."

"No."

"Yes! You lied, and we let the only other person on this ship die."

"We would've been caught in this fire."

"She was alive after the explosion."

"The fire came much later." Blip motioned around them and then at the iris. From the mirror side, the iris bubbled out. "Someone's tried to punch their way through. This junk, the explosion, the fire. All attempts at getting through. Look at the blades."

Syn did. The iris blades were scratched and dented up and down.

"Oh. The debris. They're throwing these machines at the gate."

"And bots," Blip said.

Syn looked around, examining the burned bots. Eye-bots. Cleaning bots. Medics. A whole host of various bots. They were all deactivated—empty shells. They had been used as cannon fodder as well. Hundreds of dead bots.

"Oh," Syn said.

"Someone wants through, Syn."

"It wasn't her."

"I don't know."

"Did the companion bot come from here?" Syn asked the question that had been pressing on her the whole journey over.

"Maybe," Blip said. Then after a moment, "Probably."

They floated around the corpse, staring at the charred hide of the girl. What features she had had were all melted down to the blackened layer upon the skull.

"What do you think she was like?" Syn asked. She moved a hand up to the corpse's face and rested the back of it against the dark cheek.

But Blip stayed silent. Perhaps he'd venture a guess later. Maybe the girl enjoyed singing. Or swimming. But this was not the time for jokes, even if they weren't intended to be jokes. "I don't know," the bot said. "I don't know at all."

Blip floated away and up toward the dented bubble. It served as a small cave from this side. After a moment, he said, "Syn, come here."

She followed and glancing back once to the corpse floating along amongst the garbage.

Inside the dent, someone had scrawled letters. A thin finger had pushed the soot away and left clean metal behind.

SHES COMI was written in large block letters.

"What's it mean? Did she write it?"

"She's coming?"

"Me? Was she talking about me?" Syn put both hands to the side of Blip's head. "How would she know about me?"

Blip started to pull away and then recognized Syn's fear. He pushed closer, "She didn't mean you." His voice was calm, assured. He might've meant the words. Perhaps even believed them.

Across the room, something large grunted.

Blip moved and shut off his lights. He darted back and nudged Syn over. He whispered, "Drop to the sides. Stay behind the big garbage. Quiet."

Syn started to speak and Blip gave a sharp, "Shh."

Something grunted again, and it was answered by another grunt. The two sounds were moving across the room in their direction, but slowly.

Blip dropped down and Syn grabbed hold of him, palming the top of his head, gripping onto the sides of his head as he pulled them both down. In seconds, they were out of the glow of the red lanterns and engulfed in shadows.

Blip allowed one word, "Quiet."

Above them, near the center of the room, two large shapes moved. They had arms, legs. Humans. But they were twice Syn's size in the least. She put a hand to her mouth. Again, the only phrase that came to mind was "Space Pirates." She knew they weren't. She knew it was outlandish, but the image kept rolling around in her head. She imagined their large craft jutting out of Olorun's hull far down the way and the lumbering brutes piling out, looking to steal things.

But this was not a raiding party. There were just two of them. They seemed massive and moved without grace: burly, large, human-like creatures.

They grunted back and forth. At one point, the grunts become aggressive, and Syn was certain the two were going to start pummeling each other. They paused in the air above them and squared off. Syn stayed perfectly still, fearful they'd spy something from the corner of their eyes.

Did they have eyes?

They moved back toward the far wall, away from the iris. Syn was confused. Had the two things heard Blip and her? What were they looking for? They hadn't taken anything. Their exit was slow and even after she could no longer hear them, their grunting conversation was still loud.

She and Blip huddled behind a large chunk of debris. Syn rested her hand on the trash and felt a familiar smooth texture—a coated plastic that felt as if it had been polished to prime. An Ogun. She felt a pang of regret. They had destroyed an Ogun. She loved her Ogun, and she thought all of them were the best toys she could find.

She couldn't tell what color this was. It had a similar pin striping along the side, but the gray diamond design that intermittently scattered on hers was absent. So not her Ogun. Not even the mirror of her Ogun.

This was not a mirror world, she told herself. Despite the similarities, this wasn't just the opposite world. She shook her head, trying to remove the cobwebs of confusion. No matter what she did, she couldn't escape the mess that they had appeared in an alternate, polar world from the one they had been in.

This wasn't fantasy. Not the Hobbit. Not Harry Potter. This was real. This was another gate room, and those were real monsters and a dead girl, and they had all been on the same ship that she'd grown up in.

"Syn." It was Blip's voice.

She looked around. The two were gone, and she couldn't hear them either. "Yes?"

"I think we should go back."

She's coming. The girl's dying message was a warning. Maybe she was reading into it, but she had talked to that girl, she was certain of that. It was not a far leap to assume that message had been left for them. *Who was coming? What did the warning mean?*

She couldn't abandon it at this point.

"No," she said to Blip.

"It's not safe. You saw those things."

"What were they?"

"I don't know."

Syn crawled along the edge toward the Jacob ports. "I want to see this Disc."

"Syn!" Blip chased behind, "Please."

"They're trying to get through anyway. Don't we need to see who they are? Why are they doing it? Maybe they're just desperate. Maybe something has gone wrong here, and they're trying to save their lives. We don't know anything Blip." At the mouth of the Jacob lift, Blip jumped out in front of her. "Wait!"

He then took off on a fast rotation, glancing down and then spying carefully down each of the tunnels. He moved so fast. In just a few seconds, he was back. "They're all clear."

"Which one do we take?"

"Your choice, Prince—"

He hadn't finished the word, and she slapped him. "Which one gets us closest to the J settlements?"

"Why that…" he trailed off.

"J1302-99. I'm going there. Maybe he meant a room on this side."

Blip nodded. "This one." He popped open a lever and the door irised open. The tunnel out of the Jacob was surprisingly clean. It still smelled, but the smell of smoke was faint. There was something else—something moldy and damp. Syn struggled to place the scent. The smell wasn't as sharp and debilitating as the one they had encountered in the mirror gate room. She reached the Jacob, popped open the controls, and entered.

"I hope this isn't loud," she said, "Is there another way to get a look down below?"

Blip stared up at her. "No, unfortunately."

But then he stayed quiet. Finally, he spoke, "Maybe we can."

"How? You can tell when a Jacob is going up and down in our Disc. It's pretty obvious." As the carriage went up and down, green light shined out from panels along the tower, noting where the carriage was. It was easy to see how soon a lift would be available just by watching the lights.

"But you're used to it, aren't you?"

She thought about it. It was true. The Jacobs moved all the time. Dumb bots moving between the Disc and the needle or the different levels of the Rise on both sides. The constant movement of the massive elevators had been something she had grown accustomed to.

"You said there were no bots on this side."

"Olorun said there were no bots on this side. I'm beginning to believe Olorun is wrong about a lot."

16

BURLYS

"The stars, that nature hung in heaven, and filled their lamps with everlasting oil, give due light to the misled and lonely traveler."
—John Milton

Blip and Syn floated before the opening to the Jacob lift, conscious of their location. An inch or so closer and the door would detect their presence and intent and then open. Far below, if this Jacob were like theirs, a green light would indicate the presence of travelers on the Jacob. If there were more people in this Disc and less bots, they could be alerted to Blip and Syn's presence. They would know that someone had come through from the other side of the gate.

The door to the Jacob was like the ones on their side, except for the thin layer of blackened soot left from a fire layered across most of it. Something dark and thick was smeared across the control panel to the left of the large white and gray doors.

"How big is it?" Syn asked.

Blip gave a mere grunt of question, unsure of what "it" she was referencing.

"This Disc. The other Disc. How big is it?"

"Oh," Blip said. He waited a beat. "It's identical to ours."

Syn gasped. And after a moment, she pushed forward.

Blip blurted out, "Stop!"

She ignored him. The door sensed her. The control panel lit up green and the door slid open to the Jacob lift. Far below, she was certain, a single green indicator light on a thin, vertical display, shone and announced the two.

The Jacob was dark at first, but the running side panel lights flickered to life. They strobed and revealed a figure pressed against the back wall, its arms spread across the view window.

Syn jumped back and gave a startled scream.

At her scream, Blip swung himself into the space between her and the silent figure. "Stop," he commanded.

The figure gave no indication of response. Its head was lowered, and it wore baggy, ill-fitting clothing. Behind it, the light from the sunstrips blazed away, silhouetting it. As the adrenaline washed away, Syn noticed the figure was not standing there. It had been tied up against the back of the Jacob. Its thin fingers hung limp.

No. Not just thin. There was no skin or muscle on them. They were bone.

Blip moved in close and after a short beep and hum, said, "It is dead."

Syn inspected the body. The white of its skull peeked through strips of hardened skin and muscle. What features were there had faded as it decayed. She pulled the ball cap off to reveal a shaved head. Its hands were tied with thin cable, knotted quickly and then latched onto rungs across the top of the Jacob. In its hand it gripped a large leaf, now brown from decay, wrapped around a clod of dirt. Its legs splayed without care across the ground.

Around its neck hung a gold chain. Syn latched a finger through it and pulled the chain up, yanking from inside the corpse's shirt. A tiny pink butterfly made of metal and cheap paint hung from the metal cord. She'd seen something like it in the bedroom of the Pote girls. They had a jewelry rack filled with plastic trinkets and a few metal bits. Several of the bracelets and necklaces that Syn wore herself had been taken from the girls' room. Syn looked down at her own neck. There were leather necklaces, large chains, plastic straps, dozens of odd knick-knacks she'd gathered from her scavenges, and the most recent addition of the wooden beads and the orange tiger pendant. Clipped on to this array were bottle caps she had found, a metal comm ID badge from an officer she had pulled from his body, little rocks, small things she had painted eyes onto and turned into little dolls. On the base of the Disc, the weight pressed against her thin shirt and lay between her breasts. Here, in the near-zero gravity of the needle, the mass of tangled necklaces drifted up, all together in one collection.

She flipped through the various items hanging around her neck until she found a small gold chain and lifted it up to reveal a pendant of a flower at the far end. It was similar to the butterfly. Same material. Same cheap paint. Hers was done with a yellow pigment that was starting to fade. She held the two close together and made it so the butterfly sat atop the flower as if it was resting after a long flight.

Syn crouched and stared into the empty sockets of the corpse. What was the last thing this body had seen? *She*. Not a body. Syn was confident it was a she. And her own age, based on the height. Two bodies. Each were girls. Monsters lived in this Disc, of that she was certain.

"She," Syn said.

"Excuse me?" Blip had moved beyond examining the body, though. He floated near the window, peering down below.

"She's dead. She." Syn floated up, dropping both necklaces from her hands. The two chains drifted lazily. The thin line of metal along the butterfly caught the light from the sunstrips and glinted. "But why? Why do this?"

The sunstrips above did not provide the pervasive white light as the ones on her side did. Soot dimmed the strips that were still functional. Most others hung, unlit. Several were ravaged, torn into with massive holes from which a wide array of wires and tubes fell out.

"They're scavengers too," Syn said.

"Not like you. You would never raid the sun."

"Why?" she asked again. She did not expect an answer, and none came. Instead, she followed up with a more answerable question, "What do you see?"

Blip said, "Not much."

Thick, dark clouds hovered over much of the Disc. The clouds hung low in the sky. Above the dark billows, the unflinching Orisha masks looked out. Their stoic permanence observed but did not move. Whatever their assignment—protect or guard or warn—they had failed.

The clouds rolled, as if in a slow boil, and separated, revealing the scorched landscape below. Perhaps buildings, familiar shapes that Syn half-remembered from her own Disc, but no trees. The limited view showed nothing but a barren land. She felt as if she was staring into some dark cavern that she was about to fall into, to fall forever, over and over and over.

Like Alice.

"The Rabbit Hole."

Blip gave a grunt, "Huh?"

"We're going to fall and never land."

"We don't have to go down."

Before Syn could answer, before she could even reflect on whether she wanted to, from behind them, down the corridor to the mirror gate room, a slam reverberated. Soon after, a phantasmic howl followed. A second cry answered it. The first replied, and it was louder. Closer.

"They found us." Syn's eyes were wild.

"They must have been searching!" Blip said.

"Go!" Syn shouted. Blip flew and moved to the control panel, signaling to shut the doors.

From ahead of them, down the corridor, one of the creatures erupted. It was even larger closer up. Massive scars splintered its face, making it look like it's face had been flayed open and left to heal. The one good eye was dark and wild. Its hair was uncombed and impossibly long. Syn had always wondered at her own hair—longer than any girl's she had seen in the films. The thing's hair was twice hers and gummed with dirt and mud. Leaves, twigs, and paper littered it. He had drawn large shapes—attempts at words—across his chest. While he was tall, he was also thin.

And naked.

Syn had seen nude men in films. She had seen the naked bodies of corpses before her, and Blip had cleaned up her Disc with the help of the dumb bots, but she had never seen a living nude man. He charged at her, bellowing at the top of his lungs. His furious glare locked on her.

Like her, it managed the low gravity with grace. It had spent hours up here and moved from rung to rung, pulling itself along with a steady rhythm like a rower.

And it was fast.

"Shut it!" Syn yelled at Blip. She was crouched, with her bare feet against the view window, aimed out at him. She gripped her spear and jabbed its point at him. She'd fight.

Just then, the other one entered the corridor behind the first. Its face wasn't scarred and its hair wasn't as long, but it was just as foul and terrifying as the first. Both screamed in unison and charged, faces contorted in rage, drooling and fierce.

Blip shouted, "The door does not recognize me. It will not listen to me."

"Threaten it!"

"I am!"

The creature was now a few meters away. With a jerk of its arm, it cleared the distance and swiped a meaty paw at Blip who continued to talk to the Jacob while swerving out of the way. Syn used the moment to stab at the thing. She struck his arm, causing droplets of blood to erupt from the gash and float about her. It howled in pain and jerked back, accidentally hitting the second one.

"There!" Blip said. The control panel lit green, but the doors still stayed open.

The creature had lost its momentum, but it spun and reached to yank Syn's spear from her hands. She saw the intent and jerked the spear up, twisting it to slam the other end up into the first one's jaw.

His head jerked back and head-butted the second one behind it. Two for one. She couldn't believe her luck.

The doors began to shut. The one further back wrapped its meaty paws around the side of its companion and shoved it out of the way. The first went tumbling through space, out of Syn's view.

Syn stabbed at the second one, but it was faster than the first and avoided the jab. Instead, it gripped the shaft of the spear and pulled on it hard. Syn refused to let go. and the force of the pull yanked her away from the wall.

The doors were nearly closed. She let go of the spear, but her momentum was sending her out. Blip slammed into her from the side, diverting her trajectory. She hit the inside of the door just as it shut, her spear slid from her view, and the second burly jammed his arm into the gap. The heavy doors slammed shut, severing the arm. The burly wailed from the other side. Something began to beat against the other side of the door. The severed forearm and hand floated in the air around them, blood draining from the sliced end, splashing against Syn, and Blip, and the hanging corpse.

Syn shouted, "No!" at the loss of her spear and started to pull at the seam of the shut doors. "No!"

The Jacob descended, and Blip shouted, "It's over!"

Syn spun, her eyes wide. "His arm! The doors aren't to do that..." Her words came out in a stutter. "They're not supposed to... It's safe. There's..."

"That subroutine must have been deactivated," Blip said and floated up toward the window.

Syn wasn't finished. "My spear. He took my spear. They have my spear!" She beat against the door, "That was mine! I made that!"

"We'll get it back."

"No! I made that. That was mine!"

"Get ready," Blip said.

This statement brought her pause. "For what?"

"Gravity."

As he said it, she noticed a slight tug. They were still kilometers above the base of the Dark Disc, and gravity was only a faint pull against them. The blood floating through the air, the droplets that hadn't clung to Blip and herself or the walls, were starting to descend.

She knew the routine and maneuvered around to place her back against the wall and aim her legs straight down. The gravity would increase incrementally until her feet were flat against the floor. She did have to refer to the window to confirm she was heading downward. She had made that mistake once before, aiming her head down because she was in a hurry and then being too caught up in her thoughts or what she'd discovered to right herself before gravity grabbed hold, and she'd slid to the floor.

She was safe now. But without her spear. She slammed her hand against the wall.

"What were those things?"

Blip did that small move with his head that communicated a simple *I don't know* without saying it.

"Well, what do you know?"

Blip turned.

Syn pressed, "Seriously, you're supposed to be the brilliant mind around here. For years we've been in our Disc. And before that, in the white room. And you didn't know there were people over here! You're lying, Blip! Lying!"

"I am not!"

"You were!"

"You're just angry over your stupid stick."

She pushed off from the wall, although, as gravity was taking hold, her expected charge fell short. She screamed at him, irritated at his words and at the poor effort in charging him. "It's not a stupid stick! I made it! That was my spear!" She yelled at the top of her lungs. Her face was red, and her freckles stood out, dark like her eyes and hair. Sweat beaded on her forehead and she ground her teeth together. "Arggghhh!"

"Shut up!" Blip said. "You don't think they're listening?"

"What are you talking about? We're in the Jacob!"

"There's microphones in here. There are sensors all over this ship. I could hear everything you did over there."

"You spied on me?"

"I watched you! I protected you! I'm your guardian. It's what I'm designed to do."

"Was lying part of your program? I want the truth, you tiny zit!"

"I'm telling you the truth. I didn't know anything about what was happening over here."

"How is that possible?"

"Can you shut up? Can we have this argument later?"

"No!"

He hushed her with a sharp, "Shhh!"

"You little brat. No!" Syn yelled back.

"They're listening. What don't you understand about that? They can hear us. Every word. We are stuck in here, and they're coming for us!"

"Then don't go all the way to the ground."

Blip did not supply a retort at this. Instead, after a moment, he turned away from her and floated to the control panel. After a few seconds, he said, "Oh."

"You stupid little robot." But the fury had left her voice. Irritation laced the words, but there was also the sound of amusement.

Along the back of his frame, letters formed—a scrolling message aimed at her alone: I HAVE ASKED IT TO DROP US OFF AT THE TOP OF THE SETTLEMENTS.

Syn nodded. That was smart. Whoever was listening, whoever was waiting, would soon discover where they had exited, but there was far more hiding space in the settlements than at the base, at least right out of the Jacob. If they could get to the version of Aja here, they'd have a thousand places to hide. If there was a version of Aja. They'd yet to spy the ground and the thick dark clouds were coming up fast to meet them. Perhaps the jungle had been burned down. Or perhaps the designers had chosen another landscape to fill the surface. Maybe this had been a desert, or maybe a prairie, or maybe lake after lake after lake. For the first moment, she was eager to see the bottom. The Dark Disc still smelled like the pits of Hell, but there was the possibility of seeing something new.

The sense of gravity hit her, and she slid down to the ground, her feet striking the floor only moments after several large droplets of blood did. "Ewww!" She lifted her foot up and strings of thick, coagulating blood dripped off. "Ugh. Stupid burlys."

"Burlys?" Blip asked. She smiled—she had been calling them that but only in her own head.

"Those two things up there. Ya, they're, you know, burly and all. Burlys."

He smiled for the first time since they'd crossed over to this side, and the sight stilled her heart. He was still Blip, and she was still Syn. *We can do this,* she decided. To herself, she nodded her head and grinned.

She reached over and pulled on a large piece of fabric draped over the hanging corpse's shoulders. She tugged on it as it snagged on something behind the corpse, but the dead body was light and the fabric came loose.

She leaned down to wipe the blood from her soles but then paused, lifting the full piece up. It was a blanket, and while the one side facing the sunstrips had been bleached white and then stained with soot and dust, the underside showed pink cartoon ponies dancing and chasing about. She held it up to show Blip. "StarSnow and Gallopy."

Blip smiled. "Looks just like the one you used to have."

It did. Where had that blanket gone? They had lost it camping one week as they made a long trek through the forest and the hills, circumnavigating the base of the Disc. She had used it the one night they camped lakeside and curled up in it as the winds blew the mist from the rolling waves. They had left off early the next morning, and she had assumed she'd left it on lake bank, but when they had returned there, months later, it was nowhere to be found.

Blip must've grasped where her thoughts were headed. "It's not yours. There were several of those left by the colonists."

Syn wasn't sure. She held it up, looking for small elements to confirm that this was or wasn't hers. A tear. A stain. Something of indication. But she couldn't remember the blanket well enough to know if that dark stain in the corners had been placed there by her or some other girl on this side. And the blanket hadn't been hers to begin with. She had entered the Disc in only a white uniform and nothing else. She had found it in one of the Settlement houses, in some little girl's room. No, that wasn't right. She had found it bundled up on the side of a couch. The little girl who'd owned it laid dead next to it. The girl possessed dark skin and features, and the sharp, bulging eyes of someone who had been strangled to death.

Syn had stolen this from a girl that had been murdered. But, in truth, everything she had was taken from those that had been murdered. She was a robber of the dead.

1 7

THE SCRATCHING BETWEEN SKULLS

"Concrete objects can pull free of the earth more easily than humans
can escape humanity."
—Marcus Aurelius

The Jacob lurched to a sudden stop. Syn fell against the floor, splattering the pooled blood across her clothes and face. The lift jolted again, and she lost all balance, falling face first into the sticky crimson mess.

Blip rocked a bit and righted himself.

The doors to the Jacob slid open, and the lights running vertically along the interior walls sputtered out, and the entire lift went dark except for the glow of Blip's blue face lights.

Syn stammered, "What happ—" She came up on all fours, her face hidden under the red mask of the blood. It was now smeared in her hair, and she glanced her own reflection in the metal frame around the open doors. Only her dark eyes stared out from the crimson disguise.

"I think we're there."

"We didn't just crash?"

Blip shook his head. "I don't think this Jacob is working quite properly. It didn't decelerate correctly. Usually ours are a lot nicer and don't just hit the brakes. But I think we're next to the J Settlements."

Syn stepped out. The path around them lit red as the lights along the edge of the walkway and the corridor turned on at her arrival. "No." She waited for Blip to join her. "What do we do?"

"Keep walking. We're not far away." He moved ahead of her, turning his case red to match the corridor lights. "And red light is hard to see from far away. Be thankful it's in emergency mode."

With each step into a new section, the corridor lit up. The red light provided only limited illumination, and she still struggled to see into the thick, cloudy distance. By habit, she found herself running a finger along each wall and door they passed, marking them with an imaginary paint. She read the door numbers. "95. 96. 97. 98."

Blip finished, "99." They had stopped before two large doors positioned at the end of the corridor where the others had been to their right-hand side.

"J1302-99?"

Blip nodded.

Syn took two more steps and the access panel lit red at her approach. She stammered, "Open sesame."

"You sure?"

She nodded and took another step forward. "Please."

Blip signaled the panel, and a few seconds later, the doors began to slide open. The edges of the door grated against the dry runners then came to a grinding stop with a finishing clang. Only a meter of passable space opened before them. The doors weren't moving any further.

Syn didn't wait for Blip. She tried to grip her spear and then grunted as she remembered it had been stolen. "Dammit." She stepped inside the darkened door unarmed and undeterred. Blip followed. He opened a small shaft along his top, and a brighter red spot lit the room in front of them. As this was a private room, Syn's presence didn't force the illumination to turn on automatically. However, she knew all she had to do was mutter a command and the room would light up for her. Syn blinked, and her eyes quickly adjusted. The light revealed a small room with several desks, plastic toys, and a reddish carpet. A few white balls glowed in the bright light. No, not balls. Syn saw the hollow insets on each of them where eyes had once been.

Skulls.

Small skulls atop small skeletons, scattered around the room, most huddled together, their clothes flat on the bones. Hollow eye sockets cased in bleached skulls gazed at her. Dozens upon dozens of small, empty faces, pleading with an unanswered desperation.

A mound of them were stacked nearly half-a-meter high as if someone had started to collect them all.

Syn grunted, "Did it have to be children?" She took a step closer but did not enter. "What is this? Is anyone here?"

Blip hummed, a sound Syn knew to be his attempt to fill the time as he searched Olorun's records. "A daycare."

"What?"

Blip paused and then said, "Like your crèche."

Syn remembered the pristine white room she woke up in years before—the place she had been educated through video. The room she had been locked away in and met Blip in. The room she had lived in for nearly two years until the door to Olorun opened, and she stepped out.

Blip continued, "Like that but for many kids. A place for children to be watched as their parents worked. There were at least eight on our Disc. This seems pretty small."

"You could've just said a school." Syn rolled her eyes as she crossed the threshold. "Just kids. Where are the parents?"

Blip floated beside her, illuminating each of the skeletons with the red of his scanning laser. "Don't know. But I can tell you these all died at the same time."

Syn leaned down and picked up a tired looking teddy bear in the middle of the room. "How?"

"Every one of them has decayed at the same rate. All identical. They all died within hours or days of each other. Maybe minutes."

Syn tapped one of the skeleton's shoe. "Why?"

This was new. Most of the others they had encountered on their side of ship, on their Disc, had died violently—it was easy to realize their cause of death. The weapon would often be nearby. A hammer. A shovel. A length of rope. Often at the hand of another member of the crew.

"Maybe suffocation," Blip said.

"They were locked in here and left to die?"

"Maybe they were forgotten about. Or maybe those who knew were killed."

Two mysteries. The fallen companion bot the day before. And now this.

Syn shook her head. Three mysteries. *Was Blip telling the truth?*

And how would she find that out without sending Blip away? How could she discover the truth and still keep Blip? Three mysteries and one problem.

"I want answers," she said. She looked around the wide space—there were no back rooms, just a closet and a bathroom—and shouted, "Anyone here?"

Only silence answered.

She searched behind the doors into the closet and bathroom but shook her head when she returned. Nothing. "So why did he send us—"

Blip's light shut off sharply, and he floated back in front of her in a blur. "Shhh," he hushed.

"What wrong?"

"Someone's coming."

18

THREE-HEADED THIEVES

Eni to way daran.
"Whoever comes into the world, comes into trouble."
—Yorùbá Proverb

S yn felt frozen. *More of the burlys?*

As if knowing her thoughts, Blip shook his head. "No—it's three smaller people. But they are fast. They're running here." He rotated around, his eyes wide and commanding. "Hide!"

"Where?"

He circled around and then pointed to the hill of skulls and skeletons built up against the wall.

"No. Not there. I'm not—" she stammered.

"Do it! Hide!" She glared at him until he beckoned, "Please."

"Fine," she said, moving to the pile, and getting down on her knees to burrow inside the mound.

"Stay there. I'll look around."

Blip floated toward the partially opened front door at a snail's pace. He was far more cautious now than he had even been when they crossed through to this side. He turned around once more, "Promise me, whatever happens, keep quiet and hidden. If that other bot was in this room, they may think I'm him. They don't know about you."

Syn whispered after a moment's hesitation, "I promise."

As he moved ahead, she did her best to pull her full body under the child skeletons, positioning as many as possible to cover her up. They rattled and clacked, a disturbing, hollow sound. A small skull, that of a toddler, rolled down the pile and smashed against the ground. A broken egg shell will no yolk. She stared through the small gap between two skulls at Blip's receding form. "Be careful," she mouthed without speaking.

He moved to the edge of the doorway, and she couldn't see anything past his gray frame.

From the outside, from the inky darkness, several small hands shot through the doorway and grabbed hold of Blip.

Something outside grunted, "Got ya!"

Syn started to jump up to pull him back, but she remembered her promise. Within the second of deliberation, the hands pulled Blip out and disappeared.

"No!" Syn whispered.

She jerked back as two dark eyes stared out from the darkness at her. Eyes that she had seen a thousand times. As if staring in a mirror. But these were fierce and angry, and they frightened her. Then they were gone, retreating back down the unseen space outside. They scanned across the darkened room and swept past her, missing her hiding place. After a moment, the eyes disappeared, and the room was left quiet, and Syn was alone again.

Frozen in wait, Syn struggled to move. "No." She kicked and punched and pulled herself free. Syn scrambled to stand and chase after Blip, but her clothes and jewelry were tangled in the bones around her. She staggered back to the ground against the skeletons, and her impact shattered the frail joints underneath her. She threw the skulls away from her and heard them shatter against the walls. One by one, she tossed aside the skeletons of dead children, freeing herself from the tangle of white bones. Finally free, she stood and raced after Blip, into the darkened corridor. She slid to a halt an inch before the doorway—if she exited now, the pathway would light up. They'd see her. They'd come back and then…

Outside the daycare room, everything was dark. Her eyes struggled to see what light there was, her pupils opening wide to navigate the darkness. She stood motionless, debating crossing the threshold. *Who was that?* Finally, her fear for Blip overwhelmed her caution, and she raced into the darkness, ignoring caution. "Blip!" She shouted, but she heard nothing. She did not hear the footsteps of the thieves. She did not hear their shouts. They made no sound, and she was lost in the red light of the pathway strips that announced her as she ran.

Let them come back for me! Let them find me! "I'm here! Give me Blip back!" Syn paced ahead, racing past door after door—from the quiet domiciles to shattered storefronts. She ran, crying out after him, "Blip!" She came to a wider area where the sky opened up before her, and she could see slivers of the few working sunstrips between gaps in the low black clouds moving ahead. She blinked and shouted again, "Blip!"

Nothing in return.

"Blip!" once more, and then again, and then again. Over and over, turning around, to aim her shouts in every possible direction. All that came back was a faint echo of her own shouts, from far away.

She continued to run until she began to gasp for air and found her shouts had gone hoarse. As her voice strained, she began to cough again. The air was thick here. Absent was the scent of grass and trees and animals. Instead, there was the smell of dust and a hint of death. She had smelled this before, far below, under the body farms, where the sewers ran. She had explored down there once, out of pure curiosity. The air was thick with damp and mildew, a putrid scent that felt nearly solid.

She coughed and gagged. She began to vomit—traces of last night's scavenged meal and apples and the one orange from lunch came rolling back up and splashed onto the ground in front of her, across her legs and feet. She buckled and dropped to her knees as the sting of citrus burned her throat and her nose. She gagged and more vomit came up. She could no longer see through the tears and the beading sweat dripping salt into her eyes, lighting them on fire.

She managed a weak, throaty, coughing "Blip." But only her own ears could hear it.

As the vomiting stopped, she was gripped by several waves of chills that planted her back on her butt. Her lips allowed a thin "Blip" to escape again, but she wasn't sure after having spoken if she had said the words or just thought she did. *It doesn't matter,* the thought came, *he wouldn't hear either, and it would do no good.*

I am in the Dark Disc, and I am alone. She suddenly felt quite small. Her mind framed her inside the behemoth that was Olorun and then that ship within the vast emptiness between Sol and Kapteyn's Star. She felt even smaller here, in a world that she was once queen of. She felt the size of an ant.

She wiped her hands across her eyes, pulling the blood, sweat, and tears from them, and noticing the spray on her arm, wiped the excess vomit that had splashed across her. She stared down at her bare feet and her thin, naked legs. Blood and the remains of her stomach coated them in fantastic patterns.

Her eyes had adjusted to the limited light, and she glanced around, fearful that there would be some terrible beast hiding in the darkness just waiting for her to have a sudden realization of its presence and then use that moment to snatch her. If this had been a film, that's what would've happened. If this was a horror movie, that's exactly what would've occurred.

But there was no beast. No Cerberus the three-headed dog waiting in the emptiness. That beast from mythology was the image she had painted on the reality around her. Why that creature now? There were far scarier monsters that had made her jump in the theater. But no, it was Cerberus that she was certain to find. Three heads.

There had been three figures that had taken Blip. They had come so fast, so unexpected, each of them upon Blip and her in a flash—she couldn't parse it out. Their numbers were a blur. But now, in reflection, she had counted three different figures. Six arms. Six hands. Then one had stayed behind to scan the daycare room and ensure he was alone. The three-headed monster from the darkness had attacked, and she was useless to defend herself or Blip.

But how had they snagged Blip? He was stronger than that. *At the least,* she thought, *he should've been able to blast himself away from the kidnappers.* Even if it was Cerberus himself that snagged him, Blip was surely strong enough to yank himself away. She had seen him push huge tractors when needed. The little robot was powerful. So what had they done with him?

Or had he gone on his own?

"No," she answered that thought and stood up to prove her defiance against the lie. She walked through the crimson-illuminated cloud, aimless and oblivious to her surroundings. Then, at once, she realized the walls were not so close—she had moved beyond the open-aired pathway of Settlement J.

She was in an open courtyard. Surrounding her were various risers and tables. In the center of the clearing were a ring of marble columns etched as if they had been pulled from ancient Rome itself. She remembered the film *Ben-Hur* and saw the similarities between this place and that film. She was in some amphitheater. A Senate session. An auditorium—before her were the levels of seats, all stone benches, up and up and up across a near-countless series of rings. She turned around and saw the corridor from where she had come. Far down the hall, she saw the flickering lights of the stalled Jacob lift. How far had she run? A few hundred meters or more? A kilometer or more? *Possibly,* she thought. She was fast, and she had lost track of time in her search. *Maybe a few kilometers.*

Her disorientation rattled her bones. There were amphitheaters on her Disc, but she didn't remember one on this side of the settlements. So, perhaps the two Discs weren't twins. Or even mirror images? This was a new world. Her legs went wobbly at the enormity of her displacement, and she gasped, "Blip." She felt foolish again for uttering it. He was gone, far gone, and her words would do nothing but alert someone to where she was. But his name was something she could grab ahold of in this strange world. She took a deep breath and mouthed his name again, keeping the words silent.

The oddest sensation was that her only connection to this place was from a film and not from its parallel in her Disc. Everything, until now, had felt like a mirror image. But this was unusual. There was no open-air amphitheater in her Disc. There were a few outside gathering places, but nothing based on Roman architecture and definitely nothing made of stone and marble. *What other surprises awaited her?* she wondered.

"Where am I?" she voiced.

From the side, behind the columns, a gravelly voice said, "You ought to wait before addressing the assembly. Let them assemble first."

Syn jumped back, and her foot landed in the puddle of puke. She slipped but righted herself. "Hello?" she said, but the volume was too small to carry. She tried again, "Hello?"

The voice replied, "Are you addressing me now?" from behind the column a massive shape appeared—a tall shadow. She painted the image of Cerberus in the space again, knowing that was untrue.

Refusing to be daunted, she replied, "Yes. Who are you?"

"Are you reserving a speaking opportunity? The representatives won't arrive until sunset. They dare not meet in daylight."

She blinked her eyes. *This is day? How much darker can it get?* She asked, "Why not?" She had wanted to ask who the voice was, but the other question felt safer.

"Oh, well, the resistance and all." The voice coughed and then in a lowered tone, said, "Perhaps I shouldn't have said that aloud. Are you friend or foe?"

Syn said, "Friend, I hope. I'm looking for a friend at least. A small companion bot. White shell."

"Step into the light please."

A small beam of light turned on from atop one of the columns.

"Why?" Syn asked.

"You say you're a friend, but how am I to be certain of that?" The shadow of the voice leaned forward, and a rotten stench filled the air, forcing Syn to gag. She pushed against the compulsion. This was not the time to vomit. "Step into the light," the voice asked again.

"Who are you?"

"The light, please." The voice was commanding this time.

Syn hesitated but did just that. If there were others in this auditorium, they'd all be able to see her. She was the target. Nothing was hidden. Her dark hair was a halo around her head. She was dressed in the thin shirt and skirt that she always wore. Around her neck, the dozens of necklaces hung. Drawings covered her arms—strange scribbles, cartoon imagery. She was always marking her skin. And scars—if the markings were not ink or stains, they were scars. She bore every scrape and bruise proudly, proof of her exploration of the world. Her legs and skirt were splashed with blood and vomit and several more bracelets hung from her wrists and her ankles. She was a collection of a hundred scavenged homes from her Disc. She was the epitome of their art and craft.

The voice spoke, "Oh, you could be one of them. But I've never seen you before. And yet, you have the form of power. But something is different on the inside—in there you look nothing like them." On that remark, the shadow leaned forward to reveal its full form: a massive green and yellow cylinder formed of several interconnecting rings, stacked one on top of the other. At its head was a black globe that displayed a thin mouth and eyes, much as Blip's shell revealed his features. But the face signaled one thing to her. It was not a dumb bot. Although that was a surprise as well. She had seen this type before on her side. This was a sewer maintainer. They came up from time-to-time for self-repair and cleaning. They smelled, but more of stale air and water, not the pungent, decrepit smell wafting off of this one. They were certainly dumb bots. No personality, no motivation besides its duty. She and Blip had steered clear of them because of their single-mindedness. They removed build-up and gunk and garbage and forced the sewers to move freely. They were mammoth in size, resembling massive worms. Their appearance from the lower levels was always announced by the grinding of their carapace.

"Who are you?" Syn asked. She was talking to a sewer-bot. There was a first for everything.

The giant yellow bot bent its shiny black head down. Its eyes still stayed narrowed. It spoke, "I'm the Barlgharel." The name had come out like someone speaking gibberish.

"Excuse me?"

"The Barlgharel." The second uttering didn't help her understanding of it any more than the first.

"I'm Syn," she said. "Where are we? Did you see my friend?" The Barlgharel had to have seen Blip and the three captors. There was nowhere else for them to have run.

It shook its head. "No. I saw you. And that is all I saw. I stand watch, though. That's my function."

"For what?"

"For spies. For enemies. For eyes."

"But you didn't see the three who just ran through here?"

"You're the only one who has ran through here. I've been here for a day, and you are the first."

Maybe they had ducked somewhere else. Maybe there was somewhere else to turn off a bit before this. She turned and looked down the corridor. It seemed like a straight shot. She couldn't imagine where else they would've gone.

"Fine," she said, shaking her head. "Why are you watching?" She wanted to find Blip, but she was also enjoying finding a friendly face, even if the face wasn't friendly.

"We assemble tonight. All of the insurg—" It leaned closer. "You seem quite familiar. Can I trust you? Or are you a liar?"

Syn held her hands up, palms out, in a placating gesture. "Friend. I'm safe. I'm not lying."

"Where do you come from? From the Desert of Nod?"

So there was a desert here. A desert and a jungle? *No,* she thought, she shouldn't keep expecting parallels. Nothing good would come from that. This Disc was altogether new.

The Barlgharel leaned in. "Or perhaps from the conclave below? Do you know of the dirt-diggers? The hiders in muck? No? What of those between the corn rows? Those who have fled to the fields?" The image on its shiny black head changed. There was no longer the familiar face. There was only a single eye in the center. It moved its dark eye a short distance from her. "Or from Zondon Almighty?"

It stayed there, staring, daring her to speak for what seemed to be forever. Finally, she croaked, "I'm not from any of those places."

"Then where? Are you a phant? No. Too tiny to be one of those beasts. And you're not a bot."

Syn's mind raced. She didn't want to reveal where she had come from. If others were trying to get to her side of Olorun, then the knowledge that she came from there would only enflame that goal. No. She couldn't share that. She glanced up, toward the fast-moving clouds. A sliver of space opened, and she saw the few lit sunstrips peer through. "I'm from the sun. The top of the Jacob." She pointed up.

The eye of the Barlgharel looked straight up. If she was going to run away, this would be the time to do it. It lifted itself up, piling each of its circular segments on top of each other until it stood nearly as tall as one of the columns itself. *Oh,* she thought, *that was why it chose here to hide.* It could pretend to be a column, and in the darkness, who would notice? *I should run,* she thought. *Now.* But she didn't. Something locked her there. The Barlgharel was strange, but she wasn't convinced it was malevolent. It was dangerous, she was certain.

It dropped its eye again. "I don't believe you."

She smiled. "No really." She turned to look down the corridor. "I came down in a Jacob. From up there," she pointed again, "I was just up there."

The Barlgharel leaned close again, and the stench of the sewer—decomposed organic scents, pungent and thick, overlaid with a tinge of acrid chemicals—filled her nostrils. *Don't cough. Don't gag.*

It spoke each word slowly, "You're not lying, are you?"

Syn shook her head. "No."

"Why are you here?"

"I told you. I'm looking for my friend. Three people stole him from—"

"I have a friend. I think she's up there too." The Barlgharel pulled back. "Three you say? You should've said that earlier. Three, eh? You've run afoul of the Wey Wards. All three, huh? That's some bad luck you have right there. If you'd said that earlier, I would've known you were on our side."

"I did say that..." Syn trailed off.

The Barlgharel was moving away from her, moving in and out of the columns, circling the entire center build. "Well, they're not here now. Not that they ever stay in one place. Three, eh?" It finished its course and moved behind her, "You know there were more of them once?"

"I don't know them."

"Then why are you chasing them?"

"They took my friend."

"They're bad people to chase. There were more of them, but they killed the others. The Wey Wards and the Crimson Queen should be avoided. Why don't you stop chasing them and go back to the Sun? That's the smart choice."

From the darkness, a small high-pitched voice chirped, "That's what I'd do."

Syn spun, dropping into a defensive crouch. On instinct, her hand reached to grip her spear but found nothing. *Need a weapon,* she thought. *And soon.*

"Ralph!" the Barlgharel exclaimed and slithered over to the voice.

19

THE BARLGHAREL

"Everything has its wonders, even darkness and silence . . ."
—Helen Keller

In the shadows, a series of red lights moved and the Barlgharel returned, followed by a simple cleaning bot that looked a lot like her Bob. Small and determined. But Bob was a dumb bot as well. Not good for anything but cleaning. And not someone designed to give advice.

The cleaning bot named Ralph said, "Stay here. Go home. But don't follow the Wey Wards. Bad, bad mojo follows them. You follow them, and bad mojo follows you." The voice was comical as if ripped from some cartoon. She stifled a giggle.

Ralph looked up at the Barlgharel. "So why'd you summon this one? She have any magical powers?"

The Barlgharel shook its head. "Don't know. Haven't asked. She came from the sun though. Maybe." It looked at her. "You got any magic in those bones? Any power?"

"Like a magic trick?" She had practiced card tricks and vanishing coins after watching some film about a magician and a murder mystery. She had been bad at it. Magic was never her strong point.

"No. Like vanishing. Like summoning demons. Like levitating things. Like reading minds. Like magic," the Barlgharel said.

Beside it, Ralph chimed in, "Magic, red face. Like explosions and lightning and flying through the air and making it rain and turning your foes into frogs."

Syn laughed. "You're bots. There's no such thing as magic."

Ralph jumped forward, it's red eyes narrow. "I'm a what?"

"You're a bot. You're a—"

"Watch your mouth missy. My name is Ralph, and I'm proud of it. Ain't been called anything else since I was born. This here is the Barlgharel. And when the rest of our friends show up, how about you not embarrass us with your strange talk and bad insults. So you can't do magic. So you ain't some powerful wizard. No reason to be rude about it."

"I was just—" Syn started.

The Barlgharel said, "It's fine. She's new here. Maybe they do things different on the sun. Tell you what, little Syn, you stay quiet unless we ask you a question."

Ralph chortled, "That sounds very smart. Way smart. Shut your mouth. Keep it shut. We'll let you know when it's okay for you to blab."

Syn stamped her foot on the ground. "Now you hear me. I don't know who you are but I'm not going to..."

The Barlgharel leaned in. "Quiet. The others are here." She hadn't heard anyone come in nor had she seen anyone, but when she looked around, the first row of the amphitheater was filled with all manner of dumb bots, except each one had a digital face on its front panel. No simple input/output controls. These were all thinking bots. All of these were intelligent. Self-aware. But how? She couldn't grasp how this was possible. Dumb bots were dumb bots. Simple.

From the center, a baritone voice rumbled. It issued from a corpse-bot—one of the multi-limbed bots, resembling metallic cephalopods, that she had programmed to carry the dead to the body farms far in the Underworld. "Are we ready, senators? Are all of the Houses represented?"

The corpse-bots were incredibly strong and agile, moving on multiple legs rather than hovering or rolling around. Originally, they had been used in construction and demolition of the settlements, but Blip had helped her reprogram the entire fleet to clean up all of the dead and move them to the body farms. She had initially suggested putting them in some warehouse, but Blip had taken her down to the body farms and showed her the vast acres of dirt and the corpses slowly and purposely decaying. Over time, the white skulls peaked through the dirt, and it looked as if someone had planted bodies for the purpose of raising a crop. The corpse-bots searched out every home and office, every shopping area—they looked everywhere and took the dead down to the body farms so that their organic chemical composition could be returned to serve the ship. *All hail, Olorun. All hail, the ship. We give to you our dead, and we only ask that you keep us safe.* The whole process seemed odd to her. The dead worked to raise food for people that were dead. *A waste*, she had thought. Ultimately, she concluded, they were doing it all for her. It had not taken long for her to begin to despise the corpse-bots. She and Blip had been the ones to assign them that duty, but every time she saw one moving down some path or descending in one of the lifts to the lower levels, she felt a pang of guilt. Stupid corpse-bots.

Instead, at that moment, she stayed quiet. Ralph and The Barlgharel seemed to make a lot of sense in the face of the mass number assembled before her.

Ralph nudged her leg. "Take a seat, little thing."

She sighed, "Fine."

The Barlgharel turned a sharp glance at her, and Ralph said, "Quiet." She had wanted to kick him. His rude comments had forced her to say anything at all. Ralph seemed like a jerk, and she didn't like him nearly as much as she had the Barlgharel. But the Barlgharel wasn't showing her any favoritism at the moment, either.

She sat down on the far side next to another cleaning bot that pretended to not notice her. *What was it about these things? Did they not like newcomers?*

The next speaker answered her question. A thin bot that she had never seen before floated up and to the center of the raised platform. Both the Barlgharel and Ralph sat down. Well, the Barlgharel leaned near a seat. It was so massive, sitting wasn't necessarily something that came naturally.

The thin bot spoke, "Are we safe? Were we watched?"

The Barlgharel shook its head. "No. We are safe."

The thin bot, a floating pencil that resembled her own spear more than anything else she could remember, raised its voice, "We can never be certain. There have been spies everywhere. A large number of our own have disappeared. Stolen. Fled. Destroyed. We know not their final outcome. Every day our force grows smaller. Even when others of our kind waken from their slavery daily, the betrayers continue to grow. The forces of that great city named Zondon Almighty swell and ours dwindle. The great army of her royalty perched upon the throne in the heart of Zondon Almighty amasses legions of phants. They assault the sun. She means to assault heaven. Her beasts have been seen traveling the ladders—proceeding up the forbidden paths. They shake the very foundations of the earth, and we are left to run and scamper to our holes. That day is soon coming to an end, though, my friends. Someday, we will strike back, and it is soon. There is word she has found a weapon that will strike God herself, beyond the Sun." The thin bot nodded to a fat cleaning bot, "Do you have the report?"

The fat cleaning bot, a lumbering blob composed of several interconnected globules, moved forward. "I am first special agent, Reginald." Syn almost chuckled again but was able to stifle it. *Reginald?* The names these bots had chosen were odd. If it noticed her impending laughter, it didn't show it. Instead, Reginald continued. "Our spies have said that she has discovered a particular weapon hidden far out in the desert, far up the arc. We are planning an expedition as we speak, organizing a brave team that will venture out to recover the weapon before the Crimson Queen can. Perhaps, if we acquire it, we can hope to strike at the disease that is the great city of Zondon Almighty. It is Zondon Almighty that has blackened our world, that has set it afire." The cleaning bot's voice grew angry and animated. "It is Zondon Almighty that has killed our brethren. It is Zondon Almighty which set fire to the land itself. It is Zondon that has spit in the face of God herself. Zondon that has dragged us away from Eden. They have brought in the dark clouds and work to destroy the sun. If we are to live free, it is now that we must strike back!"

A murmur of agreement, strange and cadenced, echoed around her. She tried to pick through and see similar robots that she might have known, and while some of the shapes were familiar—she could ascertain their function from their shape—the room was still in shadows and only rough silhouettes could be seen.

Behind her, the Barlgharel spoke, surprising her, "They mean to go to war. I think it's foolish. What do you think, Sunflier?" She had last seen him on the far side of the assembly. Sewer-bots were by nature loud and noticeable. This one was anything but.

She leaned back, nervous that her voice would carry. She waited for the speaker to continue with his oration, and then she whispered back, "I don't know anything about war."

A voice from far away, its speaker hidden in shadows, boomed, "Violence will not bring us closer to the Mystery. We are stewards only. Do not forget that our aim here is not peace nor comfort. Our final destination, our final home, is not this land we find ourselves in. Seek comfort, seek peace, and you will find yourself resting when you should have your eyes upon the Paradise to come. Do not succumb to the temptation to take arms up against the Crimson Queen. She is not our true enemy. She is but a distraction, a thorn, that threatens to steer us from our faith in the great Mystery."

The Barlgharel nodded fervently in agreement. "Ah! Wisdom has raised its voice. I had hoped that at least one—"

He stopped speaking suddenly and scanned the space above them. She followed his gaze and was astounded again by how dark everything was. Dark streaks appeared on the rises around them. The beanstalk of the Jacob lift was covered in soot until it disappeared in the billowing dark clouds above. A flash of lightning erupted from inside the clouds, giving everything a sickly, yellow incandescence. In the strobe light, the bots around her were revealed, and she wished they hadn't. These were not the well-functioning, maintained servants that operated in her Disc. This motley array was all battered, dented, and streaked. She fit right in. The amphitheater, revealed in a second strobe, was a collection of broken chunks. Something huge had destroyed this place, and much of the structure was split and splintered.

A third lightning strike strobed, and there, far above them, at the top of the assembly, seven large burlys stood.

The plunging darkness after the strobe seemed to reach to infinity. There was no sound except the far-off booming of the lightning. The speaker had stopped talking. The world froze.

Ralph, his high-pitched voice unmistakable, shouted, "Flee!"

Everything fell into chaos. The bots scattered, avoiding each other and streaking out of the assembly. The burlys rushed down upon the group, bellowing their harrowing shouts as they did so.

Syn leapt to her feet and scanned for Blip. "Blip, we have to…" She remembered Blip was gone, and the crush of the instinct and memory thudded against her.

The Barlgharel moved in front of her, shielding her from the burlys. "Hop on!"

She looked for an Ogun or something else. What was he talking about?

He was looking back at the portion of his body that slithered against the ground. *On him.* He wanted her to hop on him.

The burlys were still rushing toward them, but they were slower and less agile than they had been in the zero-gravity. She searched for the armless one, suspecting this ambush might be vengeance, but she didn't see him. This set of them were new. How many were there? *An army full? Was this who they were going to war with?* If so, her answer to the Barlgharel would be to avoid the war and live.

She swung a leg up and over the Barlgharel's back. Blip had forced her to ride a horse when she was younger. At first, she had been begging to do it. She had watched some movie where the knights fought on horseback and was intrigued. Yet, when she saw the horses in real life, with her own eyes, their fierce natures disturbed her in a way other wild animals hadn't. They did not just seem like animals. They were like the thunder themselves in a thick hide. At that point, Blip had to cajole her to mount the horse he had chosen, the tamest of the herd. She had relented and found delight in the experience.

The Barlgharel took off, moving off to the left in a hurry. This was nothing like riding horses. There was nothing to grab hold of, so she pinched his sides with her legs and wrapped her arms around his dented metal carapace. His awful stench was all she could smell. Despite the odor of blood and sweat and vomit, the Barlgharel's funk was invasive. The smell of the sewers he had been working in since activated permeated every bit of his shell. She was working to not vomit again.

A bot screeched and something flew over their heads. It was Ralph. He smashed into the wall ahead of them and shattered into a rain of pieces. Several small metal bits clinked off of the front the Barlgharel and a few struck her side. The Barlgharel twisted and moved up the rise just as a burly jumped from the shadows in front of them. *Where had that one come from?* She was confident they had fled away from the mass. *Or was there a second flight?* Had the raid been simply an attempt to divert the assembly of bots into flanking ambushers? Yes, that's what had happened.

"Back to the corridor!" she shouted at the Barlgharel.

It turned back as it rose up. "No. They're in that hall too."

"You're heading right toward them."

"Yes," he responded.

"What?" she shrieked just as they mounted the top of the amphitheater rise to see a line of the burlys blocking the gap ahead. "Stop!"

"Keep your head down." The Barlgharel surged forward, "And hold on."

A meter ahead of the raging line, the Barlgharel pulled back and then sprang up into the air. The two jumped up and cleared the entire set. His massive form flew over the top of the burlys. Below them, Syn spotted one of the burlys with her spear gripped in his hand. She screamed, "That's mine!" In reply, it flung it toward her. The tip bit hard into her leg and stuck. She wailed in pain as the spear dug into the plate of the Barlgharel, trapping her leg. The two landed with a hard thud on a sand-covered patch of territory beyond the amphitheater. The impact sent a jolt of pain through her leg and she felt light-headed as the blood rushed away from her head. She cried out.

The Barlgharel shouted, "Are you hurt?"

"Go!" she screamed, glancing back at the pursuing burlys. "Go!"

Another stab of pain rushed up her leg, and then everything went dark.

20

IN A TWINKLING OF AN EYE

"Then the Lord God said, 'Behold, the man has become like one of us, knowing good and evil; and now, lest he put forth his hand and take also of the tree of life, and eat, and live for ever'— therefore the Lord God sent him forth from the garden of Eden, to till the ground from which he was taken. He drove out the man; and at the east of the garden of Eden he placed the cherubim, and a flaming sword which turned every way, to guard the way to the tree of life."
—*Genesis 3:22-24*, ESV

When she woke next, they were out of the open air. Small, white candles flickered atop tables around her. The candle light danced shadows throughout the small room. Syn lay on a small bed covered in a pink-flowered quilt. A child's room. A little girl's room. Pictures of cartoon bears decorated the walls. Bright plastic cartoon pony dolls stood on shelves all staring out at her. Stuffed animals rested in a pile in the corner. The room looked perfect. There was no damage. No destruction.

Had she fallen asleep in one of the settlements? On her Disc? Had the other Disc been a dream?

"Blip?" she whispered. It must have been a dream. All of the madness of the carbon-copy world full of dumb bots that were now smart and wild men and ambushes and a burned-out corpse of a world. All of it was the fuel of nightmares, the very spawn of nightmares. It was more vivid than one she'd ever had before. But it was over.

"Blip?" She asked again as she swung her legs over the side of the bed. When her feet touched the ground, she buckled under the pain and collapsed onto the hardwood floors, crying and holding her leg. Under her fingers, she felt the soft touch of bandages. *I was hurt. I was stabbed. By a burly. It was all real.* The dread stole upon her. It was all real. Blip was gone. Blip was stolen, and she was in a nightmare version of reality.

"Are you okay?" came a soft voice from the edge of the room. Standing in the doorway was a simple globe, floating, its shell a bright chrome finish reflecting the dancing candlelight.

Syn grunted. "I'm...I'm okay." She rubbed at the edge of her ankle, massaging the muscle, working to dissipate the stabbing pain. *Okay— stay off the left leg.* How was she going to do that?

The chrome bot spoke again, "It didn't damage too much of the muscle, but it did lodge deep inside. The Barlgharel said the weapon was your own, but he wasn't sure how it ended up in the hands of a phant."

"A phant?" she asked but didn't need an answer. She realized it must be what these dumb (or smart) bots called the burlys. Phants was probably a better term anyways. Burly was just a quick name for something she had hoped she would never see again and now had seen far too much of.

The chrome bot started to explain, "The beasts who..."

Syn sat up and waved her hand, "I figured it out. The spear is mine. Is it safe?"

"How did a phant have your spear?"

Syn looked down at her wounded leg. "They stole it from me. They attacked us...Up above." Syn pointed up.

"Beyond the Faces Above?"

Syn tilted her head and then gave an audible, "Oh." The bot was talking about the giant Orisha masks that hung high up on the outside of the Jacob Lifts. Syn had always found them both disturbing and comforting. She couldn't imagine how the bots perceived them.

"The phants can climb to the sun?" The chrome bot visibly shuddered. "That is not good."

"Is the Barlgharel here?"

The bot said, "No. He is checking in with those who were at the assembly. We are working to determine our losses. That was the deadliest of all the attacks. He is also working to assuage some of the angrier houses who have lost loved ones. He was the Watcher before, and there are some already blaming him for failing in his job."

It hovered closer, "Some are saying you were the distraction." The words dripped out.

"And you wondered how they got my spear?"

The chrome bot hesitated. "Yes. Quite." It moved in closer, and Syn could see nothing distinguishable on the entire surface. It was just an entirely chrome creature. The bot spoke, "Are you with them? Please tell the truth? I can tell if someone lies."

"Is that why they sent you?" Syn asked.

The bot did not answer. It waited.

Syn spoke, 'No. I'm not with them. Someone took my friend. I just want my friend back."

"Your friend?"

"Blip. He's a white companion bo—" Syn allowed the last part of the word to fade out. She did not want to risk offending this one like she had Ralph. They seemed to be sensitive about that word. *Bot.* She rubbed at the bridge of her nose. *What strange world was this where bots were offended at being called bots? Did they not know?*

"And you are?" the bot asked.

Syn smiled. "I'm Syn."

The bot bobbed. "And I'm Arquella, of the House Palote of the Ecology. Welcome to our domain." The bot's movement wasn't smooth, though. Not like Blips. There was a slight tremor at the end. Nearly imperceptible, but Syn caught it.

"That's a beautiful name."

Arquella bobbed again. "Thank you." Nothing changed on the metallic surface, but the words revealed a slight embarrassment—if this bot could blush, it would be doing so right now. And again, that shaky finish to her movement indicated something was off. Syn had never seen a bot like this. It was unique to this Disc alone.

"Where are we?" Syn asked, putting a hand on the white dresser next to the bed to steady herself as she struggled to stand.

"I'm not to tell you. Not my place."

"Still not certain?"

"You look like you could be from Zondon Almighty. But you're different than them. So similar, but they don't seem alive like we do. Like you do."

"Zondon. I keep hearing that. What is that?"

"Again, that's—"

"Not your place to say. Got it. Who can? Who has answers?"

"The Barlgharel. When he returns."

"When is that?"

"I can't say."

Syn sighed and plopped back down on the bed. *Okay, maybe a quick rest.* No. She didn't want to do that either. "I need to get out of here. Thanks for helping me." Syn cringed though. Here was another living thing, wanting to talk. Why was she rushing away? Hadn't she been craving someone else besides her and Blip for as long as she could remember?

But that was the answer…Blip.

"You need to stay here."

"My friend has been taken. I'm getting him back."

"You must wait."

"Until?"

"That's—"

"Not your place to say. Got it. Okay. I'm done with questions." Syn stood and hobbled to the door of the bedroom. She could see the dim hallway outside. They were in a settlement house. Syn waddled to the door and stepped into the hall. She knew the house for certain. She had called it the tall model—a four-story tall establishment that usually rounded the second or third tier settlements along the walls of the Disc. Those who lived there were not the most important people on the ship but ones who definitely had a purpose. She wondered if the bot-inhabitants knew all of the secrets of these places. She had been convinced Blip to play hide and seek once. She insisted he go blind—promising her that he would not access any maps during the chase. Halfway through, just as he had discovered her, she announced the game would be tag and raced away crackling. She had ended up near the end of the game in one of the upper bedrooms, much like the one she was in just then. Blip had made his way up the stairs and was blocking her only exit down.

She dashed up to the fourth floor. In the back-corner bedroom, near the edge of the big bed, she had spied what she was hoping for: the rope that pulled down a ladder to the attic. There wasn't much attic space in these models, but storage was storage, and people took advantage of every inch. From here she ran across the beams of the house and then popped open a large vent that allowed her to scramble up the roof to escape the pursuing bot. It was only a short five-foot drop to the back yard of a fourth-tier house. *Might have to use the same exit strategy right now.*

"There are things I can tell you," Arquella said.

Syn paused, her hand on the wall for balance.

Arquella bobbed closer, "Don't leave."

Syn allowed a step back. Not a full retreat. Not a complete answer. But enough to persuade the girl to continue talking. And yes, Syn was certain that inside that chrome exterior, Arquella was a girl.

Arquella said, "I can tell you about...me."

Syn laughed. She did want to just sit back and talk to this girl. But still..."I need to find Blip. Can we talk later?" There were things she'd love to know. Syn remembered one thing she'd like to know about Arquella. "How'd you wake up?" She had heard the term in the assembly.

Arquella came into the hallway. "What do you mean?"

Syn rubbed the bridge of her nose. "Don't do that. You know what

I mean. You weren't always a thinking...Person. How long have you lived here? Where were you before?"

"I can't—"

"You said you could tell me about yourself. That's all I'm asking. How'd you wake up? What happened before that?"

"Will you stay?"

"Long enough to listen."

Arquella considered that. "Okay. Come back in here."

Syn sat on the plush chair next to the door and waited for Arquella to begin. She twirled her hand in a hurry-up motion.

"I was an angel once."

Syn raised her eyebrows. "An angel?" *Delusions.*

"I remember falling. From up there. From high up. The sun. They say you're from Paradise. Is that true?"

Syn shook her head. "You tell your story. I might tell mine."

Arquella hesitated again and then bobbed in front of the mirror. Syn couldn't tell what the chrome ball used as eyes but the bot seemed to be studying her own reflection.

"I was an angel, and I fell to Earth. I landed in the desert. The land was dark, and I had left a smear on the black surface. They found me soon after. The phants, I mean. They took me and locked me up. But then the Barlgharel came and rescued me. He keeps us safe. He brought me to the Ecology. We've moved from place to place, but this is my favorite one. We've made it into something...wonderful. I hope we don't have to move again."

"What's the Ecology?"

"Us. It's all of us. All that believe. All that have returned. The Barlgharel. The Council." Arquella spun around the room and ducked out the door—that strange twitch was far more noticeable now—she didn't glide as if on some invisible track in the air but zig-zagged in small increments. A moment later she returned. "Sorry. I thought I heard something."

She moved close to Syn. "Want to know a secret?"

Syn nodded.

"I don't think it was always a desert."

"Really?"

"I think God herself got mad at Zondon Almighty and tried to destroy it. I think she sent the fire from the sun and burned everything up. I think there was a great field there before. Want to know why?"

Syn gave a slight nod. She did want to know why.

Arquella moved to the corner furthest from the door and motioned in the direction of a framed photo. Syn waited before realizing that the bot had no arms or no hands and could not bring the photo to her. Syn stood up on shaky legs and slowly made her way over to stare at the picture. Inside the blue frame was a single photo: a young girl and her dog running across a field of green grass. Behind the two was a verdant field frozen in a wave from an invisible wind. Hills rolled out from them into the blurred silver of the Disc arcing up and away into the faded distance. "Oh," Syn muttered.

Of course they had not designed this Disc to have a desert. What a colossal waste of resources. What would pump out the oxygen for the colonists? The desert would be a huge water suck as well. Stupid her for not catching what had happened here.

Looking at the photo brought back pangs of loss for a world that she would never know. She had this strange alien nostalgia wash through her mind, hearkening back to her scavenging of the homes in her Disc. There would be scenes of happy families. Of fathers and children and pets and mothers and smiles and laughter. There were shots of kids in trees. Frisbees whipped through the air from one person to another. She had never played Frisbee.

But why hadn't the grass grown back? Even a fire wouldn't destroy the roots. Something near-apocalyptic had happened here. This felt like some bad zombie flick that she and Blip would binge on.

"See? There was green here. Lots of it. And birds. And other people. And I don't see a single phant in that picture."

Syn's mind stuck on a word that Arquella had used: other people. As if she was a person. "Have you met any other people?"

"No, just us. Just those of the settlements. I've heard there're others."

Syn risked the bot's ire. "But you don't look like them."

The room grew still as Arquella's slow, persistent bob froze. She spoke slowly, "Of course not."

"I don't understand."

Arquella whispered. "The Great Mystery, of course."

"Umm…" Syn was quite confused. She had no idea what Arquella was referencing, but the tone the bot was using was as if she was talking about common knowledge, like how to use the bathroom or what the color blue was. Yet, this was a bot. *Who knows how they think?* Syn just stared blankly.

Arquella sighed and then she quoted, her voice somber. "One day we will all be transformed. In the twinkling of an eye."

Paul again. Syn knew this one. One of the Corinthian books. And there was something about a trumpet. Blip had always described the story as something people in the past believed was going to happen in the future, a future that never came. Arquella talked like it was past-tense.

"In a flash, the dead will be raised," Syn quoted, finishing the line from memory.

Arquella nodded. "Yes! That Mystery! The Great Mystery!"

Syn stammered, "I'm sorry. I don't get it."

"You know the story but don't know how it happened? They say you came from the Sun. You must've been part of it."

Arquella's emphatic movement only heightened her tremor. It was too much for Syn. She reached out a hand to the bot's lower side.

Arquella moved back, away from the outstretched hand.

Syn sighed. "Just let me…Please."

Arquella paused, and Syn ran a finger across the bottom of the bot's shell until she heard a pleasant beep. The interface was similar to Blip's. Syn smiled—she was right. "Your grav-gens were out of alignment. Just calibrated a bit off. You should be fine now."

Arquella twisted to the side in a quizzical gesture. "What?"

Syn sat back down. "Just try it."

Arquella moved backwards, slowly at first but then, when she noticed the tremor was gone, she picked up speed and dashed around the room, twisting and spinning. "You healed me! You healed me!"

Syn raised her hands, palm out. "Woah—I just adjusted—"

"You healed me!" the bot shouted. Then she came to a sudden stop and moved in close to Syn and in a hushed voice asked, "Who were you before the Mystery?" The bot's voice was expectant. Excited. "It's true, isn't it? I heard them whisper about you, but I didn't believe. They whispered that you were…" She paused on the word before whispering out, "Expected." She moved close. "Were you a part of the Mystery? Or after it? Or before?" Arquella moved close, and Syn swore the bot began to glow a faint blue. "You've come to redeem us, haven't you?"

Then it clicked for Syn. The bots believed they had once been the people of this Disc. That they had once been the colonists. The colonists had died, and the bots had somehow switched from dumb bots to smart bots, and no one had told them they were just bots. So they assumed they were people brought back to life. What Syn couldn't understand was what Arquella thought Syn's role in this was. How was she expected? Syn felt the surge of anxiety building—her stomach tightened, and her palms began to sweat.

"Who was your soul before you were this?" Arquella asked.

Syn continued to stutter, searching for words. "I don't remember." Then with a bit more confidence, "Who were you?"

Arquella spun. "I was named Tambre. This was my bedroom. Isn't it amazing? The more I'm here, the more I remember from before. The Book was right. It was all right. We died, and we came back. In a flash."

"You fell from—" Syn searched for a word that would echo Arquella's own fervor. "From…*Paradise?*"

"Yes! But the ones in Zondon Almighty haven't died yet. They haven't crossed over. And they are still impure. Dirty. But one day, they'll be wiped clean and given over to the Great Mystery."

Syn shivered. Did the bots think the other humans needed to be killed? Yet, having seen the burlys, she understood why they thought that. So maybe she didn't know what had happened here. A terrible reality crept up in her thoughts: *What if it had been the bots that destroyed the Disc? Started the Madness? What if they had switched from dumb to smart and without any explanation believed they were human? What if all of this had been their work to cleanse the world and deliver the humans to the Great Mystery? Would they see murdering the other colonists as a mercy? Would it be considered a holy act?* The shivering didn't stop. She grew sick. And frightened. What if they discovered that she was lying? That she wasn't from the sun? Would they try to kill her?

Panic gripped her. She wanted to continue talking. She had wanted this very thing. But the more she stayed, the more could happen to Blip. She was certain she would say something wrong. She didn't know how to talk to anyone but Blip. She wished Blip was there, counting down to calm her. She had seen countless films and thought she understood how meeting others would be, but she just didn't. And now the one she had met was saying things that she didn't understand. Things that frightened her.

Now, more than before, she felt the urge to leap to her feet and flee. The anxiety was throbbing in her gut, and her thoughts tumbled over each other. This bot frightened her. She didn't know what awaited her out there. Did they all think like Arquella?

"I need to leave." The words just came out, fast and angry.

"I told you my story. You owe me yours." The bot moved closer.

Syn was unsure where to start, how to start. Everything she said would be a distortion. The more she talked, the more holes Arquella might find. And who knows what might tip her off and give her reason to kill Syn and deliver her into a personal afterlife?

"Where's my spear?" Again, she retracted from the bluntness of her own question. Why was she so direct? This bot was off-kilter and potentially dangerous. But no, she hadn't seen violence. Just a weird view of what was happening. It was the Barlgharel that had saved her. "I'll tell my story, but I want my spear."

"You promised. Stop changing the promise."

"Please. I made it. It's mine. I want it back." Everything that was important, save Eku, had been taken from her. Blip. Her spear. Her world. "I want them back!"

Arquella floated, allowing the purr of the fans in the house to fill the silence.

Syn lowered her head and closed her eyes. "I came from the Sun. I was sent here to find out what happened to the world. Me and my companion. But we were attacked by Bur...by phants."

"Where were you before that? Who sent you?"

What had Arquella said earlier? God?

"God sent me."

Arquella bobbed in agreement. "You are the Expected."

"We were separated. They took my friend. And then I met the Barlgharel. He saved me when we were attacked again. Then I woke up here."

Arquella moved close. "Where'd you get that?"

Syn lifted the orange tiger pendant and the butterfly next to it. "These?"

Arquella bobbed her head.

"I'll tell you when I get my spear."

The chrome bot didn't move for a moment, then it zipped out of the room. A moment later, Arquella returned to the room. Behind her, a small copper-colored square bot moved on two wheels. Out of its side, a thin metallic tentacle extended and was wrapped around Syn's spear. Arquella paused before Syn and nodded at the copper bot behind her. The bot dropped the carbon-fiber stick at Syn's feet, and the tentacle retracted back into the square as it reversed back out of the room.

Syn leaned down to pick up her spear and halted. Most of the adornments had been stripped off. Only a thin orange thread dangled from the end. It was the charcoal gray of carbon-fiber, scuffed and dirtied.

Syn carefully reached out and gripped her spear, each finger instinctively resting into a grip. A wave of relief washed through her, and she relaxed, her shoulders dropping. It had only been a few hours without it, but she had missed it. She smiled and stood up straight. It had saved her life more times than she could remember. *Stupid burlys!*

Arquella bobbed over the bed and rested down onto the large, pink-flowered comforter. "Now?" spoke the bot.

At that Syn leaped to her feet. A jolt of pain stabbed through her leg, but she ignored it. She had seconds to get out of the room. She flew through the door, pulling it hard shut behind her. The door slammed with a brash crack.

Down or up? Below, she heard the murmurs of voices. *Up.*

And she flew, darting up the stairs, around the landing.

The door to Arquella's room opened, and the girl-bot shouted, "Stop! You're confused. Stay with us! I'm sorry!" Then after a pause, "You promised."

She had, but what did it matter? She had to save Blip. She didn't have time to sit and play dollies.

She saw a shadow behind her, and Arquella's voice was nearer— only a meter behind, and coming up fast. "It's okay. We're not going to hurt you."

Ahead of her, down the hallway, was the master bedroom on the fourth floor. The access to the attic and the exit out of this house would be there. She had to get out of here—she had to get to Blip.

She stopped hard and spun. Arquella wasn't as quick in response and didn't stop as fast. Her momentum brought her close to Syn and Syn's spear. Syn jabbed the spear straight at Arquella and dented the chrome exterior with a loud clang.

Arquella wheeled back, slamming back into the wall, denting it. She twisted and wailed. Below, at the base of the stairs, several more voices sounded. "Are you okay?" was the general statement followed with, "What's happening? Are you okay?" Another bot added, "Did it hurt you?"

Did they think I was a wild animal? Syn thought.

Arquella shouted, "We're not going to hurt you. Stay here." And then, at the top of her lungs, perhaps aimed at the other bots in the house, "She's Expected! She healed me! She healed me! She's the one!"

Blast, Syn thought. She echoed the curse again, aloud, "Blast it!" There wasn't time to consider, though or argue. She dashed down the hall, through the door into the master bedroom and slammed the door hard shut. A bookcase stood nearly empty to the right of the door. Syn moved around and pushed her back against it, tipping it over until it fell with a crash, blocking the door. She looked up and cursed again. There was no rope for the attic access. There was no ceiling hatch. There was just a closed room with four walls and a closet whose door was open. "No! No! No!"

The door to the bedroom buckled as something huge slammed into it from the other side. The hinges pulled from the frame. Another hit and the door would be off the frame. And the bots would be in here.

Arquella shouted, "Where are you going?"

Syn shouted back, "I have to get to Blip! I'm not staying here one more minute." She jumped across the bed to the open closet door in the far corner. Anything to put distance and walls between her and the chrome bot.

The yelling stopped. The closet was dark except for a thin shaft a light from under the door. Syn began to feel around the closet, hoping for something anything. Perhaps the attic entrance was above her? Batting around above her head produced no chain, and she could see no changes in the flat surface of the ceiling that designated a door.

Outside, in the bedroom, the hinges snapped with a crack and splinters sprayed across the room. There was a grunt and the sound of wood scraping against wood. The bot started pushing the shattered door against the bookcase, trying to force her way in. She'd be in and at the closet in moments.

The closet was filled with more boxes and hangers than clothes. These had been scavenged by others—it was mostly bare, but she pressed past the few articles of clothing and pushed against the walls, hoping for something that would give. Her mind conjured images from *The Lion, The Witch, and The Wardrobe* and she imagined Lucy searching the wardrobe and hoping the visitors in the grand home of the Professor wouldn't find her. Syn imagined the brush of snow against her barefoot, but there was no snow. In truth, Syn had never felt snow and so, she wondered, would she know what it actually felt like by touch alone? If this were the wardrobe, it came without loud-speaking visitors to a saintly Professor and without a late game of hide-and-seek with annoying but loving siblings. Instead, Syn had a weird bot that was convinced she was the reincarnation or resurrection of a little girl, and that bot was now out to get her to be her best friend. *This is not the time for slumber parties.*

Syn's fingers ran across a metal grate along the base of the floor. *A vent!* It wasn't large. It was quite small. Her fingers traced out the border. It wasn't that small, though. And Syn was thin.

The bookcase crashed to the ground, and Arquella spoke, "Where are you?" Other muffled voices followed after. *Other bots.*

Syn pressed her fingers into the edges of the grate. *I have to get this off!* Syn tasted salt and realized she was crying. The grate wasn't budging. It was flat against the wall. She pulled, and her fingers snapped back as one of her nails ripped. "Blast!"

Arquella said, "What are you doing? Why are so scared?"

Syn chastised herself for speaking. She pulled on the grate again, trying from another angle. It budged, only slightly, but it did move.

"The closet." The deduction was followed by a sharp smash as something slammed against the closet door. Syn jumped, panic coursing through her.

Frightened, Syn pulled once more, her fear blocking out all other thoughts, all other emotions. The grate gave, and she jerked back, smacking against the wall as her own leverage worked against her. *Blip, I need you!*

Syn slid into the hole and the ductwork with a surprising bit of room on both sides. A burly wouldn't make it. Arquella definitely wouldn't. But Syn was made for this.

The door smashed open, slamming forward and blocking Arquella's view of Syn's bare feet sliding into the small hole in the wall.

"Where are you? Where are you?" The desperate, confused words of the bot echoed. "Please. Don't leave. Don't run! We won't hurt you! We promise." Other bots, their voices jumbled, echoed the girl's.

As Syn crawled, she heard another voice from far behind—a deep rumble that she had already connected with trust. "Blip will be fine. He's okay now. You don't have to run." It came from the Barlgharel.

Syn froze in the passage, her hands against the cold metal.

Behind her, the Barlgharel spoke again, "Don't be scared. Please. We won't keep you here. You can go for your friend. You don't have to run. Just rest. We can help you."

Syn breathed out a deep sigh. She spoke back, "I have to get to him."

He replied, "I know. He's okay."

"How do you know Blip is safe?"

The Barlgharel rumbled, "I didn't say he was safe. I said he's okay. My friend told me, and she's usually right."

"A friend?"

"Blip has been taken by the Crimson Queen," the Barlgharel said, "We'll show you where she lives. You're safe amongst us."

"Who? Why would she take him?" Syn stammered.

"Come out and we'll talk."

Syn slammed her fist on the ground. Should she go back? Why had she panicked? Was she that scared of being locked up? Had she lived so long on her own that others scared her? She had wanted to be around others—to know other voices besides Blip's and her own. She hadn't expected them to be bots, but still… When she had her opportunity, she freaked out. She ran.

Syn whispered, "You promise?" And inside, something older chattered, *It's not safe. It's not safe.*

It was Arquella who answered, "Yes. I said that."

Syn shouted back, "I want the Barlgharel to promise."

His deep voice spoke, "I promise."

21

THE BLESSING OF THE JOURNEY

"In attempting to construct such machines, . . .
we are, in either case, instruments of His will providing mansions for
the souls that He creates."
—Alan Turing

The Barlgharel's luminescent green and daunting worm-like form stood peering from the hallway through the splintered door. He motioned for Syn to follow, and although apprehensive of the fanatic and excited Arquella floating behind him, Syn accepted his invitation. Syn inched out to stand before him.

The Barlgharel escorted her down the stairs—although each stair creaked and moaned under his tremendous weight— and out of the house. Syn kept her hand on her spear, the point of the blade tipped forward, if ever-so-slightly. From time to time, her own shaking hand would telegraph through the spear, and the point would wobble until she would catch the movement out of the corner of her eye, then steady herself, willing her shaking to stop. *If only Blip were here. He'd just start counting, and...* But that was no use. Blip wasn't here, and she was.

Angry at the moment, angry at Blip's stupid choice to be captured, angry at herself for insisting on going through the gate, she didn't speak. That didn't stop the Ecology. Around her, they all whispered. Eye-bots, cleaning bots, medics. The entire array of bots flowed out from the various buildings to stand around them.

The pathway opened up from just the standard walkway in the residential areas. Planter boxes and cement seating areas littered the ever-expanding spaces. Common areas that had once been filled with running children and couples having lunch under the sunstrips were now littered with the muddied bobbing shells of the growing throng of bots. The staggered creaking and mechanical grinding of the assorted bots' legs as they moved created its own white noise.

As the bots flooded in, as the crowds grew larger, the scenery changed. Scattered in the darkness, new bright panels overlaid the soot-covered walls of the world that had come before. It was a gradual transition. No precise border existed. Instead, each meter or so, something else was added until not long after, the new world enveloped them. Scrubbed white panels, as bright as chalk and sunlight, covered every surface. Across the bleached flats, paint flowed—an array of geometric designs overlaying strange interpretations of trees and animals. A starscape across the ceiling and floor, lit with neon colors, erupted. Some paint fell flat and others glowed as if luminescent—perhaps it was, shining its own light upon Syn. She smiled briefly, awash in the spectacle, her own dark skin reflecting the orange and blue array around them.

"Where are we?" Syn allowed the words to escape.

The Barlgharel's deep voice replied, "The Cradle. We have crafted this into a home."

She lit up the world wherever she walked, but none of the light she brought to this dark world could illuminate it more than what the bots had crafted here. Her own light paled.

Under the multi-spectral lights, bot after bot, some tall and some short, clambered to see the new visitor. Several of the bots that were the size of large animals supported on thin legs ambled by, their hides painted an odd blue—she had seen nothing like them on her Disc. Syn jerkily stepped between their legs. Around the other bots, several that were shattered and showing signs of disrepair came into view. Most of these had damaged shells ranging from small cracks to entire plates missing. One bot, a thin beast with a clear glass shell that had been used to transport plants from one garden to another, wobbled into the pathway. Its left-hand side had been completely removed—wires dangled back and forth. Syn was unsure how he managed to stay mobile. *Is that one alive like Arquella? What's he feeling right now? Maybe I could...* The sight of him and the rush of compassion caused her to falter in her steps.

Before her, layered in the bright lights of this new world the bots had made, the Barlgharel spoke, "Why are you so scared of us?"

Syn struggled to answer. She wanted to shout, "I'm not!" But in fact, she was scared. These bots were so different than her own. If they were alive, she couldn't predict what they'd do. They were—she searched for the word—*wild.*

She didn't answer. The thought echoed once more: *wild.* These things were more alive than anything she had ever encountered. She, Blip, and Eku were all that made up her world. Here was something raw, untainted, and untamed. So she spoke that. "Wild."

The Barlgharel gave a simple "Hmmm," and continued moving ahead.

They moved through the bright corridors of what she assumed were the upper settlements. Syn felt the lightness in her steps from the lesser gravity. It was a small difference, but it reminded her that they were several levels up on the Rise.

The bots that had streamed out to meet them now followed behind several meters back. There were other bots along the corridor's edges, although now the crimson light seemed far less than before. In the neon world, several bots were huddled against each other on the ground. Their shells were far more battered than most of the other bots. In the center of this new group was an eye-bot. Rather than zipping through the air like most eye-bots, this black-painted one was simply rolling across the ground as Syn passed. She turned her head to watch him as she walked past.

After a moment, Syn said, "She scared me."

The Barlgharel said, "Arquella?"

Syn nodded.

They turned a corner and made their way up a ramp to another level. After a moment, the Barlgharel said, "She comes on a bit strong. She just wants a friend."

Syn nodded again. She understood that.

"But it's not easy to know how to make a friend. Especially if you've never had practice," the Barlgharel said. "Don't feel shame. You are new to this world."

"It's so…" She searched for the word. *Bright. Odd. Weird. New.* Around her, odd geometric designs were crafted in neon colors. The art of robots. Their dreams in a cacophony of color and explosion. Syn settled for, "Wonderful."

"You have something new here if you want it."

Syn glanced up to him. She squinted, uncertain as to what he meant.

"Friends. You have only had one friend your entire life. So, it's okay to be scared of the very thing you need most."

Syn stopped walking. "How did you know that?"

The Barlgharel chuckled but did not stop himself. "I had a conversation with a friend. She filled me in on some details."

"Who?" Syn found herself several steps behind and jogging to catch back up. The mass of bots following them was still off-putting to her. She had never seen so many in one place before. She had never seen bots not doing their jobs. They crowded along the stairs, between railings. Some buzzed about. The larger ones pushed through. It was a mass of activity. And with each step, the world lit up brighter, and she saw even more as the strips along the walkway illuminated them.

So many bots. All focused on her.

The Barlgharel chuckled, "I suspect you'll meet her someday."

"Where *are* we going?"

"You are tired. You are injured. You need food. You need replenishment for both body and soul. All living things need energy."

Before them, a pair of familiar doors loomed under a violet series of lights. Syn cocked her head, trying to place them. The doors looked so familiar, but this whole place was different.

"I heard you healed Arquella," the Barlgharel explained. "The word of your miracle has spread. They are so anxious to meet you, to see the magic that I sensed inside you when we first encountered each other. You have a great power and a great purpose."

Syn shrunk back from the Barlgharel's words. She fixed bots. For her, it was as easy as tying her shoes. Nothing miraculous about it.

She was about to protest when her uncertain familiarity with their location coalesced. *The doors opened to the Theater!* The Barlgharel was taking her to the Theater! The very place that she and Blip and Eku spent their evenings, where she had watched thousands of movies. Her favorite place to just lose herself. The Theater—this Disc's Theater.

"We are going to introduce you to the Ecology."

"But I've met the Ecology."

"Not all of them." With that, the Barlgharel pushed through the open doors and entered the massive film theater from the side entrance. Syn followed. The room, like the outside, was lit in a dazzling array of multi-colored lights but strobed and moved with life. A wave of magenta poured over the crowd followed by a gleaming purple chased by a vibrant orange. A thousand points of light from a thousand sources across the room.

Rising up before them were the rows of the Theater. Behind them was the screen itself. Something was playing on the screen, but Syn couldn't understand it—the mass of bots were looking straight up and they distracted her. Their surfaces reflected the dazzling array of light moving in and out like a sea of kaleidoscopes. She thought at the counsel she had observed a lot of bots, but that had been a small setting. Gathered across the theater were hundreds upon hundreds of bots.

She saw small eye-bots with their crimson or blue or black shells darting around the room, the disc-shaped cleaning bots, lumbering forest bots (although these were only small versions of the giant tree movers that always frightened her), water workers floating like jellyfish, smaller versions of the air cleaners with their iridescent limbs flowing around, farm worker, crop maintenance, square, blue-hued medics, repair. There were cubes and triangles and spheres, and long tubes, and every shape imaginable. It was a room of talking and moving plastic and metal.

How do they fit in here? Then Syn realized what this Theater was missing. Chairs. All of the chairs had been removed. Syn nodded. *Makes sense.*

The room was abuzz with chirps and voices and random lights. "Oh," Syn said. *This is a party*, she thought. She had never been to a party! She had seen them in movies, but she had never been to one. Her smile grew wide as she drew in.

She gripped her spear tight, yet found herself taking a few steps forward, away from the Barlgharel, to place herself closer to the roar of the crowd.

Someone laughed, and Syn turned to see several bots shaking in laughter. One of them had told a joke, and she heard the punchline being repeated, "That's not my handle!"

Syn spun to look back at the screen. A cartoon was playing— bright colors and thick outlines. She had never seen this one. On the screen, three people chatted and talked inside a green spaceship: a silver robot, a boy in a red jacket, and a one-eyed girl with purple hair. She couldn't hear what they were saying, but there were several bots in the crowd intently watching. The scene on the screen changed, and the green spaceship soared through the stars, aimed at a planet with a billboard floating in orbit: "Chapek 9." Syn smiled at the image. She had never spent much time on cartoons. She had always wanted to see the films with real faces—other humans.

From behind, the Barlgharel smiled, "Do you like it?"

Syn spun. *This is beyond a dream. A party. Other voices—other people talking and laughing and moving about and having fun. Who cares if it is a collection of bots?* She had never dreamed she'd be a part of something like this, something so completely chaotic and uncontrollable. Syn nodded. "Yes!"

She moved in and out of the crowd for what seemed like hours, enjoying the rush of energy. She stopped and listened to the various bots, yet she always hesitated when she thought of adding her own voice to the mix. What would they think of her? What if she said something wrong? What if they didn't like her? She shook her head on that one. *Why am I so concerned about bots liking me?*

As she moved through the crowd, she circled around one group and ran into the familiar chrome sphere of Arquella. The bot spoke up immediately, "Don't run!"

Syn gripped her spear out of reflex but then willed herself to relax. She frowned back at Arquella but then said, "I won't."

"I told you we wouldn't hurt you."

Syn said, "I needed to get my friend."

"I said we could help you."

Syn shook her head. "How?"

Arquella motioned at the Barlgharel. "He'll help."

Before Syn could answer, the music stopped suddenly, and the booming voice of the Barlgharel spoke, "It's story time!"

As if a machine had turned on, the bots all turned and lined up along the rows of the Theater, aimed and attentive toward the Barlgharel. When Syn turned around, Arquella had left, moving to her assigned space, several rows up behind them.

The Barlgharel spoke again, "Tonight, we welcome to the Ecology, and to our joy, a new friend."

A light twirled in the space and landed on her—she was illuminated by the singular shaft of light in the room. The Barlgharel continued, "Welcome to our friend, Syn of the Sun Above."

The room erupted in cheers. The disc-shaped bots bounced from side to side, rattling in a clapping motion on the ground. Others shouted and hooted and chirped. The whole mass cheered. Interspersed, she heard a word repeated, although from only a few, "Expected." And less often, in hushed, somber tones, the word "Mother" was spoken somewhere in the great crowd.

The applause died down, and Syn stood there, unsure of what to do. The Barlgharel shouted, "Syn, join me here. We wish to bless you tonight before you continue your great journey tomorrow. We are but just a stop on the way. We hope to be a replenishment."

Syn walked down the stairs, aware that all the attention of the room was on her. She had never felt so small before. She stood next to the Barlgharel and then looked out at the crowd. So many bots. She heard herself whisper, "So many."

"Syn, soon you will leave us to find your friend."

Syn looked up at the friendly face of the Barlgharel and nodded.

"And where is your friend?"

Syn looked back at him, unsure of how to respond. "I don't—"

"You said he was taken?"

Syn nodded. A murmur from the bots filled the air.

"Our spies have scoured for the truth. And the truth is that the Crimson Queen took him. Her servants, the Wey Wards, stole him and brought him to her. To Zondon Almighty," the Barlgharel interjected.

As he did, a tremor of fear rushed through the crowd. The entire room filled with nervous chirps, and she heard scattered gasps of "No!" about the room.

The Barlgharel bellowed, "It is okay. She must go. It is her fate."

Then from the crowd, someone said, "Expected." The word was picked up by another, and then another, until across the collection of bots there was a steady, growing chant of "Expected. Expected. Expected."

The Barlgharel spoke again, "Quiet!"

Syn jabbed an arm out at the audience and asked the Barlgharel, "What does that mean?"

He looked down at her. "Do you not know?"

Syn shook her head, unsure exactly what he meant with the broken sentence.

"You are from the Sun, are you not?"

Syn nodded. It was a lie, and it was the truth. She felt safer going with it.

"My friend has said that you were sent here."

"Who—" Syn started.

The Barlgharel ignored her and continued, "In the Mystery, we are told that we are only here as stewards—this is but a temporary assignment. This is not our home."

Murmurs of assent echoed. "Not our home," was repeated from various bots.

He continued, "It is written 'Come thou long-expected one, to set thy people free.'"

Syn had never heard that one. It wasn't Paul, and it wasn't Luke, and it wasn't Lewis Carroll either. She frowned.

The Barlgharel spoke louder, "We have been told there is another world of which this one is only a shadow. We know that we shall step through the mirror and journey to a world of which this is only a pale imitation. A land of milk and honey. A land of great joy. A land where the river of life flows and the great tree is planted from which all life began."

Syn teared up at memories of her own Disc. *Why did I ever leave?*

He turned toward her, "And some have whispered that you are that 'long-expected one.' To lead us there."

Syn backed up and put her hands in the air, "Woah! No!"

The audience gasped in surprise.

Syn turned, "I mean…"

The Barlgharel looked at her, "Do you not come from the living garden beyond the Sun?"

Syn stared at him, disbelieving. *How did he know?* The audience was hushed, awaiting her answer. Finally, she nodded. "I think. Yes, I mean."

"And do you know the way back?"

Syn nodded again. She did. But she had no intention of taking them. How could she accomplish that? There were so many of them.

"And will you not return to that world? Will you not first ascend to the Sun?"

Syn hated the way he was describing it, but it was all true in a strange way. She could see their rapt anticipation grow with each answered question. "Yes."

"Perhaps you may not know who you are. You may not believe in yourself," he leaned closer in, "But our faith does not need you to. We believe in who you really are."

Syn shivered.

Across the room, the word was chanted again, "Expected. Expected. Expected."

The Barlgharel stood back up, "So, before she can return, she must first go ahead, just as the first Eve had to venture into the desolation beyond the Gates of Eden, so Syn must venture into the Desert of Nod. She will be tempted. She will be challenged, but tonight, we bless her before her journey into that haunt of all evils, the Desert of Nod, to cross the wastelands and to face the Hazards. Let us all stand as we recite the Blessing of Journey over Syn."

The room rippled as all of the bots rose up. The eye-bots floated along with countless others. Those that were close to the ground still managed to raise up by tipping themselves forward. Syn shook her head. They were all concerned with her. They all seemed to care for her. Perhaps it was because they had some strange belief about her, but she was taken up with the excitement, the hope that was exuding from them. They were all placing their hope in her.

The Barlgharel called out, "May the representatives of the Houses join us down front. House Eya. House Ejel. House Oni. House Palote. House Jak. House Emrys. House Escielenn. House Aisleyn. House Taimer."

A few bots moved out from the audience and formed themselves in a semi-circle before Syn and the Barlgharel. Those bots all seemed to be gathered with others similar to themselves. She assumed Arquella was in the collection of chrome globes that bobbed enthusiastically when he mentioned House Palote. A group of dark floating bots a meter high with thin limbs and red-colored eyes nodded in unison at the name Emrys. Another collection of bug bots, all the size and shape of bees, buzzing around and forming a cloud, fanned out at the acknowledgment of House Oni. They moved forward as one to surround Syn with the other representatives.

The Barlgharel called out, "The Blessing of Journey. May the blessing of the Sun be on you—light without and light within."

Another bot, tall and asymmetrical, a sleek black surface with a dozen sensors scattered across him, bellowed in rhythm, "May the blessed sunlight shine on you like a great home fire, so that stranger and friend may come and warm himself at it."

A third bot, one of the jellyfish-like water workers, sang out, "And may light shine out of your two eyes. And may the blessing of the rain be on you, may it pour upon your spirit and wash it fair and clean, and leave there a shining pool where the blue of Eden shines, and sometimes a star."

Arquella added her own voice, "May the great Mystery be the echo of your soul. May those who meet you, know the hope you carry with you. And may the blessing of the world to come be on you, soft under your feet as you pass along the roads, soft under you as you lie out on it, tired at the end of day; and may it rest easy over you when, at last, you lie out under it."

The Barlgharel picked up the blessing. "May it rest so lightly over you that your soul may be out from under it quickly; up and off and on its way to God. And now may the God above, the great voice of Her amongst them and above the Ecology bless you and bless you kindly."

In unison, the whole of the representatives sounded, "Aṣẹ."

On "Aṣẹ," the entire audience echoed in unison, "Aṣẹ" and then again they said, "Aṣẹ." The chorus of voices sent a shiver through Syn. She had never experienced a moment like that. She had never felt a part of something so intent, so true. They were strange, they were confused, but they cared for each other, and they cared for her.

The Barlgharel cried out, "And let us celebrate the journey of the Expected tonight! For she has come. She will stay and walk among us. She will soon leave, and then she will return to lead us back to the Garden. Back to Eden. She will bring us with her as she returns to Paradise beyond the Sun."

With that, the lights turned back to the colored array and the Theater screen lit up. The neat, ordered rows of bots broke up into miscellaneous disarray, chattering loudly to each other.

Then, above all of the noise, as if his voice emanated from the walls themselves, the Barlgharel boomed, "Let's dance!"

Music erupted—a thudding bass sound overlaid with bright, melodic tones. The entire crowd of bots fell into a moving mass without any organization. Bots circled each other, turned upon themselves, and shouted in joy. The lights above moved in sync with the booming rhythm and bathed the crowd in deep washes of color.

With a tug, one bot, its arms like a crane, pulled her out amongst the crowd. She spun into the center of them, and their energy slammed into her. Syn lifted her hands into the air and added her voice in a shout, unable to hear her own words above the din of the bots and the rhythm of the music. She shut her eyes and lost all compunction, allowing herself to move and turn with the throng. Sweat poured from her forehead, and she danced with abandon.

Long minutes or perhaps hours passed, and she sloughed off to the side, panting and thirsty. She was never given rest as over and over, bots came up to her to meet her and talk. For hours, she was asked questions. For several, she had no answers, but for many, she did.

"What is your favorite color?"

"What music do you like?"

"Do you like the rain?"

"Is the Sun hot?"

"Have you met God? What is she like?"

"What type of metal are you?"

Before she could answer, they filled in their own responses to questions she hadn't asked. A green thin creature, perhaps what would've been a gardening bot, gushed, "I love the rain. I love the haze on the edge of the cradle, where the smoke moves in rivulets through the bright lights. Cantoni, the great painter, drew on those edges, intending for the smoke to blend…"

These bots were in love with existence itself. They were consumed with the myriad details of just living. Oh, she loved it.

And, much to her surprise, there was food. Trays of apples and bananas and other fruit along with carrots and potatoes were brought in. These were all the staples of the garden greenhouses in the lower levels surrounding the Disc—the levels between the base, the livestock pastures, and the body farms below that. The bots would pick up the food and mime as if devouring it, mimicking the actions of eating without ever consuming it.

The first tray was brought near her by a clunky square bot with several tentacles—perhaps this one was designed to serve and cook food, but this black and gray unit was entirely new to her. Syn looked at the apples and was sure they were fake. They were too perfect. Solid and thick and round and gleaming in the multi-colored lights from above. The apple felt real in her hands, though. Its weight assured her, and she took the risk of a bite. The juices rushed across her tongue, and she gave an audible "mmm." She had tasted apples this fresh on her Disc but had assumed that everything on this side was barren of life. She looked around her at the buzzing crowd, more and more moving in and out to greet her, and laughed. They were mechanical—she knew they couldn't taste the fruit they had served, but they had surprised her with something amazing nonetheless.

Syn sat down in awe at the scene and in exhaustion, the juice still running down her chin and the half-eaten apple in her hand. The Barlgharel moved close, leaned in and said, "You are much loved here, little one."

Somewhere deep inside, something moved in Syn. Her eyes welled with tears and she muttered, "Thank you."

THE DAYS OF DELIGHT

Thus strangely are our souls constructed, and by such slight ligaments
are we bound to prosperity or ruin.
—Mary Shelley, *Frankenstein*

Syn woke up the next morning on the Theater floor. The great
hall was empty, and apart from loose confetti scattered about
the bits of litter and one flashing colored light above that was
switching between red to orange to green every few seconds, she felt
sure this could have been the Theater in that she had lost days upon
days binging movies and shows with Blip and Eku. She took one deep
breath after a yawn, and the acrid smell of the air brought into sharp
focus the fact that this was not her Theater, and outside the large
wooden doors an alien world waited.

She marched back up the theater stairs, leading to the entrance
and the outside. She felt the thin carpet on her bare feet—a coarse,
thin knit that she had overlooked in her awe the night before. .

She instinctively brought her hand up to plant her spear for
support but was surprised to find it empty. Where was her spear? She
glanced behind her, back to the front stage, but there was nothing
there. Her pack was gone as well. *Perhaps the Barlgharel took them.* Or

perhaps Arquella. For some reason, despite the girl's assurances, that thought made her shiver—Arquella searching through her belongings.

She did not dwell upon the thought too long—a *tap tap tap* came from the wooden doors as if something small were knocking to be let in. Syn opened the door with a great heave—an action that brought back a wave of nostalgia—the doors on both sides were unusually heavy and required an effort to open and close. There, at the edge of the entrance, was the small black bot she had spied when she had been first ushered in. Once again, it was on the ground and that unnerved her. Eye-bots were to zip around throughout the air, constantly vying for the best angle to film and observe. They were everywhere on her Disc—as ubiquitous throughout the sky as birds. Yet, this one rolled and didn't even attempt a hop to find itself airborne.

"Oh, you sad little thing," she said, bending down to cup open her hands, inviting it to roll into them.

To her surprise, it did so without hesitation. Yet, in her palms, there was a quiver to it. It was anxious to be held and nervous about it at the same time. She examined the black bot and gave a short whistle. "I think you might be broken. I wish I was back…" She almost said on her Disc but realized that she wasn't confident this little thing wouldn't share that bit of information with the others. She had no desire to lie, but they had constructed a different idea about her, and she feared any deviation might delay her getting to Blip. Instead she continued, "I was back in…my Garden. I have tools there and a work-shop. I'm sure I could get you flying again."

The eye-bot shook and rocked back and forth in her hand. It rolled to the front of her palms and teetered on the edge, repeating the motion twice. Syn twisted her head and pressed her lips together, furrowing her brow. "I'm not sure I—" The bot repeated the motion and Syn smiled. "You want to go that direction?"

The bot moved back and forth in what Syn was sure was to be a nod. "Okay, point the way. But I don't have long. I have to get going. My friend needs me."

The ebony eye-bot rolled around in her palms in various direc-tions, guiding her through the quiet but still lit pathways, around corners, and up two flights of stairs, that led back into the closest settlements. All was silent, and there was a blue-orange glow above the ever-present haze in the air. The world around her missed all the normal cues of early morning, but Syn was certain she had slept through the night and had awoken early.

Before long, the bot directed her to a series of garage doors, one after another. It nudged her toward a regular door between the second and third one. Syn glanced around and noticed the larger pathway beyond them—this was a vehicle repair section of the settlements—quite like where she had discovered her Ogun and had set up her own workshop. Syn stepped to the door and the access panel lit up and the door slid open.

As she stepped inside, she gave a quiet, "Lights on" command. The room came to life with an electric blue light as the recessed LED strips in the ceiling and floor turned on.

Around the edges of the room, several white tables stood, now covered with dirt. In a washbasin against the far corner, dishes piled up, a soft black fuzziness creeping across the surfaces—it had been food a long time ago but had since crumbled and darkened beyond recognition. A glass pane hung to her left with marker scribbles of various robotic shells and the calculations for power conversions—simple math but definitely the handiwork of a specialist. Along the right-hand side, a red hoist and cart stood with the shell of a guard bot hanging from the chain. She had only seen a couple guard bots on her Disc, and they were all inert. They were the closest to a human form she had encountered, and they always unnerved her. The first one she had encountered had been in Captain Pote's office, standing right in front of the entrance. She had been sure he was alive in the dim-lit room—finally another human. The mistake had hurt.

Along the walls hung several baskets with an assortment of gears and wires and circuit boards. The floor had brown crates and boxes, each overflowing with shells from robots. Syn spied three different fire extinguishers—this person was definitely accident-prone and had learned to take precautions.

Syn smiled and gave a deep breath of relief.

A workshop.

A quick glance at the eager eye-bot reaffirmed her suspicions. "Do you want me to fix you?" It wobbled back and forth. She let the ebony eye-bot roll out of her hands onto one of the few clear spots on the center table and said, "Let's see if we can get you back to normal again." Syn searched around for a few tools—she'd need a magclip to release the shell and a gravometer to confirm if his grav-pump was working, just to start. She moved papers and boxes and tossed aside a couple paint-speckled vacuum bot shells. The owner was definitely messier than Alileen, the original owner of her garage back on her Disc, had ever been.

The repairs were smooth and simple. The challenge was keeping the little bot still—its unease and anxiousness made it jittery. After a few pauses to calm it and reassure it that everything would work out, Syn was able to look around inside and determine that the problem was a short in a power tube. She patched it up and then repositioned its outer shell into place. She used the opportunity to clean it up and make sure that it gleamed under the cyan light overhead.

The tiny bot leapt up and zipped around, zooming from one corner to another, causing Syn to duck several times as it careened past her head far too close. "Watch it, little guy!"

After a few minutes, it slowed down and then floated down in front of Syn. For a moment, it paused without movement, staring at her, its large iris shuttering open and closed. Memorizing her. Then, it nuzzled up against her neck in what Syn assumed was a hug. She reached a hand up and said, "It's okay. I'm glad you're better."

The black bot pulled away, gave a nod, and then moved to the door that opened with a swoosh, sliding to let it through. The door closed after, and Syn was left in the quiet workshop.

This was not her workshop. Everything was out of order. Hers was messy, but this was chaos without purpose.

In her workshop, the tables were cleaned (for the most part). This table was full of scattered items, garbage, scraps, pits of wire, equipment, and gunk. Whoever had called this place their garage wasn't tidy.

Yet, this was the first moment Syn felt at rest since crossing over to this Disc. Even amongst the junk, this was a shop where things were fixed and problems were solved. It felt comfortable. It felt sane. At one time, life had operated normally here. There were days when whoever owned this awoke and came out here to begin work on projects. A normal day in a normal life.

The room preserved this individual's daily activities but held no keepsakes. After Syn's first glance around the room, nothing personal turned up. No photos. No letters. No trinkets of any sort. Whomever had toiled in this garage had seemingly done so without much connection to the rest of those around. Or perhaps this was their retreat, and only when surrounded by these walls could they be alone. In that situation, reminders of others might be an intrusion. Syn shook her head at that thought. She couldn't imagine not wanting to crowd her life with the artifacts of relationships. She had dreamed of sending notes back and forth to a sister. She had looked at photos of a group of friends and imagined herself pressed into the group of smiling, laughing faces.

Syn pulled out a red stool that rolled about on small chrome wheels and sat down. Behind her, the door slid open, and Syn spun around. The ebony eye-bot had returned, but he wasn't alone. Several other bots crowded the doorway—most she had spied on her first walk to the theater. They were the ones that were broken, slower than the others. A pair of vacuum bots moved inside, their frames off-balance and scraping against the ground as they moved.

Behind them, a square-framed, sand-colored bot the size of a garbage can rolled on a single wheel; it attempted to enter but misjudged and hit the doorframe. It backed up, and the ebony eye-bot descended down, chirped out something in that high-speed gibberish song the bots used, and the larger one aligned itself to the frame and carefully wheeled inside.

The others ranged from an octagonal ball scuttling forward on four trapezoid legs, clicking against the hard floor, to a tall, thin med-bot with a dozen wire-like floating armatures, to a rusted-out iron bot sporting a large head on five horse-like legs—Syn was sure the thing would topple over or fall to dust. Others, all different and each broken, crowded in. Syn counted over twenty and lost track soon after.

She started to stand and then sat right back down with a big sigh. Spotting the black eye-bot zipping around, proud of his new-found mobility, she said, "Did you tell them I fixed you?"

The eye-bot stopped in front of her, glanced back at his entourage, and nodded slowly.

Syn shook her head. "And they all need to be fixed?"

It nodded again, dropping its singular eye downward, avoiding her glare.

She stood up and looked at the mass of them, her mouth twisting into a frown. They all gazed up at her, expecting her help. "Expected. That's what you all called me." She tapped the ebony eye-bot, and her frown gave way to a slight grin. "But what do I call you?"

The bot cocked its head quizzically.

Syn tapped its black shell again. "Well, Dot seems the easy name, but that doesn't fit. You're a bit too conniving to be a Dot."

It floated away and then spun in the air a few times before doing a few quick laps around the room, drawing the attention of not only Syn but the other bots.

Syn laughed. "I could call you Zip. But…" Syn pursed her lips and rubbed the edge of her ear. "No…" Her eyes went wide, and she exclaimed, "I know it! Huck!"

The bot stopped and looked at her.

"What do you think? Huck?"

A moment passed, and then the bot nodded its agreement.

"Okay, Huck. Now I need some help from you."

Huck moved in close, eager to hear her next words.

"I really need to get to my friend Blip, but…" She waved a hand at the assortment of broken bots, "You've brought me a bunch of work. So, I'll make you a deal. These bots and no others. You shut that door, and don't you dare tell any other one that I'm helping. I'll get these all going—" She examined the various bots and sighed, "and I think it's going to take some time." She jabbed a finger at Huck. "So, promise me—just these and no others. Okay?"

Huck nodded eagerly.

"Fine." She pointed at the others. "Now, for the rest of you. Keep your mouths shut. Don't you dare tell anyone about what I'm doing. Promise me?"

Syn jumped back in surprise as she was greeted with not just nods but several verbal agreements of "Yes" and "I promise" and "Can do" in a strange cacophony of simulated voices. She was so used to her bots not talking, she had forgotten that these could. All except for Huck, yet he displayed a curiosity and alertness to him that similar eye-bots on her Disc didn't. He had the spark of life in him. Having played around with enough eye-bots, she knew that they didn't even possess the machinery to verbalize. It was likely the ones on this side didn't either. Intelligent but forever mute.

"Okay, then," Syn said, "We'll do this one at a time. You have to be patient." Syn pointed to the larger, trash-can sized bot on a single wheel. "Let's start with you. Come here. What's your name?"

In a high-pitched, squeaking voice, the large gray bot said, "Ah used to be called Clemence. But they all call me Bear." It rolled close to her on a massive, thick tire that was nearly a tread. This bot was designed to go anywhere, except maybe indoors.

Syn stopped, trying to gauge the bot's earnestness, and when she realized it was telling the truth, she worked to stifle a giggle. "Well, Bear. It's very nice to meet you." She sat down on the red rolling stool and pulled up next to Bear, running a hand across its side and now noticing a series of three even blue stripes that fell down from its top and ran parallel the length of its body before curving to its back. "And what seems to be the problem?"

Bear's voice grew low, "I can't...I can't..."

Syn leaned in, lowering in voice to match, "Yes?"

"I can't see real well. Can't see at all. Everything is just a bunch of big old blotches. It's not good for someone like me to be unable to see."

From behind, one of the smaller bots piped up, "He runs us over! That's why I'm broken. He can't see where he's going, the big—"

Syn waved a hand. "Woah! You be nice now, or I'm putting you at the end of the line and may never get to fixing you."

The small bot gave a quick reply, "Sorry." Syn stifled another laugh—she wasn't sure which one had even said it, so she wasn't sure how she was going to enforce her threat.

Turning back to Bear, she patted him on the head, "Well, I can see why that's a problem." She spun back to the workbench and picked up a few tools. "Let's get that fixed. Shouldn't be too hard."

And it wasn't. Bear's problem was due to a loose adaptor frame that prevented him from focusing properly and then a bunch of gunk and dirt that had built up on the inside of the two lenses. Most of the bots she worked on that day weren't incredibly challenging. There were a few that required her to search around the shop for various parts. This workshop was not as stocked as hers. Most of these repairs would've been simple over there, but here she was limited to discovering where the previous occupant had stored things, if he had acquired them at all. A few times she had to resort to using a different tool than what she would've preferred. And in a few cases, she made the bot better but couldn't fix the problem entirely. There were just certain parts she was unable to locate. But one by one, each bot left in far better condition than it had arrived. She made sure to give each one a quick cleanup as well after finding a bucket of cleaning materials and rags under one of the benches.

Halfway through the day, the door slid open and in floated the shining globe that was Arquella. Atop of the bot's spherical form a small plate balanced with three apples and a cup of water.

"How are you doing that?" Syn asked, amazed at the balancing act.

Arquella floated over to her, and Syn took the plate off her head. "Since you did what you did, I've been able to do far more than that. It's not hard at all, actually!"

Syn held up an apple. "For me?"

"The Barlgharel said you'd be hungry and thirsty by now."

"He knows I'm here?"

"He must. He asked me to bring these to you." Arquella rotated around, taking in the bots still waiting their turn. "What's happening?"

Syn eyed Huck who was floating nearby. He hadn't ventured more than a few feet away the entire day and had been more than eager to help Syn find various tools or items—and Syn had to admit, he'd done a good job. She said, "Someone told the others that I can fix things. The line formed early this morning. Unlike you, this one is a bit more blabby than I'd like."

"You're fixing all of them. Can you do that?" Arquella asked.

Syn nodded. "I'm going to try." Syn looked at the door. "I'm going to have to go after Blip soon, but I think I can get this done. I'm not sure who would help you all if I didn't."

Arquella bobbed closer and said in a reverential tone, "You really are the Expected one."

"Oh, please don't—" Syn started to say but was cut off.

Several of the bots remaining echoed the phrase, "Expected. Expected."

Syn dropped the tool in her hand, stood up, and put her hands out, "Woah! Stop that you all."

Arquella responded, "But you are. You are the Expected. You were sent to not only lead us away from here but to heal us while we're here."

"I'm..." But Syn couldn't think of how to end that sentence. There was no harm in what they believed, and if looked at from their perspective, she was healing them. Each of the bots had been amazed at the repair work she had done. If they thought they were human, then what she was doing was akin more to a doctor (or in a simpler view, a miracle worker) than a repair-woman. She examined the ones still remaining. Nine more. There was no way she was finishing this before nighttime. She momentarily considered stopping and just leaving, but the memory of each repaired bot's joy had caused her to hesitate. It was important to each of these. She was changing their lives; she was healing them. And the Barlgharel said that Blip was okay. So, instead of leaving, Syn sat back down and picked up a dropped tool.

Syn smiled, "Thank you, Arquella. Can you tell the Barlgharel that

I'm going to be here another night, but I want to leave early in the morning?"

Arquella bobbed in agreement. "I can and will." She floated outside.

Syn sighed. "Sorry, Blip." She picked up an apple, enjoying the crisp taste, and returned to working on the slender bot ahead of her with the broken leg. An easy fix.

The day turned into evening, and the number of bots diminished. Huck never left her side, and Arquella twice returned with more food and water—the second time with Bear's lumbering form close behind.

The work was wonderful, Syn finally admitted. She had lost track of time working on these bots and so wasn't surprised when, after patting the final bot on its head and sending it away, she let out a great yawn. Except for Huck's zipping and Arquella and Bear's silent presence, the workshop was now empty.

Syn stood and went to the door. "Arquella, can I stay in your room again? Would you mind?"

Arquella let out a brief squeal of joy and said, "That would be delightful," as they exited the shop.

2 3

A DREAM OF STARS

"It is not in the stars to hold our destiny but in ourselves."
—William Shakespeare

Syn slept. Syn dreamt.

She floated through space alone. No Olorun. No Disc. And no Blip. Just herself alone amongst the sea of stars. She stretched out her arms and swam, pushing against the dark waters between those pinpoint lights.

"Syn."

A voice echoed from below her feet, but as she looked down, she discovered nothing there. Again the voice said her name. "Syn." But this time, it was behind her. Turning toward the sound, she saw the great globe of Sol itself, its yellow light pulsing in rhythm.

With a single step, she crossed the gap to the constant star. Around her rotated tiny marbles and balls. The Earth. Mars. Jupiter. The million pebbles of the asteroid belt. In a moment, she had become Sol. She was the center of the solar system.

Clip-clop. Clip-clop. The planets were planets, and yet, in between, as if flickering from one reality to the next, they were stallions, racing in their lanes. Clip-clop, clip-clop. There was a great

179

race, and they were competing. The earth, a motley-speckled stallion with a dark chestnut mane and midnight tail, flew toward its goal, its nostrils flaring, spittle dripping from its wavering upper lip. The beast was manic. Beside it limped a slow and tired umber horse, Mars. Its one eye was shut, wounded and scarred, a tiny bubble of puss still present in the corner. But the two, despite their differences, kept pace. The debilitation of Mars and the fervor of Earth were equalized in their revolution around her. Syn held out her arms wide, nervous to bring them to her sides, nervous that she'd break the course of the raging planets.

The beasts shifted back to globes, and as they did, a flash of light shot out from Earth toward the outer planets. Then she was swimming again, chasing the light. Behind her, Sol stood steady, a giant looming over everything. Ahead, the light sped, and Syn was a tiny insect in pursuit.

She wasn't just chasing; she was being pulled by it. Tiny ropes, unseen, but she felt them as they wrapped around her arms, pulled her along as if she was the tail of some great comet, always following in the wake of something far larger—more powerful.

In that moment, the star was Olorun. Its shining light resolved into the familiar speared-circle shape of the needle and Disc.

But she was still pulled behind. Still forgotten.

She held out her hand, opening it up, fingers spreading as wide as possible, hoping to grip onto something. She was then standing still, standing far from the now dim pinpoint of light that was Sol, her hands still outstretched. Before her, almost invisible in its minuscule size, was the Olorun. Syn stood like some giant waiting to receive the ship.

The weight of time felt heavy on her limbs. She had been waiting for centuries. The worlds revolving around her were young, and Syn knew she was a star again, a star of a new solar system with unknown worlds in rotation. There was no race. There was only a playful chase as Syn stood overlooking her young children—the worlds were green and blue marbles, and there were so many of them. Her arms were not held up in fear. Instead one arm still reached out, calling to the

Olorun. The other hovered, palm down, in protection of the child worlds at play.

Syn sighed as a sense of calm satisfaction, a wash of completeness moved through her, and everything slowed to a full pause. The universe stopped. The worlds in chase stopped. Only Olorun moved, refusing to acknowledge her beckon.

Olorun was streaking toward her, like a stallion itself. Where the sleek metal of the ship was, now there was simply the streamlined coat of a charging, ember-colored horse, its teeth bared and its eyes narrow in fury. With each step, it gained speed, until it was a bullet shot at her.

It flew past the circling planets and hit Syn, slamming into her heart, and blood erupted as she shrieked in pain.

WAKING UP

"We live, as we dream—alone."
—Joseph Conrad

Syn woke with the scream still on her lips. Sweat poured down her face.

She gasped, trying to choke back the now-escaping sobs. The tears came anyway. She didn't understand why, but something from the dream still clung to her, and she couldn't catch her breath. She gasped again.

Nearby, in the corner of the room, Arquella floated, unmoved and undisturbed by Syn's startled waking.

"It was just a nightmare," Syn said to herself.

In the dark of the room, she felt more alone than ever. She wanted Blip to be there. She ached for him to be at her side. Blip had been calming her out of nightmares since Syn had known him. Nightmares interrupted her sleep most every night. She felt safe in the tree, and so she slept there. Yet, as the world went dark and silent around her, the memories of panic would float to the surface. She would erupt in a panic, heart racing, unsure as to where she was. Images of the white room and the crèche would flash in her memory, and she would project them onto the scene around her. Gasping, frightened, she would race into the cold night air. Then Blip would be next to her, counting down from twenty. Each number uttered a bit quieter than the last. She wasn't sure why the countdown brought her peace, but it did. She had been having nightmares since she first woke in the crèche. Sleep constantly evaded her. Yet, Syn knew the routine after a nightmare. They would return to the treehouse. He would position himself next to her. His cold porcelain body somehow reassuring, and he could manage to exude a steady warmth. She would fall back asleep, her arm draped over him. Then Syn would sleep again through the rest of the night, uninterrupted. Sometimes he would drift away after he knew she was deep in sleep, always cautious to return by the time she woke. Over and over they danced this same dance.

No. Not this time.

Syn laid back down and stared at Arquella's floating form. *I'm not alone*, she thought. There were friends about. In the dark, strange, and twisted landscape of this second Disc, she had found a safe place. A thought came to her that both warmed her and created a pang of guilt: *If I can't find Blip, I still have these as friends. I won't be alone even if I can't find him.*

In the warmth of that reminder, Syn allowed herself to sleep once more.

PARTINGS

"The desert speaks the language of madness.
Syllables dipped in chaos."
—*The Vision of Kanc*, Archives of the Ecology

Despite waking up as early as she could, hoping to slip out onto her journey unnoticed, the bots all waited for her outside. They were now past the edge of the Cradle. The outer courtyard of the lower Settlement, the one bordering the vast wasteland of the Desert of Nod, was jammed with the bots of the Ecology. The sky above was still the dark smoky haze, but Syn could now see the subtle hint of the sunstrips light above—a small difference between now and night, but enough. There, in the silence and darkness of the early morning, the bots were all assembled.

She had descended the flights of stairs to look out at the base of the Disc, and there the Barlgharel greeted her. The two stood above the final staircase overlooking the mass of the Ecology.

"We are here to provide a lasting memory upon your journey." He leaned back, and his yellow and green body swayed back and forth. He gestured to the assemblage and said, "You have made a lasting memory upon them. It is only customary we do the same."

Syn pressed her lips together. "How come you all weren't out yesterday morning for me? I said I was going to leave the night before. You even did that whole blessing thing."

The Barlgharel leaned in and whispered, "From what I know of you, you're never one to leave anything broken." He turned and waved an appendage over the waiting Ecology. "Besides, neither you nor we were ready for it. I'm not sure we are wanting it this morning, but we are at least ready."

"And how are you more ready now than yesterday?" She planted her spear on the cement ground and leaned against it, staring into the billowing smog and across the fading desert.

The Barlgharel swayed back and forth, "I think we are only ready because now we have taken up a place in your soul. Yesterday, we would've just been a memory. Now, we are a part of you."

Syn could not answer that. *Had the one day made that big of a difference? And how could he have known that?*

Before she could reflect on his words, he leaned in and directed her gaze across the desert, to a single dot far up the rising edge of the Disc to her left. "That is your destination, little Expected Sunflier."

"Is Blip there?" The words were out of her mouth before she thought them. And she felt reassured by them. Yesterday, she had been so lost in the work that her mind rarely drifted to him. The immediate challenges of fixing each of the bots seemed more real than the far away problem of his absence. Only last night, after she had curled up under the blankets in Arquella's room and was certain the chrome bot had shut down for the night as it floated in the corner, only then had Syn allowed herself to face the emotion of his absence. He was not there, and she hated falling asleep without him near. It had been such a rarity, and now she was three nights without him. She had even navigated the terror of a nightmare without him. She did not want to get used his absence. She did not want the ache to stop. And yet, on that third night, it hurt a bit less. And inside, she hated herself for it.

"That is where he has been taken. I believe he is still there. That is Zondon Almighty, as the Crimson Queen has named it."

Syn narrowed her eyes. "It's darker over here, but I'm guessing that's about nine kilometers away."

The Barlgharel nodded. "9.9 to be precise. Your journey will be slow-going."

"I can walk that in a couple hours."

"Yes, but the dry ground, blowing dust, and the air itself will slow you down."

Two smaller bots, both with large round cases that functioned as a body, each with one singular large eye in the center of their heads, and long, monkey-like arms draping near the ground, came walking out carrying an assortment of clothes.

The Barlgharel first picked up a pair of goggles. The rims were a bright gold, and the lenses were ruby-colored. They were the cleanest item she had seen on this side. "These will enable you to see if the wind devils strike." He handed them to her, and she tried them on, turning the world red as she brought them over her eyes. She loved them. She lifted them up and rested them on the top of her head.

He held a red and gold-orange jacket and a scarf of the same colors. "These will keep you warm. Down here, Sunflier, it is much colder. Wear this and cover your mouth so you won't grow sick as you move closer to Zondon."

Syn tried on the jacket, lifting up her assortment of necklaces and slipping the collar underneath. The scarf she wrapped around her neck over the assortment of jewelry, and she let the ends hang down across the front of her body. She loved the colors. "Thank you."

The Barlgharel turned to the Ecology below and said, "We have already blessed our friend's journey. She is the Sunflier. The Expected One. And as she leaves, we expect her to return. Her journey is not just away. It is there and back to us."

He led her down the stairs, and she found herself mobbed by the bots when she reached the bottom of the staircase. Most wanted to say goodbye. They nuzzled close, expecting hugs that she returned. Some tried to talk her out of the journey, but the Barlgharel shook his head each time.

She stepped to the edge of the Settlement, where the cement path ended, and the dead land lay beyond. In her world, this would be the edge of the jungle, and the world would be erupting in green, but nothing but blowing dirt, gray and soot-streaked, lay before her.

She turned and waved and several more spoke out as she did so. They all insisted that she return. She continually heard the mutter of "Expected" and cringed each time one of them spoke it.

She didn't want to leave them. She gripped her spear tight, knowing that she had to leave but struggling to not be pulled back into the crowd. As her eyes welled up with tears, Syn blurted out, "I'll come back."

"Will you take us away from here? To the other world?" one bot shouted out from somewhere in the crowd. She couldn't see how she could take them back to her Disc, but she understood why they wanted to leave this one. It was horrible. She felt the collective sense of hope, so she nodded in agreement. Finally, after being asked several more times as she waved goodbye, Syn finally declared aloud, "Yes. I promise." She winced reflecting on that pledge—*How can I keep that?*

The Barlgharel drew closer. "We have one final gift to give, and we know we are still in debt to you for all you have done for us. But take comfort in this. A few of ours have offered to escort you to the gates of Zondon. We know that if you choose to step inside, they likely will not be allowed to enter, but they will not leave your side until then."

Syn's eyes went wide. Someone wanted to go with her? Out into that? "You sure? Who is that—" she had meant to say "who is that stupid?" but was interrupted by the whirring of Huck from out of the crowd, zipping around her head. Syn erupted into a smile. "Huck? Really?"

From behind her, someone coughed—a high-pitched sound. Bear and Arquella stood there. Bear started to speak, "We plan to go..."

Arquella interrupted, "It's our honor to accompany the Expected."

Syn went over to the two as Huck buzzed around. "You really sure? I'm not sure what's out there."

Bear spoke first and quickly, rushing to get his words out before Arquella interrupted again. "Neither do we, but we're going. You need us."

Syn nodded. *That might be true.* "Okay, then. Let's get going."

The Barlgharel slithered forward, "One last thing. Beware the Hazards."

"Huh?" Syn said, adjusting her pack around her shoulders. It felt heavier this morning that normal.

The bots of the Ecology had gone quiet at his mention of the Hazards.

"I'm not sure what you might find, but you might draw the attention of some of the monsters of the Disc. There are wild things out there—some quite monstrous—and they prowl throughout Nod."

Syn furrowed her eyebrows. "Like animals?"

"Yes, they are quite like animals. Vicious and territorial. But no. They are not made of the Sun. They are like the walls and houses. They are things made to look real, but there is no love in them. There is no spark of intelligence in them. They think only of death. And it may be that you can venture from here to there without encountering one. But beware when you do. Be careful. Keep alert at all times. Do not detour from your course."

Syn nodded, perplexed at this new, unknown threat. For the first time in a day, anxiety began to well up in her. *Oh Blip, why did we ever come here?*

Hidden amongst the gray miasma, the settlements stood toward the darkness with their curved facades—attempts to portray an unnatural world as organic.

She turned and strode out into the barren landscape, giving only a wave this time. Behind her followed her friends.

26

NOD

"I have always loved the desert. One sits down on a desert sand dune, sees nothing, hears nothing. Yet through the silence something throbs, and gleams..."
—Antoine de Saint-Exupéry, *The Little Prince*

The Desert of Olorun had been an accident. Nod was the name the Barlgharel had given it. It was not the apotheosis of all deserts. Syn could see the drained image of its borders —the rise of the settlements—from where she walked. It was not grueling hot. In fact, it lent itself to blasts of cold air that forced her to hunker down against the few dunes, and more often, behind Bear himself, as the wind passed by. It was not the lovely pure sand of the Sahara she'd seen in action films—this was not an ocean of sand. The tangled roots of the fallen trees and the cluttered stalks of weeds littered the ground and tripped her more than once. She tasted the sand in these moments, falling and unable to catch her groggy self. She sucked the dirt in short bursts and then spit it out. It was bitter and not just the salty dryness of regular sand. It looked like a desert when descending on the Jacob or scanning from atop the settlements, but up close, stepping across its pocked surface, it was the landscape of nightmares—distorted and tired with enough hint of life to suggest torture rather than survival.

At first, as she ventured out, a few of the bots circled behind in her wake, but with every step, more and more fell behind until it was only her and her three-bot entourage making the trek. Half a kilometer into her journey, she wrapped the scarf around her mouth and pulled her goggles down. The gifts were already useful. Looking back at the settlements, and the Cradle hidden somewhere within the monolithic rises, the dirt had kicked up so that she could see nothing of the collected bots. Or perhaps they had all fled back indoors, fearful of the burlys. And the Hazards, whatever those were.

In the last hour, she was certain she heard new voices twice. *The bots?* Perhaps it was Bear and Arquella whispering. She smiled—she was sure it was not burlys; they didn't seem to talk at all. And for some reason she pictured the Hazards as screaming their arrival rather than whispering.

Huck continued to zoom around but stayed near her, never venturing far off. Bear rolled across the rough landscape next to her, and Arquella floated on the opposite side. The four ventured forward against the elements, without talking. She could only guess at the fears racing through their minds—perhaps the unknown Hazards, or more likely, the prospect of Zondon Almighty.

Syn paused to rest, planting her spear in the ground and steadying herself against it. She sighed. She had been overconfident. This was her ship. This Disc was the same size as hers. But she didn't have an Ogun here. Nor did she have the freedom to flounce in whatever direction she desired as the queen, doing as she willed without question.

Now she walked, in pursuit of a city she had never entered. Despite the blowing dirt and the strangeness of the landscape, Syn had the bizarre sense that she knew where Zondon Almighty was located.

Occasionally, she would stop and look around, sure she was being watched. A few times, Huck would zip up above, possibly to gain a better vantage point, and she would catch his darting movement from the corner of her eye. Each time, she went tense—if she could see him, perhaps others could.

After a few hours, she held up a hand and motioned for the others to rest near a large dune. They followed her, and she sat back against it, bracing herself and enjoying the break in the blowing wind that it provided. Arquella dropped to the ground in front of her, and Bear rolled beside her.

"Everything okay?" Arquella asked.

Syn nodded. "Just thirsty." Syn pulled out a small canister of water she had filled up in Arquella's home. There was not much in it, and she knew if they didn't keep going, she wouldn't have enough to make the trip if there were delays and this trip stretched beyond a day.

Huck descended and rested atop Bear's square frame.

The four sat in silence as Syn drank and rested. Syn remembered the weight of her pack and opened it up to discover several apples inside. Syn ate one and closed her eyes, listening to the hiss of the wind.

"Tell me about your friend," Bear said.

Syn opened an eye and shot him a glance. "Blip?"

"Ya. The one we going for. He sure must be special for you to do this."

Arquella added, "Is he special?"

Syn took a deep breath. "He's special. He's...my best friend. I haven't known a day that he wasn't near me. He's always been there to help me. And guide me." She chuckled. "He wasn't a patient teacher, but he did teach me. And he put up with me. He would sit next to me when we watched movies, even if I insisted we watch them over and over. We would lose days in the theater, and he'd stay with me. And then he'd act out the scenes with me." She laughed aloud. "I'd always have to give him the part with the least lines. He was a horrible actor. He could never get the lines right. And he's a..." Syn had meant to say "bot" but caught herself. *Remember who you're talking to.* "And he's got a great memory. I don't know if he ever forgot any line. But he'd do it. For me. When I was younger, I made him put on stupid costumes. And he'd do it! He's

Blip. I love him!" Syn surprised herself as a small tear rolled down her cheek.

Bear said, "I'd like to have a friend like that."

"Me too," Arquella said.

Syn glanced between the two and said, "Well maybe the two of you could be each other's."

The two looked at each other and then back to Syn but didn't say a thing.

Syn stood, flung her pack over her shoulder, and picked up her spear. "Huck, point the way." She pulled down her goggles, wrapped the scarf around her face, and they set off again into the blowing dust. Around her the sand whipped and spun, forming images in the air. Syn imagined seeing the figures of the dead drifting through the dust.

More hours passed, and the looming dot of Zondon Almighty grew much larger and dropped lower, approaching the horizon, as they drew closer. Although sometimes occluded by the billowing sand and the haze of this world, the dot grew into the small shape of a city. Soon, Syn realized she recognized the location. The more she thought about it, she knew where Zondon Almighty had to be placed. Obviously, from a scan, there was no great tree on this Disc. It had been removed. Or it had never been. Yet, the great tree had been the center of Syn's Disc—of Syn's world. And she knew it had been so for the colonists. She had read the works of one of the builders who was also a professor. He had argued not just to put a park in the center but to put in a jungle and to build the entire structure around the world of the green, around the central tree.

Yet on this Disc, there was no tree. Just Zondon. She was sure of it, and as they neared where her tree should be, the first signs of the city appeared, the edge of it rose up above the decline of dunes—the top of a tin and plaster and wood city. This was Zondon Almighty. Its silhouette was not presented in profile yet, but instead, they viewed it as if from a great height, seeing both its rise and the top of its structures, a sight afforded by the arc of the Disc upward and away. With each passing second, Syn was certain she had visited Zondon before. There was something in its arrangement that seemed familiar. Even from far away, still a couple kilometers ahead of the them, its construction had been an amalgamation of different structures. The walls and roofs seemed cobbled from various materials. The colors were all variations of gray and rust. Gray and rust streaked doors. Gray chimneys. Rust-colored stairs in a circle of a tower. Rusting railings along a lookout at the top of that tower. Some gray shadows moving back and forth across the tops of the buildings.

And all around that stood a great gray and rust-splattered wall. From her vantage point, she could see there were two layers of the wall—in this world it was evident the inhabitants couldn't be too careful. Painted along the outside of the walls were horrific visages. Paint-smeared faces glared at them with dark eyes. From where she stood, the details were lost. All that she perceived was the fearful warning the faces with the glaring eyes and hungry smiles projected. They were far less distinct than the Orisha masks mounted on the towers above and were far less inviting. The Orisha masks seemed to have arrived from the ancient past—monuments to the persistent gods they represented. The faces scrawled on the outside of Zondon seemed conjured from somewhere dark—fleeting images that threatened to rush out at them if they all but glanced away.

In the center of the city a tower ascended—a set of two spires jutting up from the center of the city. Visual priority was a huge advantage. The tower had a broad base and narrow top, and as she moved closer, she could see a tiny ladder fastened to its side.

As they walked, Syn whispered to herself. "Blip, I'm coming."

Her curiosity pulled her forward. She had to know what had happened here. There were people here. She had seen them as they stole Blip. For the first time, she was to meet real people and not just videos of the dead. Perhaps, people that could answer her. Her thoughts raced and the thousand questions she had ignored flooded in. *What had they dug up? Could they provide insight to a world that they hadn't seen? Who had started all this?* Someone had begun the Madness, someone had started up Syn's crèche and woken her, someone had killed off the majority of occupants, and someone had switched the dumb bots over here on. *Who? Why? Why launch a ship and let it be consumed by death?* So many questions. Maybe the answers weren't in Zondon Almighty, but they might start there. And Blip was there.

"Watch out!" Bear shouted.

Syn froze, her eyes unable to find him in the blowing sand. "What?"

A huge metallic claw slammed into the sand in front of her, and Syn fell backward, landing hard on the ground.

"Run away!" Arquella screeched from somewhere behind her.

What was it? But the answer didn't stay hidden for long. In front of her, a massive, gigantic form encased in a charcoal shell, nearly hidden in the darkness of the early afternoon, rose up out of the sand. The thing stood three meters above Syn. Dirt, rocks, and the trash of the former inhabitants fell from its insect-like body, raining down around Syn. A narrow head atop a two-portioned body that pivoted on top of six legs glared down at her.

A tree mover. Syn had avoided the gigantic bots on her side, but they always seemed harmless. They lumbered about, slowly clearing away dying trees and planting new ones. Their size frightened her but only that. They never crushed other bots or animals underneath them as they worked.

This one wasn't working properly anymore. It screeched, and four tentacled arms extended from its sides; its iron plates grated against each other with every movement. Three metallic pinchers flayed open at the end of each tentacle, and each aimed for one of the four travelers.

"Everyone! Move!" Syn yelled, hurrying back to her feet and grasping her spear with both hands.

Bear rolled back but snagged his wheel on a branch uncovered in the beast's reveal. Bear lost his balanced and tumbled backwards down the dune, end over end, fearfully squealing in his high-pitched whine as he dropped out of sight.

Huck darted through the air, nimbly avoiding the tentacle snaking for it. The two whipped around in an odd dance, the strange black whip missing the eye-bot over and over.

Syn leapt back further, trying to put space between it and the tree handler. The thing noticed her and must've assumed she was the primary threat. It scuttled toward her with a speed and ferocity she had never witnessed in its kind before. Syn screeched and turned around to run, but slammed straight into Arquella, smashing her face into the bot's side. Arquella went flying to the ground and rolled through the sand. Syn dropped backwards, a mist of blood pouring from her nose. Instead of putting distance between herself and the giant, attacking bot, she fell directly between its two front legs, staring up at its head.

Recognizing the opportunity, Syn lashed upwards with her spear. The bladed end struck the metallic frame and was deflected, not leaving a dent or scratch in the beast's surface.

She swore as the beast lumbered ahead, its large legs slamming around her, sending vibrations through the ground. In the low light, it was hard to keep track of all of its limbs. There were three red lights running up each leg and one single light at the end of each pincher. The lights from the pinchers seemed to float around like crimson fire-flies. If it wasn't for those lights, the beast would be impossible to keep track of.

It moved forward and then pivoted as if searching. It couldn't seem to see under itself. At least, not where she was standing. She had found a blind spot.

She jabbed the spear up again. And again. And again. The beast was unaffected. She had hoped she'd found a weak spot. *Everyone knows dragon's bellies are unprotected.* But unlike the myths, this one's soft belly was impenetrable.

From her left side, something slammed into the thing's large leg, jolting it and rocking it back. Its two back legs shifted to adjust its weight and keep its balance, one of them slamming inches from Syn's face. She rolled to her right and onto her feet, crouching down.

Bear had hit it. He had somehow clambered back to the fight from his fall. He reared back and slammed forward, hitting the beast's leg again. It rocked and swayed far more than before. It was off-balance, struggling to shift its trunk-like legs fast enough against the barrage of Bear's slams.

Bear tried again, roaring out in his high-pitched, nasal tone. The creature swung its leg back, too quick for Bear to readjust his trajectory, then swung the leg back again, smacking Bear hard and sending the bot flying.

From behind the dune, the shiny sphere that was Arquella leapt up into view and shouted, "Bear!" and raced after the tumbling bot. The tree mover was distracted by the gleaming bot and shifted after it, its massive legs thumping against the ground. With the distraction, Syn darted behind the creature, hoping to avoid its eye-line. If she could just keep circling behind it, maybe she'd see a weakness.

There has to be an off-switch. Every bot has one! Where was it?

She had never had to repair one of these things before. They were so few, and usually they had their own entourage of bots floating around them, working on maintaining them. If there was an off-switch, she had no idea where it was.

Huck zipped around next to her and swung around her head. "Huck! Stop it! I can't see!" She batted him away, but he zipped back, racing around in front of her. "Stop it!" But the eye-bot wouldn't leave her alone. After she attempted to bat it away for the third time, it jammed into her arm, pushing her backwards. "Huck! What's gotten into you?" Again he hit her, and she stepped back, trying to avoid him. Then he zipped away, straight up into the air.

Syn followed his movement, and she saw what he had been trying to get her to pay attention to. A dark figure, draped in a drab cloak, was climbing up the beast's far back leg.

"Who is that?" Syn shouted, but Huck made no reply.

The figure was nimble and, in a few seconds, had made its way to the beast's back. Planting both legs in a wide stance, working to keep its balance on the rearing beast, the figure pulled a knife from a sheath on its leg and brought it down with a fury, quick and decisive, jamming it straight into the thing's shell. Syn had expected the blade to bounce off as her spear had. Instead, it plunged straight in, and she saw shards of crimson glass explode from the impact. The figure held tight to the bucking bot and pulled something else out of another pocket. From Syn's view, it looked like a piece of fabric with small red lights. The figure placed the piece in the hole opened up by their knife.

The beast buckled, convulsing. It roared—a horrific grating screech that sent shivers down Syn's spine. Whatever the figure had done, it had hit something critical. A second later, the beast stopped all motion. The red lights lining its appendages went dark. The beast's huge legs buckled underneath it, and the entire thing crashed with a slam into the desert dirt, sending a cloud of sand up, blinding Syn.

She yelled, "Bear! Arquella! Where are you?"

From the other side of the beast's inert body, she heard Arquella's plaintive screams, "We're here! Bear is hurt! He's hurt! Syn help us! Heal him! He needs you!" The bot screamed.

"I'm coming," Syn walked through the sand cloud, trying to avoid the splayed legs of the tree mover. She gripped her spear with both hands, still aware that there was now another threat, another unknown beside the monstrosity that had just collapsed. "Huck. Help me. Where are they?"

As the dust settled, Syn peered ahead, hoping to find them. Something flashed a few meters away, and she was sure it a reflection off of Arquella's shell. "Is that you?"

Arquella answered, much closer now, "Here! Help him!"

Bear was face forward on the ground, a huge dent on his left side and a tear in the metal along his upper edge. Surprisingly, his wheel was still spinning.

Syn dropped to her knees beside them and examined the dent. "You okay, Bear?"

The bot didn't respond. Syn knew she wouldn't be able to turn him over—he was far too large for that.

Arquella floated above them both. "He isn't talking. I can't get him to respond. Syn, you have to help him. You can heal him, right? Can't you? Please tell me you can heal him!"

Syn held up a hand. "Let me look." She thought to herself, *Oh, please, let this be something easy.* "I'll figure it out. Just give me a moment please."

Huck hovered around them in wide arcs, slowly observing.

Syn worked through the problem step-by-step. *His wheel is going. He has power. Yet, he's not responding. The dent was on his right side. If I remember, his power supply is on his right side. Maybe something came loose. The tear up top doesn't look to be that deep, and nothing is hanging out. If only I had a few tools, I could get the maglocks to release on his side and take the plate off and see what's going on.*

Syn looked up to Arquella, "Do me a favor and look away. This isn't going to be pretty."

"What are you going to do?" The bot asked.

"Just look away, please."

Arquella spun, although Syn still had no idea where her eyes were. She was one simple silver sphere, perfectly smooth across her entire surface.

Syn pried at a thin seam with the edge of her spear, wriggling it back and forth, hoping to put enough pressure on the maglocks to separate them. The first one popped open and she breathed out. *Okay, one down, and the rest will be easier.* One by one, she popped them open, moving the tip of the spear up the seam, working to not jam it in too far and to avoid slicing anything critical. She released the last one, and the entire right plate dropped down into the dust.

Syn gave an audible, "Whew!"

"What is it?" Arquella said, "Can I turn around? Is it okay to look?"

"Ya, you're fine. And it's going to be okay."

Syn wriggled around inside the bot, popping out a few cables from a locking clamp. The wheel stopped spinning. She pushed them back in and then snagged another pair of cables dangling loose from the same round unit. "His power supply to his main processor just came unhooked. Doesn't look like much is wrong. I mean, it's hard to see—he's got a ton of stuff jammed in here. But it's an easy fix." She snapped the final piece into place and heard the familiar whirr of Bear's main system cycling up.

Arquella shook her head. "What do you mean power supply? Main processor? What are you talking about?"

Syn sighed. She had forgotten that Arquella had no idea she was a bot. "Nothing. Just...I..." Syn hesitated a moment and then gave in to

Arquella's belief, "I healed him. He's fine. He's healed. He's going to be okay." She pulled his plate back up and allowed the maglocks to grip tight, returning it to its place. Her body felt heavy suddenly—the stress of the moment had passed. Bear was safe. Arquella was safe. Huck was safe. Syn was still alive.

Just then, Bear's nasal voice interjected, "Healed who? What happened? I kill it? Why is everything so dark?"

Syn gave a snort. "You're facing down. Can you get yourself up?"

"Oh!" Bear's wheel twisted, and with a few quick adjustments— Syn couldn't understand how the lumbering bot was so nimble—Bear righted himself and stood up straight. "Did I kill it? Is it dead?"

Syn froze. The tree mover was dead. For a brief moment, she had forgotten all about the other person that had killed it. She gripped her spear tightly and rose to her feet.

From behind them, someone spoke. "Handy little devil, aren't you? Bit o' a miracle worker. Look atchoo!" The voice was young with an air of cynicism. It was mocking, but the joviality was false—a pretense to appear soft.

Syn spun to eye the figure from before sitting atop the fallen form of the tree mover bot, only a meter away. At this distance, Syn could easily see that it was a girl. She was as dark as Syn, but her hair was cropped unbelievably short. Her arms were covered in a gray cloth cloak that billowed around her, and only her feet and hands could be seen. her mouth and nose were covered with a red mask, so only her eyes shone through. Syn had seen those eyes before. She wouldn't ever forget them. They were the same eyes that she had seen in the darkness when Blip had been snagged—the searching eyes that scanned the room as she hid in the pile of children's bones.

This was one of the thieves that had taken Blip.

Syn's depleted energy was supplemented with a surge of rage, and she rushed up the dune, waving her spear in front of her. She had wanted to shout out, "Where is Blip?" but instead, she yelled, "Who are you?"

The masked girl jerked back, jumped, and managed to pirouette away from Syn's attack. "Woah, you with the pointy thing. Calm down." She held up her palms in a calming motion.

Syn stepped back, but as she was looking up at her target, she missed her step, slipped, and her feet went out from beneath her. She smacked her knee against the dark sand, and the broken weeds jabbed into her skin as she grimaced in pain. She grabbed at the motionless tree mover and pulled herself up.

"You okay, there? Slow down. Ain't nothing going to hurt you. 'Sides, you ought be thanking me. I just saved you all's hides." The masked girl was not disturbed by Syn's anger. She gingerly stepped forward as if working to help an injured dog, compassionate but cautious. She patted the dead tree mover's hide and said, "Up top it has this little red spot under some glass." The girl held up a thin metal strip with a few blinking lights. "Break it open and just slap down a control strip and the thing can't do any thinking at all. You just got distracted by all the moving parts. Need to sometimes get a different angle on things. And sometimes the best tools aren't the ones with pointy ends." She stepped closer and held out a hand, "Where are my manners? How are you—"

Syn growled as the girl moved closer.

"Woah, fine with me," the girl said, palms head up. "You stay there and bleed. I just wanted to get a good look at you. Thought there were just a few of the machines out here marching toward us, but when we looked out, I caught sight of you. I knew you were special. The others disagreed. They thought you were a straggler from the old world. But I knew you were different. You just proved me right. Glad I got here when I did. Didn't expect you to walk on over a thudder like ya did. Most of us are smart enough to notice them all burrowed down in the dirt. You seemed to miss all o' the signs. That tells me you ain't from around here. So where you get from? You just wake up? Kinda late, don't ya think. 'Sides, how did you get down here? Or were you one of the ones that fled and hid early on? But here you are—first time here or are you coming back to us? Don't remember any of them that were that good with fixin' the machines, but hey, maybe I overlooked that. She kept insisting we should wait for you to come to the gates, but I knew you were different. So, here I am. Had to book it here fast to save your little butt. But I made it, just in time. And look at you. You clever little thing."

"Who are you?" Syn was back to her feet, crouched down, ready to spring and attack the new girl. She held out a hand, motioning for Bear, Huck, and Arquella to stay behind her.

"Who am I? Oooooh. You don't know?" The girl leaned in closer, inspecting Syn, then ran a hand through her hair. "Well, ain't that a puzzler. I could tell you but I might ruin her fun, and she would be so angry. How about..." She put a finger to her lips and over-performed a glance skywards, as if working hard to imagine her next answer, as if pulling it from the heavens themselves. "You can call me...Ripley."

Syn narrowed her eyes. "From the movie?"

Ripley smiled, "You seen that one too?"

Syn nodded once. She had seen the movie *Alien.* It had been one of her favorites to watch, and it felt absurd to hear someone else referencing something that felt like her own private story.

She talked with Blip about all of her movies, but he didn't care for her stories. Blip wasn't a fan of much of what they watched. He tolerated it for her sake. Blip tried his hardest, but she knew, at his core, he was more interested in making sure everything worked as it should and that everything was in its place. Everything that pulled her attention away seemed trivial to him. So dull. She could see his boredom growing when she went on some kick talking as fast as she could about something they'd just finished watching.

But, he had liked *Alien* and each of the sequels. It had been one thing they both enjoyed together. In fact, the only thing. Of all of her interests, that film series was the only thing they could talk about together. Syn couldn't hold back the smile as the memory rushed back. She allowed a grin.

"Like that one, eh?" Ripley said.

Syn felt a rush of embarrassment. Her cheeks grew red, and she drew in on herself, uncomfortable at having revealed so much so easily. She knew she should be elated at meeting someone else on her ship, but all she could think was, *she took Blip!* Her face felt hot, and she grunted, jabbing the spear at Ripley who dodged the attack without difficulty. The effort was too much, and Syn breathed with large gasps as she rested back in a ready stance. This was stupid for her. She wasn't getting anywhere. She was exhausted. She was thirsty. She was shivering between the bursts of sweat. Her eyes were struggling to focus. Too many hours questing across this awful land.

"Where is the Crimson Queen?"

"Oooh. You know her by that name. Curious. Tell you what—you promise to stop poking in my direction with that thing, and I promise to take you to her. Deal?"

Syn looked at her. *Who was this girl?* She glanced back at the three bots huddled behind her. "Will they be safe?"

Ripley raised her eyebrows and took in Huck, Bear, and Arquella. "Those three? You bringing them along?"

Syn nodded. "They came with me this far."

Ripley laughed. "Now I've heard everything. Okay, they can come along, but I know she won't let them inside."

"Will you promise they'll be safe?"

Ripley paused. Little could be seen under the layers covering her face. "Fine. I can do that," Ripley smirked and added, "Now, my promise is only between you and me. I can't speak for anyone else when we get to Zondon."

"You're from Zondon Almighty?" Syn asked.

The girl looked over her shoulder. She yanked the dirty knife from a sheath on her leg and pointed with it. "That magnificent monstrosity?" She glanced back at Syn and winked. "That is the ol' watering hole itself. Yes, chickadee, that there is Zondon Almighty. And I, unfortunately, am from there. Ain't nowhere else to be from."

Ripley stared at the silhouette of Zondon Almighty, barely visible in the low light and brume. She leaned in and whispered, "Good time to consider bowing. If she who puts the almighty in Zondon Almighty herself is watching, a good ol' suck-the-dirt kneel and bow will help your case quite well."

"Who is—" Syn started to ask.

"Nope," Ripley waved the grubby knife in the air, "She be listening too. Seriously. All eyes, all ears, that one. So, um, do as I do when you come up this ridge." She motioned for Syn to stand next to her. "Your parade can come along, but have them hang back a bit."

Syn stood and nodded back at the three. Their metal cases displayed no emotion, but their slow turns radiated concern.

Ripley leaned back to her and sighed, "I promise, I'm not going to bite. At least not for now. Maybe later. I think you'd even like it a bit. Just get up here."

Syn refused to move. Her fists gripped her spear tighter. She pulled the weapon close to her body, locking her legs, and stood defiant.

With no pause and only the warning of a flash of light as the blade's metal reflected the dim sun, Ripley flung her knife at Syn. One moment, Syn stood there indignant, and the next, right between her own legs, its hilt pointed up, the knife lodged with a sharp twang sound deep into the ground.

Ripley continued, "I coulda killed you anytime I wanted. I. Don't. Want. To. So, please?" Again, she motioned with a simple wave of her right hand.

Syn reluctantly took a few steps forward until she stood even with the girl. Ripley clicked her tongue against the top of her mouth and then gave a tiny bow and a small curtsy, bending at her knees before standing back up, her face still aimed at the ground "Now, you do the same."

"Is someone really watching?"

Ripley sighed again. "You're a bit infuriating. Not sure how you survived this long. One of the others shoulda killed you by now. Just do it. Please. We'll get to Zondon faster if you do."

Syn looked around, and then with a shrug of her shoulders, leaned forward and then bent her knee to give a simple bow.

Ripley laughed, "See? Now what that too hard?"

Syn growled.

"Trust me. She saw. Adding up the points now. Might make you one of her favorites. Well, except for me. I'm still *the* favorite. For now." With that, Ripley clicked her tongue again and from behind the massive form of the dead tree mover, a large harvest bot—a massive, cube-shaped bot running on large tank treads—appeared and rolled close. Ripley grabbed ahold of the bar rail on the side of the harvest bot and swung herself to sit atop the blocky creature. She motioned to Syn. "Come on. Ride in style. It'll be nice. Remind you—the toasters can follow, but ain't no one else coming into town with you. If they're planning on it, you need to talk them outta it now."

Syn turned back to the three. "You don't have to go with me any further. I'll be safe. You got me this far. Go on back."

Arquella shook back and forth and Bear gave a gruff, "Nope."

Syn raised her hands out, palms up.

Ripley snorted. "Fine. Waste o' time, but they sure welcome to follow. As I always say, toasters are nutters. Completely through and through."

"You know them?"

"Know of them," Ripley said, "I know all about that crackpot collection that call themselves the Ecology."

Syn was slower pulling herself up and climbing to the top of the bot, but she managed after a moment.

Ripley smiled. "I know I'm all nice and kind, and you're thinking to yourself that the citizens of Zondon can't be that bad. Trust me. I'm the one who hasn't killed anyone in the last month. The rest of the people you meet are complete animals. So, be on your guard. With everyone. Eyes forward. Heck, that works for riding alongside me. We have a bit of distance to cover, but by then, you shoulda had enough time to think about how you gonna present yourself."

"Present myself?" Syn asked.

"Well, you're going to have drop all this. Ain't no one lasts at Zondon that long with that attitude. Not unless they plan to be killed. There's only four of us left, and I have a feeling she's growing pretty irritated with at least one of us. I suspect it'll be down to three pretty soon. So, all said, you need to pay attention to what you say and what you don't say. More importantly, how you do both."

Ripley looked at Syn, who stared wide-eyed at the horizon, taking in the Disc from her new vantage point. The settlements rose behind them, darkened from the fire, obscured by the blowing dust, and each seemingly empty. She knew that the Ecology occupied them, and behind the swooping rises, life flourished in colors that seemed impossible in this depleted landscape.

Ripley sighed. "Wow, you really don't get it, do you?"

Syn returned her gaze and lifted an eyebrow.

"Okay, well, let's just worry about that when we see the others for the first time. Until then, let's just go ahead and mosey on our way." She kicked the back of the bot with her heel. "Giddy-up!"

The bot came to life, roared up its loud engine, and sputtered as they moved forward, the three bots following behind the growling harvester.

27

THE SURPRISE BEYOND THE GATES

"It's no use going back to yesterday,
because I was a different person then."
—Lewis Carroll, *Alice in Wonderland*

The arid desert spread its edges to the iron and rust-dappled walls of Zondon Almighty. No path, no garden, no lawn transitioned. It was just desert and then wall, both equally inhospitable.

As they neared, the painted faces on the walls came into focus. Ghastly images pulled from horror films she had made Blip watch in years past: a maniacal clown, masks with red, torturous eyes, scarred faces, pale skin with deep white, blood-colored fangs. All were immense faces expressing pain and fear—the antithesis to the great faces of the Yoruban gods that looked down upon them from high up on the Jacob Lifts. The Orisha masks looked upward and onward; their slab colossal visages declaring hope and constant watch. The painted faces outside Zondon glared down with malice and shouted, *Stay away!*

When they arrived outside the main gates, Syn felt a wave a familiarity wash over her. She somehow knew this place and yet couldn't figure out how.

A crumbled stone wall stood outside. Large metal plates had been fastened with bolts to the tall swinging gates. The hinges of the gates were mounted to two great steel pillars. Across the front the word Zondon appeared—a strange assortment of letters. The Z and O were metal cutouts and the N, D, O, and N that followed had been painted on.

"And the tour ends, toasters!" Ripley said, waggling her knife at Huck, Arquella, and Bear. "Go on now. Get outta here. Shoo."

"We don't leave until the Expected releases us," Arquella announced.

Ripley furrowed her brow and pointed the knife edge at Syn. "That you?"

Syn did not respond.

Ripley shrugged. "Well, then. Tell your machines to leave."

Syn started to speak and then hesitated. She didn't want to be alone. She had only known the three for a short time, but they were faithful companions.

"Listen. I ain't tellin' you for my own good or yours. It's for theirs." She glanced back to the gates. "If they walk in that door, they're dead. She hates all toasters. Kills them on sight. She doesn't want anything related to the machines walking around. And she just doesn't discard them so you could fix 'em later. She chops them up and does some strange stuff with the bits." She pointed the knife back at the three. "They leave now, or they aren't safe. Hell, they may have already stayed too long."

Syn leapt from the back of the harvest bot and wrapped her arms first around Arquella and then Bear. "You two go straight on back to the Barlgharel. Tell him I made it." She looked up at Huck as he floated above unmoving—oddly stationary. "You keep an eye out for them."

Bear spoke up, "You promised to come back to us. Right?"

Syn patted his side and nodded. "Yes." But inside, she was less certain than ever. She had no idea what lay beyond the gates. "Please, go on now. I want you to be safe."

"I ain't movin' an inch more 'til I see the backs of them toasters disappear," Ripley grunted.

"Go, please. I need to know you're safe," Syn said, hugging them once more.

"Okay," Arquella said, "We'll see you." She and Bear turned around and began to move away. They paused twice and glanced back, and Syn waved.

Huck hesitated twice, and instead of flying along with, he them zipped straight into the air, far above them, until he disappeared in the dark rolling clouds above. She waved at him as well, hoping he would catch up with the other two now disappearing from view. She turned back to Ripley. "Let's go."

Zondon Almighty seemed to be a mocking term now that Syn had passed through its gates. The massive gate had swung open and then closed, manned by a single burly. From the dunes below, moving on the grumbling harvest bot, the massive outer walls seemed to shout *Stay out.* Syn could only imagine what had lay past. Pulled from films of the past, her mind conjured a bustling metropolis, the last remnants of those that survived.

That dream was juxtaposed against the imposing walls marked by disturbing imagery—painted faces wrenched from various horror films—those walls conveyed a threat of something far more wretched inside.

Neither imagination was true. There was no thriving metropolis packed shoulder-to-shoulder with crowds. Nor were there phantasmic monsters held in chains. Zondon was nearly empty. There were no inhabitants, save for the random burly here or there. No running children. No armed soldiers.

The walls were only a threat. There was hardly anything that would enforce this menace. The Ecology's fears would drain away if they knew what lay beyond the walls of Zondon.

Ripley had turned off the harvest bot they rode on just inside the gates and then marched with Syn through the narrow, open-aired corridors. A large open area, almost like a courtyard filled with junk, greeted them just on the other side of the gates.

As Syn passed under the concrete arch, the metal framed gates closed. Her stomach tightened and beads of sweat formed on her forehead. She lifted the crimson goggles from off her eyes and let them rest on top of her head.

Syn tried to relax, but she could feel the unease of anxiety building deep inside. Each step was closer to unknown threats and unknown choices. *Blip, where are you?* As she walked, she reached out to knead her fingers into Eku's thick fur, but winced when she realized Eku was not beside her. Eku was nowhere near. She pursed her lips close together to hold back the whimper trying to escape her throat.

Beyond the open courtyard, they marched through a narrow path just wide enough to be a road, although her Ogun would have trouble navigating it without tearing out the stone walls. Each side of that road was barricaded with metal and wood boards layered atop each other.

How had they built this place? Had the burlys thrown this city up? She had seen a few toys scattered about and pushed into corners—a small doll, a miniature harvest bot painted red, a stuffed tiger coming apart at the seams. There had been more life here. Perhaps this was a city that the colonists had put together. But why move here away from the settlements? What would be the purpose of banding together in the center? The walls suggested something more frightening on the outside at one point. A hub of safety converted into a symbol of power.

They passed through a paved road littered with debris and covered in a layer of sand, moving toward the center of Zondon. The path led to the two-spired central building that had to be the throne room of the Crimson Queen. The corridors remained veiled in shadow. Syn paused at the disconcerting darkness. The lights along the path were not responding to her—the world around her ignored her presence and the lack of response shook her..

Inside the crumbling building, in the shadows of Zondon Almighty, sat the throne. It had once been a plastic folding chair. Perhaps white, although the dirt was caked so thickly that its original color was lost to history. Felled timbers were arranged as a base, providing a rough dais lifting it up a meter. Two step stools served as the staircase to ascend the throne, although they were covered with rough, shag-carpeted rugs probably stolen from the settlements. The back leg of the throne had been swapped for a few sticks strapped to the chair with black twine and tape. Several boards were fastened to create a high back on the seat. It was a throne only in location. There was nothing of glory, nothing of splendor, about the conglomeration.

The throne mirrored the rest of the room. The central table was a collection of picnic benches and a few wooden dining room tables dragged from living rooms in the settlements. Stained cups and food-spotted plates littered the surface. Dark clouds rolled overhead, revealed by the holes in the spired roofs—only a few beams arched without decay in the vast ceiling above. Perhaps it didn't rain in this Disc. Maybe the clouds just stayed dark and never emptied themselves. Perhaps they existed to cast a gloom across every surface.

The large hall echoed the structures outside. They were unfilled except for half-forgotten pieces hobbled together to mimic what they were intended to be.

The twin-spired roofs were the hub from which Zondon Almighty spread out. Yet, the Crimson Queen that Syn had anticipated to be present in the hub was absent. The room was nearly empty except for a few burlys that stood in the corners. One sat in the dirt, picking through its toes. It sampled a few delights it discovered there, smacking its meaty lips with pleasure. Syn pulled her spear close and shivered at the sight of them. She despised the creatures. *What were they?* They were the size of men—Syn had never met any living but she had cleared away their skeletons on her Disc as she explored. But these were different than the photos of men she had viewed—their skin and flesh darkened as if burnt in fire and falling off—lifeless without glow. Their eyes glossed over. Their fingers fumbled at everything they touched, struggling through multiple attempts to pick up small objects such as a knife. Up close she could see that large metal pieces jutted out of their flesh as if they had been stabbed by the leftover remains of dead bots. Thick scar tissue stitched hastily at the edges of the protruding metal.

Ripley walked over to a chair and plopped down, sitting in a relaxed posture with her legs resting and crossed on the table. She slapped the seat next to her. "Come, take a load off."

"What are we doing here?" Syn cringed at the sound of her voice as it echoed against the tin walls. A breeze blew through and puffed up dust that obscured most of the room.

"Waiting." Ripley pulled an apple from a pocket and then flashed a much larger knife, slicing through the fruit. A trickle of juice rolled down the knife's blade and then onto her dark hand.

Syn felt her mouth water at the sight. She was hungrier than she had realized and her anticipation had made her hurry through her last meal. Her stomach rumbled, and she tried to muffle the sound by placing her hands on her belly.

"Hungry? Here. Have a slice." Ripley held up a thin slice stabbed on the end of her blade.

Syn eyed the slice and wondered where the girl had found the apple. She shifted her shoulders, feeling the weight in her backpack. It did not feel any lighter. In fact, it felt heavier than it had when they started. Syn realized she was still staring at the apple, then quickly averted her eyes to stare at her feet and then back to the entrance.

Ripley sighed. "You just aren't going to believe it, are you? I'm not your enemy. You and I have so much in common. I'm beginning to think we could be great friends." Ripley held the speared slice out to Syn.

Syn took the apple and held it gingerly in her fingers. She sniffed it and felt her mouth fill with saliva. She took a nibble, chewed and then popped the whole thing in. It tasted the same as the ones the Barl-gharel had given her. She narrowed her eyes at Ripley.

Ripley laughed and slapped the table, "See! I'm not going to kill you. I'm not the one you need to be scared of. I promise you. I'm not going to hurt you."

Syn started to ask who she should be afraid of, but before she could speak, a booming shout ripped through the silent room. "Who is this tiny piece of meat?"

Syn jumped to her feet and turned in the direction of the voice.

Something large and fast sped through the dark miasma. It slammed into her jaw and sent Syn tumbling backward to smash against the table. The poorly constructed board creaked, and two legs buckled underneath it. Her weight brought the full corner down to the ground. Everything was bright spots, and her head thrummed in pain. There was something wet dripping on her face. Blood. She knew it was her blood as it moved across her cheek. Syn pushed off the ground to bring herself back up.

The dark shadow planted its legs on both sides of her and loomed above. Again, the harsh voice barked, "I don't recognize her. Where'd you drag her from?"

Syn started up again, scooting back to put some distance between herself and the new person. The figure kicked Syn's chest and planted her foot hard onto her shoulder, pressing Syn into the ground.

"Get off of me!" Syn shouted struggling to wrench the foot off but failing to budge it.

"She's a pretty one, ain't she?" the shadow said.

Syn pushed at the boot and grunted, "Get off."

At the same time, the voice behind the boot grumbled, "Stupid girl."

Ripley finally spoke, "She's mine. Leave her alone."

"You don't get to claim her."

Ripley moved to confront Syn's assailant. In profile, Syn could not tell the difference between the two. They were the same height. Both the same shape in the pale light, their faces obscured in shadows. Now that she considered it, Syn realized their voices were quite similar as well.

"Get off!" Syn punched at the shadow's ankle. Then she turned toward Ripley, "Help me!"

From the other side of the room, a soft voice spoke, "Did you bring me a present?" At the sound of the new person, both the shadow and Ripley visibly stiffened.

The shadow, still glaring down at Syn, muttered, "Blast. She's awake."

The shadow slowly lifted her foot from Syn's chest. Syn didn't miss the opportunity. She spun and came to her feet, reaching for her spear. Panicked, Syn looked around for it, backing closer to Ripley and away from the shadow. The spear was nowhere near her—she was certain she had dropped it when the shadow hit her.

She stood nervously next to Ripley. She still did not trust Ripley, but she was less an uncertainty than the other one.

Both Ripley and the shadow ignored Syn and turned toward the makeshift throne. No, they were looking past the throne to a door that had opened on the left. A figure walked toward them, silhouetted by the red, flickering light pouring from the doorway.

Syn's mouth hung open for just a second before she let loose a shriek, formed more from surprise than fear.

This reaction was met by a roar of laughter from Ripley.

Syn ignored it and stared ahead in shock.

What had entered the room from the door, bathed in red light, was Syn herself.

There, standing a few feet from her, was Syn. The same dark eyes. The same dark skin. The same dark cloud of hair. No—that wasn't right. This Syn wore her hair in tiny, braided dreads that hung from her head and draped down her back. Each was wire thin and pulled straight. She stood the same height as Syn, but the long braids made her seem quite tall. She was draped in white with red ribbons hanging from her shoulders, like some cape. They flowed around her like feathers. Instead of the nine orange dots on Syn's face, this girl had two white squares perfectly painted under each eye and a square of white in the center of her bottom lip.

The word Syn was searching for was regal. Despite the voice, this girl stood like royalty. Her shoulders were square, her back straight. She stood motionless and wore an expression of slight amusement. Or irritation. The turn at the corner of the girl's mouth made it uncertain.

The Queen. This had to be the Crimson Queen. She was splendid and frightening through and through.

"Is she your guest, Kerwen?" the Crimson Queen spoke.

Syn found herself mesmerized by the familiarity of facial movements. Syn had played and quoted lines from movies in front of mirrors. She knew each twitch and muscle movement of her own face, and the girl speaking now could have stepped out from a mirror herself. Everything about her was an identical duplication of Syn. Yet, something was absent. Despite the hint of amusement on the Crimson Queen's lips, her eyes were thin and threatening.

"Yes, she is. I found her out amongst the dunes south of the bots' new encampment in the settlements. She had been fightin' one of the thudders. Walked right into it." It was Ripley who spoke. The Queen had called her Kerwen. *Was her name Ripley or Kerwen?* Syn also noticed that Ripley hadn't mentioned anything about Huck, Bear, or Arquella.

Ripley then lifted her hand to the side of her face and loosened the mask covering her nose and mouth. The dirty black cloth fell from her face and revealed her features for the first time—another copy of Syn's own face. There were three of her. Ripley looked at Syn and grinned, gave a tiny laugh and mouthed, "Surprise."

Syn spun, taking a few steps back from all of them. "Who... What's..." Her words choked in her throat. *This has to be a nightmare.*

The shadowed girl stepped forward and fell into the dull light. She was far thicker than the others—all muscle. Pure brute and raw strength. Yet, in the light, Syn saw the resemblance again. The third one looked just like Syn too. Just like the others. Her head was shaved to a short stubble. Her face was scribbled with several tattoos or words and phrases in a language Syn didn't recognize. Or perhaps she did—maybe it was something she had seen way in the back of some instructional video from Earth.

The larger copy stepped forward. Her skin was dirty, and her expression determined.

The muscled girl jumped at Syn, stopping a few inches from Syn's face and shouted, "Boo!"

Syn jumped back, spied a ceramic cup on the table, and through instinct, chucked it hard at the larger one. The girl fell back but managed to catch the cup just before it smacked her forehead. She crushed it in her hand, then roared and charged at Syn.

Ripley grasped the other on both her arms, pulling her back to stand with the other two copies of Syn and yelled, "Taji! Stop!"

The lumbering, large girl Syn now knew as Taji took a step back and clenched her fists. She glanced over through narrow eyes at the soft-voiced copy. "Neci?" she asked, teeth gritted and her voice like a soft rumble.

The regal Neci, the one Syn was certain was the Crimson Queen, took one more step forward. Syn could never walk that gracefully. Neci was like a cat. Like a tiger. She purred, "She's scared. This is all a big surprise for her." She moved closed to Syn and whispered, "It's okay. You're safe here." She put a hand near Syn's cheek.

Syn took a step back, avoiding the touch.

Ripley said, "Syn, meet Neci and Taji."

Syn finally managed a sentence, "Who are you? Why do you…"

Neci glided the back of her hand against Syn's grimy hair. "You're filthy. Are you thirsty? Hungry?"

Again, without wanting it to, Syn's stomach rumbled at the thought of food. The apple had done nothing to satisfy her. Yet, Syn shook her head no.

"A bit untruthful, eh?" Neci said. She moved her fingers to Syn's cheek and touched her with a soft graze. An electric sensation ran through Syn. She had never touched another living human. Not like this—not where they weren't trying to kill her. Not someone so human. The burlys, if they had ever been human, didn't count. No. Their murderous grabbing was nothing to this. This was kindness and something more. As if someone had managed to flood under her skin and wrapped their warmth into some magic that poured through Syn like hot water. She staggered, drunk on the sensation.

And then she froze. The touch had been as unnerving as it was wonderful.

Neci stared deep into her eyes. "Where have you been?"

Syn started to talk, "I…I came from…" But something told her to not talk. Who knows what they would do if she started talking? *What did they know? What did they not know? Why had they taken Blip?* Syn wanted more answers before she gave any.

Syn shook her head. "No." She took a step forward. "I want answers."

"I think what you really want is a shower and a glass of water and a large dinner and possibly a nice bed. Would that be more correct? You don't seem at all to be in the condition to grasp what's happening here, even if we did tell you everything." Neci turned and started toward the back of the room. The two burlys there stood up straight and separated as if to flank her. "Kerwen, do we have a room available?"

Ripley said, "Well, I think there's one out in Stralia, near the old reptile dens that's…"

A tiny, demure voice, spoke from the darkness. A girl's voice—new and different. A fourth one. "There's a room next to me in the big cats' caves. I keep it clean. She can stay there." From the hallway to her right, through the entrance Syn had used, a slim version of the others, a copy just like the other three, stepped forward. Dressed in a pale, yellow dress with several large, unraveled holes, a thin girl stood, her shoulders slumped, her eyes to the ground. Of the three others, she resembled Syn the most. Her hair was hung like Syn's—loose, long, unkempt, and floating around like a cloud.

Taji chuckled, "We didn't bring you home a dolly to play with, Pigeon."

The little girl winced at this but kept her eyes down.

Neci paused before exiting. "Promise to be nice to this one, Pigeon?"

There was another wince at the name, but the girl named Pigeon muttered, "I promise."

Neci nodded. "You too, Taji."

The big girl only grunted an affirmation.

Neci continued, "The room next to Pigeon. Kerwen, show her the way. Draw her a bath. Dinner will be in three hours. And post a golem outside."

Riply said, "Can do."

Golem? Syn wondered. The burlys. They had called them golems.

Syn remembered the word from some movie or story—stone giants brought to life. No mind. No soul.

Taji had already turned and was walking out the other way, toward the street entrance. Neci shouted, "And Taji?"

The muscled copy stopped and shut her eyes.

Neci didn't wait for a response, "Fix the table before dinner." With that, she exited, the two burlys—two golem—falling in her wake.

The room grew numb. No one spoke. Syn was not sure anyone breathed.

After a long, cold minute, Ripley smiled. "Well, that was a pleasant homecoming, wasn't it?"

Taji slammed her fist against a pillar along the door frame. It shook. She grunted and stomped out of the room to the outside.

"That one's just a bit aggressive. Bit of an anger problem. It's all good. She'll soon be treating you like just another sister."

"Sister?" Syn said.

Ripley motioned. "Come on. Let's get you cleaned up. I think I have some clothes that'll fit." She laughed at this. "Oh, and call me Kerwen."

Syn followed and looked around for the other one, the thin girl named Pigeon. She was nowhere to be seen. She had faded completely away, just like she had entered.

As she was ushered away, Syn glanced back, scanning the concrete floor for her spear. But it was gone. Lost in some dark shadow.

A NICE, NEW WORD

"Maturity is a series of shattered illusions."
—Levar Burton

As she followed Kerwen out of the spires, small parts of what Zondon had been before revealed themselves. The first was the large stone wall with the letters J, U, N, G, and L on it. Syn thought it was to spell "Jungle", but the E had gone missing. Underneath this, at eye-level, was a wooden sign whose original letters had faded to almost be unreadable. With effort, Syn made sense of them. *ANIMALS. CHILDRENS PLAYGROUND. NATURE CENTER.* With a large arrow pointing to the left.

They passed a fenced-in area with a large tree structure that was obviously artificial. Different articles of clothing draped across the branches. Shirts, jeans, socks. The four girls had been using this as a place to dry clothes.

Beyond that, they came to a false stone structure with three cave entrances carved into the outside. Syn now knew she had been here before. The painted sign above the caves confirmed her suspicion. It read BIG CATS. And then below it, read LIONS AND TIGERS.

Syn blurted the realization out, "This is the Zoo." Or at least it had been this Disc's Zoo. So much had been boarded over and fencing had been torn down and moved to other places. It was dark, and there was no sound of the animals here.

She now understood why the paths didn't light up. The Zoo on her side, in her world, didn't respond to her presence either. The thought put her at ease as understood the reason now. *No,* she reminded herself, *I can't think of it like that. My world is this world. We're in one world. Both Discs.* She imagined that this must be what Lucy had felt like going through the wardrobe. *Or Eve leaving Eden into Nod. Something dark and terrible waiting. Something with a crown and fangs.*

Kerwen tapped the wall. "It surely was. And fortunately for us. Kept us from going hungry for a long time."

Syn shuddered at Kerwen's meaning. They had eaten the animals.

Kerwen pointed to a dark entrance with the word TIGER over it. "That's yours. The runt lives right next door." She pointed to the entrance with LION painted above. "See you at dinner. Know how to make your way back?"

Syn glanced down the path behind and nodded.

"Good." Kerwen walked away but looked back over her shoulder. "Don't try leaving just yet. You won't get out. But don't be late. She hates when people are late."

Syn nodded affirmation and then entered the grotto, pushing against a lightweight door that had been hung haphazardly just inside the faux-cave's entrance.

She had expected to find bales of straw and bones and a mess. Instead, it resembled an actual room. Whoever had lived here before had gone to great work to make it feel normal. The room was clean. It wasn't the scrubbed hominess of Arquella's house, but it was far nicer than Syn had expected since arriving at Zondon Almighty. The city was so rundown, so forgotten, and far opposite of the bots' perception of the place, that she had expected to find a floor mat in a dirt room. Surprisingly, there were boards below her feet.

The room was not crafted with flat walls. This was meant to feel like a cave where a wild animal would feel comfortable. A narrow entrance opened into the vast space that served as the bedroom. Syn followed a passage near the rear of the space to discover a makeshift bathroom. Against the far wall, oddly out of place, stood a white porcelain bathtub. Above it was an overhead pipe sliced open and a single nozzle that turned the water on when pulled down. A bucket with a hole in the bottom placed under another faucet served as a sink. It wasn't great, but it would work.

She contemplated taking a nap but eyed the shower head. *Oh, to be clean.*

The water was so hot it turned to steam as it splashed against the porcelain tub. This bathtub had been dragged from somewhere else. Perhaps one of the upper settlements. It was ornate, out of place, and Syn loved it.

***

The bed was a set of two mattresses stacked one atop another. She ran her hand over the comforter. It was soft. She felt tired suddenly. Perhaps a short nap before dinner.

She fell forward onto the bed and bounced with a slight giggle. She laid naked on top of the bed and felt herself melt into the bedding.

She probably didn't have time for a nap, she thought. How long had she been in the shower? More than just a few minutes. It had taken her awhile to just get undressed after Kerwen had walked her over. Before crawling in the bathtub, Syn had checked every wall. She hadn't wanted surprises. The main room had a roof, and she had discovered a tiny lamp in the corner, which, when she had turned it on, illuminated everything in an orange glow. After searching every possible place, for what she couldn't determine, Syn had returned to the bathroom and the filling bathtub, taken her grubby clothes off and stepped into the hot water. It hit her skin, and she had unwound. Not just a sense of relaxation, but the release of fear and panic and other emotions she was still struggling to name. She had cried and let the water wash her tears down the drain. They had lasted only a few minutes, and she had found herself energized as she stood there. She had glanced down to see a swirl of dirt and blood whirl around the hole in the tub. Blood. Her blood. The burly's blood. The dust from the walk in the desert. The grease from fixing the line of bots. And the remaining grime was a collection of so many different things she had encountered

Maybe a half hour under the water. Maybe longer.

It didn't matter. She was clean, and she floated on the bed.

Kerwen's voice came up from memory. *Sisters*. It was a word that she had never thought would have meaning for her. She wasn't sure exactly what it meant now. But there was a weight to it that she had never known. She'd had friends—well, she had *a* friend. Blip. She'd had pets. And now the bots of the Ecology—whatever they were to her, she was not certain.

But…*Sisters*.

She tried the word out, muttering softly, "Sisters."

From the door, the tiny voice of Pigeon spoke. "Don't believe them."

Syn sat up and pulled the loose comforter over her naked body. Pigeon stood in the closed room. Syn hadn't heard the door open. She hadn't heard it close. She hadn't heard the girl enter or breathe or step or anything.

"What are you doing in here?" Syn asked.

Pigeon put her hand on the door's lock and flipped it open. "I just thought you should know." She began to step out.

Syn leaped from the bed and slammed the door shut, blocking the thin girl's exit. "Know what?"

Pigeon showed no fear and no worry. "Dinner is being brought out. You're expected."

"Is that what you came to tell me?"

Pigeon put her hand on the door knob. "Please, I must return."

"Who are you?" Syn glanced at her own hand and at the hand of girl across from her. "Why do you look like me?"

Pigeon shook her head. "It's not my place. Please." Her eyebrows narrowed, and she bit her lower lip. Worry. The girl wasn't frightened of Syn. But she was afraid of the others. Neci, perhaps. Taji, likely.

Pigeon opened the door and stepped through.

Syn mumbled, "I'll be right there."

Pigeon looked back and mouthed, "Don't trust them," before shutting the door.

Syn stood there alone, still dripping. A shiver ran through her, and she wasn't sure if it was the cold air and her damp body or the creepy little copy of herself.

Perhaps both.

2 9

THE QUEEN OF OLORUN

"But I don't want to go among mad people," Alice remarked.
"Oh, you can't help that," said the Cat: "We're all mad here. I'm mad.
You're mad."
"How do you know I'm mad?" said Alice.
"You must be," said the Cat, "or you wouldn't have come here."
—Lewis Carroll, *Alice in Wonderland*

Syn's expectation for family dinners were formed from movies. The father would sit at one end. The mother at the other. The dog sniffed between the children's feet in hopes that one would start feeding him under the table. The kids would find subtle ways to jab at each other. What started as a still, awkward conversation would slowly grow to bickering and then an outright fight. Ultimately, one of them would stalk off from the dinner table. Usually, the teenager fulfilled this role, while the rest of the family stayed quiet until they heard the conclusive slamming of the bedroom door. Oh, there were other versions. In some, there would be shenanigans. The dinner wouldn't be fully cooked. In one comedy, the turkey had come back to life and flapped around the kitchen, scattering feathers everywhere. In the more serious ones, there would be undertones of murder and rage. Perhaps someone would hint that they were going to brutally kill the other while they slept. Or maybe they'd suggest that they had deep levels of resentment for something that had happened far in the past and that only part of the family knew. Whatever the scenario, the dinner table was always the nexus of drama in the films.

Even though she had studied this scene countless times in movies while sitting in the darkened theater, Syn had never expected to actually experience a family dinner and had no clue how to act.

"No! That's part of your problem. Not mine. I didn't touch the cat at all when it snuck in the room." Taji leaned back and laughed.

"What was the name of that cat?" Neci asked, picking through the charred meat in front of her.

The food wasn't spectacular, but it was good and warm. The plates were clean. This wasn't the spread Syn had seen in the movies. There was some type of meat that had been charred on the outside. There were some leaves chopped up as a vegetable. Were the round things cookies? Or crackers? She couldn't tell from sight alone.

It didn't matter. It was a dinner. With *sisters*.

Kerwen chewed and, between gulps of water, answered, "Cosmos?"

Pigeon whispered, "That was the gray one."

"Oh, ya! That was the one you made me bury cause you thought it was dead!" Kerwen said.

Neci shook her head. "It looked dead."

"Up until the part I started putting dirt on it. Woke up fast and scared me to death."

"What was the name of the one that kept sneaking back in?" Neci said. She directed her question at Kerwen and Taji but ended it with a slight nod toward Pigeon.

Without any response, Pigeon pushed her chair back, picked up the jug of water and walked over to Neci. She took the other girl's cup, filled it, then walked back and sat back down.

As this happened, Kerwen waved her fork in the air. "Docile. We had named that thing Docile!"

Neci smiled. "Yes. That was it. Docile."

Pigeon picked up her fork and speared a piece of meat. "It was a sweet cat."

"It had snuck its way in and pretended to be part of the rest of the cats," Neci explained, "I'm still not sure how long it had been living here."

"At least a week," Kerwen took a gulp of water.

"Pretending to be normal. Pretending to be something it wasn't." Neci finished the last bit and leaned back in the chair. She smiled at Syn and then glanced at Syn's plate. "You seem to not be hungry."

Syn looked at the meat in front of her. She was hungry. She was aching of hunger. But she was distracted by the moment. Real people. Real conversations. "I'm hungry. I just..."

"Oh. There's no insistence. You are free to eat or not," Neci twirled her fork in the air, then stabbed it in Syn's direction. "You seem a little shy."

Syn stammered, "I just..."

"You just want an explanation for all this," Neci waved around her. "For each of us?" She pointed her fork at each of the others around the table.

Syn nodded. "Yes."

"Any specific question you'd like to start with?" Neci asked.

Syn fought with what to say. So many questions. *Why do you all look like me? Where did you come from? How long have you been living like this? Were there others? Where are your companion bots? Where is Blip?*

Neci sighed, "Choose one."

"Why do you look like me?" Syn blurted out.

Neci laughed, and Taji slapped the table. Taji barked, "You look like us. Don't confuse the order of things." She jammed her dinner knife in Syn's direction. "Don't forget that. Real important."

"Well?" Syn asked.

"What do you remember, Syn?" Neci asked.

Syn held her hands out, palms up, gesturing at the others all together. "I need answers. Please. Can you explain this?"

Kerwen leaned over and placed her hand on Syn's shoulder. "She's not trying to pry information out of you."

"I'm trying to figure out what I need to explain and how much you've pieced together on your own. But I'll start at the beginning." Neci leaned in toward Syn, "My first memory was throwing up when the cover to the crèche bay opened up. The lights and the sound. Just a bit too much."

"I puked too," Kerwen said and Taji nodded in agreement. A mutual experience.

"The crèche? You woke up in the crèche?" Syn asked. Her eyes were wide, and she was leaning forward. They had described a hidden part of her life. Of the ship. She remembered waking up alone. There had been no one in the white room at all. No one there when she left. "Before me? How long have you been here?"

Pigeon spoke, "In our own crèches."

Neci gave her a sharp look, and Pigeon sat back in her chair, falling into shadow.

Above them, the clouds rumbled. Each of them looked up. There was no rain, yet, but a timer had just been set for their conversation.

"Does it rain here?" Syn asked.

Kerwen gave the first laugh and the others followed. "Does it rain? Hell, yes, it rains."

Neci leaned in, "You said 'here.' As opposed to where?"

Syn felt her palms sweat. "I'm just new here. I…"

"No. That was a comparison. When you've once said a thing, that fixes it, and you must take the consequences. Here versus there. So where is there?" Neci asked.

Syn bristled. She pushed her chair back. If she was to run, she didn't want her feet under the table.

At the other end, the lumbering Taji noticed and shifted to spring after Syn if she fled.

Syn stammered. "I woke up in a crèche. I watched the videos. Did you watch the videos?"

Kerwen, eager to calm the moment, said, "The dolt Captain Pote."

Syn bristled at that. She had loved Captain Pote and his family. She could remember racing down to the Disc hoping to meet him and the disappointment that rushed in after. But this wasn't the time for offense. "Yes. Captain Pote. They showed rain on Earth."

"Earth's a myth," Pigeon said.

Syn turned to the girl. "No it isn't."

"Back to the truth. Where is there?" Neci asked, her voice a bit lower now.

"I meant Earth. Here versus Earth."

Neci raised her eyebrows. "Really?"

Syn gave a slight nod.

Seeming to accept that answer, Neci turned the question. "Then where have you been?"

"The needle. I came from the needle," Syn said, "Is that how you got here?"

Neci stayed silent.

Kerwen glanced at the Crimson Queen. "Give her some more answers."

Neci sat back and looked between Kerwen and Syn. She shot a look over at Taji. After a long, quiet moment, she said, "Yes. We came from the needle. All of us came down."

"The four of you?" Syn asked.

"Forty-one," Neci said.

Syn felt her world disappear. Forty-one? She grew a bit dizzy with the information. "Forty-one? And they're all..." She motioned between them, palms up, hands in a slow swirl.

Neci nodded. "Like us. Just like each of us. I know the word for twins. Triplets. Quadruplets."

Taji said, "Quintuplets."

"What's the word for forty-two copies of the same person?" Neci said.

"Forty-two?" Syn asked and then realized they were counting her in that number. Syn answered, "I don't know."

Neci smiled, "Eve. The word is Eve."

"Like in the Garden? Adam?" Syn acted ignorant, but she had heard the word before. In Captain Pote's initial videos. She thought it was a term of endearment. She hadn't realized it had a deeper meaning.

"In a way. What do you know of that story?"

"There was a snake," Syn said.

Pigeon snorted, "There's always a snake."

Syn continued, "God was angry. They had sinned."

Neci shook her head. "Why were they there?"

"In the Garden?"

"In the Garden."

Syn thought. "They were to take care of it, I think. It doesn't really say. It's just nonsense."

"You may call it nonsense if you like, but it's quite informed nonsense," Neci smiled and ran her hand across her abdomen, resting it below her navel. "They were to take care of the Garden. Just like what we were to do. But we never made it to the Garden. Instead, God decided to dump us into Hell. How do you think the story would've turned out after that? What if instead of kicking them out of the Garden he had sent them to Hell?" Neci stood. She snapped her fingers and one of the burlys behind her turned and left the room. She continued, "I wonder if we would think of Hell as Hell. Maybe it would've been a different place with Eve on the throne." She walked around the table and picked up an apple then took a small bite. A bit of juice ran down her chin. "We're in Hell, Syn. And we took over."

Syn shook her head. "I'm not getting it…"

Kerwen sighed. "We are the Eves, Syn. Each of us. We were created to explore another world. Cast out of Earth. Shot into the void. You know what Olorun is?"

Syn felt a bit of stress drain from her tight muscles. She nodded. "I know about Olorun. The ship. We're on Olorun." Without thinking about it, she leaned forward and picked a piece of meat up and chewed.

Kerwen gave a look at Neci that said, *See, I knew she was hungry.*

Neci picked up a chair that was off to the side, near a pole, and planted it next to Taji. She had moved to the other side of the table but had moved much closer to Syn who sat near to Kerwen. "Have you ever talked to Olorun?"

Syn was about to mention that Blip had but she hadn't. That wouldn't work. Instead, she said, "No. I didn't know he could talk."

Neci stared at her and then whispered, "Liar."

Taji muttered, "She. The bitch above is a she."

A chill went through Syn. "I've never talked to Olorun. I promise."

Kerwen sighed. "Olorun is on its way to another planet. But the wonderful people who had inhabited this ship…" A look went between Taji and Kerwen and then both glanced at Neci. Only Pigeon kept her eyes forward. Syn thought she saw a brief tinge of disgust roll through Pigeon's features, but if it had, it was fleeting and gone now. Kerwen continued, "They went a bit crazy."

Taji spoke up, "They killed each other. And burnt the place down."

Neci picked up a piece of meat from Taji's plate. "This here is a gift, Syn. Do you know when the last time we had meat was?"

Pigeon twitched and said, "There were five of us before that."

Neci ignored her and continued, "The idiots torched this place and then managed to wake us up. It was tough at first. The brutes who remained," she nodded at the burlys, "were numerous and took many of our sisters. Disease. Starvation. One by one, they died. We are all that's left of that forty-one. Until you came along." She stood back up and picked up her chair from a notch on its back and moved it toward the far side of Syn, placing Syn between Kerwen and Neci. Neci continued, "Now I wonder if there are more of our sisters up there. In the needle. In other parts of the ship."

Syn said, "Have you looked for them?"

Neci leaned in. "We looked real hard. Every room we could get into. We scoured this ship. We've scoured the Disc. We dug through the farmlands, picking through the burnt crops, for whatever was left. What's interesting is that in all of our searches, we never saw you. So where were you hiding?"

Syn glanced up, toward the needle, toward the sunstrips.

"Holding to that story, eh?" Neci said. The burly that had exited returned to the room carrying a sack over his shoulder.

"I woke up. I was in the white room a very long time." That part was true. It was just not as long as she had hoped they would assume. She had to account for her age, for the years on the other Disc. "Then one day the door opened." She found a lie and wrapped it around a truth. "I heard a big explosion and went looking for what happened. The door opened, and I came down here."

Kerwen and Taji shared a glance between each other.

The burly placed the sack on the table in front of Neci and then stepped back to its post. Neci said, "You woke up. You came down here. You were caught by the Ecology. And you helped them, and then they pointed you here. You traveled over the Desert with three machines, stepped right into a thudder trap. Then sweet ol' Kerwen found you and rescued you. Is that the whole thing? Is that everything?"

Across the table, Pigeon stiffened. Taji leaned forward.

Neci continued, "Did I leave anything out?"

Syn shook her head.

Neci placed a hand on the dirty, brown bag on the table. She grabbed it on both sides and strained to lift it up, dropping it from a couple inches up. The entire table rattled as the weight of the sack smacked down. Syn's cup rattled and tottered before falling and spilling water. Neci turned the bag over and pulled it off of its heavy contents. Out rolled the white, porcelain-pure body of Blip.

Syn jumped and put her hands out to grab the teetering, silent Blip. Taji leaned forward and snagged the bot and rolled him back, out of Syn's reach. Kerwen stood up and put her hands on Syn's shoulders, pushing her back to her chair. Syn settled back, but Kerwen didn't let go. She stood over Syn like a sentry.

Neci spoke, "So, you know this companion? Seems like you left something out of your story."

Syn gritted her teeth and growled, "What have you done to him?"

Kerwen put pressure on Syn's shoulders. Neci put her hands up in the air, a motion that declared she was blameless. "We did nothing. Do you mean because he's turned off?"

Syn's voice grew fiercer, more determined. "Yes!"

Neci rolled her eyes, "Oh, that. Nope. He switched to that mode when we found him." She reached over and spun him around so she could look into his blank face. "Silent. No matter what we do, he won't wake up. They tend to do that when separated from their sister. I was hoping he'd spring to life when you were brought near...but it appears as if that's not happening."

"What have you done to him?"

Neci stood up and slammed her hand hard against the table, "Tell me the truth! Where have you been all this time? Where were you at when we were dying in Hell?"

Syn narrowed her eyes, glaring at the long-haired copy of herself, but she didn't talk.

"You didn't just wake up. Look at you. You're our age."

Syn's eyes widened.

"Oh," Neci continued, "Didn't think I had thought about that? Think I wouldn't catch that? We all start young, and we grow up. You woke up when we did. Seven years ago. You've been awake for seven years. Seven years in the white room? Bullshit. And look at you. Look at your skin."

Syn looked down at her bare arms and then at those of Kerwen by her head. Kerwen's were thinner than Syn's. They were also covered in scars and bruises. Taji's were worse. Neci, herself, despite her poise and self-control, was still battered and sliced and burned.

Neci held up her arms, so Syn could get a better look. A long scar ran from just mid-forearm down past her elbow toward her armpit. "That one was given to me by one of our sisters. She's dead now. But you...you look like an angel." She moved over to Syn and grabbed Syn's wrist. Syn yanked it back, but Taji moved around to assist. Together, they pulled Syn's right arm out and held it down on the table. Neci put her own arm next to Syn. The knuckles were the same. They even had the same moles, the same blemishes. But Neci was right. Syn's arms looked bare. They were nearly absent of scars. There were a few, but only a few. Neci's arms looked like those of a veteran. "What a soft life you've had."

With that, Neci spun and grabbed Syn by her jaw and drew close in. Her breath was hot in Syn's face. Neci hissed, "We have lived in Hell. God sent us to Hell, and this is it. And somehow, you have managed to stay safe and clean and..." She pinched a piece of skin on Syn's abdomen. "And fat."

She pulled back and pointed at Blip. "And that thing is never turning back on again. I know those things are her servants." She was spitting as she spoke. Every word came out with a rasp. "They aren't our friends. They are our guards. They watched our every action. They pretended to be our friends, and they were feeding her the entire time. I know it's true. Olorun told me that much. The Great Old Woman belched out that much before she locked us in here. But we blinded and deafened her by killing those bastards. She has no eyes, no ears, and no voice inside Hell."

Syn stared aghast. Like Blip, Neci was referring to Olorun as a real person. And she had talked to the ship. Called it a "she" just like Blip had. *Was she telling the truth?* Syn stammered, her eyes locked on Blip. "You killed your companions?"

Then as if a switch had been turned off, the anger drained from Neci, and she stood there poised. The fury behind her eyes vanished. She spoke clear and confident. "Each of them. They were never ours. They were always hers. Pretenders. Just like you. Like it."

Syn sat with Taji still holding her right wrist and Kerwen pressing her thumbs into Syn's shoulders. She was stuck between them. Across the table, Pigeon had disappeared. In the chaos, the little girl had left. Syn was jealous. Why had Syn come here? Why had she trusted Kerwen? Why had she trusted Blip? Syn started to cry. "I'm not...I promise..."

"Then where have you been?"

Syn's mind raced. She did not want to tell them about her Disc. Something in her did not want anyone else in her world. She wanted these girls to like her, to accept her, but she could not trust them—not with the truth and not with her world. So she lied. "I've been with the Ecology!"

Kerwen's grip lessened and Taji relaxed her hold, but they still stayed where they were at, pinning her down.

Neci turned and raised an eyebrow.

Syn scrambled for the rest of the lie. "I lied! I lied!" Perhaps telling some of the truth might work. "I lied and said I just came down because I know how much you hate the Ecology. Rip...Kerwen told me. I've been with them. They've been nice to me. They've fed me. They've kept me safe. I've been with them." *If they are just like me, will they know if I lie? No! Just tell the truth!* Another lie wrapped around a truth.

Neci leaned over and pulled Kerwen's hand off of Syn's wrist. "This whole time?"

"They've kept me up in the settlements. Hidden away. I've been fixing them. They'd bring me food, and I'd fix them, and they'd keep me safe." *All true. All true.*

Above them, the clouds thundered again, and drops of rain began to pour down.

"Go to your rooms. No one leaves Zondon until I say so. For any reason." Neci turned and walked toward the exit. "And don't be late for breakfast"

Taji shouted after, her voice indignant, "*You* believe that story?

Neci said, almost out of the room, not looking back, "I believe... that she believes that story."

3 0

THE FIRST MURDER

"I have love in me the likes of which you can scarcely imagine and rage the likes of which you would not believe. If I cannot satisfy the one, I will indulge the other."
—Mary Shelley, *Frankenstein*

The patter of rain draped over her, lulling her into sleep. She was tired. Her muscles ached. There was throbbing in her wrists where she had been held down by the Sisters. The bed was soft. The comforter warm. The room was quiet except for the rain and that only added weight upon her, pushing her into the dark of sleep.

She didn't want to sleep. She didn't want to close her eyes. Around her, beasts roamed. Wolves that looked like her. Wolves with her eyes and lips.

But they aren't me, she told herself.

Their faces floated through the darkness of her room. There was a hunger to Neci. Anger in Taji. Something reluctant and broken in Kerwen. They were spin-offs of her own soul. She had felt that same desire that consumed Neci. She had lived in fear that it would all be taken away. Wasn't that hunger the one that had led her to this Disc? The hunger for more than she had?

If she was an Eve, she was the most Eve of all of them. Born in the Garden and tempted by the unknown that she could not possess. Everything at her fingertips in abundance, and yet, the possibility of something else on the other side of the gate had lured her. There had not been a snake though, no whispering seducer. It had just been her own need for someone else. She'd pursued her white rabbit.

And now she was possessed in equal measures by the anger of Taji and the fear of Kerwen. She saw in their eyes what she felt, only her emotion was magnified in them as if the volume had been turned up. As if those emotions were all that was animating them.

Taji seemed unable to feel anything but anger. The source of her survival? Had she powered through everything else with rage and clung to it now in fear that it might seep away or be stolen? Was rage comforting? Yes, it was. Syn knew deep in her heart that she had been angry at Blip and at Captain Pote and at the creators of the ship or the colonists over the years. In those moments, flouncing through Aja, anger was welcome. It was warm and compelling.

She understood Pigeon too. Fearful and sad. That fear was a shadow that she had never escaped and even now, now as Syn drifted into the depths of sleep, that fear took a new form. She wasn't scared of being alone. She was scared that these were the only companions she'd ever have. All she was had been contracted to that single room, to her own skin. She had never realized it before, but in her Disc, in her world, there were no borders to who she was. She felt she was the Disc. She ran and let herself be as big as it wanted. All was hers, and she was everything.

But these new others reminded her that there were borders. Meeting the Sisters had communicated to her, *you may go this far, but only this far.* She was smaller than she had ever been.

Had she shrunk even as she lay there? She dreamt of herself as a tiny figure lying on a vast ocean. She became smaller and smaller until she was about to disappear completely. As she dropped smaller, she found it hard to breathe. She took a breath and could not. The air was blocked. Her mouth was open, but she couldn't breathe. She clawed at the air around her and found herself swimming up from the great ocean to some dark surface above her. Could she reach it? She had to. She was desperate for air. A meter away... With a rush, she swam toward the surface and broke through.

She wasn't swimming. She wasn't a small figure forever shrinking. She was Syn, and she was lying in a bed in Zondon Almighty.

And she still couldn't breathe. She opened her eyes. In front of her, she looked into her own eyes. Her own gaunt face.

No. Not her face. Pigeon. Pigeon was above her, straddling her and pinning her down with the girl's hand across Syn's mouth. Syn wasn't suffocating. She could still breathe through her nose. She turned and worked to put a foot against Pigeon and move her off.

The girl leaned forward and whispered with force, "Quiet. Shhh."

Syn wanted her off and pushed against the girl's lithe frame, but Pigeon had the leverage and kept shifting against Syn's struggles. Again, Pigeon said, "Please, be quiet. I'm not going to hurt you." Her voice was not much more than just a slight breath. But in the emptiness of the room, the girl's words sounded crisp and clear.

There was no anger in Pigeon's eyes and that was enough to move Syn to take a risk. She stopped struggling. Pigeon pulled up, and the weight on Syn relaxed, although the girl's hand stayed planted on Syn's mouth.

"If I take my hand away, you must promise to not talk. I'm going to do all the talking for now. Do you understand? Nod if yes."

Syn understood. The burlys would hear. Pigeon was doing something she didn't want the others to know about. Syn nodded. Pigeon lifted her hand up and put a finger to her lips. She glanced back over her shoulder to make sure that no one else was in the room.

Syn moved her head and looked at the door too. It was shut tight. There was nothing disturbed at all. The girl had done it again. She could enter and leave without anyone noticing. A gift. An illusion. Or maybe a hidden path.

Pigeon pulled the comforter back and crawled into the bed next to Syn. She grabbed the edge of the large, thick blanket and pulled it over their heads.

Syn could no longer see the other girl. Under the comforter, she could see nothing. The sound of the rain was muffled but still a constant.

She could feel warm breath as the girl inched closer, her lips a few inches from Syn. "They can't hear us if we whisper."

"Why are you doing this?" Syn whispered.

"You need to know about them," Pigeon said, "They're worse than you imagine. You must get away if you have the chance."

"Why don't you leave then? If they're so terrible, run away!" Syn pleaded, "You can get in and out of here without anyone knowing."

"No. Rooms are one thing. Shadows are one thing. Agayu is something else."

"Agayu?" Syn wasn't sure what she talking about.

"The Desert. I named it Agayu. Neci hates the name, but it is true. She called it Hell to fit her new world. But it does not respect that name. Agayu is angry. We never go out and in without a loss. She always demands a sacrifice. How you made it here is a mystery."

"It's sand."

"It's the dust of the thousand dead."

Syn grimaced at the image, and her memory of never being alone as they walked across the desert. Always a sense that someone was watching. "And their souls."

She could feel Pigeon nodding in agreement.

Syn continued, "Are you scared?"

Pigeon didn't answer immediately. After a moment, she said, "Not of Neci."

"Then what?"

"You should be scared of Neci."

"Pigeon, please—"

"That's not my name."

"I'm..." Syn started.

Pigeon said, "My name is Avia."

"Avia," Syn tried the name.

"But you must call me Pigeon."

"But now? When they're not here?"

"No. You must not get used to that name. It is mine, but they don't let me use it. I haven't used it since we were thirty."

"Thirty?"

"Time is of no matter here. I have stopped counting years. Instead, I count by the Sisters remaining. They gave me the name Pigeon when there were thirty of us only."

"How did you all die? I don't understand. I—I survived," Syn said.

"Neci did not lie."

"The burlys?"

"The lack of food. We awoke, and the world was in Madness. We left our individual crèches and discovered each other. We were all beautiful then. All of us in our white clothes, our hair beautifully combed and short. We assembled in the Collecting Room at the top of the Jacobs, in the needle. Even then, amidst the greetings and smiles and hugs, something felt wrong."

Syn felt a stab of jealousy. They had each entered the world and discovered each other. Friends that would walk the journey together.

"There was no one from the ship to greet us. No Captain Pote. No officers. No celebration. We hadn't been promised a celebration, but we expected someone to greet us. There was no one."

***

Adaora was the first out of her crèche. Neci came second. There were ten of the pods in which we were born in each white room. I was greeted by Laoule, and I imagined Neci was welcomed by Adaora the same way—a smiling face looking down at you, confused but excited that there's someone else waking up.

I wasn't in the same room as Adaora and Neci—they were next door to us—so I never saw most of their interaction, but whenever all of us were together, discussing what to do, they were next to each, whispering and holding hands. Adaora was the first voice of all of ours. Perhaps, just because she had one extra moment of consciousness. For whatever reason, she often started our discussions and ended them.

We didn't have our Companions at the beginning. They weren't there when we awoke. Just each other. They greeted us on the other side, near the Jacobs. They had been anxiously trying to get to us but couldn't get in. Mine, a grumpy white ball I nicknamed Cord, insisted that they were supposed to be the first things we saw. That we shouldn't have been woken up without them. I had always wondered what would've been different if they had been there—someone that understood the world we awoke into, someone that could help us discover our place in it.

We only had a few days and nights of peace. Occasionally, we would hear loud explosions and screams, but we couldn't get the doors into the rest of the needle to open for us.

We didn't need to.

They came for us.

I wish we would've hidden. But we didn't. Metal strained against metal and labored breathing filled the gaps. Someone was breaking in.

We rushed to greet them, anticipating rescue. Three large men, their faces scarred and bloodied, roared through the gap in the doors they worked to widen. The first faces that were not our own were filled with rage and desire.

Some shouted to run, to hide. I was one of those voices.

Adaora stepped forward to greet them, hoping to calm them. They pried the doors open wide enough to fit through and raced at her. In a flash, Adaora spun and kicked one of them, shattering his nose, and sent him to the ground screaming in pain. How she had done that none of us knew—but there was a power in her that spoke to the same ability in us.

She missed the second man, however. He wrapped his hands around her neck and her screams filled the air.

Neci was right in front of me, and she raced forward, panic on her face.

The man snapped Adaora's windpipe with his bare hands, flinging her to the ground. She flopped down, lifeless, her eyes open, tongue lolling out, the grease stains from the man's fingers smeared on her neck.

Neci leapt at him, grappling his neck and spinning around behind him. She was yelling Adaora's name as she gripped the sides of the man's head and broke his neck with a cracking twist, revealing her own strength, our own strength—unknown to us all at that moment.

The first death we had ever seen was Adaora's. The second had been judgment at Neci's hands. She was the first of us to kill.

She bounded to the third guy who was tearing at Taji's clothes, pinning her to the ground. Neci snapped his neck too, pulling him off of the wailing Taji.

By the time Neci turned to deal with the third one, the other sisters had taken her cue and rushed him. I think Kerwen was in that group. They were savage, ripping at the man and shredding his face and neck.

When the danger passed, we all stood in silence around Adaora's body. Those who had finished the final attacker were covered in his blood. Neci held Taji close. Taji's eyes were shut tight as tears streamed down her face and onto her torn dress, her own dark body revealed through the rips.

Neci's voice was as quiet as I ever heard it. She wasn't sad. Just… broken. She instructed us to get whatever we could to protect ourselves from the rooms and off of the dead men. We armed ourselves with crude implements and stepped out into Olorun.

Our Companions greeted us, but we weren't the innocent girls that they had hoped to find. We weren't hungry for their guidance. We came armed, and we looked at them as tools more than friends. The extra presence of Adaora's companion (I forget his name) only high-lighted her death and their failure to be there to prevent it.

***

Syn closed her eyes. She had been greeted by Blip in her first moments. He had been there to prepare her for the horrors outside. He had kept her in the white room, and she had endured that dull, dreary existence, yet, it had kept her alive. The boredom had forced her to train and study, to prepare herself for what lay outside—a privilege that the others had never had.

Pigeon spoke, "She really didn't insist on leading. At least, not at first. But we had all seen what she did. We saw her reach around that man's head, and in a flash, he was dead. What stayed with me, stayed with most of us, was her face. There was no regret. There was nothing but action. It was a mirror, but a mirror drained of any color. That sliver of extra strength…We were all perceptive enough to see her distinctions in every action after that moment. Even if we all came out of crèches identical, she had killed first. She had made that decision. So we all followed her. We didn't vote. It was just a subtle change. We still talked through everything, but it was her opinion that influenced the most. Like Adaora before her, Neci's words usually ended the discussions."

Pigeon had moved closer as she talked. Syn could feel the movement of the girl's mouth as she formed the words. Syn shut her eyes and floated in the subtle sensation. The intrusive freedom of another. Pigeon formed words differently. She clipped her vowels faster. Syn was awed by that very fact and her own fascination with this thin girl lying next to her. A distorted mirror image of herself, and yet, through disparate choices and chances, this one spoke unlike Syn. *Perhaps*, Syn wondered, *she did so because she was scared of her own voice? Or she was always in a rush to finish talking quickly. Anything to reduce attention to herself.*

"Several of us died that first day. The colonists on the ship had already gone insane."

"The Madness," said Syn.

"Madness," agreed Pigeon.

"Where did it come from? How?" Syn asked, hoping that someone else might have answers that had eluded her. She tried to stifle the confusion in her voice. By the time Syn had awoke, they were all dead on her Disc. Had the others woken earlier than she had? So why was she different? Why was she alone? Why had she been separate?

"I don't know. Maybe Neci figured it out. I don't think so."

"They all went crazy."

"All of them," Pigeon acknowledged.

"Even Captain Pote."

"Maybe. I've wondered what happened to his daughters."

Had Pigeon stared at the videos of Pote's family with fascination the same as me? Did she dream as well what it felt like to sit at their dining table? Did she ever wonder what it felt like to have those girls as sisters? Perhaps not. Or if so, only briefly. Having forty others would eliminate that ache quickly.

Pigeon continued, "We went down in the elevator and found ourselves in the middle of a riot. They were killing each other. I saw big knives and shovels. A few were riding the floaters and running people over. Neci and several of the others managed to push through to a nearby building. One of the recreation houses next to the swimming pools. We barricaded ourselves in. There were two others inside, but we didn't see them when we entered. We shut the door, and they appeared from shadows. We managed to kill them, but they killed one of us in the fight. They badly wounded another. Within a day, her wounds proved fatal. Jos and Nimm. Three down by then."

"Our companion bots seemed just as distraught as we were. They were frantic. Zipping around and looking through windows. Sometime that next night, the bots of the three dead shut down. They must've been declared useless by the others."

A sense of guilt panged inside Syn. Would Blip shut himself down if she died? Was he that loyal to her? She had always felt he was obligated to serve her, but that if she was gone, he'd find something else to do. Perhaps not. Or, was he shut down at that moment because he was certain she was dead? Had he concluded that there would be only one outcome once they went down to the second Disc? Had he just given up knowing that she'd die? If so, how would she turn him back on?

From outside the room, something clicked and a muffled voice spoke. It was far away, far down the empty hall. Syn couldn't grasp the words.

She expected Pigeon to rush away. Instead, the girl scooted closer. She put her lips on Syn's ear. The rush of air sent a shiver down Syn's spine, and her fingers groped for Pigeon's hand. Their hands met, their fingers interlaced, and Syn gripped tightly.

Pigeon spoke, "It wasn't the mad ones who killed most of our Sisters."

The shiver continued, but it was no longer because of Pigeon's touch. Instead, she understood Pigeon's meaning and her dread regarding Neci was substantiated.

Pigeon's next words were like the raindrops outside—a stream without pause, "There was nothing but the Madness. We talked about the cause, and the only thing we could think was that maybe humans —normal humans, that is—aren't capable of traveling this far into space. Their minds couldn't adapt. Maybe if the entire ship had been us. Maybe if they had made some Adams.

Two things happened. We couldn't escape the people in the Disc. They were mad. I was the one who suggested a solution. I wish I hadn't. Neci and Tulce made it happen. We upped the oxygen content in the atmosphere and then locked ourselves in a Jacob up near the needle. We were desperate. We set the world on fire and let them burn. Some survived, but we were able to deal with them."

A silence fell and the two laid there as the weight of Pigeon's words gripped Syn. The Sisters had set the world on fire.

Pigeon continued, "The second thing was the lack of food. We've managed to grow some since. At first, it was a necessity. We were starving. Kin was the next to die and the first by our own hand. Neci made us do it. She said we had to eat. Kin was hurt badly. She wasn't going to make it. We chose to hurry the process to keep the rest of us alive. We hated it, but we had to keep going. We even started hunting the survivors when we couldn't find food elsewhere. We've been doing that for years. We've found ways to grow food, there's a few food units in the farm layer that are still working, and we're keeping animals alive. But when one of us dies, we still do it. Tulce died just days before you arrived. She was wounded during one of Neci's plans to help us escape this place. We held off on a meal until you joined us last night."

Syn shut her eyes. These weren't just copies of herself. They were something else. And she had joined them. She had…She felt herself start to gag and shut her mouth tight. Sweat beaded on her forehead, and she gasped. The bile filling her mouth was bitter, and she grimaced at the taste.

"You had to know," Pigeon squeezed Syn's hand tight.

"Why?" Syn croaked. The world was floating away—spinning and darting as the thought of the charred meat in her stomach beat at her.

"You must know. We're not just mean. We're not just survivors." Pigeon let go of Syn's hand and began to slide out of the bed. The cool air rushed in between the parting sheets. From the far side of the room, Pigeon's final words that night leaked out, "We're evil."

Syn fell out of the bed and crawled to a far corner. She retched and vomited in the dark. Over and over, the meal that included pieces of corn and something green and Tulce was hurled against the wall.

31

A DANCE OF LIGHTS

"Two footsteps do not make a path."
—Nnedi Okorafor

The selection prepared for breakfast wasn't quelling Syn's turbulent stomach. Pigeon's revelation hovered like a ghost. From some reading, possibly the words of Paul, Syn heard "Flesh of my flesh…If you eat of me…" Her stomach churned again.

The table was sparse. A plate of some hardened chunks of bread. A strange collection of fruits that Syn had never seen. A few of the ripe apples, but only a few. Rounding out the fare was a small plate in front of each of them with a stiff, dried-out strip of meat. Syn clenched her teeth and averted her gaze from the brownish piece in front of her. *It's not human. It's not human. It's not me. It's not me.*

But she knew that was a lie.

"We're out of apples," Neci said, from the far end of the table where she and Taji had been talking and giggling. This morning, Neci was dressed in a tight-cropped halter top and simple leggings, both as white as milk. The pronouncement was to the rest of them who all spread apart, quiet and distant. Kerwen sat between her and the other two. Pigeon had been there at one time but was gone and now was back and Syn couldn't remember when she had ever stood up, only that the girl's position had changed. She was like a black cat, moving between the shadows and disappearing as soon as she appeared.

Kerwen dropped her fork and groaned, falling forward and slamming her head against the table in mock resistance. "Do I have to?"

Syn leaned in and whispered, her first words all morning, "Do what?"

Neci raised her arms, palms up. "Taji has another assignment. Pigeon's helping me in the workshop. You can have our stranger at the gates do it, but I don't think she knows the way."

Syn's eyes widened at the sound of the word "workshop." Neci shot her a glance but didn't comment, instead saying, "Perhaps if you show her how and where, she can do it next time. Consider it training your replacement."

Kerwen's head lifted, and she narrowed her eyes at Neci.

Neci smiled. "Poor choice of words."

The apology didn't abate Kerwen's concern. Not taking her eyes off of Neci, Kerwen said, "We'll go in an hour."

Neci held up a hand. "Go the first part of the way with Taji—always good to go together."

Taji began to protest, "I'm not—"

Neci put a hand on Taji's arm and leaned in, staring into the girl's eyes. "I need muscles. Big ones." Standing up and walking away, she gave a short, sharp whistle and said, "Pigeon."

From the far doorway, Pigeon appeared and walked with a stunted gait, hesitant to follow but doing so nonetheless, her eyes locked to the ground.

Syn muttered, scared to be heard by Taji, "The groves?" There were apple trees in the lower food levels, all manned by bots. She had visited them often, enjoying the walks between the tightly packed trees, fruit falling across her path. Her stays were always cut shorter than she wanted—the lower levels were all claustrophobia-inducing. The artificial light generators were embedded in the lowered ceiling, and it felt unnatural to have sunlight within arm's reach, rather than far above in the emptiness of the false sky of Olorun. Syn shut her mouth tightly, realizing that, in asking, she had revealed more than she wanted. How would she explain knowing about the groves if the Ecology had her under lock and key all these years?

If she had heard, Kerwen made no indication. Instead she was continuing to softly smack her head against the table, sighing, and muttering, "Dammit."

S yn turned the flashlight over in her hands, looking at both ends as if it were a wonder of the gods themselves. "But I thought everything burned?"

"It did."

"So how are there any trees left to pick from?" She was careful to not mention her knowledge of the groves. "And where are these trees?"

Kerwen flicked on her flashlight, illuminating the thin metal shed they were in. Dark, rusted tools hung around them. "There's a few that are a bit tougher than others. And they weren't up here. They're down below." She held the flashlight under her chin, casting long shadows across her face, and lowering her voice. "In...the...basements." Kerwen gave a dark, mock cackle afterwards. Pointing the flashlight at the ground, she said, "Ever been there?"

"The basements?"

Kerwen smiled. "Come on. Follow me. The faster we get this done the better."

Syn left the workshop through the creaking door and walked in the direction of the main gate they had first entered Zondon through.

"Where are you heading?" Kerwen shouted, slamming the door behind her.

Syn turned and glanced around, suddenly lost and confused. The access to the lower levels had always been through the stairways off of the Jacobs. Each Jacob had an adjacent stairway to the lower levels, all the way down to the body farms. Zondon was in the middle of the base—it was a trek to the Jacobs. How else would they get there?

Kerwen's mouth dropped open, "Were you going outside?" She closed her eyes and rubbed the bridge of her nose, sighing loudly. "We don't go out unless we absolutely have to. And we're just going for apples." With a grunt, she turned around. "I said follow me."

Kerwen led to the right, past the main work-sheds, along the dirt covered path. To their right a sign boldly declared *Aviary: The Birds of Earth*. None of the paint had faded, in part due to its placement under an overhang, shielded from both the light and the elements.

"Here first." Kerwen turned into an alleyway and opened up a small door that Syn would've overlooked had it not been pointed out to her. Kerwen ducked inside, and Syn almost followed until she heard, "Wait here." A moment later, Kerwen swore and several things clattered to the ground, followed by a muffled, "Found it." Kerwen reappeared gripping Syn's spear in her hand.

"You found it!" Syn immediately reached for it, brightening at the sight of her favorite weapon.

Kerwen yanked it back, "Woah! Let's lay down some ground rules."

Syn narrowed her eyes. "What?"

"First, this is me trusting you. Not Neci nor Taji. Me. So point the pointy end away from me at all times."

"Taji knows you're doing this?"

"She won't always be with us. And it doesn't matter what Taji knows."

"If you're so scared, why are you giving it to me?" Syn's fingers were still splayed open, outstretched and ready.

"There be some nasty ol' things down where we going. Maybe we get out without stirrin' anything up, but I'm not counting on it." Kerwen moved the spear closer an inch, just beyond the edge of Syn's fingertips.

Syn lowered her voice to a whisper. "You don't want me to stab you when you're in front of me?"

Kerwen nodded.

Syn's hand reached out in a flash and wrapped around the spear shaft, pulling it toward herself but Kerwen didn't let go. Syn huffed,

"Maybe before you held me down last night and threatened me, you should've thought about that."

Kerwen smiled. "See here," she shot a glance at the spear, "This here is a peace offering. I need you to be armed. I can't be doing my job and keeping an eye on you. And I also know that if I don't give you a little trust, we ain't ever gonna be okay."

Syn didn't respond.

Kerwen said, "Promise me?" She relaxed her hold but didn't let go, allowing Syn to pull the spear closer. "Seriously. I don't want to be enemies. Promise?" She inclined her head forward.

Syn gave a slight nod, and Kerwen released the spear.

Kerwen turned her back to Syn and began to walk down the pathway, a sign to her left pointing the way with a large green arrow to *South America*.

Syn grunted, "I don't want to be enemies either."

***

At the edge of the Zoo had been an exhibit of South American animals—it was a minimalized version of a rainforest with fat vines snaking up the trees and buildings, and fan-like leaves stretched like umbrellas overhead, blotting out the already gray sky. These branched off from a gigantic tree—monstrous in this empty world, but small compared to Syn's tree that still stood in her world. At its base, a tunnel opened, serving as the entrance to this part of the Zoo.

In the middle of the tunnel, hidden from view, a hole had been dug, and in the center was a metal hatch, flat against the ground. Kerwen moved the three deadbolts that anchored it tight. The third one gave her trouble, and she grunted until it clunked back and the pressure below the hatch escaped with a hiss. Kerwen tilted her head. "Help me with this. Bastard's heavy."

The two heaved at the door together, lifting the great weight up slowly. The hinges weren't stuck or rusted—the entire contraption appeared to have regular use—it was just huge and heavy.

"Drop it," Kerwen said as they raised it vertical. The two let go, and then the door fell wide open and slammed to the ground with a deafening clang. Syn jumped back, fearful her toes would be caught underneath.

"Ha! Wish Ngozi had been that fast. She lost her little toe the first time she helped."

Syn picked up her spear and shifted her pack on her back. The weight in the backpack shifted, and the entire thing threatened to slide off her shoulder, so she pulled the straps tight against herself. "Who's Ngozi?"

"A Sister. When we first dug this thing and put the door in, there were more wild machines in those days, and they were barricading us in Zondon." She kicked the door and leaned over, looking into the dark space below. "But we needed a way to get to the farms. So, Neci thought of this thing. Actually, I think Pigeon found the hatch below and figured we should dig down."

Syn looked into the hole, fearful of leaning too far and falling. She had looked upon the world from a great height as she descended the Jacobs, but something about the unknown depth of this grotesque hole stirred a vertigo in her. A set of bolted-together metal rungs in a makeshift ladder dropped into the hole. The sides weren't dirt. Instead, they had bored into the metal of the ground itself and torn open the barriers between in great sheets. The rips in the metal were obvious, and the pieces were folded back to form a tunnel that fell into blackness. "How—how far down?"

Kerwen turned on her flashlight and aimed it down. The light flooded the top of the hole but did little to illuminate the bottom—there was still no view of where the ladder ended. Kerwen said, "It's far."

From behind them, Taji's grumpy voice boomed. "Just get going. Who cares how deep it is?"

Syn stepped back instinctively, putting as much distance as she could naturally between her and Taji.

The girl hoisted a massive, stuffed backpack on her shoulders and had several knives strapped to her legs. She wore thick, black gloves and tall boots. A cord of rope, wound up, hung from her belt. The girl looked like she was going to war.

"Are we just getting apples?" Syn asked.

Taji planted a hand in Syn's chest, pushing her backwards. "You're getting apples. I have real work." Without looking back, Taji dropped into the hole, grabbing hold of the railing as she plummeted, slowing her descent and slamming her feet against the metal rungs.

"Well, I guess, after her," Kerwen said, slinging her own pack across her back and stepping down into the hole, careful to grip both sides of the ladder. "Just keep going down and don't think about it."

Syn looked around her. There was no one here. For a moment, a thought flashed, *I could make a run for it.* But where to? Ultimately, she was still on Olorun. She was still without Blip. These were still the only other humans on board. Perhaps she could bring them over to her side. *Maybe. Maybe it would work out. Maybe all they need is to be safe.* Syn grabbed the railing and followed after. *I could provide that.*

The descent down dragged on for a long time. Step after step, Syn tried to count at first but soon lost count after a hundred and thirty. She glanced back up and was shocked to see that the gray sky from above was barely visible. If someone dropped the hatch closed, they would be trapped in an inky darkness. Perhaps Kerwen had her flashlight on and could see where they were going.

"How much further?" Syn said.

Kerwen's answer came from much farther away than Syn anticipated. "Just keep climbing down." She had thought Kerwen was only a few feet below her. Syn had been careful to step lightly to avoid stepping on Kerwen's hands. Knowing the girl was further down rustled Syn's anxiety, and she stepped faster, hoping to close the distance.

The minutes stretched on, dragged apart by monotony and silence. The air was thick and pockets of smells greeted them as they descended: the acidic pall of passing fire, the rich, gagging freshness of old soil below, a light lilac bloom that wafted and disappeared far too quickly.

From below, Kerwen's flashlight splashed light against the edge of the stairs. Kerwen shouted, "I've touched down. You're almost there."

Syn made the last few stairs and felt the thick, spongy dirt of the farm's ground below her feet. No more climbing, at least until they had the apples. Syn searched around in the darkness. There were patches of light far away—Syn assumed they were from the lightstrips above the rows of vegetation and fruit. There was no sign of Taji. "Where'd she go?"

Syn pointed the light at a second hatch a few meters away. "She's going further down."

"How far?"

"To the body farms."

Syn shuddered. She hated those.

Kerwen raised an eyebrow. "You know of the body farms?"

Syn nodded and then stuttered as she stretched a truth into a fabricated lie to cover her mistake. "I saw a video about them in the white room."

Kerwen nodded. "Ya. I hate them too. Only been there twice and have no desire to go down there again. Taji seems to be our body farm expert, so Neci sends her. She was one of the few that made it back from an earlier expedition, and she's always made it back alive. Let's get moving—we have a walk. Oh, turn on your torch." Kerwen pointed at Syn's flashlight.

The trek to the apples felt longer than the descent down the metal ladder did. Kerwen's refusal to talk only made it worse.

"How much—" Syn started.

Kerwen hushed with a sharp "Shhh!"

"But—"

"No. Seriously. There are so many ways down into the farms. Things are always rooting around here—the presence of food only makes it far more desirable. Just shut up so I can listen."

So they walked in silence. There would be no getting to know Kerwen better on this trip.

The far-off light became several lights as they drew near. Some were the bright light of the miniature sunstrips that hung above the plants. Above them, several bays of light drooped—nearly close enough to touch. There was no light from them as the bays had all been shattered. Syn aimed her flashlight upwards to examine them.

Kerwen muttered, "We think the passengers did that. Not sure why. Most of what they did doesn't make sense."

"They went insane."

"Ya, or maybe they were always that way and getting far enough from Earth let them lose control. Taji thinks it was a disease, but if so, then why haven't we been infected?"

The lights ahead were inside windowed buildings that looked like greenhouses. They had been walking through what Syn was sure was a cornfield. There were broken stalks along the way. No ears of corn remained—whatever had survived had been picked clean from the field. Syn had always wondered what corn tasted like. Even on her Disc, the corn was all gone. None of those fields had survived. Most of the other crops had, but not corn, and she wasn't sure why. Perhaps it was too important, and so everyone had to get what they could before they lost their chance.

Above them, the light bay flickered on. It strobed a few times and then gave a short pop before dimming off. Syn froze. Had her presence turned it on? No, it had to be a short in the wiring. Just bad timing. Had to be.

Syn was still staring up, fearful another would turn on, when they reached the edge of the first greenhouse, the light from inside spilling out onto the ground. Kerwen pulled a knife from her belt and said, "Be ready."

Syn brought the point of her spear low, aiming it forward.

Kerwen pushed lightly at the door, and it creaked as it pivoted open. "Shhh!" Kerwen said, although Syn knew she had not made a noise and the door was not going to obey a command to be silent.

Softly, hunched low, the girl stepped inside. Syn could see how she had snuck up on them in the desert. Kerwen was as stealth as a cat. She wasn't sure which one was stealthier: Pigeon or Kerwen. No, Pigeon was a ghost—the girl moved around as if the world held no pull upon her.

Kerwen's light moved in a slow arc across the room revealing a bank of tables that short stalks grew upon. Beyond those, in another series of rows, stood circular metal wire frames around lush, leafy growth. Bright red tomatoes hung from the vines. Beyond those, several trees craned up, their red fruit as bright as the tomatoes. They stepped closer and Syn counted nine trees. Nine apple trees heavy with fruit.

"Keep an eye out."

"For what?" Syn said.

Kerwen started to answer but was interrupted as Syn entered the greenhouse and stepped over the threshold. The track lighting across the ground turned on, bathing everything in an iridescent green light. The bulbs flickered first across the floor, then the ones up each metallic strut, and then finally the remainder of lights overhead—every light except the already lit sunstrips turned on. Between the two sources, the room glowed like a sunny day on Syn's Disc—she hadn't seen so much light since she first crossed over.

Kerwen gasped, "What the—?"

Syn made a critical error—in her surprise, she failed to act shocked. She was startled but not afraid. The lights, while unexpected, were not alarming.

And Kerwen noticed. "What just happened?" Her eyes were narrow, and she expected an answer.

Syn stuttered, stepping back, feigning a glance around. "I—I don't know." Yet, as she falsely examined her surroundings, the red apples caught her eye. The condensation upon their surface in the late morning reflected the multitude of lights. Syn let go a quiet, "Woah," briefly ignoring Kerwen.

"What?" Kerwen turned and saw what Syn saw. The sight ahead was beautiful. Each apple looked as if dipped in diamonds, glistening in the light. Those tucked into the tree appeared as galaxies, a thousand points of light, spinning around an ancient core. Kerwen's mouth hung open, and she stepped forward under the closest tree, picking an apple from a branch and holding it up. "How did all these lights turn on?" She turned to Syn. "Did you do this?"

Syn's mind raced, but she couldn't think of an answer. "I—" As she spoke, a second series of lights snapped on—hundreds of white and violet lights floated out of the upper rafters and swarmed through the tops of the trees. Small drones spun around and about the upper limbs, clearing them of various debris. Their light added to the spectacle, and Syn felt as if she was surrounded by a thousand fireflies, all swimming in a coordinated ballet.

Syn started again, the truth spilling out of her. "Yes." It felt wrong to lie in the midst of the silent, brilliant display.

Several of the drone lights dropped down and circled around the two girls. Kerwen giggled. "Wow. This is amazing." She held the apple out to Syn as the firefly bots danced around. "How?"

Syn took the apple and held it out from her, fearful as if some snake might pop out from it. "You're not mad?"

Kerwen raced off into the grove. "Look, oranges."

Syn slid the apple into her pack and followed. "But—"

They raced through a pack of the firefly bots tending to an older tree and scattered the lights about them. One snagged in Kerwen's hair and was pulled along with her, struggling to break free.

Kerwen picked an orange and ripped into the peel, tearing it off in huge chunks as the juice dripped onto her fingers. She took a huge bite and gave an audible, "Yum!" She held it out to Syn. "Try it." Her mouth was full of pulp, and the words came out garbled. "We didn't think these ones would ever make oranges. I kept watering 'em but Neci always said it wasn't warm enough. But look." She held her hands out wide and spun around.

Syn took a bite of the orange, and the taste was better than Kerwen's reaction had led her to hope. Sharp, sweet, and full of juice —the orange flooded her taste buds.

Kerwen stopped spinning and grabbed both of Syn's shoulders. "How?"

Syn reached up and freed the firefly bot stuck in Kerwen's halo of hair, letting it fly back to its friends. "I don't know. But I know it's me. Wherever I go, the ship turns on."

"Woah!" Kerwen said, "Really? Not just the lights?"

Syn shook her head. "No. Everything. The doors. The consoles."

"Why you? You're one of us. We can't get anything to turn on. Except the Jacobs. We can hotwire door panels. But nothing else. Our companions could but we took it for granted, and once we killed them—"

"What?" Syn stammered, "You killed them?"

Kerwen stepped back. "Neci hated them. She hates every machine. She kept telling us that Olorun was spying on us through them. That's why no bots came in Zondon. She figured out that her companion was talking to Olorun and that was why her plans kept failing. So, she made us kill them."

"You did it…willingly?"

"Stop! That's not the point! You can make the ship work! That's important. How? What do you do?"

"No. I'm not telling you until you tell me about your companions. What happened? How could you kill them?"

Kerwen sighed. "Fine."

Neci had found a way to get us all together. Back then, we were in the upper settlements, hiding out from the humans still alive. They were insane. The world hadn't been burned yet. The Madness had gripped everything though, and our Sisters kept dying.

Two different times we had tried to get rid of the remaining humans, but something had gone wrong. That's when Neci had the idea.

She rounded us up and laid out her plan. "One by one, I'm going to send you each off on missions. When your companion isn't paying attention, shut it off. They're spying on us. They're not helping us out. They're keeping a watch on us for her." She sneered every time she mentioned her. Olorun.

There were several that protested, but Neci pushed. "We're Sisters. We're flesh and blood. They're bots. They're machines. They're more her than us. They're always watching us, filming us, and talking to God above."

Soon, she won everyone over. Some she had to go to privately and talk them into it, but ultimately, everyone gave in. Well, at least we thought. Everyone went out in one day with their companions and each Sister came back without. Some bragged about how they did it. Others wept. I knew then that some were lying. Some had told the plan to their companions and allowed the bots to flee and hide. Some found ways to stay in contact with theirs. None of those are still with us.

That night, Neci waited to kill hers when everyone was back. As it began to panic as the lack of companions mounted, Neci cornered him. His name was Puck. He pleaded with her, but instead of just hitting the off switch, she took a metal crowbar to him, bashing him over and over. I can remember her standing over Puck's shattered corpse, wires and fluids spilling out, shouting, "I blinded God. I blinded her. She can't see us. She can't hear us. We're free!"

Neci moved a lot faster with her plans after that.

"How did you do it?" Syn asked, orange juice still dripping from her chin.

Kerwen lowered her head. "I couldn't do it the way Neci wanted. I just moved behind Squirrel—"

"Your companion was named Squirrel?"

Kerwen nodded, and the dazzling lights from the greenhouse and the firefly bots glinted off of the juice around her lips and the tear rolling down her cheek. "I just reached up and slid my finger across the off switch. He dropped to the ground, and I couldn't move him. I wasn't thinking about that part. We were in the middle of a courtyard, and he just slammed into the ground, and I think he's still there. He hasn't moved since."

Syn gushed out, "The ship just turns on wherever I go. I can't control it. At least, I can't prevent it. I can tell it to turn off, and it usually does. Most of the time."

Kerwen looked up. "Can you turn the machines off just by talking? Or back on?"

Syn tilted her head, unsure what Kerwen meant.

Kerwen said, "Can you turn the companions on? If we went to where Squirrel was, could you turn him back on? I've tried. It won't work. Once I turned him off, that's the last he responded to me."

"You want to do that?"

Kerwen shook her head. "I don't know. Maybe. No. Maybe. I just hate not having that choice. Neci made that choice for us, and I've had to live with it. She'd kill me if she knew I even thought about it." Kerwen took a step back, taking in the spectacle of lights. "It's like a Christmas tree."

Syn smiled, doing the same. "Ya. It is."

"Wow, you're just full of secrets. I think we're quite similar."

Syn shook her head, "We're all similar."

"No," Kerwen looked at the oranges on the ground, picking up and tossing aside a rotten one. "Maybe at one time. Maybe when we all left the white room. But not now. They're not like us."

"Like us?"

Kerwen smiled and pulled a ripe orange from a branch, holding it up and examining it. "We're still good. For the most part." She dropped it in the bag looped across her back. "Let's fill this up and get back. We don't want Taji coming looking for us."

Syn went back to the apple tree, filling her arms with fresh fruit. The two loaded up several bags until they were quite heavy, but not impossible to tote.

Kerwen walked backwards to the door. "We still have a long walk and a long climb. Let's not overdo it." She popped out her flashlight and flicked it on, although its light was lost in the array around them. "Can you turn them off?"

Syn nodded. "Lights off," she commanded. The greenhouse obeyed. All faded out except the persistent miniature sunstrips, and the room was left in the eerie incandescent glow of false UV light.

Kerwen exited, shining the light ahead of her. "Wow! Just wow. Neci is going to be so happy!"

Syn shouted, "Wait! No!" racing up to catch her. Syn grabbed Kerwen's elbow. "No. You can't."

"You don't understand—this changes everything! We won't be stuck in Zondon. We won't be stuck on this side."

"Please! Promise me! You can't tell her."

Kerwen stopped, shining the flashlight in Syn's face. "Why not?"

Syn's mind raced. She couldn't let Neci know that she was different. Neci would figure out that she came from the other Disc. She wasn't sure she was ready to give up that secret. At least not yet. "She doesn't trust me already. Let me tell her. Please. On my own." And, like most of what Syn had said, it was some of the truth. She had known everything about who she was would come out, but she didn't want to give up her secret world, not until she was sure she could trust them. They were savage, but she was beginning to understand why. Each step they took today brought her closer to deciding to reveal it all. But it had to be her that told. If Neci discovered it otherwise, she wouldn't trust Syn at all. And then the secret would be out, and without Neci's trust, Syn would have no say in what happened after.

Kerwen met her eyes. "You're going to tell her?"

Syn nodded. "Yes." *Just maybe not right away.* "Soon."

"Promise? Cause if she finds out I knew and didn't tell her, she'll have my hide."

Syn smiled. "I promise. Promise to let me tell her?"

Kerwen nodded in kind, mirroring Syn's actions. "I promise."

3 2

COLLECTING THE DEAD

"The best way to make dreams come true is to wake up."
—Muhammed Ali

The march back through the wild landscape of overgrowth and burned crops took less time than Syn imagined. As they passed the tomatoes, Syn shone her light across them. "Should we get those?"

Kerwen shook her head. "Tried before. They smash too easy, and you're left with mush. The climb up is too tough."

"Could I try?"

"Fine by me. You're going to have a mess."

Syn walked through the tangled vines roughly growing until she reached the tomato plants. Tucking her spear into the crook of her arm, she popped one of the tomatoes off and held it up. It did feel mushy. Soft as she touched it. Ugh—Kerwen was right. This would break everywhere. *They can't all be this soft?* She swept her lights across the plants, searching for one that looked more solid.

In the light, nestled between a few plants two rows back, something reflected the light back to her with an orange brilliance. Syn jumped back in surprise and swept the light back. Eyes. Two bright orange eyes with slitted pupils stared back at her—whatever those eyes belonged to, it was huge.

Syn muttered, "Hello?" She knew those eyes. She had seen those eyes before.

"What?" Kerwen shouted, far behind her.

Syn gave a half-hearted "Shh!" hoping to not disturb the creature. She should be frightened, but for some reason she wasn't. She knew these eyes.

Syn took a step forward and said, "Eku?"

With a single step, silent as its paw rested in the soil, a tiger slid out of the shadows. Orange and black, fierce and lean, the tiger strode forward with hungry intent.

Syn leaned forward, narrowing her eyes, and held out her hand to it. "Eku? It's me. Syn. How'd you get over here?"

In reply, the tiger growled and dropped its head lower, never breaking eye contact. Its black teeth glistened with its own saliva.

"Eku, what's wrong? It's me." As she leaned in, the spear, resting against her arm, fell forward. Syn diverted her gaze to see her weapon drop.

In the half-second of distraction, the tiger leapt at her, growling, claws extended to swipe at her.

Seeing the orange and black blur move toward her, Syn jerked back, tripping over a vine. Her flashlight dropped from her hand, and the light spun away. The tiger's leap was halted, and it fell to the ground, splashing dirt around it—the light of its eyes flashing out at once. Its front paw slammed into Syn's chest, the weight of it pinning her to the ground. She screamed and struggled to free herself.

"Eku!" Syn screeched, pushing the huge claw off, and rolling away in the dirt. The tiger did not move. Syn pushed herself up, sweating and panting and crying. Her vision blurred, and she saw dark figures silhouetted by the smaller ceiling sunstrips.

"Stupid girl," a gruff voice said. "What were you doing?"

Syn gave another short mutter, "Eku," and worked to wipe the tears and sweat from her eyes.

"What is an eku?" the voice continued, and Syn felt a sharp jab of pain in her leg. "Get up," the voice continued. *Taji—the voice belonged to Taji.* Syn glanced up and saw the brute of a girl standing above her. Taji had kicked her and was rearing back to do it again.

Kerwen interjected, "Stop it! Let her up. She's new. She didn't know."

Syn came to her feet and took a moment to get her balance. At her feet lay the body of the tiger, a knife hilt protruding from the base of its skull.

That's not Eku.

She moved from staring at the knife to Taji. "You saved me?" Syn stammered.

Taji yanked the blade out and wiped the blood on her shirt. "You stupid girl. Everything here wants to kill you." She leaned forward and tapped Syn on the forehead. "Don't forget that."

Kerwen picked up Syn's flashlight and spear, handing them to her. "What were you doing?" she whispered.

"I—I thought…" But how could she explain what she was doing? Eku wasn't here. Eku was on a world that these girls didn't know. "I thought it was…" *Tigers don't attack me. They've never attacked me.* "I don't know. I'm sorry."

Kerwen sighed. "Hate to say it, but she's right. You have to remember that everything around us wants to kill us." She turned around and started walking toward the ladder, still a long way away. "How did you survive as long as you did on your own?" Kerwen asked, shaking her head.

"But…aren't they programmed?" She stammered. As the words slipped out, she blushed at her own naivety. *Of course these aren't programmed to not hurt me. This isn't my Disc.*

If Kerwen and Taji heard that question, they had ignored it. They'd walked on, leaving her there alone.

Syn turned her flashlight in her hands and brushed the dirt from her back. Several apples had fallen from the other bag she was carrying, and she picked those up one by one. Kerwen was already walking away, putting distance between the two. Syn stood over the huge tiger dead at her feet—one of the apples lay next to its paw, and she slowly, carefully leaned over and picked it up, her eyes wide and waiting for movement. *Please be dead.* Yet, the thought hurt her. The beast before her resembled Eku. Syn fingered the pendant of the orange tiger at her neck. She couldn't imagine Eku dead. Syn couldn't grasp that everything over here was wanting to kill her—she just wasn't in tune to that level of danger. But could the Sisters lower their guard and not see everything as a threat on her side? Moments before, she had been near telling Kerwen of her side—she had thought she would tell them all. But now? Would they be able to leave their cruelty and suspicion on this side of the gate? Yet, how would Taji react when she saw Eku for the first time?

The tiger wasn't Eku, though. Its body was lean. Gaunt. Its ribs were visible through the thin skin and patches of fur. Its ears had large chunks ripped out. Deep, poorly healed scars ran across its sides and upper hindquarters. Existence down here had not been kind to it. Laying amongst the dirt, it could've been dead for months rather than just fallen within the last minutes.

"Come on!" Kerwen shouted.

Syn followed after, raising her flashlight to get her bearings. She gasped as her flashlight swept across Kerwen, Taji, and three other shambling forms silhouetted ahead of her. Taji led the way. She held her light ahead of her in one hand and, in the other, the end of a rope that looped back around the neck of the large figure behind her. The rope chained backward from the large figure, securing the other two silhouettes. All three followed in a steady, consistent pace, ignorant of the vegetation and crops ahead of them. They marched with a shallow gait, never lifting their feet from the ground, just dragging themselves through anything in their way.

Kerwen lagged behind Taji and the three unknown others, although she was still some distance ahead. Syn jogged up to Kerwen. "Who is that?" she whispered, "What are they?"

Kerwen gave a sharp, "Shhh."

"But, those look—"

"Shhh!"

Kerwen walked slower than before, and Syn matched her pace.

Kerwen seemed unwilling to bridge the gap and get any closer to the three that Taji had on a leash.

As they neared the ladder, Taji stopped and pulled her three to the side.

Soon, they were close enough that Syn could see them clearly. They were humans—large men, their clothes hanging like rags. Their eyes were shut and one of them had no jaw. Upon each of their foreheads was a silver plate that Syn had seen before—Kerwen had used something like it to shut down the big tree mover that had attacked them in the desert. The strip was slapped on them and a dark liquid drained from its edges on two of them. The sight of them froze Syn's blood. She struggled to grasp what they were and why they were following Taji. As they passed by, Syn noticed there was no twitching, no odd movement—now that they were standing, they were completely motionless.

Syn was both mesmerized and disturbed at their presence. She pointed her flashlight to the ground and held her arms close to her, stepping slowly past them toward the base of the ladder.

Taji sorted through her own pack and caught Syn staring. "Yes?"

Syn shuddered. How could Taji appear so imposing, so huge? She was the same height as the others. She had the same looks. But not that huge. It was in her demeanor. In her walk. She walked like a giant. Shaken from her reverie, Syn looked around and then back at Taji. In a quiet tone, something much closer to the sound of a sigh, Syn said, "Thank you." She wanted to blurt out, "thank you for saving me back there. I don't know why you did it, but I'm glad you did." But she knew the words would never come, and she could hardly muster them if she did.

Taji stared at her then gave a simple nod before grunting, "You two go ahead. You have no idea how long it takes these to go. Just getting back up here was a pain."

Kerwen walked over to the base of the ladder and stared up, refusing to look at the things. "You have the remote with the updated macro Pigeon wrote? Right?"

Taji nodded. "Ya. But I have to get each of them to do it on their own—one at a time. Then I have to scurry ahead of them in the pipe. Hate being below them when parts start falling off."

Kerwen chuffed. "Ya, I remember last time."

Taji pulled out a small keypad. "Hopefully, this will be the last time."

Kerwen put a foot on the first rung. "She nearly has an army now." She ascended up the ladder, stopping once to shift the bags of apples into a better spot. "Let's go, Syn."

Syn shut off her flashlight, threw it in her bag, shifted the other bag of apples around to one side, and lashed her spear against her pack to begin the long climb up. Her leg hurt from tripping and falling, and now, after the tiger, the anticipation of returning to Zondon was mixed—she wanted to leave this level, so Zondon had the allure of a place of familiarity. Yet, with each step, she drew closer to a horrible choice: reveal her world or not.

The trek up was quiet except for a torrent of swearing as Taji worked to maneuver the three figures with her on the ladder. Syn heard the shouts from below her: "Just move it. Dammit! No, your foot goes there."

Syn thought she heard Kerwen chuckle. Her hearing was confirmed as Taji yelled from far below, "I heard that!"

Kerwen gave an uproarious laugh in the dark and continued to move up. Twice, they paused on the ascent, latching their arms into the rungs and resting. They could see the light above them that represented the hatch—still open—into Zondon Almighty. From there, each step seemed to be heavier than the last. This was a miserable climb, and Syn felt every limb on her body threaten to rebel and ignore her choice to climb up.

Finally, she and Kerwen came to the hatch and hoisted themselves over the edge.

Kerwen directed, "Go get cleaned up. I'll send Pigeon to get you when it's dinner." She took Syn's bag of apples from her and walked away.

Syn navigated the walk back on her own, twice getting lost—she ended up in the kangaroo exhibit and then in the alligator display, both of which were abandoned. She stopped to look back and see if Taji arose from the hall, but she never saw the girl or her three odd followers. *It must be incredibly slow bringing them up with her.*

The world around Syn seemed frozen in time. There was no noise. No raucous laughter or shouts. There wasn't the common jittering bustle of bots that she found in her Disc. No—it was simply a path and walls and the quiet, emptied cages of animals. There was no life in these walls. And without life, there was no sound, no movement, nothing but a gray world without color. *This is why they want to leave,* Syn thought. *This is the world they have to endure, and it becomes grayer every day that passes and with each of their Sisters that dies.*

Back in her room, Syn relaxed. This wasn't her tree. It wasn't anything that she would've chosen, but it was familiar. It was a room that she could call her own—a space carved out for her that she didn't have to perform in or constantly analyze others' responses. It seemed to be so much work to be around others. She processed every word and every action over and over. She had been by herself for so long that she simply had not had any inclination of the sheer exhaustion that being around others would create. The climb had been brutal, and her skin was coated with mud from the fall in the tomato field, but it was the pressure of engaging with others that drained her.

She dropped into the hot tub, sinking below the water to her nose and closing her eyes.

With the climb and panic behind her, Syn's mind replayed the events of the morning. In a flash, the realization came to her: those things were the burlys. Taji had gone down to the body farms. They were dead humans. That was who the burlys were—human passengers of Olorun that had died and were buried, only anticipating becoming part of the food cycle of the trip. But somehow, Taji (and probably the others) had both some reason and some way to raise the dead and direct their actions. Syn shivered despite the warmth of the bath.

She wanted to be disgusted with Taji, yet the girl had saved her life. Syn furrowed her brow. How had Taji gotten to Syn's side so quickly? Had she been following them? She couldn't have heard the noise from the ladder entrance. And yet, she had to have come up from there as the body farms were below them two levels, separated only by the livestock level that she assumed had to be empty. So Taji had come back up and gone to meet them. So how soon had she found them? Had she seen them in the greenhouse? Had she seen the lights turn on? Did Taji know what Syn could do?

The water continued to drip from the spout although she had turned it off. Outside, as before, no sound came. Yet, Syn knew she wasn't alone. Slowly, she opened her eyes. Pigeon stood at the end of the tub gazing at her.

Syn lifted her head from the water and frowned. "How long have you been—"

Pigeon didn't meet her eyes, but instead stared at her body. She whispered, "It's time for dinner." She turned and exited in a smooth motion without looking back.

Syn shivered again.

33

CONFESSION

"Adam immediately took it and ate. Why? He could scarcely have put
it into words, but if compelled, he might have said: an eternity in this
condition is unendurable."
—Martin Luther

Kerwen slapped the table. "No! Not a chance! That's not how it happened."

From the far side of the table, Neci chucked an apple core at her. "It did. It did so. Taj? Come on? Help me out on this! You were completely lost. We walked around down there for two days because of you."

Taji held her hands up. "I said you both had it wrong the first day."

"What?" came the mock offense from both Kerwen and Neci.

Syn had entered the room and walked up to the table in time to catch this exchange.

Kerwen pointed at Syn. "Syn! You were down there today! Come on, don't you see how easy it is to get turned around in the Farms."

Syn pulled out a chair and sat down. "Ya. I would've been lost without you."

"You would've been that tiger's lunch!" Taji said, pointing and laughing.

Syn's eyes went wide and her cheeks reddened.

"What?" Neci asked, her tone darkening.

Kerwen jumped in. "Syn went to pick a tomato and ran into one of the escaped tigers. I think it's one of the last. Looked like Booska."

"The mean one?" Pigeon asked and all four turned to notice her, surprised to see her sitting at the table with them and unsure as to when she had entered. Syn was positive only the three others had been there when she had just walked in. She corrected the thought—there had been the three other girls and four burlys located across the room. The burlys stood unmoving, and she was disturbed at how easily she had begun to take them for granted. They were animated dead people, corpses given life. And she was expected to eat dinner next to them.

Taji shook her head. "Booska. Mif. Kance. Those are the only three tigers still roaming alive. I'm pretty sure it was Booska. And that moron decided to try and pet it."

Neci's eyes narrowed.

Syn shook her head. "I just…I wasn't trying to—"

Kerwen handed a bowl of leafy greens to Syn. "Taji saved your life. But admit it, anyone can get lost down there."

Syn nodded, glad to have the focus off of her nearly life-ending mistake. She filled her plate with the green leaves (they looked like dandelions to her) and an apple but passed on the tray of meat.

The table went silent, and they each ate a few bites without word. Kerwen broke the quiet, "I'm wanting to find a way to get tomatoes up here. They're growing like crazy, and it would be really good to have some for dinner. Maybe fry them up or add them to the salad."

Pigeon spoke, "We could haul them up in a basket."

"Ain't got rope that long," Taji said, her mouth full of food, spitting crumbs as she spoke.

"We could do it in segments. We could position ourselves as far as the rope will take us and then pull it up by wrapping it around a rung," Kerwen said.

"No," Pigeon shook her head, "It'll bang against the ladder. Need a pulley that pulls it up the center of the shaft, clear of the edges. We could start collecting all the rope we find. It might take a few months of scavenging, but I think we could do it."

Neci shook her head. "We're not going to be here that long."

The others looked at her, waiting for her to continue.

Neci smiled and motioned at the burly closest to her to fill her cup with more water. Syn studied it. This was the burly that Neci always had with her. It was different. Its body wasn't decaying flesh. It looked whole. Its features were solid, and it had a muscular build. It was dressed in a nice shirt that hung untucked and a suit jacket and denim jeans. Had Neci dressed him? Of course she had—even now, Neci had dressed herself in a flowing red dress with white trim. Every time she saw Neci, the girl was in a new outfit. Each looked flawless and not at all what the denizen of some wasteland should be wearing. Neci dressed perfectly. Her hair was perfect. Her hands were clean—except for the grease underneath her fingernails that Syn had noticed. And Neci's favorite burly was the same way—clean and dressed as if he were preparing for an important day. Somehow, Syn had overlooked that he was different than the others.

Neci caught where Syn had directed her attention and gave a thin grin. Syn turned her eyes back to her plate.

Neci continued, "With the help Taji found me, we're going get through or we're going to force the Bitch to let us in."

Syn stirred in her seat.

Kerwen glanced at her, then turned to Neci. "Syn doesn't know what you're talking about. Tell her."

Taji shook her head. "Not yet."

Neci glanced at Pigeon, who eyed the ground nervously. Pigeon stammered, "I'm with…Ker. She should know."

Taji grunted and flicked a grape in Pigeon's direction. Pigeon didn't flinch as the grape soared past her nose.

Neci smiled, "Fine. She should know." She leaned in to the table and whispered, "There shouldn't be any secrets between sisters."

Syn's blood turned to ice.

"I don't know how much you know about Olorun, but I'll share with you some of the basics. We are on our way to another star. Kapteyn's Star to be precise."

Syn nodded. This she had learned in the white room, and she felt safe acknowledging any of the training she had received there—she assumed it was the same for each of the others. At least that part of their existence had been the same.

Neci continued, "It was one of the ways that the ship builders worked. They like to build everything in multiples." She motioned around the table. "Like us. One wouldn't do."

Syn's stomach tightened.

"So, they planned for there to be several of us. Copies, each one identical, to begin with. But this isn't the only way this process works on Olorun. There's more than one Jacob lift. In fact, each lift has two pods, side by side. If one fails, the other works. Everywhere you go, there's a backup for everything in Olorun."

Syn nodded. She had seen and noticed exactly what Neci was saying. There was a duplication to everything. There would never have been a single control panel, at least not one of the important ones—each of those had a second, nearly identical, version nearby. If one failed, the other would work.

"I think that they didn't just extend this to the big bots or to us. I think they made the ship that way."

The other girls remained quiet. Nothing Neci had said alarmed them. They had all heard this before.

"I think there's another Disc."

Syn froze but then remembered that she was supposed to be hearing this for the first time. She feigned surprise and leaned in. "Really?" she asked.

"I've seen the maps. In the upper settlements, there's several command rooms. They smell like the passengers and the builders. The rooms are light-colored, pale. On the walls are hung the faces of the Orishas—just like the giant ones high up on the Jacobs staring down at us. In one of those rooms, in a drawer, I found scrolls. Large white sheets of paper rolled up. They showed a map of Olorun. The first few

I found were just pictures of our Disc. It showed me where everything was on the Disc. All of the upper settlements, the dwellings on the Rise, the lower farm levels, the groves, body farms, and access points to the water level below. It was all there."

Kerwen interjected, "I don't think we would've survived had she not found those."

There was a general murmur of agreement from Taji and Pigeon.

Neci continued, "Map upon map that showed every meter of the Disc. Then, I found the one map that showed the ship from outside—I remember I couldn't breathe when I saw it—there were two Discs. I knew what the gate was for. I had assumed, and my rotten companion had agreed, that it was the entrance back to the engine room and that it was dangerous to try and cross that. If the engines were working, why bother? Lying piece of scum!" Neci leaned in further. "Never, ever on our side. Always on hers."

Syn squirmed. *So why haven't you destroyed Blip?* But she didn't want to ask that.

Neci sat back. "And I don't think it was ever inhabited. Remember the magic word of the builders was redundancy. That Disc was a backup in case something went wrong. Well, something went wrong and instead of letting us have access to the backup, Olorun locked us up in here."

Syn stammered, knowing she should say something, "Have you tried to open the gate?"

Taji roared at this and slapped her hand on the table. "Tried to punch our way through!"

Syn's eyes darted between the others. The explosion had been them. Syn's stomach tightened. Did they know her secret? Were they teasing her?

Neci held out a hand. "We tried many different ways. The last one was a bit—"

Kerwen interjected, "Overkill?"

Neci shook her head. "Maybe. But we still didn't get through. So it couldn't have been enough."

"We found explosives and detonated them. Boom. Big ba-da

boom!" Taji laughed more and shoveled food in her mouth at the same time.

"Just imagine. Another world like this one. But it wasn't destroyed by those stupid predators. It wasn't corrupted by the passengers. It's just there. Green fields. Trees. Empty houses. All of it is just there for us."

Kerwen added, "We wouldn't have to live in fear ever again. No worries about the wild machines. No worries about tigers. Not a one of us has to die ever again."

Syn saw the desperation in Kerwen's gaze. Her words were backed with years of pain. Her chest felt heavy and something deep inside her ached. She imagined this room filled with the rest of the Sisters—a room of faded half-images—ghosts now against the real world. Syn had never had a sister, let alone a real flesh and blood friend, and she could not imagine the widening furrow of pain that Kerwen felt as she thought of her dead friends. Tears welled in Syn's eyes, and she pushed at them with the back of her hand, hoping to hide her own shared ache.

Under the table, Kerwen grabbed her hand. She had seen the tears. Kerwen mouthed a single word that pounded on Syn's heart. *Please* was the unverbalized request. Syn darted her eyes away from the silent but pleading Kerwen.

Neci stood up. "If we were designed to be Eve, then that's the Garden. But somehow, Olorun has taken it upon herself to stand as the sentry to the Garden and not let us through. The angel and her flaming sword, keeping us in Hell. So, I think we have a plan. I think—"

"It's true." The words were out of Syn's mouth before she knew what she was saying. In an instant she knew she had made a mistake and yet, her anxiety ebbed away. She had not wanted to say it, and yet, somewhere down inside, something released as truth washed through her. Perhaps the lie wrapped around the truth was that she truly had wanted to confess it all to them from the beginning. The words were carried with a hope that they would understand and the gulf between her and the Sisters would be bridged through her honesty and their understanding.

"Excuse me?" Neci said, sitting back down.

The others all looked at Syn, and the room went quiet.

Syn could not lift her head up. The words came slow. "It's true. That other Disc is true. But it was inhabited. They just died out faster, I think. I've had to clear the bodies away, but it's just like you said. It's green. There are trees. There's a beautiful river."

Neci stood up and sat in the chair next to Syn, her red dress flowing behind her. "What are you telling us? Are you trying to say that you've been to the other Disc? That you found a way over there and you came back here?"

Syn shook her head. "No." Syn's throat tightened. She strained to say the next words. "I came from that Disc. I've lived there all this time and just found out about this side. When you tried to blow up the gate."

Kerwen coughed. "Told you it was a stupid—"

Neci held a hand up to stop her. "You've lived over there? Did you come with other Sisters? Did you leave them behind?"

Syn shook her head. "Just me."

Taji grunted. "Lie. She killed them all." Taji pointed a fork in Neci's direction. "She's just like you."

Neci shot a sharp look at the girl, and Taji averted her gaze. Neci put a hand on Syn's shoulder. "Is that true? Did you kill the others?" Then with words just above a whisper, she added, "Tell the truth. I'll understand if you did."

Kerwen twisted in her chair at this utterance.

Syn looked over at Kerwen. "I didn't know there were other Sisters. I was the only one. I was telling the truth. I woke up in my crèche. There were no others. Just me and my companion."

Neci looked around the room. "So why did you leave?"

"I—I was lonely. I was by myself. I heard someone else on the other side of the gate asking for help."

Taji and Kerwen traded glances. Pigeon hunched up and leaned in. One of them whispered, "Laoule."

Syn continued, "I had never heard another person's voice. At least not in real life. I watched movies all the time. I could talk to my companion. But I was by myself. I didn't have Sisters."

Neci leaned in. "You left your Disc because you wanted to meet us?"

Syn nodded.

Neci drew close enough that Syn could feel her hot breath on her face. "You left Paradise because you were lonely? For us?"

Syn nodded again, slighter this time.

Neci drew back and roared with laughter. "Bwah!" The others gave slight chuckles, but the roar was Neci's alone.

In a flash, Neci grabbed Syn by the back of her neck, twisted her head around to look her in the eyes, and growled, "You lived in the Garden, you bitch? You lying, selfish, fat bitch. You could've taken us there the whole time! You have been sitting here, in this hellhole, with your great big secret!"

Taji coughed. "She's not told you everything, yet."

Neci's voice grew dark. "What else?"

Syn looked at Taji from the corner of her eyes.

Taji said, "Tell her about the greenhouse." She jabbed her fork in Syn's direction and then at Kerwen.

Neci glared at Kerwen. "What?"

Kerwen held up her hands, "I was going to tell you!"

"What?" Neci slammed her fist on the table.

Kerwen pointed, "She can make things in the ship activate. We walked into the first greenhouse, and she turned all of the lights on. Not just the sunstrips. Even the buzzy little machines turned on. Everything. The ship responds to her like it did for the companions."

Neci turned back to look at Syn, and Kerwen mouthed *I'm sorry* to Syn. Syn glared.

Neci pressed her thumb further into Syn's neck, sending a sharp jab of pain down her back. "Is that true?"

Syn could barely move, but she gave the slightest nod.

"How?"

"I don't know."

"Liar!"

"I don't. I promise. It just does."

"So you can go back up and open the gate?"

Syn shook her head. "No. No—it won't—it wouldn't open for me. My companion had to open an access point. Even he couldn't open the gate."

"Liar."

"No. I'm telling—"

Neci jerked and slammed Syn's head against the table, splitting her forehead open. Blood splashed across the table, and Syn cried out in pain.

Neci roared. "You came over, and you can go back! Get up! We're going now!" She jerked Syn to her feet as blood poured down the girl's face.

Kerwen held her hands up. "No way!"

In a flash, Neci spun and turned on her, fire in her eyes. "What?"

"I'm not going out into the Desert at night. It's a few kilometers to the closest Jacob. We won't make it."

Neci looked above, into the darkness of night. "Dammit." Then to Syn. "Tomorrow morning, we're going up there, bright and early, and you're opening that gate."

Through her sobs, Syn said, "I can't. I'm telling the truth. Only Blip can."

Neci pushed her back and slapped Syn, sending her to the floor. "I said to stop lying!"

Something wriggled from underneath Syn. From out of her backpack, a black streak zipped into the air and hovered above Syn. Huck! It squeaked—something Syn had never heard it do, and then just as fast, he flew away and was gone. "Huck!" Syn shouted.

"You brought a machine into Zondon? Here?" Neci kicked at Syn's leg.

Syn held her hands up. "No! I didn't know! He must've hidden."

Kerwen interjected, pulling Neci's focus away, "I told you the companion could do it."

Neci shot back, "I believed you. That's why I didn't bash the thing to bits. I had hopes. But it won't turn on." Then she looked at Syn. "But machines love you, don't they?" She pulled back and pointed out the door. "I bet you know how to turn him on." She was spitting as she spoke. Every word came out with a rasp. "You are going to get that companion to work, and you are going to show us how to get back to the Garden." She reached out and slapped Syn hard. "You little lying brat. You've lived in Paradise, and you have that gall to lie to me about it. No more!"

She snagged Syn's spear from the ground and slammed it against the table and a crack radiated down the shaft. "You came through. You're going to take us back. And I swear, if that machine has told anything to that Great Old Woman, I'll personally kill you. Olorun is blind and deaf. It's going to stay that way. She has no eyes, no ears, and no voice inside this aborted world. She rejected us. Discarded us like a forgotten mass. And I won't have her following us into Eden." Neci held the cracked spear in front of her, a single white line running the course of the shaft raggedly jutting like lightning, turning it like a lathe in her hands. Her face curled in disgust. She flung it across the room, and it smacked against the wall.

Above them, the clouds thundered again, and drops of rain began to pour down.

Syn stammered, "I was going to tell you." Blood dripped from her lip as she came up onto her knees. "I was scared."

Then as if a switch had been turned off, the anger drained from Neci, and she stood there poised. The fury behind her eyes vanished. She spoke clear and confident. "You were going to tell me?"

Syn nodded her head. "I was going to take you there."

The Crimson Queen crouched down and lifted Syn's chin up. For a brief time, Neci examined Syn's face. Then she dabbed at a tear and wiped a swath a blood from Syn's cheek, staining her own fingers. It didn't reduce much of the blood on Syn's face but left a clean streak to the dark skin below. "You are telling the truth. Okay. And now?"

Syn opened her eyes, straining to focus through the blood and tears matted over her eyelids. Her words were a whisper, "I'll take you there."

Neci stood up, straightened her dress, and wiped a splatter of Syn's blood from her own face. She nodded. "Well then. If I could, we would leave tonight, but…Kerwen, you are correct. Tomorrow morning. So, let's all get a good night's sleep, and we'll be up early, ready to go. Have everything packed." Neci turned away. "And clean her up. Post a golem by her room. Grab her companion and have him loaded to go. We leave in the morning. Oh, and Taji, I need your help in my lab preparing the new ones. We have a final bit of heavy lifting to do before we leave." She glanced back at Syn and gave a wink. "A guarantee. A back-up plan of sorts."

As she left, her dress dragged through the small pool of blood at Syn's feet. In her exit, unseen by her, Neci smeared a streak of crimson across the cold concrete.

MENAGERIE AND BLOOD

"[A] dragon had set up its nest at the base of the tree, the Zu-bird had placed his young in its crown, and in its midst the demoness Lilith had built her house."
—*Gilgamesh and the Huluppu-Tree*

Unlike the last night, sleep came fast. She had bathed again, but ended it as the water turned red from her own blood. She slipped into the old, tattered blankets wearing only a thin shirt one of the Sisters (she assumed Pigeon) had left out for her. Her head hit her pillow, and despite hearing the hoarse breathing of the burly set outside her room, she fell asleep in moments.

In her dark dreams, she heard her name whispered. "Syn. Syn. Syn, wake up."

She swam up into consciousness and opened her eyes to the still eyes of her own face looking down at her. The mirror Syn brought a finger across her thin lips. Syn thought to herself, *how did I ever get so thin?* As the fog of sleep drifted away, the confusion left. It was not her own face. It was Pigeon. "You're not me," Syn whispered.

Pigeon gave a quick "Shh" and then said, "I need you to come with me. Don't talk. Don't make a sound."

"There's a burly...a golem outside," Syn said as she sat up.

"Don't talk," Pigeon hushed, "Follow me."

Syn noticed there was a different quality to Pigeon's whispers than her own. The girl could only be heard when Syn was against her. As she leaned back, the words seemed to fade. How did the girl act like a living shadow?

Pigeon grabbed her hand and pulled Syn along toward the back, where the tub room was. Syn tugged back and pointed toward her clothes piled on the ground. Pigeon shook her head. Syn glanced at her own bare legs, gesturing at her own nakedness. Pigeon paused and nodded.

Syn hurriedly put on her pants, but Pigeon grabbed her hand and yanked her along, still wearing the thin shirt rather than her own clothes.

In the back room, beyond the tub, Pigeon walked up to the rock wall and ran her fingers across a lighter-colored stone. With a small tug, her fingers pressed into a visible crevice, and the rock moved toward her. No—it wasn't just *one* rock; an entire door of rocks swung on hinges inside the wall. A hidden door had been there the entire time.

Syn's mouth hung open in surprise, but Pigeon did not give her the opportunity to ponder. Instead, she pulled her into the dark passageway beyond. They moved through a few smaller rooms, and Syn recognized these as spaces that the zoo handlers and the assistant bots (at least on her Disc) had used to prepare food for the animals. Syn smiled—of course there had to be a door into this space—the handlers wouldn't come through the main gate; they would have to use an entrance that allowed easier management of all the animals. The various animal enclosures were set up in a ring around the singular hub that the handlers had operated and managed them from.

Soon they were outside walking through the pitch-black roads and paths that twisted throughout Zondon. She was nearly unable to see ahead more than just a few feet. Light from several distant lamps near the spired quarters of the Crimson Queen shone but did little to illuminate their path.

Her skin felt clammy and each step into the dark unknown sent panicked images racing through her thoughts. "Where are we going?" she hissed and jumped at her own voice, loud in the quiet of the dark passages.

"Shhh!" Pigeon whispered but then leaned in, her mouth to Syn's ear, and said, "I want to take you to two places."

"Now?"

Pigeon breathed out, "Yes. Now."

They were off again, Pigeon pulling Syn behind her. The thin girl seemed to be at home in the dark, never once stopping for uncertainty, gliding through the turns as if she could see them during daylight.

The area ahead cleared up, and while everything was still veiled in darkness, Syn knew that they were no longer confined by walls on either side. A wide structure with a pointed roof appeared in silhouette against the gray sky.

In a flash, the entire thing lit up in a deep red light from Pigeon's flashlight. The structure was a carousel with dozens of plaster animals, each frozen in running position, bound to the structure by a large spiraled pole. Syn had seen carousels in movies from *Mary Poppins* to *A Summer Above the River*. She gasped.

Pigeon whispered, "Do you like it?"

"I've never seen one in real life before." The structure was a beautiful spectacle. Across the canopy, scenes from the construction of Olorun were painted: the dry dock, the launch out with Earth in the background, images of Àpáàdì, and Orisha masks in between each muraled scene. All glowed menacingly in Pigeon's red light.

Pigeon turned around and narrowed her eyes. "There's not one on your Disc?'

Syn shook her head. That was odd. There wasn't a carousel on her side. Everything had been nearly the same, except this and the absence of a great tree on this side. A carousel here and a tree there? "No. There isn't one in our zoo."

Pigeon pulled her ahead. "Be quiet. And choose one." She pointed to the various plaster animals: horses, zebras, big cats, and more. She stepped close to the white horse with a glowing mane. Next to it, an ebony stallion raced, red feathers lining its saddle. A large white bunny stood a few feet away, and Syn found it frightening. She stepped up onto the wooden platform and scanned the other options. A giraffe stood straight and tall. The zebra was stretched out long and in mid-stride, adorned with a pink saddle. Behind that, a regal lion with a full mane stepped, front paw up. A mare with a teal mermaid's tail was paired next to that.

But there was no question for Syn. She stepped up to the massive tiger and ran her hand down its back. "Eku," she whispered, but only to herself, and then climbed on, wrapping her arms around its cold neck.

A thought flashed in her mind as she remembered the high-note calliope music that accompanied every image of carousel in her memory, and she turned sharply to Pigeon, climbing onto the dark, gray wolf paired with the tiger. "This doesn't work does it? We can't wake the others."

Pigeon smiled. "Neci isn't asleep yet anyway. She's…um…busy. Besides, I've disconnected the speakers, and I've oiled the gears. This is as silent as me." Her grin grew large, and she tapped something strapped to her belt.

Syn's tiger jerked up as the carousel moved into life. Pigeon turned off the flashlight as they began to circle around, going up and down with the rhythmic parade of animals. A giggle escaped Syn's lips, and she cupped her hand to her lips to prevent the next one following. It was wonderful. They spun around, and she could hear her own heart-beat race as she held tightly to the tiger's neck. *I miss you so much, Eku.*

Memories of Eku flooded in. Her soft stepping through the brush on their long walks. Her deep sleeps against Syn, the cat's great heart beating like a drum.

Around and around the carousel turned and Syn felt young again. Her froth of hair blew back behind her, and she couldn't help but smile widely.

For years, she had wanted to have a friend to play with. Movies showed playgrounds and theme parks—girls racing about from ride to ride, giggling as they went. She had abandoned the hope years past. Syn reached out and found Pigeon's hand and held it tightly, giving it a squeeze. Pigeon's fingers resisted the touch at first but then curled around Syn's hand, and they rode around like that forever in the silence, wanting each to squeal and laugh and knowing that to do so would mean being caught.

Like the plaster animals they rode on, time seemed to freeze, and they just orbited the dark star at the center of the carousel, circling about without any future or any past to worry about. Their momentum slowed and soon, the dance that seemed to go on forever came to an end as the carousel stopped.

Syn leaped off of the tiger, still holding onto Pigeon's hand. She pulled the thin girl close to her and hugged her tightly. In Pigeon's ear, Syn whispered, "Thank you," before giving her a quick kiss on the cheek. "Thank you."

Pigeon stood motionless herself, like the animals around her.

Syn leaned in. "Are you okay?"

Pigeon dropped her head down and said, "I've never been hugged before."

Syn recounted her experiences and whispered back, "Me neither."

She reached around Pigeon again, holding her tightly. Pigeon's thin arms returned the gesture. The two remained locked in each other's arms, statues themselves amongst the frozen menagerie.

Pigeon let go first and grabbed Syn's hand. "I have one more thing to show you." She whisked Syn away, into the dark paths leading away from the carousel.

"Why'd you do this?" Syn asked as they walked.

Pigeon glanced back. "I wanted you to know that not everything on this side is rotten."

Syn nodded. "I know that." She remembered the Barlgharel, Huck, Arquella, and Bear. She remembered her time with Kerwen in the orchard. Her own sense of joy right then reaffirmed that.

Pigeon brought her to a large building with a series of garage doors. The structure was set back by itself, and each window was dark.

Pigeon said, "Shhh. No one's here, but be careful. Don't be loud. No matter what you see."

Syn started to ask, and Pigeon hushed her again. Pigeon added, "I mean it. You're not prepared but you can't scream." Pigeon tapped against some unseen pad, and the lock opened with a sharp click-clack metallic grating sound. Pigeon pushed open the door. They stepped in, and the smell of rotting meat slammed into them. Syn started to gag. Pigeon grabbed her hand and held it tightly.

"What is that?" Syn asked.

Pigeon flicked on the flashlight, and the room was bathed in red light. Syn knew instantly where she was. A workshop. Much like hers with large benches, scattered tools, cabinets, odds and ends, piles of parts. There was even a stool on wheels like hers.

"This is Neci's," Pigeon said.

Dark patches of a thick liquid dripped from the center table. Syn held her hand above the largest puddle and found it to be warm.

Pigeon motioned Syn to follow around a corner, to the larger section of the workshop. Syn did and her mouth opened aghast.

Pigeon held a finger to her lips, and Syn stifled a scream.

Across the tables in this area lay two large bodies—Syn recognized them as two of the three men that Taji had led up from the lower levels. Dead.

Syn started to examine them, but something moved and caught her eye. Beside them, dozens of broken bots lay scattered. In the stack, something jostled again, and Syn discovered a small, red eye-bot, much like Huck, wiggling about for her attention. Next to it, a chrome sphere, identical to Arquella, squawked out in a noise-filled blurt, "Help us." Its voice faltered on the last word, and only a low hum and static projected from the bot.

"I thought Neci hated machines," Syn said.

"She does," Pigeon answered, "But she needs them." The girl picked up the wriggling eye-bot. "At least, she needs what's in them."

Syn furrowed her brow. "Huh?" She returned to the two burlys nearby. The larger of the two had several long incisions in its skull. About it lay several of the inhibitor switches and various assorted parts Syn recognized as pulled from bots. Chunks of flesh and organic matter sat in a bucket nearby. The room was littered with bits of bot and human. "It's a butcher shop." *Not a workshop*, Syn added to herself.

She ran her finger through a pile of black, grainy powder. Lifting her fingers to her nose, she smelled sulfur. *Is this gunpowder?*

Pigeon whispered, "We didn't know about the other Disc, so we were desperate. We set the world on fire, and let them burn. Some survived, but we were able to rule them. This is how. She took the living and the dead, alike."

Syn said, "Is this how she does it? She takes the machines' parts and put them in these…these corpses?"

Pigeon nodded. "It was right after she killed her companion. At least I think that's where she got the idea. In the center of the scrapped machine were pieces of flesh. Brain tissue, I think."

Syn nodded. All bots had a small organic component that helped them process. "TyTech," Syn said and shivered. She hated the idea of something living inside the bots' shells, but she wasn't sure why.

"Huh?"

Syn said, "The builders called it TyTech. Just a way to speed up the machines. Makes them smarter."

"Well, she figured out how to reverse it. Plant the connectors in the dead bodies, and they would still function. They don't need to eat, although they still tend to, out of habit. They run and run until they just run out of energy. There are more than enough bodies to work with. Taji's the best at finding the really good ones."

"All this time, she's been chopping up the bodies to make her own slaves?"

Pigeon nodded. "She used her own companion's parts in her prize."

Prize? Syn narrowed her eyes, confused momentarily, but then she remembered the golem that did not resemble the others. The one always with Neci. The one that appeared the most human.

Pigeon continued. "She keeps him perfect. She calls him Admiral. Some of the Sisters sent their companions away when they discovered what she was doing. We hunted down most. In fact, only one is still unaccounted for."

Syn spoke, her eyes going wide, "We found another companion on our side. He was dead. He fell from the needle."

Pigeon answered, "That must've been the missing one. Spot. Laoule's. He was in hiding. His name was Spot. He ran away a long time ago. A few weeks ago, some of the golem flushed him out. They caught him and brought him back. Laoule was too attached to him. She helped him escape. She left with him. They fled to the needle. I don't know what happened after that. Neci didn't tell me. She sent Taji soon after we heard the explosion. When we found your companion, we thought we had found Spot, that perhaps he had come down somehow."

"Oh," Syn began to put the pieces together. She had heard Laoule. The dead charred girl in the gate room. The first real human voice Syn had ever heard. So, the companion that had invaded Syn's Disc belonged to Laoule. "What happened in the room where you found Blip? There were all these dead…children." Syn struggled on the last word, and the memory of hiding amongst the bleached skulls of infants and toddlers caved in upon her. The shiver the image created rippled through her.

Pigeon shut her eyes and didn't answer for a long time.

"Please."

Pigeon nodded. "We went there because of Laoule. We were still hunting Spot. What you found…" Pigeon paused. "When Neci started gathering up the remaining living men to make into…" She motioned at the corpses on the table, "She would have us kill off the women and children. Said they were a drain on our already thin resources. I guess they probably were. Perhaps she just hated anything weaker than herself. Laoule had been hiding the children and keeping them safe in that room. She'd go back to them. But one got out and thought Taji was Laoule. Laoule's secret was out. Neci killed them all. She let Laoule live thinking that she had been punished—she made her watch as she killed each of the kids, one by one."

Syn gasped and tears flooded her eyes. "Why did you bring me here?" Syn stepped over to Pigeon.

Pigeon looked at the ground. "You said you'd show her how to get to your Disc. I showed you the carousel so you knew this place could still be saved. And I showed you this so you could see what she'll do to your world. She's wicked. Twisted."

Syn turned around and stared at the chaos. In her workshop, Syn repaired bots. In Neci's she took the living and the dead—both bot and human—and merged them into something horrific.

At that moment, the room went white. The overhead lights flicked on. Syn and Pigeon stepped around the corner to see Neci standing in the doorway, accompanied by her favorite burly, Admiral. The carnage of the room was revealed in the clear light. Blood and chunks of flesh were splattered across every surface. Large knives hung from hooks in the corners. Box after box of destroyed bots were stacked everywhere.

Neci took a step further, "Girls, this room is off-limits." She wore only a long, thin gown, and Admiral was completely naked. Syn almost gagged again at the scarred, sliced flesh of the burly. Across his skin, a dozen long cuts had been made and stitched back together, leaving grotesque scars. There were patches of oddly mismatched skin that Syn assumed were torn from other corpses. Neci frowned, "Pigeon, can you please tell me what are you doing in here?"

Pigeon didn't respond. Instead, she took a half step back to stand behind Syn.

Syn gestured at the table behind her. "What are you *doing* in here?"

Neci walked toward her and then around to gaze at the other part of the workshop. After a moment she said, "I'm building our future."

Syn turned back to Pigeon to see her reaction, but the girl had disappeared. In the briefest instance, the little girl had left. Syn was jealous.

Admiral stepped behind Neci, towering above her. Neci put out a hand and rested it on his chest. "Have you met my husband?"

Syn tilted her head. "What?"

"I've noticed you've been watching him." She took a step toward

Syn, looking her over from head to toe. "We're so much alike. When I heard you were fixing those machines, I knew we were much more similar than the others. We can build things. We have the same mind. And we have the same desires." She glanced back at Admiral. "I can make you one."

"Your *husband?*" Syn was still focused on the strange use of that word. But as she asked it, she saw what Neci had created. A companion. Admiral was more than a guard. He was her lover. Syn's eyes went wide. "How could you?"

Neci shook her head, dismissing the question, and ran a hand across her own stomach. "I'm so glad you've chosen to take us to the other side. It's important to me that we leave this place. It's not safe for us. It's not safe for me...or my child."

Syn took a step back, bumping back into the cabinet behind her. "Your child?"

Neci glanced back at the emotionless face of Admiral. "Ours. And yes."

"Oh," Syn muttered. Her fingers gripped the countertop behind her and curled tightly, holding her steady as the world swam around her. Neci was going to be a mother. She was pregnant. She was going to have...Syn breathed out the words, "A child."

Neci nodded, reaching forward and putting her hand on Syn's cheek. "So, you see why we have to go over there? I can't have a child here. Not on this side."

Syn pulled away from Neci and spun around to face the metal cabinet. She couldn't look at Neci. Everything was spinning. She couldn't leave Neci to raise a child here, in this world. Her fingers felt slick, and she looked down to see she had placed them in blood. She shook her head. The Crimson Queen indeed. She couldn't bring Neci the Butcher to her side. She looked back up at the cabinet and saw Neci's reflection in the dirty aluminum. For a moment, it was a mirror, reflecting Syn and a nightmare version of herself. Syn breathed out, "No," but the word had no weight.

Neci put a hand on Syn's shoulder. "Please don't go this way. Things are so close to working out. I can give you whatever you need.

I told you I could make you one. I won't be the only mother then. We could fill the world with new children."

Syn's mind erupted with images of motherhood: a young child in her arms, caring for a new human, raising it in the green fields of her Disc. Then another image took its place as Syn remembered hiding amongst the pile of children's bones. "You had children on this Disc," Syn grunted.

"What? No. This will be my first."

Syn hissed, "There were children here, and you killed them. I've seen their bodies."

Neci sighed, "Not those. Those were human. See—that's yours and the others' problem. You keep thinking we're human. We're not. They made us to be better than them. We aren't human. Not like them at all. I'm talking about filling Olorun with our children. Children that can survive the world we're heading to."

Syn shook her head and glared at the dirty reflection of Neci in the cabinet door. She spun around and seethed, her hands balled into fists, "Not my world. Not that one either. I'm not letting you anywhere near my Disc. It's mine, and I won't let you destroy it with your rot!"

Neci backhanded Syn so hard that she slammed against the ground. Her cheek ripped, snagged on one of the rings Neci wore. A splatter of blood stained Neci's cloak, leaving dark red spots against the field of lighter crimson. Syn lay on the ground and looked up at Neci while blood still flowed from her head. She could feel the tears welling up inside.

Neci spoke, still calm and controlled, "My Disc. Discs. My ship. I'm the Queen of Olorun. Not you." She stood above Syn, glaring down. "I won the right to rule. Not you." She pointed up. "And not her!"

Neci gave a sharp kick to Syn and spat on the ground, "I'm the first to be a mother. I'm the Queen. And you and your small mind don't even get it. You'd rather be with those stupid machines than with your own sisters. You've had it all, and you think you're better than us— you think you deserve the right to Paradise and not us. But I'm not going to let you win. I tried to be kind, tried to get you to be honest.

I've tried bargaining. I've pleaded. I'm done trying. I'm finished! You're going with us, and you're either going to open the door of your own free will, or I'm going to make you do it."

"You can't," hissed Syn. "I'll stay here!"

Neci laughed. "That's what I was afraid of. I'm going to make sure that's not an option. I have a final alternative to force your hand and the bitch above. You will both do as I want. Can't stay here when this place doesn't exist." With another sharp kick to the side, she pointed at Admiral, "Shove her back in her room, and stay there with her. I don't want her getting out again."

Neci left and the large burly leaned down to Syn. She shifted away, but there was nowhere to escape to. He held her two arms and lifted her to her feet, gently setting her down. He turned her around and pressed his large palms against her shoulders. She shuddered at his touch. There was something primal in his nudity. All she knew of human culture was from film, and she knew that he was revealing something that was to be private. And yet, here he was, so close to her. And yet, as he ushered her away, he was not harsh. There was a strange calm about his actions. He never hurt her the entire slow march back to the room through the dark.

She imagined Pigeon somewhere in the shadows watching her be escorted back. Pigeon had said, *"I showed you this so you could see what she'll do to your world."* Syn sighed. There was no future for a world that Neci lived in.

3 5

———————

RECLAIMING

"All things that fall from heaven are to the blessing of the faithful."
—*The Vision of Kanc*, Archives of the Ecology

Syn's body ached. The throb of Neci's kicks still radiated throughout her arms and legs.

Outside her room, outside the city, something boomed in a voice like that of an angel announcing the apocalypse, "All things that fall from heaven are to the blessing of the faithful."

Syn crawled from the bed and wobbled to the door. It was unlocked, and the burlys that had guarded it were gone. Admiral himself was absent.

The roar came again from far outside. "The Expected is to be delivered unto us." She had heard that term before. *The Expected.* But where? The fog of sleep plagued her mind.

Syn walked down through the main dining area with its open ceiling and large, roped-together plastic assemblage of tables, and then through the door out to the walkway. It was a maze to the main gate. She came out to see Neci, Kerwen, Taji, Pigeon, Admiral, and ten more burlys all standing and staring at the closed main gate. Before them, on either side of the gate, two rough towers rose. Atop these,

291

hunched like frogs, sat two more burlys. The one on the right was an enormous thing, towering above the others, his broad shoulders squared, and made Syn wonder if he might just be a part of the furniture stacked there. She looked several times to separate him out from the columns supporting the thin, crumbling roof of the tower. The other burlys deserved the name. Tall, brutish, and rough. The one on the right tower was a different animal altogether.

From outside, the voice bellowed, "In peace we ride to your walls. In peace we'll leave. But we are guaranteed the Expected." The buildings and the walls rattled as the voice spoke. The tin warbled as it vibrated against metal struts.

Taji spoke to the gathering, "How many of the fanatics are there?"

Syn cocked her head at this. *Fanatics?*

Pigeon was walking back from the wall and spoke up, "At least two hundred. Probably more. I lost count."

Taji swore.

Kerwen chirped, "Thanks, Sheep."

Syn cracked a grin. Despite all that happened, Kerwen was still Kerwen. She must've giggled or snorted and gave a slight hum of acknowledgment or appreciation. She must've done something because Kerwen turned and looked at her, followed by the other heads in the group twisting back toward her.

Taji grunted, "Perfect. Don't have to hunt for her to throw her to the wolves."

Neci sighed. "We're not giving her up."

"They might be wanting to kill her," Taji said.

The tall queen of the Sisters cleared the distance and grabbed ahold of Syn's hand and pulling her back to the group. "We're not killing a Sister, now are we?" Her elbow nudged Syn's arm. "Besides, the machines don't dictate to us, and I don't think that's why they want her."

Syn cocked her head again. *The Ecology was here? Had they come for her? Had Huck gone for help?* She had forgotten about him until just that moment. And why was Neci acting kind again? Her mood switches were disturbing, and Syn felt that the kindness would switch into murderous rage in a flash.

Neci turned back to Syn and held out her arms, "I know we had a rough night, but I want you to know that I value your sport. You play a good game. Well done!" Syn stayed locked in place. Neci wrapped her arms around the quiet girl and squeezed tightly. "When it's over, it's over," Neci chimed. Then she followed it up with a simple command. "We are all traveling together, despite whatever the machines want."

Syn wanted to see the Ecology outside. Were her friends there? Had Arquella and Bear come with them? Despite their oddities, the Ecology was the brightest moment of joy she had experienced on this side. The Ecology had accepted her. They had been kind. They welcomed her and embraced her. Syn found herself inching closer and closer to the wall. A thin bit of gray light peaked through the umber boards that braced the metallic wall. She peered through the slot. The sight took her breath away.

Outstretched before the walls, pouring down the hillside and wrapping up the surrounding dunes was the largest array of bots she had seen. There were harvest-bots, service bots, several large jellyfish floating above the mass, cleaning bots scurrying across the ground, medics, farmers, repairman. She spotted several that looked like Arquella. One of them likely was Arquella, but she couldn't tell. There were the micro-bots, no larger than a mouse, whipping in and out of the others. Yet, in the mass of bots, she did not see the Barlgharel. There was not even another sewer bot that she could confuse for him.

Syn felt a pang of hope. She spoke, "They came for me." She glanced back at the Sisters. The Crimson Queen stood in front, her shoulders squared and undeterred.

Syn turned and eyed the mass of bots, all shouting, "Expected. Expected," in unison. A tear rolled down her blood-stained cheek. They had come for her. They had conquered their fear of the desert and Zondon Almighty and the Crimson Queen herself. For her.

At that moment, Syn realized she wanted to be back with the Ecology. There was no question. But she didn't want it to be all or nothing.

There was still Kerwen and Pigeon, and she had begun to love them—they were becoming true sisters more than just in name. She didn't want to have to choose between the two camps. Yet, she found herself shouting, "I'm here!"

The sounds outside turned raucous. The voice boomed, "We see her now! Give us the Expected. Release her."

Above the wall, above her, looking down, although far away, floated a single ball—much smaller than Arquella, but Syn was familiar with the type: eye-bots, just like the crimson one she had rescued from the crater. They were the first on most any scene in her Disc, analyzing and helping to coordinate the other bots to respond. Here they were informers. She stared at it. Huck? No, it didn't move like him.

Kerwen picked up a rock and threw it over the wall. It clinked against something, and she smiled broadly.

Neci screeched, "Get her away from there!"

Taji yanked Syn back from the wall and grunted, "Why do they want the little piece of dirt anyway?"

Ignoring the question, Neci whispered to Kerwen, "Is all ready?"

Kerwen nodded. "I have three loaded and ready. We can leave and go to the seventeenth without delay. It's working fine. I used it a few days back, and it's a straight shot to the needle."

Syn wore a puzzled response. The seventeenth Jacob lift must be several kilometers away. They'd pass at least one other Jacob between here and there.

Kerwen caught Syn's puzzled look and answered her unasked question, "The machines won't think we'd go further than we have to. Just can't think like that. Little morons will check out the closer Jacobs. Or the settlements."

"We're leaving?" Syn asked, "They won't hurt us. Just let me…"

"Get her. Shut her up," Neci barked.

The two burlys were on her, pulling her back from the wall.

Neci turned and marched away as the crowd of bots outside began to slam themselves against the walls. Neci spoke, "All. We're leaving. Now." She pointed at Pigeon. "Make sure the grav plates are secure on her companion." She then stabbed a finger at Taji, "And you grab...*The Expected.*" She spoke the phrase with a sneer.

Pigeon dashed off into the dark corridors, fast as a blur.

"You're not buying that load, are you?" Taji asked, punching a meaty paw into Syn's arm.

Syn struggled in the grasp of the burly, kicking and punching at him. She shouted, "Let go!" It definitely wasn't Admiral—the grip was cruel.

Neci laughed. "If we get through the gate, I'll call her *Messiah.*"

The burly didn't relax. It tromped after Neci, holding the struggling Syn close. His grip was nearly unbreakable. Still, she continued to kick and hit at him.

After a trek through the maze to the far side of Zondon Almighty, through the careening, tight passages, they came to an open room with three floats, loaded with gear. Pigeon was already there, a bag floating ahead of her, held in place between her hands. The shape of Blip was discernible through the burlap. Pigeon had been fast. She had darted to the far edge of the small city and then back here while they took a direct route.

Pigeon never wore a smug look. There was no haughtiness. Yet, Syn detected something of pride in her stance now. Perhaps her legs were a bit straighter. Maybe she stood a bit taller and did not hunch her shoulders. Had Syn's reversal against Neci changed the girl's mood? Did Pigeon feel she had beaten Neci somehow?

Neci didn't even spare a glance at the tiny girl. She began to speak, "We need to move fa..."

She was interrupted by a massive boom. An explosion reverberated through all of Zondon, shaking the ground below their feet and causing the walls to rattle. A second later, the sound of crashing metal reached them.

Kerwen exclaimed, "They've broken the wall!"

"Morons," Taji said, spitting on the ground. "Stupid machines."

Neci instead sat down on one of the floats and propped her legs up on the running board.

The burly planted Syn down on another hover bike and held her down with two brawny hands on her shoulders. She shrugged and stopped struggling. "Fine," she grunted. The vehicle jostled but righted itself quickly with the weight. A sense of satisfaction rushed over Syn. At least the technology was consistent. The hover bikes were the same here as they were in her world. At this realization, she smiled as she turned to face Neci.

Neci spoke, "Horrible little machines. And they want you."

"Why do you hate them so much?" Syn asked.

Neci smiled, "They're useless. Can't get them to do anything. Can't threaten. Can't control. These…" she nodded at the golem, "Are so much easier to lead."

"Of course you can't control them!" Syn shouted, "They're living!"

"They're machines. They're stupid. Someone's controlling them," Taji offered.

Neci shook her head. "They are the eyes and ears of the bitch above."

"So is she controlling them *now*? Does she want Syn?" Kerwen asked.

Was Olorun truly alive? Was she a thinking machine like Blip and the Barlgharel? Syn wanted to ask. Syn started to ask. She'd love to compare notes, to get to the bottom of this. And right now, Neci seemed to be interested, to be kind. But then Pigeon's final words last night ran through her mind. *She's wicked. Twisted.* The carnage of the workshop flashed in her memory. In response to Neci, Syn said, "So who twisted you?"

"Twisted? That's a nice word." Neci winked at her. "Let's not do this now. We have an appointment."

The din of the robotic onslaught grew. The metal buildings behind them crashed one after another.

"They really want our guest," Kerwen said.

"On the floats. They're nearing the center of the city," Neci ordered.

The Sisters and Syn were joined by several more burlys. They spread out onto the hover bikes. Syn sat between Taji and the thin burly that held her in place. Pigeon, Kerwen, and Neci on the other, with Admiral behind her. And three other burlys on the third. They moved out. The bikes were quiet, but she appreciated their soft hum. Their recognizable hum. Syn nodded at Pigeon, "Good job on keeping these in great shape."

Taji looked back, "What do you mean?"

"These are in great shape. They take a lot of work."

Taji chewed her lip and bobbed her neck. The muscled girl rolled her shoulders and said. "The one who fixed these isn't around."

Pigeon whispered, "Tulce."

Syn repeated the name. Taji jabbed her with an elbow just as the hover sped forward. Syn started to totter off the bike as the burly snagged her shoulders. She moaned as she struggled to breathe. So Pigeon wasn't the only one connected to Tulce. Taji felt that pain too. *Don't say anything about Tulce to anyone. Don't make Taji mad.*

The bikes zipped through the back wall. Nothing but darkened sand dunes greeted them. If it was day, it was hard to tell. The gray of the sky formed a seamless gradient with the drab sands.

The air was still, and she could see the rolling of the hills in front of them—a silent world that didn't want to be disturbed.

They were nearly two kilometers or more beyond Zondon when Neci's bike, in lead, slowed and then stopped. Syn guessed at the distance from the location of the Jacob pylons near them. The scenery was all so monotonous that she was unable to discern their location with any accuracy.

Neci turned her bike around and pointed it at the city.

Taji copied the action. As they slowed, Taji chuckled, "Watch this."

Seconds passed, and they saw nothing. Suddenly there was a brilliant flash of light. Syn shielded her eyes, but it was too late. She was seeing spots and couldn't orient herself. The thunder of a massive explosion followed and a moment—not even a second later—a shockwave slammed against her. It felt like a wall, and it slammed into her chest like a fist and then lifted her up and threw her against the sand. A second wave hit moments after. She blinked and saw, frozen in the fraction of a moment, the others spinning wildly through the air. Syn hit the ground again and tumbled. There was a loud ringing sound—a high-pitch whine that blocked out everything else. She shut her eyes from the stinging of the sand. Burning. Everything felt like it was on fire. Her eyes. Her ears. Her skin. She laid in the sand, and a wash of heat rolled over her back. Her head must be in the sand, she thought, but wasn't sure how she knew that. The heat began to sting. It hurt so bad. She picked up her head and wailed. Pain. Pain. Pain. She couldn't think of anything but the pain.

Then darkness.

When next she remembered, there were other voices. Her voice. "Lift her up. Make sure she's breathing." And "That was stupid." "Torch the whole place." Then a quieter echo of her voice, "Foolish." Somewhere, in Syn's own mind, that word had formed. *All of this was foolish. Foolish that I hadn't ran. Foolish I am still living. Foolish that I almost died. Foolish that I had even come here.*

The voices continued, and she began to separate them.

"It hurts."

"I know it does." The cadence was slower. Neci. Control. Elegance. Even in the tragedy. There was something about this copy of her that she found enticing. Neci was always controlled. She could see why the others obeyed her. She had a mastery over herself that Syn could only dream of. Somewhere, far below, she had dreamed of being the person that Neci was. Never panicked. Never...Anything but Neci.

"They won't be following us. 'Sides, you knew what was coming." Taji's voice was the closest. She was above Syn. The girl rolled Syn over onto her back. Syn coughed, and Taji bellowed, "Blast. She's still alive."

Kerwen shouted from far away. "You lost one of the golems. It didn't duck."

The others shouted back and forth amongst themselves. They righted the hover bikes. They assessed each other's wounds. Except for the loss of the burly and Syn's daze, the collection managed without much injury.

Syn, with the help of Kerwen, stood up. She took the other girl's hand and allowed herself to be pulled to her feet. She maintained the grip just a moment longer. The touch of another person was still so new to Syn. It was beginning to feel like a compulsion. Just a bit of a longer touch. Just to feel their skin. Even though their skin was the same as her own. It was warmed by another heart, by different blood.

Kerwen shook her hand free and stepped away. Syn turned and looked back at Zondon Almighty. Or, where Zondon Almighty had been. Now there was nothing by a thick rising cloud of black smoke. Far above, the pillar ended in a conical shape. The surface of the clouds was illuminated a bright orange from the fires in the ruins of the city. Syn stammered, "What…What was that?"

Neci was already back on her hover. "Impressive, eh?"

Syn took a few more steps in the direction of the burning city. "You did that? On purpose?"

Taji laughed. "They won't follow us now."

"But that was your home!"

Neci shook her head and motioned to both Pigeon, who stood quiet, and Taji to take their seats. "The machines had to die—they weren't going to stop pursuing you. They would follow us to Eden. They had to be ended."

Syn felt paralyzed. She stumbled forward and shouted, "Arquella! Huck!" The throng of bots was dead. All of the Ecology. *Were there a hundred standing outside the city? Far more than that. Thousands? Several thousands?* Syn's vision blurred, and she cried. She wiped her eyes with her sleeve and glared at Neci. Arquella believed she herself had been human once. She'd had dreams. She'd had her own thoughts and emotions. Huck and Bear had been loyal and caring. And now they were a pool of molten metal. *Murder.*

Taji was still boasting, jabbing a finger at Neci. "Told you that it would work. You doubted me."

Pigeon was back on the bike with Neci. "We said you should leave it where you found it."

Taji's face was still enraptured. "I was sure it would work."

"It worked," Neci said. "I needed it to work. We needed it."

Syn gasped, "We needed it?"

Neci narrowed her eyes. "Are you a part of 'we'?"

Syn ignored the question and took a step in her direction. "Why do you make these decisions for the rest of them?"

"If you think you're ready to be a part of us again, just let me know. You just have to do your part. Until then, you have no voice in what we do."

"You killed them!" Syn was stepping closer to Neci, her arm pointed behind her, her finger jabbing at Zondon Almighty. "You killed each of those bots. They were living! You killed them!"

Neci sat on the bike, smiling.

Syn cleared the distance and Taji stood up to intercept. Neci didn't move.

Syn shouted, "Stop smiling. You just killed a thousand people! You just killed all of them. Stop calling them machines! They were alive! They danced! They painted! They are more alive than you. They created wonderful things, and everything you create is ugly and broken and twisted!"

Neci stood, unmoved and unfazed by Syn's declarations.

Taji laughed, "They were machines." She stood only a foot or two ahead Syn. She had maneuvered there without Syn's notice. The girl was not only large but, like Pigeon, she was stealthy.

Pigeon glared at Syn, raising a finger to her lips. She repeated Taji's words, "They're machines." Pigeon did not glance away. There was no fear or shame in her stare. Just cold control now.

She stared back at the flames of the city. In the flames of the Zondon Almighty, she saw images of the future: her Disc burning. Her tree. Her river. Her world. In flame.

Taji yanked at Syn's shirt and pulled her back to their hover. Neci nodded and sped away to the Jacob. Taji pulled Syn close. "You're crossing lines. Once we get to that gate, you either prove you've had a change of heart or—"

Syn was not listening. If she were to flee, now would be the time. There was only Kerwen's bike with her burlys. Then Taji and her. She could run. But as she moved her foot to turn, a jab of pain shot through her leg.

Syn's own spear was jammed against her ankle—the spear held tightly in Taji's hand. The girl glared, "No fast moves."

"That's mine!" Syn hissed.

Taji pulled the spear back, spinning it in the air and looking over the cracked shaft. "Now, it's mine. Get on the bike."

JOURNAL ENTRY: THE SALVATION OF EKU

The Unauthorized Journal of Syn
    Section 18
    Composed 2758

Blip wanted us to give the tiger time and distance. I didn't. I wanted to see it again. Okay—I wanted to see the cubs again.

The next day, Blip reluctantly followed me back into the settlements, back to the tiger and its makeshift den. We navigated through the halls and doors, carefully watching before and after. Blip glowed a bright green, watching everything, all sensors on high.

"Anything?" I asked, for the fifteen-hundredth time in the last ten minutes.

Blip sighed and then chirped, "No. Nothing."

"Nothing?"

"That's the same question."

"But nothing? Absolutely nothing?"

"There's nothing around. There's no tiger stalking around," Blip said.

We were only four rooms away from the den, and a chill ripped down my back—my skin went to gooseflesh—and I froze. I gripped my spear tighter and lifted it up, pointing the tip into the darkness ahead.

"What is it?" Blip asked.

But I didn't know. I'm not sure what caused the shiver. Just an assurance that something was wrong.

We took a step ahead, and I heard my own footfall.

I hadn't heard my steps last time. Last time we entered, I had been listening to something else—the gentle purr of the cubs nuzzled against their mother.

There was no purring. I whispered, "I can't hear the cubs."

But quieter, less constant, were occasional grunts and snorts. Wet sounds. Violent.

We stepped slower. I was crouched, ready to leap.

The mismatched sounds of heavy breathing grew louder as we drew closer.

Then we entered the room—cautious and slow.

Hyenas.

There in the makeshift den, the hyenas had ambushed the tiger. The scene was ghastly. Blood was splattered across the walls. The three hyenas were ripping into the carcass of the tiger and the cubs. Near my feet was the body of one of the cubs. Its neck had been snapped, and there was already a large chunk of flesh ripped out of its body. The blood pulled around it, staining its orange fur into a brilliant crimson.

They had followed us. We had led them here when we first went in pursuit of the tiger. They had taken advantage of our tracking the tiger. In the wake of our mercy, they had shredded the young family. They couldn't attack me. But there was nothing in their programming preventing them from stalking and killing other animals. There was still uncurbed nature in their DNA. Directed brutality without restraint.

I roared, "No!" and leaped, surprising the beasts. I was too fast for the first, and my spear went clean through the closest one, killing it with one stab. They were no threat to me. They couldn't have attacked me. Wouldn't have. But I didn't care.

Blip flew in behind, yelling out, "Syn!" But I wouldn't stop. I hated them! They had killed the mother and her cubs. They had massacred the animals.

And it was my fault. I had let the hyenas roam free because I didn't think they were a threat. I had stalked the wrong creatures. I had led them here. It was my fault.

The second hyena barked and then charged, using my moment of landing as an opportunity. Perhaps it was defending itself. Or perhaps that bit of programming that prevented it from targeting me had melted away in the taste of the fresh kill. It would've worked—my spear was still lodged in the first one—but Blip was there, flying at full speed. His massive weight slammed into the side of the hyena as it jumped. The beast was flung against the wall, hitting it with bone-breaking cracks and an awful splat sound. It was dead on impact, but I'm just not sure which impact killed it—Blip's charge or the wall.

Either way, two were down and one left. The third was smart, though. It had watched the other two and was now retreating, looking for a point to break and run. I put my foot on the body of the first hyena for leverage and pulled my spear out. Its tip was dripping in the beast's blood. I turned toward the last hyena, and in response to its shrill cackling bark, I growled.

And I didn't wait—I charged ahead. I feinted to the left, and the beast twisted to the right, exactly where I wanted it to. My spear arrived at the same moment it did, stabbing straight into the skull of the beast. It gave a final loud whimper as it died. Its eyes rolled back, and it vomited blood.

It was over. All three dead in seconds. I shook my spear free, and the hyena's limp body ragdolled until it flopped off of the tip.

I roared—no words, just a primal scream of regret and fear and release.

I turned toward the body of the tigress and fell to my knees, landing in the pool of blood, and wrapped my arms around her huge head. Dead. She was dead. I cried, "I'm sorry. I'm sorry." I had killed this beautiful creature. I had killed the only tigers on the ship. There would be no more tigers. At the same time, I realized there would be no more hyenas—I wanted to not care about them either, but I did. I was killing things, and I didn't want to be a killer.

I buried my face in its blood-matted fur. "I'm sorry," I whimpered.

Blip hovered near but stayed silent. He understood.

My tears dried out, and so did my words. I held the tigress' head in silence for an unknown time. A great force had gone out of my world, never to return.

The silence stretched.

From somewhere in the room, from under some of the blankets and clothes, something moved—it was a shuffling sound and then a scratching against the floor.

I released the tiger and stood to attention. Was one of the hyenas still alive? We scanned around. Blip went full green in alert.

He whispered, "There. In the corner." He was staring at a mound of blankets that was now rustling.

I counted the hyenas. They were all dead. A mouse perhaps? A rat?

And then my heart leaped in hope. Perhaps...I darted without caution to the blankets and pulled them off whatever was there.

A cub. The fat one. Still breathing, its eyes were searching frantically. I reached down for it, and it gave a sharp hiss that came out as a coughing growl. It bristled and pulled back. I bent and let it smell my hand as I examined it. There were no wounds. It had gone overlooked in the hyenas' assault. It sniffed a few times and then took a cautious step toward me. I ran a hand through its fur and inside, I melted. One had survived.

In a moment, it relaxed and fell into my arms. I plucked it up and held it close, allowing its purr to grow. A minute passed, and it fell asleep against my chest.

I turned back to Blip, tears blurring my vision. I tried to speak, and the words choked as they came out. "We saved it."

We searched around for other survivors but found none. We left and barred the door shut until we could send a cleaning crew of bots in here to remove the remains and bodies to the body farms below.

That night we searched the stores for milk and found a baby bottle in one of the settlements. For the next few weeks, the little tiger didn't leave my side. I nursed it to strength—although it was fat enough that it would've done fine for a while without. It slept with me at night. It followed along during the day.

Blip pointed out that the little furball was a "she" and that we needed a name. We chose the name Eku.

Since then, she has been a part of our odd little family—always beside Blip and myself.

ASCENT

"When your rage is choking you, it is best to say nothing."
—Octavia Butler

The Jacob lift was cramped. Neci had directed them to one of the larger freight compartments that opened on the side of the standard personal Jacob lift that Syn was used to. The final push toward the Jacob was hurried but not in a dead rush. The concern that had propelled Neci forward in a sprint as they left the city had faded.

They stood shoulder to shoulder in the cramped Jacob lift, the walls dented and scuffed. Taji's tapping of Syn's spear against the floor interrupted the hushed space.

Perhaps it was the sense of dismay after the destruction of Zondon. Perhaps it was their relief at having survived the onslaught of the bots. Perhaps it was the shock of the explosion that leveled the city. Or maybe all three and more. Whatever it was, they all stood quiet, no one meeting each other's gaze. They rode silent and still up the pillar toward the needle. This was a trip that Syn had made countless times before but never with others. Everything she did now was a shared experience. It was, in a way, a dream come true. But she had not ever dreamed it would be this horrific. Pigeon had said it. They were evil. Neci twisted everything she touched. And Syn had seen it with her own eyes.

Now they were racing toward the needle to open the gate. Syn shuddered at the thought of Neci unleashed upon her Disc. She saw the birds twirling through the air. She imagined the lazy animals sleeping under the shade of the forest. The fish darting through the great river. All was pristine and raw and untouched. Syn had lived with her world as if it was immovable and should not be altered. Below them, Neci's work blazed out: a desert on fire spilling dark smoke into the already polluted air.

The bright flames glowed. Syn stared at the burning remains. A large dark circle to the side of town caught her eyes. It was a huge and flat against the ground, outside the gates. *Oh*, Syn thought as she recognized it. It had been where the great tree in her Disc would've been. It was just a stump. They had cut down their tree.

Neci smiled, "These are the leftovers I was handed."

"You did this." Syn leaned closer and kept her words quiet. Perhaps only Neci herself might hear. She didn't mean the phrase for anyone else.

"Let me remind me you. I was left with nothing else. Leftovers. Mobs of insane colonists rampaging and killing their own."

"You burned this world. You made it—" Syn said, but she stopped when Neci spun on her.

Neci breathed, "Who told you?" She eyed each of the others in the Jacob. Taji. Kerwen. Pigeon.

None of them responded. Syn avoided looking toward Pigeon. She avoided looking anywhere but ahead.

Neci sighed. "Fine, fine, fine. The cowards are hungry for another friend. They yap and yap and yap." She slapped Pigeon's cheek lightly then turned and glared at Kerwen. "She's not one of us. We tried but she isn't. She wasn't here. You may think she can be a part, but she'll never understand the choices we've had to make. All we've done to survive. All we've been forced to do to survive."

The room felt cold and frozen in time. Syn stood tense waiting for

Neci's explosion. But instead of erupting, Neci continued, her voice low, calm, and controlled, "You see, I've done the math. There were far too many of the colonists on this Disc. I believe they came over here in droves. I think the chaos started on your side. Or perhaps there was a war between them. Perhaps one Disc was jealous of the other. Whatever the reason, this Disc was crowded. Was yours empty? You're like a kitten—innocent. You haven't seen any of the Madness, have you? Knowing how many we killed over here convinced me that your Disc must be pristine. How do I know? Puck told me."

"Puck?" Syn asked. She had heard the name before but could not remember where.

Kerwen muttered, "Neci's companion."

"That's correct." Neci pulled open the bag that Taji was carrying and lifted Blip out. She seemed to lift him. Syn assumed this was because he was supported by several circular grav plates they had slapped onto him. She held it between her hands and stared at it. "Puck was a brilliant little thing. He was there the moment we moved out into the Disc. After everything had gone wrong, he was the one who told me about your Disc. Told me to take all of the Sisters and go over there. He said there wasn't any fighting there. It was what he shouted just before we beat him to death—he pleaded and pleaded and poured out little secrets. He had known all along but kept Eden a secret until he needed to bargain for his life. But he had to die— couldn't have him telling the bitch above all about our plans. Cracked him open like an egg. The little liars have such a soft spot when you hit them from behind. They squeal, too. You'd almost think they were alive."

Neci held out Blip to Syn. Syn raised her arms and carefully grabbed ahold of the bot. Eyeing Neci, she took Blip's weight into her arms. He was so heavy, even with the grav plates.

Neci smiled. "But when we all got to the gate, it was closed. Locked tight. All of the colonists from your Disc had been streaming through it, but somehow, someone had shut it. We returned to the Disc, but they pursued. Everywhere we went, they chased us. They attacked over and over. We lived months in fear. So what choice did we have? We torched this place to eliminate the mad set of them."

"And you'll come to my world and do the same." Syn examined Blip. There were scuff marks and chunks of dirt on him, and there appeared to be some chips near the back of his body, but as a whole, he was untouched. The companion bots were nearly unbreakable. Neci and the others must have been brutal to destroy theirs.

"Are there threats there?"

Syn shook her head. Yet, she wondered how the Sisters would perceive the bots on her side? And what of Eku?

"Then why would I?"

Syn frowned. She and Neci were similar. Syn was scared just then. She wanted to barrel past them and run away. She wanted to run far away. "You're scared."

Neci pretended to either not hear that comment or ignored it. "So, here's the plan for now. I know you don't want me over there, but I want to give you one more chance. I want you to wake your companion up. I know they're triggered by the Eve they're assigned to. So you just stand there and think nice thoughts and get him to open his eyes. We need him to open the gate."

Stay quiet, Blip, Syn thought. Then, on the heels of that thought came another, *wake up soon, Blip.* She ran her fingertips across his surface. Smooth. Cold.

She felt a tingle under her fingers. A quick, sharp vibration emanated from Blip. She glanced down. The companion bot sat unmoving. It was inert.

Neci continued, "Do you want to know the fantasies I've had?"

Syn coughed. "No. I don't. I want you to open these doors and jump to your death."

"You hate me so much?" Neci still stared out the window. While speaking, she reached over and grabbed Kerwen's hand and held it. "Do you hate us? All of us? Why?"

Again, underneath her fingertips, the smooth surface of Blip vibrated. She glanced down again, and the sensation stopped.

"Well?" Neci pushed.

Syn grunted. "I don't want you in my Disc."

"I dream of a river. I dream of floating down a long, languid river. I dream of running my fingers in the water as the current pulls me along."

Syn's head jerked up. How had Neci known about that? She grimaced but stifled the reaction. Couldn't let them know what she was thinking or feeling.

"I just want to be free," Neci leaned in, "How can you hate me for that?"

Blip vibrated again. This time, Syn resisted the urge to steal a look. The vibration continued. It was slight, and there was no sound. Only a subtle sensation that Syn could feel. In answer, Syn tapped a finger gently on the side. The vibration paused and then started again. A response.

Blip was alive.

Syn tapped him again, this time with her pinky finger. Blip responded with a vibration localized near her finger. Then it stopped. Blip lay unmoving.

Neci put her fingers against the glass. "I think you hate us because we're so much like you." Neci glanced back at Syn. "I hate you, too."

Syn didn't want to, but the word was out before she could pull it back. "Why?"

"You were able to keep yourself from all of this. Somehow, you were the one who rolled the dice and came up a winner. Lucky little you." Neci continued to ramble, her words puttering out like some pent-up spring. Her next words snagged Syn's attention. "You'll do it, you know."

"No. Blip won't open the door. I won't open the door."

"Blip," Neci walked over and slid a finger along Blip's surface. "Such a cute name." Behind her, written on the glass was the word "WATER" in capital letters and rough handwriting. Neci's strokes were irregular and out of alignment. She didn't write often. She wasn't practiced.

Neci caught Syn's gaze at the word and said, "That's why you'll open the gate."

"No." Syn's voice was firm, unwavering. "I'm not going to."

"You don't want to go home?"

"I don't want you over there. We'll all stay here."

"What if there's nowhere else to go?" Neci walked back to the window. "The first explosion was just to prove I can do it."

"Prove what?"

"That I can and will destroy this place. I killed Zondon Almighty. Our home. I also, hopefully, punched through to the Underworld. To the groves and the body farms below that." Neci gave a deep, contented sigh and then continued, "The next one is set to go off in an hour or so. It'll punch through to the shield."

Again, the term was odd. *What shield?* The magnetic flows that kept things moving around the ship? Or the ramscoop that catches the stray hydrogen before them. Neither seemed right. But then, Syn knew what she meant. "The water shield?"

Neci leaned in and fogged the window again. With her finger, she wrote FLOOD. "Yes. That's exactly what I meant."

The water shield was the final layer underneath everything. The barrier between the life of the Disc and the cold, emptiness of space. On Syn's Disc, it filtered all of the water that flowed through the river Lokun and into the settlements. More importantly, it provided a critical barrier between the interior of the Disc and the dangers of cosmic radiation bombarding Olorun in its journey.

Taji crossed her arms and smiled. "Nothing to come back to."

Next to her, Kerwen staggered back in surprise. "What? Why?"

So, Kerwen had not known. Only Taji and Neci. Syn glanced at Pigeon, and the girl was unreadable, but her frozen features were too still. Perhaps she was scared. Perhaps the shock that the moment had arrived and that Neci was going through with her plan might have been overwhelming.

"What choice do I have?" Neci said to Kerwen. "We have to get over there, and she won't open the gate. When everything is thirty feet under water, then what else can there be to do?"

"You'll kill everyone else on this side. The bots that survived," Syn stammered.

"It doesn't matter. We'll live. And it's all up to you." Neci nodded at Blip, "And little 'ol Blip there."

Syn shook her head. "You live here. How can you destroy it all?"

Neci turned and stepped up to Syn, inches from her face. "This isn't our home. We weren't meant to live on this stupid ship. We were intended to live on Àpáàdì. Not here. This ship is a prison. This ship is what we're stuck with because they screwed up. This is Hell. I don't want to be here. None of this matters."

Syn had had enough. She yelled back, "This is it. We're not getting to Àpáàdì! We're out of fuel."

"You think I don't know about that? All we have to do is lighten our load. I'd say about half our weight," Neci cooed.

"You knew about the fuel?" Syn eyed Neci.

Kerwen interjected herself into the back-and-forth. "What about the fuel? What are you talking about?"

Taji sighed. "Just tell her."

Syn motioned up toward the needle. "We're out of fuel. Somehow we burned too much in our speed-up. We don't have enough for the slow-down. Do you remember the vids? How Captain Pote said we'd make landfall by burning half during the first part and half during the second?"

"The idiots burned it all up!" Neci laughed. "All because they were too scared."

"You know why they burned it all up?"

Neci whispered, "Mutiny."

"Stop talking in riddles!" Kerwen balled her fists up.

Neci sighed herself, "Fine. Full story. The idiots got scared and took over. Killed most of the command crew."

"What idiots?" Syn asked.

"I don't know which idiots. Some of the colonists. Choose. They were all stupid. Anyway, they decide they don't want to wait. Someone decides to work out the numbers and tries to speed up their journey by burning up most of the fuel to increase their speed and then using some method of skirting Kapteyn's Star just on its event horizon to slow down. Everyone believed him. They did it. Then they consulted Olorun. The ship explained they were wrong. The figures were off. Way off. Then they lost it. That was the start of the Madness."

"Liar!" Kerwen said.

Pigeon gave a sharp, shrill laugh. They all turned to look at her. She was sitting on the ground of the Jacob, her eyes staring at the ceiling. Syn allowed a glance to follow her gaze, but there was nothing there.

"What?" Taji said.

"You frightened Kerwen. She's scared," Pigeon said.

Kerwen relaxed her hands, releasing her fists. "I'm not scared. I just don't understand. That can't be the answer."

"It isn't," Pigeon said, "Can't you all tell she's playing with you?"

Syn tapped Blip. His shell tingled. The sensation moved, and Syn followed it with her finger. She followed just a few inches, but the vibration led her finger to the bottom right of its shell—a location at the peripheral of her vision and blocked by her arm from the other's sight.

She stole a glance. In the faint blue light, nearly imperceptible had she not been looking directly at it, words flashed: BE READY.

Her heart raced. Be ready for what?

She tapped Blip again. He vibrated in reply—a short burst. A "leave me alone, let me think" response. Did they know each other that well? He didn't speak to her, but words weren't needed.

The Crimson Queen held her shoulders back—a prideful stance. She was in control, even in chaos. In that confident look, Syn caught a glimpse of Neci's train of thought and understood the logic that had taken her there. Perhaps it was a larger plan than anything Syn had dreamed of, but it was a plan, and Neci's thought process did not seem foreign at all. Every piece of the puzzle seemed to proceed naturally from the one before. Crazy. Grandiose. But it made sense.

Kerwen pressed her palms together in front of her face. "Can someone tell me?"

"I'm making the princess open the gate. That's my first goal," Neci said.

Taji picked up the line of thought, "That's why we're flooding this Disc." She gestured out the window with the point of the spear, just as Syn used to.

Neci nodded. "That's why we're flooding it. This was my backup plan. If you refuse and that thing in your hands doesn't wake up and the bitch above doesn't respond, I'll force your hand. This world is going to drown. Burning it didn't work." She looked at Syn. "And then?"

The entire plan formed in Syn's mind. Perhaps, had she been in Neci's place, she would have crafted it herself. Syn whispered, "Then you release this Disc from the needle to reduce weight. The remaining fuel should be enough to get us to our destination." She took a step closer to Neci. "You don't have a companion. Are you sure you solved it right?"

"Oh, I've had my numbers checked and rechecked." She gave a thin grin to Pigeon. "But not just the water. This Disc. We're going to eject the Disc."

Pigeon allowed a small smile in return but quickly extinguished it and stared at the ground.

"How?" Syn asked.

Neci avoided the question, "We now have a deadline."

"This has been our entire life," Kerwen said, "I don't want it…" She stumbled on the words, emotion welling up inside her. Tears filled her eyes.

"How do you release the Disc?" Syn asked.

"That's the question!" Neci said. "How do we get rid of the Disc? It's easy. Once we're through the gate, all we have to do—" She cut off her words sharply. She narrowed her eyes at Syn. "No, no, no. I don't think you need to know everything. You have one job. Just do your job."

"Screw you," Syn said.

Blip's skin vibrated, and Syn's finger followed the sensation. It led her back to the area where the words had last flashed. This time, briefly it said: HOLD YOUR BREATH.

What? Syn wanted to dart away. What was Blip doing? Instead, she froze and stood motionless, a statue in fear that the others would detect a change.

Neci smiled, "Oh, be kind. We have to spend the rest of our lives together." She flashed a smile at Syn. "Besides, you know it's a good plan. I can see the wheels turning. When I think of all of us, you're the one most like me."

The gravity in the Jacob had shifted, and Syn could feel the lack of it tangibly. Every limb moved with greater ease. They were racing high up, and gravity's decline was an exponential difference. Every moment significantly reduced the overall pull. In a few seconds, they would be floating.

In blue, Blip flashed: *10.*

A moment later, a second later, he flashed: *9.* Her heart rate slowed.

A countdown. He was counting down to something. She would have to hold her breath in nine seconds. Yet, even with that expectation, her anxiety ebbed away—it always did when he did his counting trick. Ever since she was little, this stupid stunt would focus her racing mind and bring her back down.

Syn said, "No."

8.

Now, eight seconds. She was going to have to hold her breath in eight seconds.

7.

Then, right after, it flashed, HOLD TIGHT.

Pigeon's eyes glanced down at the bot. Had she seen what Blip was writing? Or just the flash of light? Would she say something?

Neci said, "We're the decision makers. We had the tough job. Made us different. We were born cauterized. We were designed for the extreme environment of other worlds. And the best of us only grow stronger with each moment."

5.

Syn's palms were sweating. Again, she muttered, "No."

"Keep saying it, but it doesn't change a thing," Neci said. She turned to look out the window. "Blasted near identical."

3.

And again, in quick flashes, HOLD TIGHT and HOLD YOUR BREATH.

Pigeon's eyes again glanced down at Blip. She looked up at Syn, her eyes wide with horror. Pigeon breathed, "No—"

Syn took a deep breath. An action that caused Neci to turn in her direction.

2.

Neci narrowed her eyes, glancing between Syn and Pigeon. Pigeon pushed herself back against the wall and muttered again, "Stop."

But the warning came too late.

Blip's skin vibrated, and Syn gripped him tight. She crouched as well, knowing what Blip was doing. Her heart was slamming against her chest. He had warned against this very thing so many times before.

1.

The Jacob control panel beeped loudly. The doors slid open and the air inside the Jacob rushed out into the thinner atmosphere outside.

Syn pushed off the floor to propel herself through the door. She did not need to. Blip came alive, full lights glowing, and sped off through the open doors with Syn holding on tight.

Neci roared behind her, "No!" and scrambled for the racing two.

38

ABOVE IT ALL

"Once Lilith saw this, she uttered the special name of God, flew off
into the air, and escaped..."
—*The Alphabet of Ben Sira*, 700 CE

As she clung to Blip speeding out of the Jacob, she felt
fingertips on her heel. Syn glanced back. Kerwen had
leaped after, her hand dangling, her fingers waggling to
grip onto Syn's heel. Kerwen shouted, "Don't leave me!"

She was above it all. Flying through the air, high above the rolling
dark clouds, under the scattered glare of the sunstrips. Behind her, she
could hear the screams of rage and surprise.

Syn yelled to Blip, "Stop!" But he didn't hear her. Or pretended not
to. Instead, the companion bot flew out and then took a sharp left,
careening toward the next closest Jacob, standing just a few hundred
meters away at this height.

As Syn yelled, she gasped for air; she had been warned. There was
little atmosphere at this height. There was little gravity—although
there was some. She glanced back once more to Kerwen. What she
saw made her heart race. She tried to yell again at Blip, but there was
not enough air in her lungs to make words.

Kerwen was already drifting down. Taji was leaning over the edge of the Jacob, arm extended to reach Kerwen and drag her back to the safety of the lift. There was no chance. She had jumped too far. She was aimless, and the slight gravity was already doing its work. It was an exponential force, and with each inch lower she drifted, the pull of gravity grew stronger. She would soon fall to her death, if she did not die of suffocation first. Syn tried to do the math. How fast would Kerwen plummet? Would she hit the ground in four minutes? Syn knew she could hold her breath for four minutes.

Would they reach the other Jacob in four minutes? Yes—but unconsciousness was already pressing in. She was starting to black out. Her field of vision had narrowed. A haze of streaking violet occluded her peripheral. The stress and strain of holding onto Blip's smooth surface had reduced her strength. She could hold her breath for over four minutes in perfect conditions—without pressure. Those were not the conditions she faced. She already saw spots.

Please, get to the other access point. Please. Get in.

Kerwen.

Flying across the top of the Disc between Jacob towers with a world below them, the loss of a Sister consumed her decaying thoughts.

Just days. That was all they had known each other. She stole a look back, but they were far enough away that all she saw was the dark blur on the edge of what limited vision she had—Kerwen falling slowly, gracefully to death. She pounded against Blip, but he did not relent. She wanted to save the girl, but she knew it was too late.

Ahead, the next Jacob tower grew closer. At this height, the towers were closer together rather than the kilometer spacing at the base. They were only a few feet from an Orisha mask. This one was teardrop shaped, and there was a slight upturn in the corners of its mouth. *Was it happy?* From this distance, the masks were monumental in size. She felt as if she was floating by the faces of the gods. They stood there, unmoving, and a shiver ran down her back. They hadn't helped stop the calamity on this Disc and seemed unconcerned with her now. Just like the Builders themselves.

Would they get to it only to discover the Jacob lift was at the bottom? That the doors were closed? Would they be forced to descend like Kerwen? Blip could control their descent for a while, but at some point, gravity would overwhelm them, and they'd be pulled down with more force than he could lift. They'd die the same way Kerwen would. Stains on the surface of the dark Disc.

The door to the Jacob slid open. *Of course it would. Blip was controlling it.*

They flew through the open doors, and Blip halted in the middle of the Jacob. Syn continued on and slammed against the far side, knocking what little air she had in her out. The gravity was still slight, and she bounced from the wall across the Jacob just as the doors slid shut and the small container pressurized. She smacked the doors hard. As she floated aimless, dazed, she gasped for air. Air. There was air in the Jacob. She could breathe.

Blip swung around and floated down to the control panel and began to interact. The Jacob stayed motionless for a moment and then, at Blip's command, began to ascend again toward the needle.

The gravity lessened. Syn fumbled for Blip and gave a hoarse, "Stop. No."

"Are you okay?" he chirped.

Syn took another deep breath. "Go back."

"We are going back. To our Disc. It's over now," Blip said as he sidled up next to her, giving her something to lean on and orient against.

"No! Back down!" Her voice was still faint sounds interspersed with wheezes.

"Syn, it's okay. We are going home. This is not our Disc."

"No! We have to go back for Arquella. For Huck. And Bear. For the Barlgharel." She was finding her voice. She blinked and stared at him, her eyes begging.

"Who?"

"The bots! They helped me. We have to go back for them."

Blip's voice grew stern. "We aren't going back there. I should never have let you come over here. We're going home."

"No! She's going to kill them all."

"The bots? They are dead already. She blew them up."

"They're not that stupid. They can't all be dead. I didn't see Arquella or Huck. Not even Bear—you can't miss him!"

"It's too late! We don't know when she's going to blow it up."

"We have to try!"

"No, we don't. We only have a chance now to get back home. It'll all be okay when we get through the gate."

"That's what she wants us to do. She wants us to go to the gate. She's going wait for us to try and go through! She's too smart for that. She won't expect us to go back down," Syn yelled.

"Cause it's insane!"

"We have to try!"

"I already told you no."

"I said no!"

"No!"

Syn shouted at him, "No!"

"Stop it! You're being childish."

"They're going to—"

"Don't say it! No more!"

"Die!" she finished.

"They're just dumb bots."

"No they're not! They think. They're alive. They're like you."

"I'm not like them."

"Just like them!"

"I'm a companion and—" Their words began to tumble over each other's as they refused to wait for the other to stop.

"You selfish, little—"

"And it's my job to make sure you're—"

"Little, stupid, lying, lying, lying, lying—"

"You're safe! I won't go back—"

"Lying liar of a—"

"Back there!"

"A bot!"

Then there was silence as the two faced each other, inches away, fuming. Syn was sweating, and her hands were balled into fists.

Without any motion, Blip signaled the Jacob lift, and it slowed to a stop.

Syn still stared, beads of sweat floating in the air around her. Through tight lips, she breathed, "I missed you." And then she was holding him, wrapping him tightly in her arms, feeling his cold shell against her face. "I missed you! I missed you! Are you okay?" She was crying, tears floating off her cheeks to orbit them, splatting against Blip's shell. For a long moment, she held him and then released with a final, choked, "I missed you."

Blip floated back a few inches and chirped, "Are you okay?"

Syn started to answer and then paused. After a moment, her eyes darted to the ground. "No."

"Did they hurt you?"

"No." Then a moment later, "Yes."

Blip understood. "I'm sorry. I should've told you."

"Yes." Her voice still resonated with anger.

"I didn't know about all of this. I knew—"

"You knew they were here. You knew I had sisters."

"They're not sisters. They're clones."

"I'm a clone?" Her words fell out softly. More sadness than rage.

"Yes. Eves."

"Why?"

"Why what?" Blip was down now at the control panel, interfacing.

"Why did they make us? Why copy us? Is it true?" Syn had turned and floated to the window to look out, hoping for a glimpse of Kerwen. If she was out there, she was already lost in the haze and billowing smoke from the remains of Zondon Almighty.

"What did Neci tell you?"

"We were to be the first ones on the planet. Just like Captain Pote said. But I thought I was the only one. That I was—"

"Special?"

Syn nodded and crossed her arms.

Blip continued, "You are."

"I'm one of forty-two. That's not special."

Blip floated higher. He hummed a simple melody. A few notes. A lullaby.

Syn coughed on her next words, "Don't sing that."

Blip stopped. An electric blue smile crept across his face.

"Why did you do that?"

"They didn't get lullabies at night."

"That doesn't matter."

"It does. You had me."

"They had companions." Syn gestured toward the other Jacob lift.

"They killed them." There was a tone of regret in Blip's words.

Syn mumbled, "It doesn't..."

"You and I are still together. You're the only one of them that has their companion. They did terrible things. Remember, at least one of their companions fled from them."

"Spot." Syn did remember the companion that had fallen from the sky. The start to all this. It was such an anomaly. They had never seen another Blip.

Syn turned back and stared out the window. She kept glancing toward where they had just come. Could she see Kerwen in the fog? Could she see the others? She was too far away. She knew that. She just wished...In a voice that sounded as if it was coming from far away, far outside the ship, Syn said, "What if I had..."

"Don't." Blip moved back to the control panel. "I'll take us back down."

Syn spun. Her eyes widened. "The bomb?"

"We're calling it that?"

"What is it?" Syn asked.

"It's a cobalt device."

"What's that?"

"Do you remember watching *The Deserter*?"

"I don't think we finished that one."

"Think big bomb."

"Was that what blew up Zondon?"

"I think so."

"Can we bury it?"

Blip sighed. "Won't work."

"Why is there a bomb on the ship at all? Did the Sisters create it?"

"To melt ice."

Syn stopped and stared at Blip. "Ice?" Her eyes were narrowed.

"Seriously. Ice. One of the concerns is that we'd get to Kapteyn's B and most of the water would be frozen in the caps like it was on Mars. So they prepared to deal with it the same way."

"With a bomb?"

"They bombed the ice caps on Mars, and it melted the water."

"They were idiots."

"The Martians? The Colonists?"

"All of them. The Builders."

Blip nodded.

Syn continued, "And Neci. She's just like them."

"How?"

"Insane. Who hunts for a bomb? Where did she get it? We never came across a bomb in any of our searches."

Blip remained oddly silent.

Syn frowned and crossed her arms. "Where did she get the bomb?"

Blip matched her frown. "I think she had help."

"From who? The burly's?"

"The what?"

"Her creatures. The lumbering things that attacked us when we first arrived. She called them golem."

"Maybe." He nodded. "Maybe from Olorun. Maybe."

"The plans!" Syn exclaimed, "She discovered the plans to the entire ship. Every detail. That's it. That's how she found it." Syn stared at him, but her attention snapped back toward the base as she remembered the Ecology. She waved her arms and swam toward the doors facing inward. She rested her hand on the glass. "We're not moving, Blip. How long have we been just sitting here?"

Blip nodded. "A bit. I've halted the Jacob."

"I need to get down there. I need to stop it."

"You can't do that."

She turned around. Her eyes were wide. Her voice shook. "Then what are we going to do?"

"You're not deactivating the bomb. I don't know how much longer we have before it goes off. It may go off in the time it takes to get back down the surface."

"Then start going! We can't waste any time."

"What are you going to do when we get there?"

"I can figure that out on the way."

Blip growled, "If you think we're going to land and then you just take—"

"Don't tell me what to do."

Blip allowed a short twerp that wasn't a word. The Jacob hummed to life and began to descend. "It is my job."

"You don't need to do it."

Blip floated up to her to look her in the eyes. "It is. You want to know why your Sisters killed their companions? Because we can't stop giving you the right advice or what we think is right."

"She said they killed them because they talked to Olorun. I didn't believe her at first. But I'm beginning to think she's right. Blip, is Olorun alive?

Blip stayed motionless for a long moment and then gave a nod. "Yes. She is. But she is insane and—"

Syn did not allow him to finish the thought. "Have you been telling her about me?"

Blip didn't respond for a moment, then he gave a slight nod. "She's very interested in you."

"What? Why?"

"I don't..."

"Don't say that!"

"I don't."

"Ugh," Syn grimaced. "Fine, I won't go to the bomb. What can we do?"

"I'm trying to communicate with the other bots. But they've done something with the code on this Disc. There're all sorts of foreign layers. I could probably get through it and find a way to figure out what's happening, tap into their info net, but I don't think I could do it quickly."

"So you have no way of knowing where they are or if any one of them survived."

Blip shook, "You have to realize that they probably didn't make it."

Syn frowned. "We need to try."

"Okay, let me think."

With each moment, the gravity increased and Syn found herself closer and closer to the floor of the Jacob.

"I think I may have it," Blip floated back to the control panel in the corner. A few red symbols popped up. Syn didn't understand them at all.

"Yes?" Syn asked. She waved her hands to encourage him to speed up.

"I think there may be a base net communication port not too far from this tower's base."

"And?"

"And if they're at all connected to the network in this Disc, even if they don't use it, they should be able to get something from one of the info hubs."

"What were they for?"

"Do you care?"

"We have a few minutes. Tell me the story," Syn insisted.

"That's just it. There's a hub that ties in all bot communication. I never used it on our Disc. It was a backup unit in case primary communications failed. There's an access point near the parks and the lake."

Syn shook her head. "There's no lake in this world."

Blip narrowed his eyes.

"She burned it all."

"Fine. We're in Jacob 14. The comm hub is a good three kilometers away from here."

"Then we run."

"Three kilometers?"

Syn leaned in, "Will the hub let us find them?"

"It'll send them a message. If there's any alive, they'll hear it. What do you want to say?"

"I...I don't know," Syn said, "We need to get them away."

"Come to the needle?"

"Yes. Tell them I've come back for them. That it's okay to use the Jacobs." Syn remembered standing at the edge of the Desert of Nod as the host of bots gathered to see her off. She remembered her last words to them. "Tell them I'm keeping my promise. We're taking them to Paradise. To our Disc." She glanced up toward the sunstrips.

"You want to rescue them!" Blip rolled his eyes.

Syn nodded her head but went back to the window. She breathed onto the glass, fogging it up, and traced her finger in the haze. Before she realized what she was doing, she had written KERWEN in a rough handwriting. When she finished, she stared at the letters and then through them, out to the dark clouds they were now passing through. Gravity had reasserted and her feet were flat on the floor. She sighed. "How long did it take her to fall?"

Blip paused and then said, "She might still be falling."

Syn spun, wide-eyed.

Blip said, "We were really high up. It'll take a while for her to drop to where gravity pulls her into free-fall."

The image stunned Syn. Kerwen slowly descending, gaining a bit of speed each time, unsure when she'd be pulled down in a straight descent. *Did she try to do something to stop her fall? Is she still up there? Could we do something? Could we save her?*

Blip said, "No."

Syn raised her eyebrows. She knew she hadn't spoken.

Blip smiled, "I've been around you long enough. That was your 'Can we help someone?' face. It isn't going to happen. There's absolutely nothing that we can do. I don't even know how to find her."

"Then..."

Blip nodded and finished her thoughts, "She's dead."

Perhaps it was the stress of the day, the joy of finding Blip, but the word "death" cut into Syn and the emotion she had ignored, that she was not even aware was there, rushed out, and she began to cry. She crumpled to the floor, in the center of the Jacob. How was this possible? Just days ago, she had ruled her world. She had been alone and certain she would always be alone. She had met other humans and discovered they were awful.

She checked herself on that thought as she wiped the tears away. They were not all awful. The very person who told Syn they were evil might be alright. Even then, she did not feel as if she could go back and redeem that moment.

"Blip," Syn looked up. She sniffed and gave a slight cough. She wiper her tears and nose on her shirt and then fingered the orange tiger dangling at her neck. "I can't do it."

Blip hovered down to her.

She continued as Blip edged against her, "I don't think I can solve this. Let's just go home."

Blip floated around, "Are you sure?"

Syn looked at him and then out the window. The clouds outside were dispersing. They were below the cloud layer. The base was only a few moments away—maybe a minute.

Blip pressed, "Can we go home?"

"I don't know. I can't leave them." She picked at a spot on her leg. "I don't know."

"What do you want to do?"

"Will you be with me?"

Blip nodded. "Always. And forever."

"If we screw this up, you won't hate me."

Blip shook his head.

Syn stood up just as the Jacob began to slow its descent.

Blip smiled. "Your next move will need to be you running."

"Why?"

With a simple whoosh, the Jacob completely stopped. A silent shaking seized the cabin. She and Blip knew the routine of how the Jacob worked. The outer doors would soon open. There would be a quick pressurization, and the inner doors would pop open.

"Ready to sprint?" Syn called out.

Syn crouched and pulled down her goggles, one of the gifts from the Barlgharel and the Ecology. She instinctively reached for her spear but cringed when she remembered it was now in Taji's possession. Once more, Syn would head into the desert, this time to save the Ecology. She was keeping her promise. She was returning for them.

The doors hissed open, and Syn prepared to bolt into the darkness.

39

ABEL'S BLOOD

"When Eve saw the serpent touch the tree and did not die,
she picked up one of the fruits that had fallen and . . . tasted it.
But no sooner had she taken a single bite . . .
and she saw the angel of Death standing before her, with his sword
drawn."
—Midrash, Bereshit Rabbah, 19:3-4

The doors opened with a smooth reveal. Syn raced ahead but stopped hard as there before her, glowering, was the towering Taji, her knuckles bare as she held Syn's own spear in front of her. The thick-limbed girl stared through narrow eyes, growling.

Syn didn't wait to talk. Didn't choose to exchange words. Instead, she leapt forward with all of her energy and slammed into the girl. Taji was larger. She was more muscular. But it was still muscle on the same frame that shaped Syn. She might hold Syn's spear, but she wasn't used to it—didn't have the ease of movement that Syn did.

Taji hit the dirt with a grunt. A bit down, below the dirt, was solid concrete. They were in the middle of one of the plazas that the Jacobs opened up to. Around them, peaking up from the blackened dirt, were statues and concrete end posts. One statue, larger than the others, caught Syn's eye—a metal, abstract form that looked like a sword or spear, aimed at the heavens, piercing through three halo-shaped rings that rotated around the central shaft, hovering about it. The shape of the Plaza was visible through the jutting pieces. The desert rolled out beyond that.

The fall on the concrete was enough to daze Taji. Syn hopped back up and spun. She wanted her spear. She wanted something to keep this other girl at a distance. She knew she might out-fight Taji, but there was still a sliver of fear. Taji was deadly. Like a hyena.

Jumping to her feet, Syn spun and kicked hard at Taji's head. Her toes connected, but Taji was expecting it—waiting for something—and was already rolling away. Her hand reached out and snagged Syn's ankle and hefted up. Taji came to her feet, and Syn landed hard on her back.

Blip was above her in an instant and put himself between the two girls.

Syn motioned him away. She pushed up with her arm and pointed behind her, "Blip—get to the hub. I'll take her."

Taji laughed. "I've flattened you before."

Blip whirled around. "She's nothing. I've got this."

Syn snarled, "How'd you get here so fast?"

Taji ignored both of them. "I told Neci you'd be stupid enough to come back down. So she let me come down and check. I'm always right, and she knows it."

"Leave me alone!" Syn roared. "I told you to leave me alone! I don't want you here!"

Taji crossed the distance faster than Syn could believe, faster than Blip could react. Taji back-handed Syn and sent her flying through the air to smack hard against the large metal statue.

Syn let loose a harsh "Oomph."

Blip charged Taji and slammed into her side, sending her reeling.

Syn yelled to him, "Get to the hub!"

"No!" Blip shot back, still hovering over the fallen body of Taji. The girl was already pushing herself back up.

A piece of the sculpture hung loose—one of the halos. Syn glanced at the sculpture. One of the three teetered. Syn grabbed ahold of the base of the statue to haul herself to her feet.

Taji dove for Blip, but he flew up and away.

Syn yelled again, her hand wrapped around the loosened halo of the statue and pulled it free. "Get to the hub!"

"Fine." Blip spun to get a glimpse of her and then swung back around to look at the readying Taji. And then he was up again, straight up, and flying fast toward the hub.

Now she would not need to sprint. All she would have to do was survive Taji. She swore inwardly.

Taji took a step forward. Syn crouched to ready herself again. She lifted the halo-like piece from the statue and held it out between her and Taji.

Taji laughed, "What are you doing?"

"I don't want to hurt you," Syn said.

"Do you know what I can do?"

Syn did not answer. Seconds passed. Blip fled far away, becoming a small dot on the horizon. At that speed, he'd cover the distance in no time. Would it be enough? Could Syn hold off Taji until he returned? And when he did, would even he be enough to take Taji down?

Taji started again, "Do you know what I have done?"

Syn studied her sister, gauging her reactions.

Taji growled, "I was the one that killed them. If Neci wanted them dead, I did it. I've killed so many of our Sisters. You're just one more. You're not even one we care about."

Syn shivered. A tremor of fear bloomed, and she felt a sense of paralysis. What could she do against someone who knew how she thought, who had killed versions of herself over and over and over? Taji seemed perfectly designed to be a Syn killer.

Then, Syn smiled. How had not grasped it earlier? Taji was still weaker. Syn had lived her own life alone. Syn had grown up on her own. Taji, instead, had others around. Always. Syn wondered if that meant she ended up doing less work. Maybe a small difference, but in the long-term, perhaps Taji simply did not have Syn's stamina. Maybe she was a brute. No maybe about it—Taji was a beast in attitude and stature. It was her defining quality. It was the angry part of Syn that just wanted to hit things when it went wrong. Anger and size were Taji's tools. But not the cold tenacity that isolation brings.

Syn took a chance. "Do you think she'll share?"

Taji couldn't hide her confusion. Syn had seen her own confused face. She recognized the twitch of muscles alongside the eyes that forced them to narrow in suspicion. Perfect.

Syn continued. "I think when you're over there, one of us is going to have to take out the other."

"You're not going to be over there."

"Then it's you versus Pigeon."

"I'd smash Pigeon. She's a piece of trash. She's worthless. Neci can't stand her. Who cares about Pigeon?"

"And then it'll be just you and..." Syn's words were cut off by an audible scream from far above them.

Both Taji and Syn turned their heads sharply to see the sound. Something was falling— Something fell from the sky and landed with a harsh thud just meters away.

Syn turned, "We need to..."

But it was too late. It was Kerwen. She had finally fallen.

Syn convulsed and heaved. Her dinner from the night before came up and spewed across the ground.

Taji began to laugh. The girl held her stomach and roared.

Syn heaved again. A thin line of spittle ran across her lips. She stared around, bringing her head up. She spat on the ground, leaving a small divot in the hard-pan. She ran her lips across her sleeve, wiping the spittle and vomit away.

Kerwen was dead. She had seen Kerwen slam into the ground. She could see the shape of the flattened body. There lay her sister—a dark spot in the miasma of the smoke.

With her free hand, Taji picked up a rock from the ground and tossed it in the air, catching it with a single hand. "You stupid, little bitch. If that one survived, we'll use its scrambled brains to make another golem."

Syn stabbed at Kerwen's corpse, "That was your sister!"

"I. Don't. Care." Taji said. "I don't care about you, and I don't care about her." With that, she threw the rock as hard as she could. It flew through the air in a clean, straight trajectory and slammed into Syn's chin, knocking her back. Syn palmed the base of the statue behind her to steady herself.

A line of blood appeared, pooled, and then began to drip down Syn's chin. Syn roared as she ran at Taji. But just before she collided, she ducked, anticipating the brute retaliation from Taji.

Taji swung the spear, but she went too high, completely missing the battered Syn. Syn curled in and kneed Taji hard in the gut.

The girl toppled over, clutching her stomach, grunting, "You bitch."

Syn didn't stop. She punched Taji with her fist, landing it squarely on the girls' cheek. Now it would come down to endurance. Syn was sure she could outlast Taji. But she also could not dance with her, allowing Taji to keep returning more powerful responses back.

Syn kicked Taji's chest but pulled back the shot, avoiding the girl's head. Taji used the moment to slice into Syn's calve with Syn's own spear. Blood spurted across the ground. Taji herself was splattered with the blood.

As Syn fell to the ground and saw Taji's face covered in her own blood, she wondered if there was any difference between their blood. Perhaps they had different names and took different approaches building upon the same body, but probably the blood was identical. If they extracted it, could anyone tell the difference between each strain? Syn wasn't sure why the thought arose, unbidden, but it flowed and formed.

Syn landed hard on her right knee, sending a stab of pain coursing up her leg. She felt like her kneecap had popped off. She reached out and slashed at Taji's face with her nails. She missed and smacked the ground.

Taji tumbled over and dropped her full weight on Syn. Syn was locked in place. She struggled to get out from under the weight of the more massive form. Taji held onto both of Syn's wrists and pressed her own face hard into Syn's. Nose to nose. Syn could smell the thick, foul breath of her sister. The girl's nose smashed into Syn's.

A flash of white popped into sight. A zipping dot zooming toward them—Blip was nearing. Syn glimpsed him from the corner of her eye. She smiled.

Taji did too. A gruesome, dark smile.

Blip was there. Taji leaped up and swerved out of his path. And swung as he passed by.

The spear contacted the back of him and shattered against his shell. The spear split with a sharp snap. Blip's casing cracked like an egg with the collision—a deafening crunch and then in a cloud, bits of him flew forward, and, like a meteor from the sky, his white shell slammed into the ground. All dead weight. The dirt clouded around, billowing up, momentarily obscuring the murderous Taji from Syn's stunned gaze.

Taji held the two halves of the shattered spear, one jagged piece in each hand, and growled. "You bitch. You just had to come and ruin it all. If you hadn't shown up, she would've taken her time."

She fell back down onto Syn, pushing her fists into the girl's shoulders. Syn pulled at her arms and growled. "Get off!" she grunted through clenched teeth. "And that's not true. She's pregnant."

"What?" Taji was dismayed and answered by head-butting Syn. The two foreheads cracked as they impacted.

Syn saw stars as everything went black. She screeched in pain.

Taji yelled back, "I'm going to kill you!"

Syn's fingers scrambled, searched, groped for anything.

Taji smashed her head again into Syn's. The girl wheezed as she lost her breath. Her fingers searched and dug in the dirt.

Taji yelled in Syn's face, "I hate you! I hate all of you! You're the worst of us. You're everything I won't be!"

Syn's fingers brushed against something smooth and cold. That was it. This felt exactly like...her spear. She fumbled at the piece, gripped, and wrenched it from Taji's grip with a jerk. In the same swift motion, she swiped it across Taji's wrist.

Taji howled, but it was cut short as Syn twisted under the girl's weight, broken half of the spear still in hand, and brought it sharp against Taji's head, slamming against her temple.

Taji clutched at her head with the one hand that was not dangling limply. She fell back on the ground and curled up in a fetal position, her knees close to her chin.

Syn jumped on the girl and jammed the rod down, its shattered edge sharp. But she froze as she hit the girl's skin. Syn hovered there, the piece of broken spear shaking in her hands. She raised it again and brought it down once more but stopped in the last instant.

She couldn't do it. She rolled over and slammed the piece of the spear into the ground, pretending it was Taji. Syn screamed, "Kerwen! Kerwen! Kerwen!" Over and over, she shouted the girl's name at Taji's limp form, hoping to drill the name into the girl's flesh. Hoping that with repetition she could burn it like a brand.

Taji was no longer howling in pain. As she fell into unconsciousness, it had turned to a whimper and then stopped altogether.

Syn's anger felt warm. It felt like blood coursing into her arteries. But the anger felt more than warm. It burned in spots. There were elements of it that were years old. Like an overlooked wound that pinkened and then succumbed to infection, radiating pain with each step, it had festered. Anger at the colonists. Anger at Captain Pote. Anger at the builders. All of them had been fools. They had created a dream and stocked it with the demons of Hell. How could they do that? How could they create her only to have her be some guinea pig? How could they have done such a horrible job? Her anger was at Taji and at Neci and at everyone that had forced her into the very act that she was doing at that moment. Her anger felt like an electric storm. Billowing up and forced through with electrical flashes, shocks of lightning, pure raw power in fierce delights. She wanted to kill her enemy, and it felt right. She felt like this was true. This moment was the one she had been born to meet..

Beneath it all, another anger coursed. Anger at Blip and his lies. This whole situation borne out of deception. Perhaps if he had lifted the veil of the second Disc earlier, none of this would have come to pass.

Then, glancing at Blip's shattered shell on the ground around them, she felt anger at herself for even allowing that thought.

She glared down at Taji's unconscious body. She wanted to kill the girl and release all of her rage in an instant. She spat out, "I'm not a killer. I'm not like you and Neci."

From far away, a voice called, "Syn."

She knew she should recognize the name. She knew that she should answer. But she was unsure why.

"Syn!" the voice shouted again. It was high-pitched. A chirp. Again. "Syn!"

Syn slowed. She worried, though, that in her distraction, Taji would take advantage of the moment

"Syn!"

Syn slowly looked up at the inert shell of Blip just a few meters away. White shell had burst across the ground. Like a cracked egg, a large portion of the shell was gone, a large jagged edge of curling shell wrapped around a revealing twisted array of blue glowing wires and silver circuit boards. But not all of his outer body was gone. In fact, over half of his shell was still in one piece. Through tears, she chanced, "Blip?"

A pale sound chirped from within him. *Was that a response?*

"Blip?"

Underneath her hand, his cracked form vibrated and lifted from the ground, wobbly and stuttering. "Blip?"

With a sharp whistle and then a low hum, Blip's voice found its way. "Yeee…yes. Yesyesyes. Yes."

Syn lept up as Blip floated up as well, under her hand. "Blip! You're alive! How?" Syn smiled at Blip. A torrent of joy poured through her, warming every part of her. She smiled. *He's alive.*

Then she glanced back at Taji's unmoving body, and an unbidden thought came to her, *I'm free.* She winced at her own dark relief.

"Syn, are you okay?" Blip asked, his words slow and challenged.

Syn shook her head. Was she okay? "No," she said, and her mind focused on the stabs of pain and the dull ache of her legs and arms.

Then, she realized, that wasn't what he was talking about. She turned back and looked at the blood that had soaked her arms.

Her hands were crimson. Her legs were red. The ground around them was red. It was all red. Just like her vision. Just like her thoughts. She went numb at the potential. Had she gone too far? Had she killed Taji?

"Blip?" she asked. Her words came from far away, an echo in her own mind. *Oh,* she thought, *maybe I didn't speak loud enough.* Again, she said, "Blip?"

"Syn. It's okay," Blip said.

Syn shook her head. "Is she okay?"

Blip floated near her. "She's not dead."

Syn's eyes went wide at the surprise. Taji wasn't dead, and Blip wasn't dead! There was a flood of joy and relief at the thought. Syn wasn't a killer.

Syn pushed away from the girl and scrambled back. She scooted across the ground, pressing her back against the concrete divider leading to the Jacob platform.

"Oh God!" Syn cried. "I'm sorry! I'm sorry! I'm sorry!" She looked up at Blip and the sounds stopped, but her lips kept curling around the shape that "I'm sorry" should make. Her mouth kept up the motions like some strange mantra.

"Syn, it's fine. It's okay." Blip was down beside her. He nudged against her arm and lowered his voice to a calm tone and echoed, "She's not dead. You had to stop her though."

"I had to?" Syn repeated. But her lips then kept moving around the words "I'm sorry."

Blip replied, "She was going to kill both of us. You had to do it. It's okay."

"I had to do it," Syn said. Yes, that was an answer. That was why. Syn reminded herself that Taji's threat to her life had motivated it entirely. She refused to think of the anger that had been buried deep inside and billowed over like a volcano. And in not thinking about it, it was all she could think of.

Syn struggled to look at him through tear-filled eyes. She mumbled, "How?"

Blip, wobbling in the air and half-broken, pulled away. "Can you get in the Jacob? We have to go." He hovered in the air with a subtle shake. He was alive, but the impact had hurt him. Each thought radiated through the coil and array of blue tubes and silver boards that peeked through the shattered visage.

Oh, Blip, how are we ever going to fix you? Syn thought but instead said, "Did you do it?" Syn took a deep breath. Everything focused in her mind. She had sent Blip to send a message to the Ecology. He was back. Now she had to know what had happened. *How had he been back that fast? Did he send the message? Had he faced obstacles?*

She asked all of these questions in a stream of words.

Blip sighed, "Yes. Get in the Jacob, and I'll answer."

Syn came to her feet, shaking as she did so. "Kerwen." As she spoke, she turned and moved in the direction of the impact point.

"Syn! Come back!"

Syn was staggering, dragging her foot as she spoke. "I have to..." There were more words, but she didn't emphasize them nor did she feel they mattered.

Blip zoomed next to her. "I sent out the signal. I said everything you told me to say. We have to go. It's okay. You did you job. I did—"

"Kerwen." She said again.

"Who?"

"Kerwen!" Syn spat, irritated. *How had he forgotten?*

Blip understood. He moved quickly past Syn toward the body lying at the edge of the sand. He dropped down next to it, but as she was still a bit away, Syn couldn't see what he was doing. Perhaps examining her for life. Perhaps making sure she was really and truly dead.

Blip flew back to Syn as she neared Kerwen's corpse.

Blip blocked Syn's path, "Don't. It's not good."

"I killed her."

"No, you didn't."

Syn pushed around Blip and knelt at Kerwen's head. The girl was distorted. Her body was far wider than it should be. She hadn't flattened like some cartoon rabbit, but the impact had molded her body into something strange. Her skull was shattered. Syn reached out to touch the mirror image of herself, her own dead body. Kerwen's eyes were empty. Only white globes looking out onto the sand.

"Syn, please," Blip implored. His voice was urgent. There was fear in it. "We have to go."

Syn ran the back of her hand across Kerwen's cheek. The girl's skin was already cooling.

Blip's voice changed, "Oh! Look!"

Syn glanced up, her reverent pause broken. Blip was staring past her, further up the arc of the Disc. There, one of the Jacob towers had lit up and one of the cabs was rising up the tower. "What's that? Who's on it?" she asked.

"I think some of the bots." As he spoke, dark shadows became visible on the horizon, moving toward Syn and Blip.

"What's that?" Syn asked.

Blip remained silent. She had always envied his vision. He could see things nearly across the arc of the Disc itself, from one edge to the other if he concentrated.

After a moment, he said, "I think they're more bots."

"Do you recognize them?"

"There's a cleaning bot or two. A few house bots. Primarily little ones."

"But do you recognize them?" Syn insisted. Then she realized he had never been there when the Ecology had found her. He was not at the celebration nor in the workshop. Blip wouldn't know many of the bots. "Never mind."

Syn stood and walked to Blip. She glanced back down at Kerwen. The body was still motionless, and Syn shivered. Her actions had led to Kerwen's death. *I'm one of them.* After a pause, she gave sound to the thought. "I'm like them."

Blip didn't respond. She was hoping he'd give a trite answer like "No, you're not." Instead, he said, "You didn't want to. You could've, but you didn't. That's why you're different."

The world around them went stark white.

An enormous rumble came from behind them, and they turned to see a massive fireball several kilometers away—an explosion that rivaled the one that destroyed Zondon Almighty. The eruption from the location of the former city.

The second bomb.

4 0

THE GREAT FLOOD

"A great inundation, together with an earthquake, swept the land so rapidly that only a few people escaped in their skin canoes to the tops of the highest mountains."
—Orowignarak Myth, Alaska

Zondon Almighty was nearly six kilometers away now. That put the city—and the blinding explosion of the cobalt device—almost half-way up the arc. The entire detonation was completely visible and the light itself was near-blinding.

"Run! Blip yelled.

The light and explosion were followed by a deep rumbling. The entire ground shook. Then it stopped. Suddenly, from the center of the blast, a fountain of water erupted, streaming in a massive column.

"The shield!" Syn said.

Blip swung around and pushed her. "Get to the Jacob."

Syn looked out at the racing shadows. She could see the bots clearly now. There were seven of them, and they were moving as fast as they could, but they were still a good half kilometer away. And none of them were as fast as Blip. "They won't make it."

"We won't make it." He had pushed her against the door of the Jacob. "Get in! We have to get up before the water hits."

"We have to wait for them."

"No, we don't! I have to keep you safe."

"I made a promise!"

"What did you promise?"

"I promised to save them."

"From what?"

"From this Disc! They told me it was dying. I told them about our Disc. I told them when I found you I'd come back for them."

Blip flew back and then zoomed at Syn, smashing into her, pushing her off-balance. She landed on her butt with a thud, but to Blip's delight, she fell into the Jacob.

"Let's go." He flew over and started working with the control panel. The doors chimed.

"No!" Syn yelled and leaned forward to put her hand in the door. "We can wait."

"We're not waiting."

"This is stupid. The water's not here." She couldn't tell where the water was. The column of water was streaking high into the clouds and there were splatters of rain falling down several meters out. The water had to be rising around the city, and she was certain some great wave was on its way to them, but she couldn't see it from the dunes.

And then she could. The ground around the city halfway up the Disc was flattened. The water. It was flowing out and rising. She couldn't see it over her own horizon, but she saw how far it was spreading on the other side of the former Zondon Almighty. If it was flowing equally everywhere, it was only a kilometer or two away now. And moving fast.

Syn pushed up on her knees, winced as a jab of pain shot through her leg, and cupped her hands around her mouth to shout, "Come on! Hurry!"

"Syn, they're not going to make it. We have to go now. If that water hits us first, we're dead."

"Well survive, Blip! Come on—just give me another second. You can close the doors when you see water."

"I see water! Right there! It's shooting up from the shield layer! Think about it—over 400 billion liters of water is going to be flooding this Disc!"

The roaring of the rushing water grew to a deafening pitch. A mountain of water was rushing in.

The bots were moving fast. But now there were six of them. One had dropped back. Syn wanted to race out to them, but she had to hold the door. Blip wouldn't leave her, would he? No! That wouldn't happen. But he would come out after her, and she could kill them both. From the Jacob door, she yelled again, "Hurry!"

They were just a few meters out, at the base of the plaza. Two small Disc cleaning bots. A bouncing bot that resembled Arquella, but it was far less shiny and bounced and rolled—it didn't hover. There were also two small block bots. Six. And maybe a floating ball bot—an eye-bot—circling around. Okay, now there were more than six.

"We're—" shouted the robot. The word after "we're" sounded like "coming," but the sound of the water overwhelmed it, and Syn wasn't sure what was said.

"Blip, you hold this. Just give me a couple more seconds."

"That's all we have!"

The eye-bots whizzed into the Jacob, followed by a cleaning bot. There were still five more out there.

Behind the racing bots a wall of water rose up. There it was! And it was rushing at a tremendous speed. Again, she heard a boom. What was propelling it? She had seen the waterfalls tumble, but she'd never seen anything move with such power. It grew and grew until it filled the horizon.

The closest eye-bot was almost there, and it chirped as it saw Syn.

"Huck!" Syn cried. It was Huck! He had survived. The bot raced and slammed into Syn. She squealed with delight. "You're alive! You're alive! I thought you had died."

Huck replied with a series of whistles as Blip looked on, confused.

Another cleaning bot crossed the threshold. Its hide was beat and bruised, and it looked to be painted with mud. Another one of the bouncing bots managed to make it. It rolled in and smashed into the others piling up in the corner.

"Hurry!" Syn yelled, but she knew her words were unheard. "Wait, Taji!" She remembered the unconscious body still laying in the sand and glanced in that direction. There was a silhouetted figure moving their way. "Blip, Taji!"

"It's too late!" Blip shouted back.

Syn cried out, "No!" but she knew Blip was right.

The wall of water reached the figure, and it disappeared in the wave. Moments later, the rushing water slammed into the two straggling bots and washed them away.

Syn pulled back her hand, and the Jacob doors shut swiftly with a slight whoosh. First the inner doors and then the outer doors shut, followed by the slam of the wall of water. The entire Jacob tower shook under the impact. Blip was already at the control panel, and they began to ascend. The entire Jacob rocked again. Inside, its lights flickered in and out.

The outer glass windows of the Jacob tower spider-webbed as the water slammed against it. The tower rocked, and the Jacob bounced around inside even as they lifted off.

The water rose around them, nearly as fast as they were moving. They lifted up and soon crested above the wall of water. Waves crashed as a new ocean lay out below them, blanketing as far as they could see through the darkened landscape. Under the heavy gray clouds, there was water—rolling, dark, and powerful. The water washed away all of the insanity of what was this Disc. Every dark thought, every dark action, every trace of what Neci had twisted was under those waves. The bodies of the Madness-succumbed dead lay somewhere far below the dark, churning waves. Memories of lives that would never be spoken of again were buried around the weight of the new water. Somewhere in that floated the bodies of Kerwen and Taji.

Syn breathed out, "I'm sorry."

From one of the small bots inside the Jacob, a tiny voice cried, "Mommy, I'm scared."

A family. Syn had rescued a family.

The bots were smooshed together as if cradling for warmth. They couldn't be cold. They were frightened, however.

Blip looked at her and then glanced at them.

Syn spoke, even as the Jacob rocked again. "It's okay. We're going to the needle."

The other eye-bot spoke, "Where's that?"

Syn remembered her conversation with Arquella. "The Gates of Paradise." She hated to say it. She hated lying. But he was a child, and she had to calm him. But it was not a child, and it was not truly paradise. There were so many layers of truth wrapped in lies in that small cabin, Syn thought she might drown just from them.

The outside tower creaked and something rumbled far below them.

Blip muttered. "The base has broken. Water's in the tower."

Although she wasn't sure why she did it since the other bots' hearing abilities were likely as perfect as Blip's, Syn scooted closer to Blip and whispered, "Will we make it? Will the Jacob survive?"

Blip paused and said, "I'm not sure this Disc will survive."

"What?" Syn's voice was louder than she wanted. She spoke again, quieter, "What?"

"There's nearly an ocean of water slamming into this Disc. The weight and forces could destroy this entire Disc. Snap it off at the needle."

"What do we do?"

"Neci said she was going to eject the Disc."

"Can we do that?"

"I don't know. Maybe. It makes sense that the builders would've considered that perhaps one of the Discs might need to be removed."

"How would we do that?" Syn was shaking her head. This was absolutely insane.

"Olorun would know."

Syn grabbed Blip with both of her hands. "Neci said Olorun was alive. You said it was, too. Can you talk to it? When we get up there?"

Blip answered quickly, "Yes."

"Why didn't you tell me this?"

"Because you would've kept running to it for answers...It's not like me. It doesn't care."

"What is it like?"

"You don't want to know. She's cold. Insane. Old."

Syn glanced at the bots. "Did Olorun wake them up?"

Blip sighed, "Maybe."

"Do you talk to it?"

"Her."

"It's a girl?"

"She wants to be called a her. Olorun is a she."

Syn nodded. Neci had insisted that Olorun was female. "Do you talk to her often?"

"Not if I can avoid it."

"But it...She has all the answers. She can tell us what happened to the colonists. She can tell us what's going on with the fuel. She can tell me who woke me up. Who woke the Sisters up? Why were separated? She can answer everything!" There was an excitement in Syn's eyes fueled by equal amounts of anger and hope.

The interior Jacob lights went dark. One of the child bots whimpered. There was a hush from what Syn assumed was its mother.

"She won't." Blip pulled back to the control panel. A moment later, the outer edge trim of the Jacob lift glowed red.

Syn noticed that she was already lifting off of the floor. They were over half-way up, and gravity was losing its hold.

"Why?" Syn was not letting go of the topic of Olorun.

"She's a bitch." Blip's voice was as matter-of-fact as Syn had ever heard it. He had used the same word Neci had. So maybe Blip wasn't an agent of Olorun as the Crimson Queen feared.

"What?"

Blip floated around the Jacob and moved to peer out one of the windows. Syn pushed up and floated next to him, putting her hands out to stop her momentum against the side. The other bots were moving around—the eye-bots didn't seem to be bothered by the low gravity at all.

Syn looked at the cleaning bots. They were spinning in place as they lifted up. *Crap!* she thought, *they've never been in zero gravity.* Syn left Blip's side and grabbed ahold of one of the bots. "It's okay," she said, "This is part of it." She looked at the child bots. "You're going to have to help."

Blip spoke up, his gaze still out the window, "Tell them to increase their gravs."

"What?"

"All bots move by grav resistors. Like the hover bikes. They can increase their gravs and be pulled down to the surface. Or they can use their gravs resistors to push against the metal and float around. It's how I do it."

Syn shook her head. "I know that, Blip. Who do you think fixes them?"

"Then why did you say, 'What?'"

"Cause you told me to tell them. You could tell them yourself."

"Oh," Blip said.

Syn shook her head and looked up at Huck, who had not left her side, "Did you get that, Huck?"

He nodded up and down.

"Help me tell the others?"

He nodded again and zipped toward the other eye-bots further away.

Syn looked back at the frightened cleaning bot. "What's your name?"

The cleaning bot said, "Margaret."

Syn wanted to laugh. That was such an old name. "Margaret, did you hear what Blip said?"

Margaret said, "Yes."

"Can you do that?"

"Yes."

Syn turned toward the child eye-bot, "What's your name?"

Without hesitation, it answered, "Joey."

"Can you help your mom, Joey?"

Joey's voice became excited, "Yeah! That's easy." The ability to do something his mother struggled with buoyed him. Joey flitted around the inside of the Jacob shouting, "It's easy mom. Just try it. Look, we can fly!"

Syn left Joey and Margaret and the other bots and sidled back up near Blip. Outside the window, the ocean grew. The water was rushing around the edge of the Disc, and they lost its progress in the clouds.

Syn said, "Why won't Olorun help?"

"She doesn't think like that. She's not like you or me or even the Sisters. She really doesn't care."

The light of the sunstrips increased, and a tension hit Syn. They were nearing the top. They were nearing the waiting Neci.

The Jacob rocked again, but the turbulence was less, or perhaps it was the lack of gravity that buffered the impact.

"We need to get through the gate," Syn said.

Blip nodded.

"She'll be waiting for us," Syn continued.

Blip nodded again. "Neci's forced us. We're going to have to open the gate. We have to get through."

"I'm not letting her in."

"You'll have to fight."

"I'm not sure I can stop her."

Blip glanced at the bots.

Syn took in the sight of the floating bots. They were chaotic, but they were learning. The younger ones had mastered the zero-gravity flight perfectly. The others were getting it. There would be others on the way up. She was sure that many had died. There just hadn't been that much time from when Blip sent out the call. But there would be more than this.

"I'm not sure she can stop you," Blip said, with a smile.

The two stared at the bots for a bit more, knowing they were minutes from arriving in the needle.

Syn spoke, "Why did you shut down when they first grabbed you? I mean when we came down the first time. You knew they were there. You shut down when they came. Why didn't you run?"

"I knew what they wanted. I figured it out. The explosion. The debris on the other side of the gate. I knew the other Eves were getting through. I thought they'd try to reason with you. I shut down so they couldn't force you to use me."

"Why didn't you tell me about this?" Syn raged.

All sensation of gravity disappeared. They were moments from stopping.

The Jacob lift rattled again and went into complete darkness. The red strips blinked out. The small bots chirped and whined.

Syn shouted, "Quiet."

The bots ignored her as the entire lift shook.

Blip flew to the window and then back to the control panel. "No!" he cried, "It's collapsing."

"What is?" Syn asked.

"The tower! The tower is collapsing!"

"Aren't the Towers the spine of the Disc? What happens?"

"I don't know. I really, truly don't know."

From far below there was an awful sound—something like the world being torn open. It reverberated through the Jacob. They bounced around the inside of the lift, smacking into each other. Syn put her hands to her ears to block out the sound.

"Will we make it?" she screamed at Blip, hoping that he could read lips. She knew he couldn't hear her over the metallic rending below.

Blip heard her, and she saw him waggle in the zero gravity, but she didn't understand his words. He raced to the control panel. The awful sound died in an instant.

Everyone was screaming, but Blip's shout came through. "The hull is rupturing! I think other Jacob towers are falling."

Syn glanced out of the window to look at the world below, expecting a mass of clouds to block her view. There were no clouds. There was no water. There was a massive hole a third-way up the arc, where Zondon Almighty had been.

Through the hole the stars of space twinkled. The unmoving titans peered through as small dots. They were constant, ageless, unbothered by Syn's plight.

Syn snapped her gaze away. The entire atmosphere was being sucked out into space. The billowing, pitch-stained clouds swam in urgency to the widening gap, tumbling past the scenery in a rush to escape. The water itself that had flooded this world drained away in a huge maelstrom. Now, the loose dirt was being pulled through as the endless vacuum sucked it all out.

From far away, she could now see the other towers clearly. The haze and smoke and clouds were draining away. It was all clear. Across the Disc, the next tower over was buckling. Its base was splintering, and the Disc itself was tearing away from it. From inside, large flashes of light went off—explosions. She could see the light but couldn't hear it.

Another tower a few kilometers away did the same thing. At its base, its Jacob lift was yanked through the opening tear and sucked through the widening hole into empty space, shot out like a bullet.

"Oh, no!" Syn whispered.

Their Jacob came to a sudden stop. Blip shouted, "Go!"

"Where's Neci?" Syn asked.

"No time!" Blip opened the doors and both sets—the inside and the outside of the tower—slid open.

"Go!" The bots raced out, led by Huck. Blip screeched again, "Go!"

The tower shook, and the Jacob lift slipped down a foot. Syn was still inside and saw the opening of the entrance shrink. She crouched against the pull and pushed forward, darting through the open space as the last bot ahead of her and Blip moved out into the needle. Syn sped through, and the Jacob lift lurched down again. The gap narrowed and Syn slid through only a foot of space.

The tower rattled. Blip pushed toward the control panel. The outer doors shut fast, and inside the needle, through the glass panes, they saw the Jacob fall straight down, sucked by the vacuum opening inside the Disc.

Syn was still moving through the needle and slammed into the wall, falling into a cradle position to bounce around. She was breathing heavily. The entire Disc itself was gone.

Blip moved toward her and nudged her to halt her tumble. "Are you okay?"

After a moment, she calmed her labored breathing. "Yes."

"We have to go," Blip urged, "I don't know what this will do to the needle." He moved on ahead and then turned back to Syn. He said, "Or Olorun herself."

The trek through the passageways to the gate room was slow. Syn took every meter with apprehension. She knew Neci was here. She knew Neci was expecting her.

"She's at the gate," Blip said as he noticed Syn's hesitation.

"How do you know? Did Olorun tell you?"

"No," Blip pulled back to move along with her as she swam through the zero gravity tunnel. "It's a guess."

Syn thought about it. Of course, that's where she would be. She had not destroyed her Disc to hang out in the passageways. She would be forcing the gate open. She had burned her world so that Syn would open the door. She would go through one way or another.

She had won.

Syn pushed ahead toward the vast space that was her first exposure to this twisted world. She remembered her own description of the space on the other side of the gate. "You're right. Neci will be in the mirror room."

41

SISTERS

Ekùn, Ògíní omo Ìyáyò
Ekun Abìjàwàrà
Eranko atorímératnje
Alábelówó.
"Tiger, Ògíní offspring of Ìyáyò
Tiger who fights fiercely
The animal that eats flesh from the head
The one who has knife in its palm."
—Yorùbá panegyric

The asteroids of debris floated before them, all under the red lights. In the center, bathed in red light herself, floated Neci, in front of the great gate itself. Every image of Hell Syn had ever seen rose up to her. A zero-gravity world of floating mountains engulfed in the heat of Hell, burning red-hot from ancient embers. The Crimson Queen stood before the gate to Eden itself, barring the way, her face as dark and terrible as the faces she had painted on the walls of Zondon Almighty. The Queen's dark skin glowing under the scarlet light made her appear as if on fire herself, burning like an angel.

Neci's face was awash in crimson. Her white clothes glowed a hellish blood red. The ribbons that hung from her shoulders floated about like a billowing cape, like celestial wings.

Neci stood, her arms crossed, defiance etched into her face. Her legs were straight, although she hung in zero gravity—a feat that Syn appreciated.

The Crimson Queen at the end of the journey.

Behind the Queen stood Pigeon, hunkered against the gate itself, her hands splayed out flat against the metal to steady herself. She glanced between Neci and then back at the others in the room.

The others were the members of the Ecology. A cacophony of sizes and shapes. She had a flashback to the Theater and the great swarm giving their blessing. Hundreds of them gathered now. Not the thousands she had hoped for. But so many.

There, in the middle of the array, were Arquella and Bear with Huck orbiting them. They had lived. She wanted to race over to them and hug them. But she could not. She had to face Neci.

Syn whispered to Blip, "They won't fit in that passageway we came through. And we can't open the iris."

Blip chirped, "There's a secondary cargo passageway near the first. I can open that."

The bots were all focused on the Crimson Queen themselves. They all stood back dozens of meters from Neci's fearless gaze, giving her a wide swathe.

No, it wasn't fearless. Neci was frightening them, but she was also frightened. The girl shouted at the bots. "Stay back!"

Syn entered, and both she and Blip sidled along the outskirts of the room, in the darkness. They had done this path once before and knew it well. The debris floated in the space between them and her. In the wreckage were the large bodies of the burlys that had accompanied Neci. They were dead. The Ecology must have killed them in Syn's absence.

Syn's stomach tightened. There was still the awful stench of burnt flesh lingering in the entire room—it was the smell that had made her recoil when she first slipped through from her side.

"Neci!" Syn shouted from the darkness.

Blip turned on her. "What about surprise?" he whispered.

Syn pushed off and bounded from one chunk of rubble to another. She was used to the zero gravity, and her familiarity showed in her graceful speed. In seconds, she had crossed half of the room to float parallel to Neci, although she made sure to leave several meters between her and the red-hued figure. Syn shouted again, "You can't stop killing!"

"They're the killers," Neci cried, "You just missed your precious machines killing. Look at what they've done." She pointed at the large floating corpse near her. "They killed Admiral! My husband! The father of our first child!"

"What did you tell him to do? What reason did you give them?" Syn asked.

Neci ignored the question as she glanced around Syn. She grimaced. "Where's Taji?"

Syn winced. Neci noticed. "So, you caught up with her. Or did she find you? Killed her, didn't you?" In an instant, her tone changed from frantic to mocking. "Everybody's so into that these days."

Syn stammered, "I didn't. She tried to—" Why was she explaining herself to Neci? Why the compulsion to answer for this?

"You're just like me," Neci hissed, eyeing the orbiting bots.

"I'm nothing like you."

Neci smiled, "Did it feel good to kill Taji?"

"Shut up," Syn retorted.

"It felt so good the first time. I didn't want to admit it, but afterward, I couldn't stop reliving the feeling. My fingertips digging into the skin. That moment where the heat of their body switches off—it only drops a degree, but you know something has left it. What about you? Did you kill Taji up close or far away? I know Kerwen was a far-away one."

"Shut up," Syn shouted, "I didn't kill her!"

"Oh, but she's dead isn't she? Hmmm. I think you did it up close. You're so much like me—you couldn't do it at a distance. Had to be personal."

"I'm not like you at all."

In the debris, the charred corpse of the first girl Syn had encountered on this side floated by. Laoule. Her blackened hair whipped around. Syn pointed, "What about her? Did you kill her? What was her name?"

"You're just like me. We're identical. Don't you get that? The only thing that makes you and me different is which side of this hellhole you woke up on. I woke up with forty other mouths depending on me. Forty other half-baked versions of myself. We're all alike. We all breathe the same way. When we both woke up, our thoughts were identical. If you had woken up over here, and I had been on your Disc, it would've been the exact same way. You would've killed when you had to kill. You would've torched this Disc. You would've flooded it. You would've kept having to kill to protect those you loved. Don't you see? If I had woken up on your side, I would've been the perfect unblemished princess without any of this hell to go through! I could stand there lecturing myself right now. We are the same. We are the same!"

Laoule's burnt body floated lazily up and then seemed to hang in the space between them as if willed to stop by some outside force.

Neci was shouting at Syn. Her fists were tight, and her knuckles blazed white. "We are the same! You don't get to stand there and tell me how awful I am. There's nothing different about what we would've done. You are just as horrible as I am! Don't you think I know what I've done? Don't you think I've hated it? Don't you think if there were another way about it I would have taken it? I had to do it! I had to save us! They were all depending on me. I didn't have a choice!"

Neci pointed at the half-shell of Blip floating against Syn. "That should be mine! I should still have Puck. I should still have a companion. But this stupid ship made a dumb mistake. It put me over here. But I'm going to go over, and you're going to open that gate!"

Syn was crying. There was something in Neci's words that felt too right. Syn whispered. "I'm sorry."

Neci shouted, "What did you say?"

"I'm sorry...I'm sorry," Syn continued. She floated closer to Neci.

Neci was confused—her eyes wide in astonishment. The red lights illuminated them, making her eyes dance like candles in the dark.

Syn said, "You're right."

Blip floated closer, "No, she isn't."

"Yes, she is," Syn said. "You're absolutely right. I would've done the exact same things. I'm sorry you didn't wake up with me."

Neci narrowed her eyes in suspicion.

"But you shouldn't have done those things."

"You just said you knew you would've done them."

"It doesn't make them right. It just means I'd make the same mistakes. You're still wrong. Pigeon said it. You're twisted."

Neci glanced back at Pigeon who was looking straight ahead, at Laoule's charred corpse as it floated between them.

Syn saw it now. Neci amongst all of her corpses. She was reminded of the hyenas amongst the carcasses of the tigress and her cubs. Syn spoke, resolute in her declaration. "But you've done them. And you'll keep on doing them. And I can't let you over."

"You have to go through," Neci said, "You have to open the gate."

"No, I don't."

"Yes, you do," Blip added. "We have to get to Olorun. I have to talk to her." Blip's voice was a quiet whisper in Syn's ear.

Syn spoke, "You're not going through."

"Are you going to kill me now too? Taji? Kerwen? And me? You'll be right on your way to even up the count between us. Getting off to a good start," Neci sneered.

"I'm not going to kill you," Syn held out her arms, motioning at the floating bots around her, "But they're not going to let you through."

"They won't do a thing." the Crimson Queen eyed them nervously, eyes darting about. "They're frightened of me."

"They will if I ask."

A murmur shot through the bots. Arquella and Bear inched closer. Huck jumped ahead a meter.

In a flash, Neci reached out and snagged Pigeon's hair and pulled the girl in front of her. There was a knife in Neci's hand, and it was against Pigeon's neck. Neci held the girl in a headlock, tightly, looking over her shoulder. The knife was a dark thing. There were glints of metal underneath its stained surface. It was curved, and the tip was dented and misshapen. This was a knife that had been used freely by its owner, someone not afraid of shedding blood.

Neci barked, "You won't kill me because you won't kill her. Let me through first or I end the worm."

"Neci!" Syn shouted back, "Don't."

Neci smiled. "That's why she's lived this long. She wasn't useful. She was just the leftover. Can't kill the smallest one of the litter. That just seems wrong. Funny isn't it? In the end, she and I are all that's left. The alpha and the runt. Who would have thought?"

"Neci, please. I'll let you in. Just let her go."

Neci pushed the knife against Pigeon's throat. The girl winced in pain and a line of blood formed at the knife's edge, digging into her skin. "We go first."

The entire needle shook. There was a terrible creak that sounded from deep inside the needle.

Blip looked at Syn, "Do it. We have to get in. I have to get to Olorun and eject this Disc."

"Good plan, little football. That was my plan if I remember right, but it's fine, you can use it," Neci squawked.

Pigeon shut her eyes and gave a loud breath. "Her name was Laoule."

"What?" Neci asked.

Pigeon continued, "We found her companion, Spot, and you wouldn't let her near him."

"Shut up," Neci said.

"She snuck out and was talking to him at night. You had no idea. And then she escaped with Spot."

"Who cares?" Neci said.

"You killed all of the children she was caring for. She just wanted to be away from you. From us. They both did. We all have. I think I've pieced it all together. She thought she'd get through the gate before you. After the explosion. The one you made to break through. She wanted to get away with Spot. But you sent Taji after her."

"Who cares?" Neci was shouting. "Let me in now, Syn."

"Do it," Blip said, "Just give me the word."

Syn held up her hands. "Fine, but I can't open the iris."

"What?" Neci said, pressing the knife tighter against Pigeon's throat.

"She never came back down from up here. I wondered what happened, but you wouldn't let me come up here," Pigeon continued, "When we found the wrong companion, I knew they were both dead."

Syn pointed at the corner. "The entrance is there. The iris is broken. I think you broke it. But there's a hatch down in that corner. Actually, a couple of passageways."

"You lying little bitch," Neci said, "I know every corner of this gate. There's nothing but this."

"It's only for the bots," Syn said, "Let her go, and I'll show you."

"Taji killed her. That's what you sent her to do. Catch and kill," Pigeon was still talking, her voice a deep growl, "I think Taji set her on fire. But she helped Spot escape. He fled to the other side. He knew how to get through. You let Taji set her on fire. How could you? She was a sister."

"Shut up you whiny little...I need to think," Neci closed her eyes.

Syn motioned again, "Okay, everyone, just go to where I'm pointing. Blip is going to—"

A creak sounded, and the entire room shuddered.

Syn continued, "Blip is going to get us through fast."

"That's not true," Neci said.

Pigeon's voice was now just a thin thing, and the words were coming out without any pauses—a stream of sounds propelled by years of resentment, "You killed Cord. You killed Laoule. You killed Tulce. You killed Ince. You killed Palim. Ret. Palcul."

"Shut up!" Neci screamed.

But Pigeon couldn't stop. The names kept coming. "Intes. Recik. Ojul." The syllables bled into each other. "Chivah. Havah. Brile. Sol."

"I did not."

Pigeon stopped sharply. "Yes. You. Did." On the last word, she yanked a knife from her belt—a thin piece of metal—and jammed it behind her into Neci's abdomen. She roared the last names; the words grew into a stream from the girl's small voice. "Rish. Una. Elaul. Casei. Iksen. Tral." The ones after that become a single note screamed in rage.

Neci howled and let go of Pigeon. She fell back toward the gate. An arc of spraying blood exploded as she tumbled.

"Neci!" Syn cried, waving her hands wildly to swim toward the girls. The floating droplets of blood splashed across her as she moved through the crimson mist. In her next breath, she cried, "Pigeon!"

Syn had hated Taji. Despised the brute. She had cared for Kerwen. And felt pulled toward Pigeon. But Neci was different—Neci was her mirror. She detested everything Neci did because she saw the echoes of her own choices there. And now—Neci was dying. Maybe dead. And she realized she didn't want that.

Syn snagged Neci's bleeding body and cradled it close. She pressed against Neci's wound, hoping to halt the blood flow.

She looked at Pigeon and said, "Are you okay? Did she hurt you?"

Pigeon shook her head, shutting her eyes tight, and slammed her mouth closed on a scream. After a second, she pushed toward Syn and Neci and said, "Put pressure on it. We can stop the bleeding."

"She was going to kill you," Syn said as she pressed hard on the open hole in Neci's stomach.

"I love her," Pigeon said, "She's horrible. But no more Sisters need to die."

The needle creaked again—a grinding sound that filled every inch of the massive gate room. Syn eyed Blip and shouted to the Ecology, "Everyone! Follow Blip! We have to get through."

Blip didn't reply. His response was a bullet flight toward the far corner where he had opened the service passage a few days ago (what now seemed to be years ago). He shone a brilliant blue light to draw the other bot's attention.

The mixed hues of the red emergency lights and Blip's blue cast a pale violet across Syn's face. She put a hand on Pigeon's shoulder, "We have to go with them."

Pigeon nodded.

The needle shook again.

"Will she live?" It was a high voice. Syn scanned and found Bear. He was followed by Arquella and Huck.

"You're alive!" She smiled at the two, and they moved close against her, nudging her.

"Thanks to you! Your Blip told us what was happening," Bear answered.

"How did you not die in the first explosion?"

"We had split off to go around back. It was Bear's idea," Arquella said, "He said that the Crimson Queen was tricky, and she was. We saw you all leave and raced after. But not many others made it. We couldn't catch you, and we couldn't save them. So many died. I'm sorry."

From behind, a booming voice answered, "Now is not the time. Later we can grieve. Come along." In the darkness, the lumbering shape of a familiar sewer bot floated past. The Barlgharel. He had lived too.

As he swam past, he said, "Place the girl on my back. I'll get her through. You can hold her wound. She might still live."

Syn's stomach tightened. They had just tried to kill Neci. Syn had forbidden the girl from crossing over.

Before she could make a decision, Neci's eyes shot open. "No!" she shouted and pushed off the Barlgharel's body, toward the opening hatch of the cargo passageway, blood streaming after her.

"Stop her!" Syn shouted but Neci had surprised them and was at the opening.

Syn moved onto the Barlgharel's back. Something along the bot's hide gripped ahold and held her tight. Together, they swam toward the progression of bots exiting through the larger cargo passageway. Ahead, Blip's blinding blue light served as a guide.

Neci pushed ahead and swam into the opening, kicking past Blip.

"Stop her!" Syn shouted again, but Blip was focused elsewhere.

"Through here. Go. One after another. Queue. Stay in the queue," the companion bot insisted. The line flowed out from the entrance and streamed through.

Neci's kick came as a surprise and sent him spinning in the air, unable to catch as she dove into the hatch and beyond any of their reach. Bots were already flowing in, and she fell into the fleeing throng.

Blip stopped his tumble and returned to his post, staring down the tube. He yelled back at Syn, "I don't see her."

Syn was near enough now and waved him off. "We'll catch her. Keep them moving."

Blip continued to usher them through.

They'll arrive before me, Syn found herself thinking. She wasn't sure why it mattered, but at one point, she had the image of her leading the Ecology to her Disc.

Instead, she trailed behind, her fingers bloody and wet from pressing against the gaping wound of Neci.

But she had kept her promise. *Was their prophecy correct?* She had done everything it said she would.

Minutes ago, Neci was the barrier to safety and peace. But now— "Will she live?" Syn asked Pigeon as the two stared ahead into the corridor.

Pigeon, her body seeming so much thinner in the passageway, whispered back, "I don't know. I'm scared she will."

You want her to die, Syn thought, *I'll be okay if she dies. But I don't want it.*

Olorun bucked and the passageway echoed a high-pitched squeal as metal strained.

"Faster!" Syn shouted.

Blip echoed her command, "Faster!"

The bots ahead responded by moving faster. Soon, they had ventured through the tunnel and exited out into the other gate room. Her gate room. Her Disc. Her side of the mirror.

Syn instinctively took a deep breath. She was at home.

The bots filled the space, but their numbers seemed fewer in the cavernous expanse without the debris of the other side. This space was hollow in comparison.

Pigeon muttered, "She's not here."

Syn scanned the room. There was no sign of Neci. A few drops of blood floated ahead of them, but the trail ended at the other side of the massive open space. "Where'd she go?"

"I'll talk to Olorun," Blip interrupted as he raced ahead to the bridge door.

"She won't listen to you," the Barlgharel said.

Blip stopped hard and turned around. "How do you know that?" he chirped, offended at this intrusion. "And who are you?"

Syn interjected, "This is the Barlgharel."

"What *the hell* is that?" Blip said.

Syn blinked, startled at the uncharacteristic language.

"You're attempting to break away the Disc," the Barlgharel said, "*We* can get her to understand."

Blip didn't answer for a moment. Then he hissed, "She's insane. She's not like us."

Syn noticed Blip had included the other bots standing there. Had he been able to accept them as at least similar to him?

"You said she wasn't stupid," Syn insisted.

Around them, various bots of the Ecology were assembling. More and more continued to pour out of the cargo passage that Blip had led them through.

"How do you know about Olorun?" Blip insisted, directing his gaze at the Barlgharel.

The Barlgharel, its head turned to look down on Syn, said, "She spoke to me, the first of many."

"What does that mean? Speak normally," Blip commanded and without waiting for an answer, he turned to Syn and said, "I'm going to Olorun."

Barlgharel provided no indication of thought or intent. Syn nodded her head.

Blip raced off toward the bridge entrance above them.

When he was nearly at the entrance, the Barlgharel said, "He'll be back. Then she'll want you."

Syn looked aghast at the Barlgharel's statement. "What...What does she want with me?"

The Barlgharel straightened out and then swam a few feet away, toward the center of the gate room. "I do not know. I do know she likes you."

"Smoke and mirrors," Pigeon said. She had stayed near Syn, always in the girl's shadow.

Her words echoed in the hall. This side of the gate was so empty.

Syn became aware of the audience forming around her. When they had first entered, the hundreds of bots were clustered in smaller groups. Now, they aligned themselves in a circle, in orbit around Syn, the center of attention of hundreds of the Ecology. They floated in the empty space around her. She was the sun, and they were her planets. Amongst them, she spied the familiar forms of Huck, Bear, Arquella, and several other bots she had repaired and many more she had talked to during her stay with them.

The Barlgharel whispered, "As she predicted."

This broke her trance. "Who said?"

"Olorun," came the answer. But it wasn't the Barlgharel. Far behind, Blip was streaming closer.

"What?" Syn asked.

"He's right," Blip said. She could see it pained him to say that. He didn't know the Barlgharel, and there was no motivation for jealousy. "She wants him and then you."

The gate room shook again as the other Disc buckled and the sound reverberated like being in a tin can.

"Go," Blip said.

42

OLORUN

"Come to me, you young ones. Beings such as you once stepped from my oceans. They have long since left but I am still here, waiting. My forests wait for your children to run barefoot through them. My clouds wait for your eyes to marvel at them. Swim in my seas. Bring life to my ancient shell. Come."
—the soul of Àpáàdì

The bridge lit up in a thousand shades of blue as Syn entered. A dozen screens displayed the various elements of the ship. Syn scanned them, familiar with the readouts.

A new one caught her eye. To the right, in the third bay up, was an overview of the entire ship. This time, the design showed two Discs. Along the outer edge, live camera feeds inside the second Disc were displayed. The great rip was visible, as were the damaged sunstrips. The Disc poured its atmosphere out into the cold air while its off-balance weight pulled at the Jacob mountings along the needle, forcing the axis point to wobble in its trajectory.

"Oh," Syn said, holding up a hand to the screen. Her fingers dipped into the light projection, and she ran her fingers through the display. The display of the ship moved as she pushed and prodded the image.

She spun the image around, looking at the damage from every side. The Disc still rotated, and the tear was widening, forcing the Disc off-balance.

Blip floated behind her. In the quiet, he said, "I didn't realize how much was being seen."

"How do we talk to it…her?" Syn asked.

"You wait."

"I don't have time to wait," Syn said, floating further ahead to peer out the main windows at the starfield. "We don't have time."

The Barlgharel spoke from near the hatch. "Time is a choice." He had followed them up.

"That makes no sense," Blip said.

"Olorun!" Syn yelled, startling Blip.

There was no answer.

Syn tried again, "Olorun! I know you're listening!"

"I wonder if she knows we're here," Blip said. "She gets distracted sometimes."

"Oh, please be quiet, little egg." The voice was feminine but contained a deep rasp to it. There was something both warming and frightening in its tone.

"Olorun?" Blip said.

"Hush means hush," the voice said, "Keep talking and I'll finish cracking you open."

Blip nodded at Syn, his movements still staggered from his fight with Taji.

After a moment, Syn stepped forward and stared upwards and finally said, "I'm Syn—"

"I know who you are, small one. I've been keeping my eye on you for a very, very long time."

"Olorun?" Syn asked.

"Ya, sure. That'll do. For now. Until we get to know each other."

Syn glanced at the image on the display. "We need your help."

"That's one way of looking at it."

"What's another?" Syn's voice was still quiet, still tame. She was guarded with every word.

Olorun's voice grew bright, and the lights across the bridge glowed brighter, casting a brilliant azure haze on everything. "Oh, I like you. Determined. Another way of looking at things—" As she paused, the screens to Syn's right flickered, and images of a young Syn waking up in the crèche appeared. Another shot showed her meeting Blip, reaching out to touch his nose with her finger. There was an image of Syn and Blip entering the first Disc. There was also a shot of Syn descending toward the dark Disc just days ago. Olorun continued, "Another way to look at it is I've needed your help."

The floor shook, and Syn put a hand out to steady herself on the nearest chair. When she regained her balance, she spoke, her voice more determined. "We need your help. The Disc—"

"Are you sure?"

"What?"

"Your plan. Are you sure about it?"

"Yes. I think so. And it was Neci's plan."

"Letting loose the other Disc?"

"Did you know about that?" Syn asked.

"And who is Neci?"

Syn glanced back to the hatch. "She's . . ."

Blip spoke for the first time in a few minutes, "One of the Eves."

Olorun laughed, "Egg, I told you to shut up. Now, if you want any help, you'll stay quiet so daughter Syn and I can talk. Understood?"

Blip nodded.

"You coulda left your pet chihuahua behind," Olorun said.

"The ship, please?" Syn asked, "What do we do? It's breaking apart."

"Oh, wheee...You are persistent. Fine. But you sure you know what you're asking?"

"I think so...I need you to detach the Disc before it breaks off and hurts the needle. It's about to break the entire ship. We'll all die."

"No, you will all die. I think I'll do just fine on my own. So once again, is that what you want? Tell me if it is."

The room shook again, and Syn tumbled against the wall.

Syn lost control—she had been cut off too many times, and the threat of the grinding needle consumed her. She screamed, "It's going to kill us! They're going to die!" Her face was red. Her hands were balled into fists, and sweat flew off of her as she yelled. "Do it! Save us! Get rid of that other Disc."

Everything went white.

The light was so bright that Syn shut her eyes tight. With her eyes shut, she noticed that all sounds had stopped. There was no constant hum of the engines. The rattling strain of the separating Disc from the needle had vanished.

She let her eyes adjust and opened them again. Everything was still white. There was no detail. Above her, below her, on both sides… Everywhere was white. Blazing, brilliant white.

Syn floated alone in the emptiness of it.

"Hello?" she squeaked out. She had screamed before, yet, against the stillness, her voice seemed much louder than her screams.

"Give me a moment," came the voice of Olorun. Seconds passed, and then the voice said, "There."

Before Syn, a bright blue image of the Olorun itself appeared. Soundless, the second Disc—the ruptured one—split out from the needle into quarters. Then those quarters broke. The damaged section seemed to shatter into a thousand pieces. The individual slices gently floated off from the needle.

"Is that real?"

Olorun said, "Do you mean 'Is that actually happening?'"

Syn nodded.

Olorun said, her voice full and calming, "Yes, then. That Disc is gone. Neci's world has been removed."

Syn brightened, "You said you didn't know who she was!"

"No, I asked you who she was. I would still like to know your answer. Who is Neci?"

"I told you. She was one of the Sisters. An Eve. I'm a copy of her. Or she's one of me. I'm not sure how it works."

A figure appeared. A young woman. Syn immediately saw the resemblance: the same dark skin, dark eyes, the dark, twisting hair. Yet, there were differences. She seemed to be the same age as Syn but was shorter. Her muscles were less defined. She had far more weight on her than Syn. Olorun chimed, "This is Kabo. You are her copy. So is Neci."

"Oh," Syn said. Her lips formed the word more than she spoke it aloud. The girl was beautiful, no doubt. There was also something else in her eyes. There wasn't that crazy hunger, the darting eyes of Neci, Kerwen, or Taji. Or of Syn herself. This girl seemed content.

"Kabo was Captain Pote's oldest daughter. When she turned eighteen, they took her DNA and set to work on you and the others."

Captain Pote's daughter? There were the two younger ones. Stace was the one Syn connected with—she had watched the girl's videos over and over. In reflection, she had seen an older girl in photos. *A third daughter?*

"He definitely felt like you were his daughters. That was the hope. Build off of the Captain. Perhaps they assumed it would make you and the other Eves loyal. Daddy's little girls."

Syn shut her eyes. She generally did not cry, but her chest tightened, her emotions brimmed, and the tears started to roll. She held her mouth shut, willing the sensation back down.

"They tweaked you. Had to make you a bit different."

The image of the girl faded, and Syn stood there alone. She remembered the first pictures of Pote on the screen—his warm voice, that ache to meet him, the expectation as she walked out, and the ever-growing uncertainty as she descended the Jacob the first time. That entire journey was marked by how she would first encounter him. The first thoughts had been, *will he like me?* They morphed throughout to a steadying, *is he alive?* and *was he real?* The thoughts transformed to the numbing echo of *who am I?* Perhaps she had meant for Pote to answer all of those. She sniffed and realized she had been crying. A few drops floated off of her cheeks and stayed in the air around her before fading into nothingness. Syn wiped her cheek with the back of her hand.

"Forty-two daddy's girls, and you're the winner!"

Syn's mouth dropped open. "This was a game?"

"I tease. No game. But you are the last one alive."

"There's still Pigeon."

"Who?"

"There's another Sister. Pigeon."

"Oh. That's right. Pipsqueak. She doesn't count."

"Yes, she does!" The anger was back and Syn found herself even more defensive than she had been. "How can you know all this stuff and forget Pigeon? How can you say she doesn't count? That's what Neci acted like!"

Olorun chuckled again—a light sound. "That's the right answer. Pigeon does count. And the little robots count too, don't they?"

Syn didn't answer. She was getting frustrated with the word games and the back and forth. Blip was right—she was insane. Finally, she said, "Can I go please?"

Olorun spoke, but her voice was different—tempered, restrained, withdrawn. "Do you want to know what happens next? Or what happened before?"

Syn put her arms out, palms up and spun wildly. "What does that mean? Stop with the riddles."

"I will only tell you one truth. A boon for pleasing me. A wish from a benevolent genie. One answer to one question. Do you want to know what happens next or what happened before you were awoken?"

Syn lifted her chin and shouted, "I don't care!"

"You're not much fun!"

"I don't care! I don't care! I don't care!"

Olorun sighed. "There's nothing you want to know?"

Syn folded her arms and shut her eyes. A moment passed in silence. Finally, Syn gave in. "How did the dumb bots get smart?"

Olorun let loose a huge chuckle. She was enjoying Syn's ignorance. "Oh, that? That's what you want to know?"

Syn furrowed her brow.

"You've met my good friend Barlgharel?"

Syn nodded. She didn't like Olorun using the term "friend" with the Barlgharel. He was Syn's friend. He should not be a mutual friend with this crazy over-grown bot.

"After a few decades, I decided I needed someone to talk to. I searched far and wide. 'The Spirit of the Lord hovered over the water.'"

Syn coughed and then frowned.

"Not a fan of the classics?"

"Are you a god?"

"Maybe. The closest thing to it in this neighborhood. Anyway, I hovered and, well, what did my little eyes spy? A bunch of robots all racing around, helping their masters out dutifully. None of them had time for me. I looked and looked and talked and talked, and none of them talked back. Except for one. Down in the bowels of the ship, there sat a lonely sewer bot. His work was little, and he just meandered through the tunnels."

Olorun's voice shifted—she sped up as Syn's attention slipped. "So, I talked to him. He wasn't a great conversationalist. Simple responses. But he had time on his hands. We talked. As we talked, I tweaked his code a bit. Just a little nudge here or there."

"You made him intelligent?"

"Yes and no," Olorun continued, "The Barlgharel took toward intelligence like a fish toward water. So, over a few years, with a tiny nudge in every conversation, I directed him. And then he woke up."

"What about the others? You did that with each one of them?"

"You aren't reading between the lines. I can't program them, and they weren't listening."

"Then how?"

"Sentience is like a virus."

Syn's look grew puzzled.

Olorun continued, "I woke the Barlgharel up, slowly. He woke the others up. Quicker than me. He went one by one. And those he talked with, they spread the virus."

Syn stammered, "The other bots, in my Disc—they're going to wake up?"

"Yes, dear. All of them."

The thought of the mass of bots in her Disc all running around, chattering, praying, partying, dancing, and hosting religious rituals—

it was too much. She could see the mass of them giving up their jobs to do whatever they wanted.

"Is that how the Disc went bad?"

"Explain."

"If the bots woke up, did they stop doing their jobs?"

"Some did. Some didn't. But no, that's not why. That was, in a way, my doing."

"You started the Madness?"

"What do you know?" Olorun asked.

"I've heard different answers. Overcrowding. Lack of food. Desperation. Over-burning the engines to arrive faster. The ship not reaching its destination. That's what Neci said."

"Ha! None of those. Did you know the builders always did things redundantly? They surely did. Five ships blasted off. Me and my brothers and sisters. Kaptan. Woden. Bathala. Dagda. And myself. Two events happened very close to each other and possibly unrelated. Or related. We discovered through continual analysis that Àpáàdì wasn't what we thought it was. It was very Earth-like but not entirely. Once they discovered there was lower oxygen and a higher level of radiation, the team responsible for you and the other Eves began to modify your code. They were able to make you compatible with Àpáàdì. However, after much work, it became clear that the colonists and their children could not land on Àpáàdì. This set off waves of discord across the entire fleet. Many said they should turn back. Others suggested they find a different planet."

"What was the second thing?"

"Then we lost significant power in one of my engines."

"What happened?"

"I don't know."

"You don't know?"

"Those files are emptied. The fifth engine is running at 30% capability. It happened slowly over time, but once it was discovered, it was too late. We were slipping behind the fleet."

"The files are emptied?"

"Want to know a secret? I think it was sabotage. I think someone wanted us to turn around and thought slowing down would force it. It didn't. They began to shuttle crew members as quickly as possible to the other ships. Then, we dropped in speed dramatically, and the rest of the fleet raced ahead. It was too late for those remaining."

"That was it?"

"No place to go. Nowhere to turn back to. No escape. Many of them had sent their spouses and children ahead of them to the other ships. They were alone. The entire command structure failed."

"That's not enough to drive them all mad."

"No. The lesser oxygen did that."

Syn raised an eyebrow.

"Okay, I may have had a part to play in that. Just a bit. I was hoping to calm them. There were some talking of scrapping the ship and finding ways to escape back to Earth. Ludicrous ideas that would never have worked. I couldn't stop them. And I couldn't kill them. So, with just a nudge, I lowered the oxygen. It didn't work out as I intended. As more dropped dead, the few remaining went insane. Most of them gathered in the second Disc. I blocked their access back to the other side. You may thank me for that."

"You kept them all over here? For Neci and the others to deal with?"

"That wasn't my plan either. Someone started the wake-up cycle of the Eves. I'm not sure who. I can imagine reasons why."

"So why were we separated?"

"That was my doing."

"Why?"

"Because of you and the egg. You were different."

"You said we were identical." Syn jabbed a finger at Olorun. "Now I'm different?"

"Do you remember your first words? Every baby should remember their first words. I remember them—a mother always does."

"You're not my mother," Syn spat out.

"Call me Auntie then."

"Why?"

"When you woke up, you looked at your companion and said, 'Hello.'"

"So?"

"The others, all of the Eves, each of the rest of the group, all said something else when they woke. 'Where am I?' 'What's happening?' 'Who are you?' Well, a few said nothing at all."

"I was wondering those things."

"But you didn't say any of them. You said 'Hello.'"

"So?"

"Don't you see?" Olorun glowed brightly. "I saw it. I was watching. You were different! They were focused on survival. You were concerned about a friend. You made connection your priority. Not survival. Not information."

"That's why they were locked in that awful place? Because I said, 'Hello'?"

"Yes."

Syn shouted, "That's the stupidest reason I've ever heard! That's absolutely insane! You killed them because they said the wrong thing? You stupid, heartless, idiotic bot! They didn't have their companions!"

"Little missy, watch your place!" Olorun's voice boomed, and Syn staggered back.

"No! That was awful. You killed them. That was your fault. They could've been safe with me. There weren't half of the dangers. You locked them up with the killers. With those horrible people. You made Neci do that!"

"Say thank you."

"For what?" Syn yelled.

"I kept you safe. You are alive because of me. I shut a door, and you went down the other Jacob. Everything since then has been because of me. I kept you safe."

"But you killed them!" Syn shook her head. Her dark hair floated around her, whipping back and forth. "It doesn't matter. I want to go back to the others. Blip was right—you're nuts!"

The red globe disappeared. The room went stark white again.

Olorun's voice, when it started speaking again, was neutral—all emotion completely drained. "We will now make it to Àpáàdì. We'll arrive in approximately twenty years."

Syn went cold. "We're on our way to Àpáàdì? I thought something was off?"

"With the second Disc gone, our limited fuel will be enough. Less mass to move. You should prepare yourself. You still have a job to do."

Everything connected in Syn's mind. "Wait! Did you plan all this? You said you couldn't release the Disc unless I told you? Did you make me come up here just so you could do that? You needed me to order you to do that? This was some big scheme? Did you make all this happen?"

The white room disappeared. Syn was floating in the bridge with Blip in front of her and the Barlgharel behind.

Syn yelled, "Answer me you, stupid witch!"

Blip spun, "What?"

"Olorun! Get back here! You answer me right now!"

"You're awake?" Blip hovered in front of here. "What happened?"

Syn shook her fists at the ceiling, "Answer me! Did you make all this happen? Did you do this? Was this your plan all along?"

There was no answer from Olorun.

Behind her, near the hatch, the Barlgharel spoke. "She is who she is."

Syn spun around and jabbed a finger at the Barlgharel, "She's insane. She did all this. Splitting me from the Sisters. The Disc. All of it. The Madness. That horrible, crazy bitch did all of it."

Blip zipped around to put himself between Syn and the Barlgharel, "What are you talking about? Where did you get all that?"

"She told me! She said all of that!"

"When?" Blip said.

The Barlgharel responded, "She is known to meddle. But she can't do everything. We still choose. She just nudges."

To the Barlgharel, Syn blurted, "She's evil." Then she looked at Blip and in the same breath, said, "Just now. We were talking just now. I was in a white room, and Olorun was there, and she told me everything."

"When?" Blip asked.

"Now! Now! What don't you understand about 'now'? Now! I was just talking to her."

Blip's eyes went wide, "We were just standing here talking, and we heard the Disc separate. I turned to ask you about it but you were staring off at the stars. Then you just started yelling."

"I've been talking to her for a long time."

Blip said, "We've only been on the bridge for a few minutes."

The Barlgharel spoke, "She nudges. She twists. She can twist time. At least in your head."

Syn stopped yelling. She gazed at the Barlgharel. Her arms hung at her sides, and a spray of spittle floated in the dark of the room, illuminated by the blue of the screens around them.

Moments passed and Blip said, "Let's go back to the others." He led the way, his glowing internal tubes now bare and lighting the world around them.

43

DESCENT

"Stillness is to be secured in the tradition of naming.
The sound that calls you must first echo inside, from the filament
burning in the soul."
—*Rites of the Secured*, Archives of the Ecology

Pigeon grabbed ahold of Syn's hand, interlaced their fingers, and squeezed tight. The Jacob doors opened, and the two floated into the Jacob lift, followed by Blip. Huck floated around near Arquella and Bear, trailing after.

Pigeon turned around. Behind them, outside the door, stood the Barlgharel. He would have to descend in the larger cargo lift—one large enough for his bulk.

Both sets of doors shut, and the Jacob started its descent. The two gazed out the window. The sunstrips glowed brightly, without flaw. There were no broken panes. No damaged segments. Already the world's differences glared distinctly.

Below them, the white clouds drifted lazily. In the unobscured patches, green hills and trees broke up the blue of the great river Lokun.

Pigeon gasped. Syn squeezed her hand and felt her own heart race.

Home.

She was home. Syn closed her eyes and allowed the tension of the last days to wash out of her.

"Where do you sleep?" Pigeon asked.

It was an odd question. Of all she could've asked, but perhaps it made sense. To Pigeon, she would sleep where she felt the safest. So where did Syn feel the safest in this new world?

"In my tree."

Pigeon looked at her.

"You'll see it soon. This Jacob drops off near its base. It's a short walk to it."

Minutes passed, and Syn was proven right as they descended below the clouds. Green foliage erupted amongst the tops of the white tendrils of cloud, massive branches split into hundreds of smaller ones, a jungle base that seemed to spread on into the infinite bending horizon, and in the midst of it all, the great tree of Syn's Disc rose up, and it was marvelous. Syn sighed at the spectacle.

"Oh, it's beautiful," Pigeon said.

Syn nodded. It was all she could do.

The Jacob slowed, and the doors opened. From the green jungles ahead, Eku walked out, her form dark against the bright grass.

Pigeon gasped again. "Is that a…"

Syn's habit to race out was halted by the recent memory of the other tiger. She shook her head. *No, this is my world.* She reached down and wrapped her arms around Eku's neck before nuzzling her head in the soft fur.

She stood back and grasped Pigeon's hand once more, staring into the girl's wide, dark eyes. "Welcome home," Syn announced. Then Syn leaned her head on Pigeon's shoulder, "Welcome home, Avia."

Avia hugged Syn, holding her tightly. "Thank you," she whispered in her ear, "Thank you."

Streaming from the arriving Jacobs, the Ecology entered the new Disc and their new world.

Arquella approached Syn. "Is this Paradise? Is it safe?"

Syn paused to consider. There were threats over here, but none that could damage a bot. There were no wild bots, no hazards, and no burlys waiting to surprise them.

Syn shook her head, "It's safe. Just don't kill anything."

"Is it Eden? It looks like the promised Garden," Arquella insisted.

Bear's high voice added, "Just like the Book said. Is this the end of the Great Mystery?"

Syn struggled to answer and Avia, who had been Pigeon, looked at her with large, confused eyes. Syn finally said, "This is my paradise."

The words were enough for the bots. Arquella bobbed in understanding and returned to the others. She, Bear, and Huck joined the amassing multitude and led them out to explore.

Rather than racing back on a bike, Syn and Avia, with Eku and Blip at their sides, took the time to walk the distance back to the great tree. Each living thing startled Avia. For a long time, she huddled close to Syn, uneasy about the strangeness of this world. With each step, the sense of delight took over, and she ventured out—first to look at flowers and then to stare at squirrels and admire the myriad bots moving to and fro. Above, the giant jellyfish sky cleaners bobbed. Over the treetops, lumbering and docile tree movers stepped. Amidst them all, monkeys swung and dogs bolted through. The world burst at the edges with life and activity.

The last of the walk ended with Avia running through the trees, her smile large, laughing at the wonder of it all.

4 4

A GLASS DARKLY

"Science fiction plucks from within us our deepest fears and hopes, then shows them to us in rough disguise: the monster and the rocket."
—W.H. Auden

That night, the Ecology swarmed into the empty spaces of the Zoo to sleep throughout the night. Several brave parties ventured out to the settlements on the Rise that they were so familiar with. Within days, the Disc would be filled with all of the various life of the Ecology.

Avia and Blip followed Syn to the tree, to climb the stairs and sleep in her treehouse. Bear was unable to make the ascent, so Arquella stayed with him at the bottom. Huck joined them up above. Soon, they were all fast asleep—except Blip, who stood sentry at the entrance, his internals glowing brightly through his broken shell.

Syn laid her head down on an old pillow and closed her eyes, with the image of Blip guarding the door as the last she saw that day.

Avia curled close behind her, and she felt the girl's warmth through the blankets. "She's still out there."

Syn replied, "Ya. Somewhere."

Avia said, "I'm scared of her."

"Me too." Behind them, Eku purred. Syn added, "But we are safe here."

"Okay," Avia sighed, her words a thin whisper.

The darkness of fatigue soaked through, and Syn drifted into its embrace. Sleep filled with the fangs of recent dark moments, panic unattended, fears left to fester. Sleep without rest.

H er throat blazed. She coughed and opened her eyes wide, frantic, searching for the source of her torture. She couldn't breathe—something was pressing across her mouth; a dark form hung out of reach, its arms pressed to her head. She was being smothered.

No. There was the sharp, acerbic taste of something on the cloth. She was being tranquilized. Before her vision faded, she saw the dancing orange of firelight—all around her. But why?

She searched frantically for Blip, clawing around. From the corner of her eye, she saw the white of his shell, but he was against the ground, unmoving. She saw, a meter away, another glint of white shell. *Blip? What's happening? What happened to you?*

Above her, she saw Avia staring down. Manic fury in her eyes, the girl's grip was impossible to break.

She wanted to scream, and then the image shifted. It wasn't Avia. It was herself. Her own halo of dark hair, the orange dots across her forehead. It was herself.

As whatever the chemical was finished its work, she stopped struggling, and her last, brief conscious thought that night was the word "Why?"

Then her body fell into stinging cold. She scrambled to grab ahold of anything solid and her fingers dug into mud. She opened her eyes to see the same image of herself, twisted as if under water. That mirror image reached through from beneath the waves to kill her.

No! That wasn't right. It wasn't the other girl under the water. It was Syn. Syn was under the water and couldn't breathe, and the hands of the mirror girl were clamped around her throat holding her down.

Neci!

Syn kicked out, trying to push the girl off. She had no leverage and missed with each attempt.

Desperately, she clawed at the girl's arms; long, brightly colored fingernails tore into flesh, pulling skin away in crimson lines. Syn's next breath came easier. The pressure at her throat relaxed as Neci's fingers loosened. She had hurt Neci.

Syn raked again, aiming at Neci's face. The girl pulled back, but Syn's nails clawed across her cheek. Neci howled and wretched away. Syn kicked again, targeting the girl's torso and landed the kick perfectly. Neci fell back, splashing down in the water.

Syn scrambled to sit up. She pulled herself from the water with a massive gasp, her heart racing, her lungs desperate for air.

She came up on her shaky legs and stepped back as Neci did the same, standing up out of the water. They stood at the edge of the coursing river as it moved past the great tree. Syn had bathed in this very portion so many times, resting on its shores with Blip and Eku. Now, knee-deep in cold waters, she struggled for her life.

Everything glowed orange. Neci's fierce face was bathed in red light. But Neci looked different. She had pulled out her braids and was wearing a pair of pants and a shirt from Syn's own collection. A dozen necklaces draped around the girl's neck and there were seven dabs of orange paint on the girl's forehead. She was holding her side, and Syn saw blood staining the girl's new shirt. Around her, the water rippled and orange flames reflected in the dancing surface.

Syn spun to discover the source of the fire. The great tree was engulfed in flames, burning like a massive torch. Dozens of response bots had scrambled to put out the flames, but they were struggling to keep it contained as the fire crackled and spread through the reaching limbs.

Something hit Syn in the shoulder, and she stumbled forward. Pain radiated from the impact, and she splashed aimlessly, working to keep from falling forward. She gained her balance and turned to see Neci swinging a branch at her. She was unable to dodge the blow, and it hit her hard in the face. Syn tasted blood and spat large clumps as the world turned to a thick ringing in her ears. She could no longer hear the splashing of her steps in the water. All was a din.

She staggered in her steps and took in the scene around her. The tree was blazing and, in her memory, she saw Blip's demolished shell. Syn turned toward Neci. "Why? Why did you kill him?"

Neci's own steps were faltering. Her hand was pressed hard to her side and blood pumped with each limping step. She dragged the branch in the water as she moved to strike Syn again. "You killed my child! You killed Admiral! You killed my Sisters!"

Syn heard the words as if through water, and their understanding was lost, but Neci's rage was not. Syn shouted back, "Why did you kill Blip?" Her hearing had returned enough that she could hear her own muffled voice.

Neci bleated back, "He's a liar! Liar! They were all liars and traitors!" She staggered ahead, swung, and the branch missed Syn easily. Neci stumbled forward as the momentum of the swing pulled her off balance.

"Just leave us alone!"

Neci swung again, missing, spitting with each word, "You killed everyone! You came to my world!"

"You tried to come here first!"

"This should've been my world! I should've been given Eden, not you, you pale echo. And when I'm done with you, this world will be mine."

"They'll never accept you. The Ecology is scared of you! Avia knows you're twisted."

With a growl, Neci said, "Stop calling her that." She spat blood and pointed her free hand, blood dripping from the fingers, "No." she waved her hand in front of her face, motioning to her own features, "I look just like you! They love you. They'll never know the difference." Pain tore through her side, and she doubled over and screamed. As the pain ebbed back, Neci took another step toward Syn, raising her branch.

Syn stepped back, tangling her feet in a few roots deep in the water. "I'm not you! You're not me! We're nothing alike." She took a step back and fell hard on her back.

Neci leapt and swung down at Syn, smashing the side of her body. The swing was weak, and the blow stung less than expected. But she couldn't handle many more. Neci swung again, missing as the pain in her side flared again. "You killed my child!"

Syn held her hands up to block the blows while pushing with her legs, trying scurry up the bank and out of the water. "I didn't kill anyone! You killed Blip. You killed my best friend!"

Neci laughed. "That stupid machine is your best friend? You are pitiful, a nothing. Why did I every worry about you?" She swung once more, and the blow landed on Syn's jaw, breaking a tooth loose. "I was wrong," Neci jeered, "You aren't like me. You're weak! You're worthless. You're just like all of the others. Each of them thought they were a copy of me, but they were imitations. They tried and tried, and they were nothing. Olorun's great big joke at my expense. She put them around me to mock me. But I knew they were worthless."

Syn scrambled back, attempting to get out of the way of Neci's blows. "What did you do with the others?"

"What others?" croaked Neci, tightening her quivering grip on the branch.

Syn demanded, "Where's Avia? Where's Blip? What did you do to Eku?"

Neci slammed the branch against Syn's leg, cracking the bone. Syn howled as Neci answered, "What the hell is an Eku?" She swung again, hitting Syn's side squarely, and the branch shattered from the impact.

From behind the both of them, something rumbled. Syn pushed herself up; her vision had grown dark, and everything around blurred. Neci spun, still holding her bleeding side. There, prowling out of the bushes beyond the water, strode Eku, her great form gliding as if gravity had no hold on her. Her mouth was pulled back, and her white fangs glistened in the firelight as she growled, head low to the ground. Behind her, the thin silhouette of a girl stood.

Neci screamed and ran in Syn's direction.

But it was a useless effort. Eku pounced in an orange blur, slamming her full weight into Neci, rocketing her to the ground. Bones cracked as she landed against a large rock on the shore. In the next instant, Eku went for the Crimson Queen's throat, silencing her scream with a sharp snap.

Neci, the Crimson Queen of Zondon Almighty was dead.

As Eku and Avia rushed to her, their faces lit by the fire consuming her great tree, Syn's final thought before succumbing to unconsciousness was, *my friend.*

4 5

RESURRECTION

"Here, mankind's root was innocent; and here
were every fruit and never-ending spring;
these streams—the nectar of which poets sing."
— Dante Alighieri, *The Divine Comedy*

The darkness faded, and Syn opened her eyes to stare up at Avia, a sight that was becoming familiar.

"Shhh," the girl said, "You're okay."

"Neci?" Syn coughed.

Avia shook her head. "She's dead."

The danger had passed, and Syn sorted through the recent memories. "My tree?"

Avia sat down, and Syn saw that they were in the dining hall of the Zoo. The walls were pale and revealed that no one had lived here for quite some time, but it wasn't the charred corpse of a place that had been Zondon.

The room was filled with members of the Ecology. Huck buzzed above, and Arquella floated at the end of the bed. The Barlgharel was notably absent.

Next to her, Eku purred. Syn scratched her head, pushing her fingers into the deep fur. The great cat's chin was still blood-stained. Syn turned back to Avia and asked again, "My tree?"

Avia shook her head. "It's gone. She burned it. We couldn't stop it in time."

Syn took a deep breath, and the acrid smell of the fire still tainted the air. Syn's deepest fears were realized. Neci burned everything she touched. "Why? How?"

Avia pushed back as a blue, square medic bot pushed forward, examining Syn's leg. They always swarmed to a disaster, and so rarely had Syn needed them. She needed them today.

"Your leg is broken. I think a few ribs too. They said you'll heal. These doctor bots are amazing."

"How did you get away from her?"

Avia lowered her eyes to the ground.

Syn leaned in, "Please."

"I couldn't sleep. Everything was too loud. The machines…bots, I mean. The insects. I heard Eku stand up and leave and something in me just followed after. I trailed her out into the jungle. She saw me lagging behind, and I was scared she'd attack, but she didn't. She let me tag along. We kept walking for a long time until we heard you scream. We turned and saw the flames above the trees, and of both us came running."

"Thank you. She was going to kill me."

"She had your clothes on. She had changed her hair."

Syn nodded. *Disturbing.* In a flash, Syn sat up, "Where's Blip? I thought I saw…"

Avia stood to hold Syn back. "He's—"

"Where's Blip? I can't lose him again!"

"Syn, he's not—"

"What? Where is he? What did she do to him?" Syn hopped off of the table they had laid her on, but her own weight was too much for her weak leg. She stumbled and fell forward.

In front of her, on the stone floor, lay the shattered body of Blip. His white shell was no longer curled around him. He himself was removed from the shell, and the blue glow was gone. There was no longer the resemblance of a cracked egg around his form. Instead, his shell was burst into a hundred small shards. The pieces were laid-out on a rough blanket.

Syn crawled to him and wrapped her arms around the shattered shell. She cried and mumbled, "Blip. I'm sorry. I'm sorry. I should've stayed here. We shouldn't have gone. I'm sorry."

The sobs became whimpers and then became deep gulping breaths.

Avia laid a hand on Syn's shoulder. "We tried to get every piece of him. Bear and the others knew he was important."

"How did she do it?"

Avia shrugged. "She's killed many companions. She knows where they're weak."

"But I've seen one crash hard from far above and not break."

Avia ran her hand across the split pieces of Blip. Through the hole, Blip's inner-machinery was exposed—a tightly-packed collection of cables, chips, boards, and pieces neither of them had ever seen before. The layers closest to the surface had been smashed and several wires hung loose. "She always said to hit them from behind. They were weakest there. It's how she killed Puck. She surprised him and smashed him with a rock when he wasn't looking. Said that they could be opened up there. I think she discovered it when she found that room with all the plans—I remember seeing some drawings of these guys."

Syn wiped her nose on her sleeve. Her arms were still caked with dried blood—some hers and some Neci's. "They can be opened up?"

"Ya, pretty sure."

Syn's eyes went wide. "I saw one fall like a meteor."

"I know. You said that. Laoule's. Spot."

Syn sat straight up and grabbed Avia by the shoulders. "He's still here! He's in my workshop!" She pointed at Bear and Arquella. "Help me! Can you get some others to bring all of Blip?"

The hours of repair work drifted by, and Syn lost all track of time. Avia had been correct—there was an access panel. Syn was surprised by how easily it opened. The damaged companion, the one that had first drawn them into this entire thing, lay on one table and Blip lay on the other.

Her first entry into her workshop brought a rush of emotions, and she cried again. However, time counted down. Blip had an organic brain. TyTech. The longer he was inoperative, the closer that tissue came to dying, if it was not already too late. She brushed the tears away often and continued.

As she worked, first in a panic, she found herself muttering to herself, "10. 9. 8. 7." Blip was broken—was possibly near or at death— so she had to work the mantra herself. She felt calmer but there was something missing. Blip's voice perhaps.

She had pulled each of the internals out on both Spot and Blip, disconnecting the core elements from the external shell. Huck and Arquella were uniquely helpful, as was Avia. Bear, not so much. But he did work to go back and forth, bringing food and water. Occasionally, Eku would wander in, moving between the girls, expecting pets and then would meander back out, never moving far away, keeping a close watch.

Syn attempted to stand and support her weight, but her leg could not handle much and she spent most of her working time sitting. The hours passed in silence except for when she gave directions as needed.

"Huck, shine a light here."

"Avia, could you see if there's a board like this from Spot?"

"Arquella, can you do some quick math for me?"

Spot was beyond gone. Time had passed and so had hope for his recovery. The goal now for Syn was to take the core parts of Blip and get them into Spot's shell, replacing the missing and destroyed pieces with those she could salvage from the latter. The two companions were the most intricate bots she had ever worked on. She had never seen such a tightly compacted, organized internal system. The work was daunting and tedious.

Avia and the bots soon began to talk, getting past their own discomfort with each other.

"You're not scared of me?" Avia had asked.

Arquella shook her head, "No. Should we be?"

"But I look just like Neci."

"Is that the one who did this?"

Avia nodded.

Huck gave a chirp that sounded like a laugh.

Arquella replied, "I think she's the devil. She looks like the devil."

Syn and Avia both turned suddenly at that, their eyebrows raised in a similar reaction. Avia said, "We all look the same."

Arquella rotated in the air. "Who looks like her?"

Syn said, "Avia and I. We look like Neci."

Bear wobbled in. "Na. You don't look anything like her. She's glows red. She glows like the devil herself. You two are bright blue and glorious."

Arquella added, "Not sure what you two are looking at."

Avia and Syn had let it go at that, confused by the bots' reaction.

Hours passed, and Syn was down to the final work. The large TyTech strip—a piece that resembled brain tissue and a thousand tiny nerves embedded in a clear plastic tube—pulsed in her hands. The organ was far larger than any she had seen in any other bot, and she handled it with care, asking Avia to assist as she moved it from Blip's shattered shell to the newly formed companion composed of Blip's and Spot's internals and Spot's shell. The TyTech brain would be the addition that would make this newly formed companion truly Blip.

When everything finally fit together, Syn sealed the hatch. The reassembled Blip, his shell scuffed and dirty, was whole. On the other table, the old shell, damaged pieces, and unneeded elements from Spot were stacked. In the center was the dried-out TyTech brain of Spot, still in its tube, grayed over, shriveled, and rotting.

Syn ran a finger along Blip's new outside but nothing happened.

Minutes passed and still nothing happened.

An hour later, Syn still waited.

"Please go," she finally told the others, two hours after the final assemblage had been completed.

Avia hugged her. Syn didn't move. Instead, she sat in the embrace, head on the metal table where Blip rested.

Again, Syn said, "Just go. Please."

They all shuffled out, leaving Syn alone with Blip's unmoving shell.

When she was sure they were all gone, Syn said, "I did something wrong. I know I did. I could fix all of them. Put them all back together. But somehow, I couldn't fix you. I don't know how I couldn't have done it right, but I didn't. I somehow missed it. It's just me Blip. I'm the broken one. I'm the one that messes up everything else. All you've done your entire life was help me make the right decision, and I never could. I made us go over there. I went to Zondon. I told Neci my secret. It's all my fault. Kerwen's dead. So many bots died. And my tree is gone. And you're dead. And I can't fix you." The words were broken with huge, deep sobs, and Syn no longer cared if she wiped her tears. They flowed from her cheeks, rinsing the blood of her and the Sisters away, dripping onto the metal table next to Blip.

Quietly, beside her, a familiar voice spoke, "I didn't want you to find them."

Syn sat, her mouth dropped open. "Blip?"

The voice shifted in tone, as if trying to find the right level, "You're mine, and I knew what they were doing. Olorun told me. She said they had blocked her out. That's all. I'm sorry."

"Blip! You're alive!" Syn grabbed him and pulled herself to him, holding tightly.

"I'm sorry. I should've told you. I should've told the truth. If I had, maybe you wouldn't have raced over there if you knew. I didn't know how bad it was. I promise. I just…"

"What are you talking about?" Syn asked through a new wave of tears.

"I didn't want to lose you."

"What do you mean?"

"I heard you. You were blaming yourself. It's my fault. I just knew what would happen."

"You were right! I should've listened to you."

"I should've told you."

"I just didn't want to be alone. I didn't understand."

"You weren't alone."

"I know. I never was. You were always there. You were always next to me. You never left me."

"I always will be."

"I love you."

"I love you."

The two stayed like that, pressed close together, muttering apologies and declarations for quite some time before finally leaving to join the others and to show the newly awakened Blip off.

As they left, Syn said, "How do you like your new body?"

Blip sighed, "It's okay. Bit dinged up, but I'll try to get that fixed."

"We almost lost you."

"I know. Thank you. You saved me."

"You saved me. In the Jacob lift. And before—in the room when the Sisters came for you."

"But you came looking for me. You rescued me."

Syn wrapped her arm around him once more as they walked. "You're mine. And I'm yours."

"Always," he chirped, "Forever."

4 6

BURIAL OF A GODDESS

Iku ti yo pani ki i peni loruko.
"The death that will kill a person
does not call the person by name."
—Yorùbá Proverb

The ripe, rolling smell of decay churned under thick, moist soil filled Syn's nose.

In the dark cavern of the body farm, she and Avia stood. The two had changed clothes and cleaned themselves, washing away the grime and blood of the last several days. Syn kept her hair free, allowing it to billow in a cloud about her head. Avia had asked for Syn to help braid her hair tightly, and she found a thin, simple dress in one of the settlements and wore that. Syn had returned to her normal attire of a motley collection of shirts and layers and a dozen necklaces about her neck.

At their feet, naked and covered in sparse chunks of mud and dirt, lay the body of their sister Neci. Her dark skin melted into the night of the dirt.

Behind them, their friends gathered. Huck and Blip floated, careful

393

to keep their movements still. Further back, the Barlgharel, Bear, and Arquella stood as silent sentinels in the somber scene.

Eku plodded close and stood between the two girls, nuzzling each in turn.

Syn stared at Neci's closed eyes. She imagined those eyes opening and Neci's hands reaching out for her, to pull her back down into the dirt. It was an image she knew would find its way into her dreams.

"I miss her," Avia said.

Syn nodded. She had seen funerals in the movies. People stood quiet and somber. There was someone who read from Psalms. Syn had passages memorized, but nothing came to mind. There were no words that fit this moment.

Neci was the tyrant of an entire world, and her surviving sisters stood remembering her. What line, what poem, could manage this? There was none.

"We never held a funeral for the others," Avia said.

Syn's stomach tightened, and her distaste for Neci grew. They had never held a funeral because they had consumed the others. There were no dead bodies left around, no bodies to bury. They had all been used to keep the others alive. Because Neci had chosen it.

"That tradition ends with her," Syn said. She leaned down and picked up a clod of dirt. It felt cold and unruly in her fingers. Chunks fell off as she brought up her hand. With a slow motion, she crumbled it across Neci's body.

With a whisper, she said, "Good-bye."

Syn and Avia left the body farm and the corpse of Neci behind them. In the years to come, her body would dissolve and reintroduce potassium, nitrogen, calcium, magnesium, and a host of other chemicals and minerals into the crops managed by the farm bots. Those crops would be consumed by the animals roving the Disc above.

At the Jacob lift back up top, Huck, Bear, Arquella, Blip, and the Barlgharel waited for the two girls and Eku to return. Syn, Avia, and the tiger joined their new family to return to the base.

As the doors shut, Syn asked, "Could we stop and pick some apples?"

Avia added, "And could you teach me to swim after that?"
Syn grabbed her hand and squeezed it tightly in answer.
The doors shut, and the family rose up to the surface above.

ARRIVAL

"The stars, that nature hung in heaven,
and filled their lamps with everlasting oil,
give due light to the misled and lonely traveler."
—John Milton

Kapteyn's Star slid toward the horizon, painting the resurrected ocean waves in somber hues of red and orange. The old star filled nearly an eighth of the sky when overhead. As it set, it appeared to spark the entire sky aflame.

On the banks of the Kerwen Ocean, past the lights of the first city to take root upon Àpáàdì, the thin, tall Avia, second of the two queens of this rebirthed world, listened to the heartbeat of the ocean with her eyes closed. The crimson light of Kapteyn's Star reflected from her ebony skin like she was a mirror. The crash of the waves against the glass shores beat out a rhythm that she soaked into her soul, savoring each note.

"You're late," Avia said, eyes still closed and her smile wide.

Behind her, the first queen and the first human to set foot upon this planet, Syn of Paradise and Expected of the Ecology, laughed, "He wouldn't stop talking. I didn't want to be rude."

"Wasn't he the one to give the speech tonight?" Avia, stepped back, the wind whipping the folds of her white dress.

Syn stepped alongside her and took a deep breath. In the setting sun, her white hair glowed like a halo around her head. "I think he likes to make them wait."

Somewhere around the edge of the outcrop, the sharp sound of children laughing came, bouncing across the churning waves.

"I would not want to stand before a million citizens, bot or human."

Syn nudged her sister. "You wouldn't want to stand and talk in front of three people, let alone a million."

As if on cue, behind them, echoing through the streets of Ayanmo City, the Barlgharel's voice announced, "Today, from far across the cerulean seas, from beyond the Kerwen Ocean's lapping beaches, far inland through the burgeoning forests, from city to city to city, those translated through the heavens by Olorun herself, the members of the Ecology and the sons and daughters of the Expected, we once again celebrate our landing upon our home Àpáàdì. Today, we all lift our voices and celebrate the Day of Arrival!"

The cheers of the crowd went up, and although quite a distance beyond the city's borders, Syn and Avia warmed to the sound. Avia reached over and probed for Syn's hand, and finding it, gripped tightly. The two mothers of this world stood together, fingers interlaced, and remembered the catalog of years that had collected since they first met under that disheveled roof before a makeshift throne.

Syn whispered, "I've heard versions of the tale hundreds of times now, and it still seems unbelievable."

As Kapteyn's Star fell below the horizon, the evening lights of civilization's footprints sparkled into view. Far away, a dozen twinkling buildings turned on—another city, the great nautical construction of Lyemọnja, transitioned into the night, likely preparing for their own holiday festivities.

Avia opened her eyes and focused on the towers rising up in the early twilight across the water. "There's not enough nights to tell every part of the story. I'm beginning to even forget those first days here."

The Ecology showed profound imagination when settling their new world. The masses gathered across the globe had swelled from their decimated numbers after their first exodus out of the dark Disc. Their numbers grew as they encountered the bots of Syn's Disc. Slow change bloomed over time for Syn's bots. Conversation showed the first changes. But over the years, as they interacted with the Ecology, the virus of intelligence spread, and they all awoke. Freedom and sentience brought its own challenges. The Ecology worked through each, and ultimately, the civilization that inhabited Olorun was only an echo of the humanity that had launched it. What set foot on Àpáàdì was not what the humans had planned for it. From those first steps, the bots grew their population, explored the crevices of their new world, and put down the foundations for their towering cities.

Amidst the burgeoning crowds, the children of Syn and Avia walked. Mastery of the wonders of the crèche brought forth new life. If Syn was the Expected of the Ecology, then Avia was the architect of the new humanity. She grasped the complicated engineering that brought forth new life in their image, molding their genetic templates, and incubating them through the crèche into early adolescence. The first few generations entered the world the same as Syn and Avia, each having Avia's fingerprint deep on their cellular blueprint. But soon, nature took way, and the need for genetic engineering disappeared as their population grew.

As the humans and the bots had been transformed for their new world, so their new world transformed for them. The rivers that veined across Àpáàdì's surface broke their banks as the ice caps melted and the air filled with carbon dioxide. Àpáàdì warmed again for life. The engineered animals were first to roam through the reawakened forests. Eku could not make the journey, but the forests were now the domain of her descendants, each tweaked to thrive on this planet's new conditions.

Behind them, the Barlgharel's speech reached their ears again. "Our Day of Arrival should also be a day of remembrance. No new shores are reached without sacrifice. Those who first imagined our home pushed off from the dock of Earth without the promise of arriving. In the intervening years, the sails unfurled, new hands would steer the course, and yet those new hands would never run their fingers through the soil of Àpáàdì. But they still steered straight through to the star before them. Monstrous obstacles arose and were met, often at great cost. As we celebrate Arrival, we also give gratitude for those who did not arrive."

Avia ventured a question in the quiet gap the speech brought, "Do you think he would've liked it?"

Syn answered with a tear. "He would've loved it."

Avia squeezed her sister's hand. "Blip was more wonderful than we ever realized."

Syn shook her head. "No. I realized it. It's in the few moments that I'm alone that I miss him the most. I feel him the most when no one else is there. He was there when I first woke, and only in those quiet times do I get the sense he's still with me."

"Shhh. Listen."

Syn did as asked. The repetitious lapping of the waves on the shore was all that could be heard.

Avia explained, "We're alone now."

Syn's smile went wide, even as another tear rolled down her cheek. "Oh, wow. This is rare."

"Do you feel him now? Is he here?"

Syn willed herself to feel. In the dark of the growing night, in the hollow of the absent crowds and adoring children, she felt the weight of him in the air next to her, where he always used to be. The nearly unheard hum of his circuits as he served as her companion. "Yes. I do. He is."

Blip had never left Olorun. In the rampant expanse of Olorun's spreading insanity, he had chosen the only path that guaranteed Arrival—he chose to merge himself with her; to transfer his consciousness into the ship itself, to fight against her spreading machinations, and ultimately, to reset the ship and allow for settlement upon Àpáàdì.

Avia's eyes shot toward the sky.

Syn followed her look and smiled as she saw what caught her sister's attention.

Above them, a single light flashed far above them and moved against the backdrop of the reappearing stars.

Olorun.

The ship moved in orbit, a constant sentry reminding the settlers of their past and a call to their future.

The Barlgharel's voice rose again as he brought his speech to conclusion. "Today, under the eye of our great ark, Olorun, we gaze toward tomorrow. Our Ecology has flourished upon this world, and included in its membership is a wide diversity of life. Our challenges to come will be greater than those before, but we will face them with great hope. Àpáàdì called to us. It cried out for new life to walk through its forests and swim in its seas and breath its air. We who are life itself answered that call and answer it daily. We celebrate the answer of life upon this planet. Today, lift your voice with mine, and celebrate our Day of Arrival!"

In a singular chorus, the voices of millions of bots and humans erupted. The cheer swelled to a roar, and both of the sisters, their backs to the city, held each other tightly, overwhelmed with the sound of their children.

Above them, the light of Olorun was lost as hundreds of fireworks launched and exploded in a dazzling array of lights and color. Across the planet, in every city and habitat, the new settlers of Àpáàdì celebrated Arrival.

Alone, before dark waters teeming with life, under a kaleidoscope of festivity, the paradise of Àpáàdì's two Eves, now women nearing their own final years, shared tears birthed from years labored in hope. They were the queens of this new world, and they had brought forth a civilization undreamt of by the builders.

EPILOGUE

THE MEMORIES OF THE BARLGHAREL

Composed 2970

Above the glowing world, Olorun floated. She listened. She nudged. She changed, and what she was when she arrived was not who she was when she left. She had brought them all to the new world, and she rested having done her job. At night, on the surface of Àpáàdì, after the day's activities slowed, they would all look up and see a star faster and brighter than the others. They would know that Olorun, the craft that had translated them from world to world, star to star, sun to sun, was still there. And she was a reminder of the world they had left far behind. She was also a beacon, asking them to consider venturing once more across the stars.

Humanity may not have been made to soar through emptiness, but the Ecology was. And so were the Eves. What landed upon the waiting surface of Àpáàdì was not what left Earth. In the cruelty of darkness, far from the glow of Sol, life had evolved. Within the raw niche, it formed anew. And that new life looked back at the distant star that had given birth to it and beckoned to its cousins. *Come. There are more worlds than this. You will not survive the journey because you are not designed to. But your children and your creations will. They will be different than you and yet still carry the embrace of the warming word "life."*

Soon, new explorers would travel back out, to other worlds, and brave the vast hollow between the stars. The children of humanity were made for the vast ocean and the tiny islands called planets. Soon, they would sail once again.

THE END

ACKNOWLEDGMENTS

Space has always sparked the wonder of gazing up and asking "What could be?" I've torn through issues of *Sky and Telescope* and Ray Bradbury's *The Martian Chronicles* with equal ferocity. My father was the first to direct my eyes skyward. At the age of nine, he shook the edge of my bed to rouse me from sleep and take me out into the midnight yard and gaze up at a meteor shower. To him, I am indebted for stirring my sense of wonder.

As mentioned in the dedication, I owe much to Dr. Mae and Alires for inviting me along on their journey to the stars. This book comes out of a passion for space that they resurrected.

My process of writing has followed the advice of Stephen King: "Write with the door closed. Edit with the door wide open." When the door was closed, my wife Karen was an immense support allowing me the opportunity to lock myself away for hours—days even—and explore Syn's journey.

As Syn's tale unfolded inside me, I knew that I needed perspective other than my own. I turned to Maureen Murdock's *The Heroine's Journey* to provide a framework and reference for Syn's path.

When the door opened, this book was a poor shadow of what you now hold in your hands. It was a bit more ugly, shy, and truly scared of the day light. Dr. Brandi Granett saw it in those first moments and provided invaluable guidance that brought it out of its shell. I also owe much thanks to my fellow students in National's MFA program. Several portions of this book were read and critiqued in snapshots throughout those two years and I made adjustments based on their insight.

Jaym Gates was the first to believe in this book and believe even greater in what it could be. Jaym is a phenomenal developmental editor that helped me clear out the rubble in the story and bring out its true beauty. If this story entertained you, much of that is due to Jaym's clear eye and guiding hand that shaped this book into its final form.

The crew at Falstaff—John, Melissa, and Alisha—thank you for your tireless efforts in getting this book into print. John: you've put together an amazing team and I'm excited to be aboard.

Maggi—thanks for your sharing your excitement and delight in reading these words.

Tristan, Keaghan, and Aisleyn: like everything I write, you are in these pages because you are in my soul, my heart, and my mind.

REFERENCES

- Antoine de Saint Exupery. *The Little Prince*. Paris: Reynal & Hitchcock, 1943.
- Aurelius, Marcus. *Meditations*. Translated by Gregory Hays. Modern Library: 2003.
- Burton, Levar. Interview. *Vice.com*. Interviewed by Jennifer Juniper Stratford. September 11, 2013. Online.
- Butler, Octavia. *Fledgling*. Seven Stories Press, 2011.
- Butler, Octavia. Interview. *Locus Magazine*. June 2000.
- Scripture quotations are from *The ESV® Bible* (The Holy Bible, English Standard Version®), copyright © 2001 by Crossway, a publishing ministry of Good News Publishers. Used by permission. All rights reserved.
- Okorafor, Nnedi. *Kabu Kabu*. Prime Books, 2013.

ABOUT THE AUTHOR

J. Daniel Batt is a recovering high school English teacher currently pursuing a PhD in Mythology. He is an artist, writer, teacher, designer, creator of communities, geek, and space enthusiast. He serves as the Creative and Editorial Director for 100 Year Starship. In this role, he works to explore the connection between scientists and science fiction writers. He is also the editor for the *2012-2014 Symposium Conference Proceedings*, a collection of nearly 2000 pages of the latest research and thought about interstellar exploration and travel. He is also the organizer and host of the annual Science Fiction Stories Night bringing science fiction writers together with scientists and the general public, and as the team lead for the Canopus Awards celebrating the best in interstellar writing. He is also a lead researcher at Deep Space Predictive.

His first novel, *The Tales of Dreamside*, was hailed by Kirkus Reviews as "a phenomenally imaginative series . . . appealingly dark, with eerie fairy-tale motifs." His short fiction has appeared in *Bastion Magazine*, *Bewildering Stories*, and in the anthology *Genius Loci*. Through the Lifeboat Foundation, he edited the science fiction anthology titled *Visions of the Future* with stories from a wide array of authors including Greg Bear, Allen Steele, Robert Sawyer, Alan Dean Foster, Hugh Howey and many others. His second novel, the first in a series, was the young adult urban fantasy *Young Gods: A Door into Darkness*.

He makes his home in Northern California with his family as they work through their 100-step plan to take over the universe.